P9-EDL-346

BONES

An Irene Kelly Mystery

JAN BURKE

A SIGNET BOOK

SIGNET
Published by New American Library, a division of
Penguin Putnam Inc., 375 Hudson Street,
New York, New York 10014, U.S.A.
Penguin Books Ltd, 27 Wrights Lane,
London W8 5TZ, England
Penguin Books Australia Ltd,
Ringwood, Victoria, Australia
Penguin Books Canada Ltd, 10 Alcorn Avenue,
Toronto, Ontario, Canada M4V 3B2
Penguin Books (N.Z.) Ltd, 182–190 Wairau Road,
Auckland 10, New Zealand

Penguin Books Ltd, Registered Offices:
Harmondsworth, Middlesex, England

Published by Signet, an imprint of New American Library,
a division of Penguin Putnam Inc.
This is an authorized reprint of a Simon & Schuster hardcover edition.

First Signet Printing, February 2001
10 9 8

The author and the publisher gratefully acknowledge permission to use an excerpt from *Parzival: The Quest of the Grail Knight* by Katherine Paterson. Copyright © 1998 by Minna Murra Inc. Used by permission of Lodestar Books, an affiliate of Dutton Children's Books, a division of Penguin Putnam Inc.

Printed in the United States of America

PUBLISHER'S NOTE
This is a work of fiction. Names, characters, places, and incidents either are the product of the author's imagination or are used fictitiously, and any resemblance to actual persons, living or dead, business establishments, events, or locales is entirely coincidental.

To Judy Myers Suchey and Paul Sledzik
and the AFIP Forensic Anthropology Faculty
for their compassionate work
and for teaching me to see more than bones
and
in memory of Shadow and Siri

The gate was open and the drawbridge down.

He galloped across, but when he got to the end of the drawbridge, someone yanked the cable so abruptly that Parzival was nearly thrown, horse and all, into the moat.

Parzival turned back to see who had done this to him. There, standing in the open gateway, was the page who had pulled the cable, shaking his fist at Parzival. "May God damn the light that falls upon your path!" the boy cried. "You fool! You wretched fool! Why didn't you ask the question?"

"What do you mean?" Parzival shouted back. "What question?"

—*Parzival: The Quest of the Grail Knight*
by Wolfram von Eschenbach,
as retold by Katherine Paterson

▲ ▼ ▲ ▼

He paid cash for the book, as he had all the other books on this subject. He spoke to no one, did nothing that would make him memorable to a clerk or customer.

There were many customers in the store when he made the purchase; he always chose times when he knew the bookstore would be busy.

Even if the store had been empty, he would have had little to worry over. When he chose to hide his powers, he was a nondescript man in a world full of people who could seldom describe more than what they saw in the mirror each morning.

Oh, perhaps they could also describe close friends, their own children, their spouses, people they worked with every day. At a stretch, their neighbors. But not quiet strangers in bookstores. Not a stranger who had never been there before, who would never come in again.

He found mild excitement in buying these books, knew this was how some men felt when buying pornography. Seeing it sitting in the bag on the car seat on the way home, he knew the book's subject matter would arouse him, Not as much as the real thing—nothing ever excited him as much as the real thing.

This one was about Dahmer.

We don't share the same appetites, he thought to himself, and was hard put to control a little fit of hilarity at the joke he had made.

When he had finished reading and rereading the book, he would place it with all the other books about his brethren. Books about Bianchi and Speck and Bundy; about earlier ones—Mors and Lucas and Pomeroy—and others; books about killers and their minds, about killers and their victims, about killers and those who hunted them.

At first, he had read the books because he wanted to understand the drive, the need that he feared would consume him. But now it was merely entertainment of a sort. By now, years after he had begun his little library, he knew he understood all there was to understand: he knew that only a man of his genius could cope with the demands of his desire.

He did not lack daring or creativity. Every new aspect, every heightening of the experience, merely confirmed what he already knew: he was unique in history.

Thinking of this, he was a little sad that he wouldn't be caught, because he knew he was going to miss that one additional thrill—the only one that eluded him. The acknowledgment.

Notoriety beckoned. He dreamed of it, fantasized about it almost as much as the killings.

Why did he kill?

Everyone would want to know.

Why did he kill?

Everyone would ask.

And he would speak—quietly, and with authority—and all would hear the answer.

1

▲ ▼ ▲ ▼

FOUR YEARS LATER

Monday Afternoon, May 15

The sensation of being watched had been almost constant on this journey, and now I was feeling it again. I tried to ignore it, to concentrate on the paperback I was reading, but my efforts were useless. I lifted my eyes from the page and looked toward the prisoner, three rows up, expecting to see him staring at me again. He was asleep. How he could manage it over the loud drone of the plane's propellers, I'll never know. How Nicholas Parrish could sleep at all—but I suppose that's one of the advantages of being utterly without a conscience.

So if Parrish wasn't the one eyeing me, who was?

I glanced around the cabin. Most of the men—even those who were not sociopaths—were sleeping. Two of Parrish's guards were awake, but not looking at me. The other two napped. I turned to look behind me. Ben Sheridan, one of the forensic anthropologists, was looking out the window. David Niles, the other, sat across the aisle, reading. There, sitting next to him, was the starer.

He wasn't staring so much as studying, I decided. No hostility there. Actually, of the all-male group with me on the small plane, he was the only one who didn't object to my presence. While most of the others snubbed me, he had taken an immediate liking to me. The feeling was mutual. He was handsome, intelligent, and athletic. But then again, nothing excited him more than discovering a piece of decaying flesh.

He was a cadaver dog.

Bingle—named for his habit of crooning along whenever he heard his handler sing—was a black-and-tan, three-year-old, mostly German shepherd dog, trained to find human remains.

And that was what this expedition into the mountains was all about: finding human remains. A very specific set of them.

I looked into Bingle's dark brown eyes, but my thoughts had already turned to a blue-eyed girl named Gillian Sayre; Gillian, who had spent the last four years waiting for someone to find whatever remained of her mother.

Four years ago. One warm summer day, the day after her mother failed to come home, Gillian was waiting outside the building which houses the *Express*. I was with a group of coworkers on our way to lunch. I saw her right away; she was tall and thin and her hair was cropped short and dyed the color of eggplant. Her face was pale; she was wearing dark brown lipstick and lots of eye shadow, which only accentuated the nearly colorless blue of her eyes. Her lashes and brows were thick and dyed black and her left brow was pierced by a small silver hoop. Seven or eight pierced earrings climbed the curve of each ear. Her pale, slender fingers bore silver rings of varying widths and designs; her fingernails were short, but painted black. Her clothes were rumpled, her shoes clunky.

"Are any of you reporters?" she called to us.

Never slow to grasp this sort of opportunity, my friend Stuart Angert pointed at me and said, "Only this lady here. The rest of us just finished an interview with her, so she's free to talk to you."

The others laughed, and the words "call for an appointment" were on my lips, but something about her made me hesitate. Stuart's joke had not gone over her head—I could see that she was already expecting me to disappoint her, and she looked as if she was accustomed to being disappointed.

"Go on," I said to the others. "I'll catch up to you."

I put up with another round of chiding and some half-hearted protests, but before long I was left standing alone with her.

"I'm Irene Kelly," I said. "What can I do for you?"

"They won't look for my mother," she said.

"Who won't?"

"The police. They think she ran away. She didn't."

"How long has she been gone?"

"Since four o'clock yesterday—well, that's the last time I saw her." She looked away, then added, "She went to a store. They saw her there."

I figured I was talking to a kid who was doomed to learn that her mom was throwing in the towel on family life. But as I let her talk, I began to feel less certain of that.

Julia Sayre was forty years old on the night she failed to come home. Gillian's father, Giles Sayre, had called his wife at a little before four that afternoon to say that he had obtained a pair of coveted symphony tickets—the debut of the symphony's new conductor was to take place that evening. Hurriedly leaving their younger child, nine-year-old Jason, in Gillian's care, Julia left the house in her Mercedes-Benz to go to a shopping mall not five miles away from her affluent neighborhood, to buy a slip.

She had not been seen since.

When he came home that evening and discovered that his wife hadn't returned, Giles was more anxious about the possibility of being late to the concert than his wife's whereabouts. As time went on, however, he became worried and drove over to the shopping center. He drove through the aisles of the parking lot near her favorite store, Nordstrom, but didn't see her blue sedan. He went into the store, and after questioning some of the employees in the lingerie department, learned that she had indeed been there—but at four o'clock or so—several hours earlier.

When Giles Sayre reported his wife missing, the police gave it all the attention they usually give an adult disappearance of five hours' duration—virtually none. They, too, looked for Julia Sayre's car in the shopping center parking lot; Giles could have told them it wouldn't be there—he had already made another trip to look for it.

"Sometimes, Gillian—" I began, but she cut me off.

"Don't try to give me some bullshit about how she might be some kind of runaway, doing the big nasty with somebody other than my dad," she said. "My folks are super close, happily married and all that. I mean, it would make you want to gack to see them together."

"Yes, but—"

"Ask anybody. Ask our neighbors. They'll tell you—Julia Sayre only has trouble with one person in her life."

"You!"

She looked surprised by my guess, but then shrugged. She folded her arms, leaned back against the building, and said, "Yes."

"Why?"

She shrugged again. "You don't look like you were some little sweetcakes that never stepped out of line. Didn't you ever fight with your mom when you were a teenager?"

I shook my head. "No, my mother died when I was twelve. Before I was a teenager. I used to envy the ones—" I caught myself. "Well, that's not important."

She was silent.

"If she had lived," I said, "we probably would have fought. I got into all kinds of mischief even before I was a teenager."

She began studying one of her fingernails. I was wondering how my memories of my mother might have differed had she lived another five years, when Gillian asked, "Do you remember the last thing you said to her?"

"Yes."

She waited for me to say more. When I didn't, she looked away, her brows drawn together. She said, "The last thing I said to my mother was, 'I wish you were dead!' "

"Gillian—"

"She wanted me to watch Jason. She wanted me to cancel all my plans and do what she wanted, so she could go to the stupid concert. I was upset. My boyfriend was upset when I told him I couldn't see him—so I yelled at her. That's what I said to her."

"She may be fine," I said. "Sometimes people just feel overwhelmed, need to take off."

"Not my mom."

"I'm just saying that she hasn't been gone for twenty-four hours yet. Don't assume that she's—" I stopped myself just in time. "Don't assume that she's been harmed."

"Then I need you to help me find her," she said. "No one else will take me seriously. They're like your friends." She nodded in the direction Stuart and the others had walked. "Think I'm just a kid—no need to listen to a kid."

I pulled out my notebook and said, "You understand that I don't get to decide if this story runs in the paper, right?"

She smiled.

Once I argued my editor into letting me pursue the story, I drove over to the Sayres' home, a large two-story on a quiet cul-de-sac. Giles answered the door after scooping up a yapping Pekingese. He handed the squirming dog off to Gillian, who took it upstairs. Jason, he told me, had been taken to stay with his grandmother.

When I first approached Giles Sayre, I thought he might resent Gillian's recruitment of a reporter for help with what could turn out to be an embarrassing family matter. But Giles heaped praise on his daughter, saying he should have thought of trying to enlist the *Express* himself.

"What am I going to do if anything has happened to Julia?" he asked anxiously.

Like Gillian, he was tall and thin and had pale blue eyes, but his hair was a much more natural color, a dark auburn. He had not slept; his eyes were reddened from tears which, by this point, could come easily, and which he didn't try to hide.

He hurried to hand me several recent photographs of his wife. Her hair was dark brown, her large eyes, a deep blue. An attractive, self-possessed woman, she appeared to be perfectly groomed in even the most casual photographs. Gillian did not resemble her so much as her father, but Jason, I saw from a group photo, took a few of his features from each—her dark hair and aristocratic facial structure, his pale blue eyes.

"Which of these is the most recent?" I asked.

Giles selected a photograph taken at a Junior League event.

"Can I keep it? I can try to get it back for you, but I can't make any promises."

"No, that's all right, I have the negative."

This level of cooperation continued throughout the day. He met my involvement with a sense of relief, anxious to do whatever he could to help me with the story. The benefit was mutual—I gave him a chance to take action, directed some of the energy that up until now had gone to pacing and feeling helpless; his help made much of my job easier. It occurred to me that his anxiousness to spread the word was not something you'd be likely to find in a man who fears he has been cuckolded.

So I talked to neighbors and friends of Julia Sayre. I talked to other members of her family. The more I heard about her, the more I was inclined to agree with her daughter—Julia Sayre wasn't likely to disappear of her own volition. Julia seemed fairly content with her life, content with just about everything except her relationship with her daughter. The universal opinion on that matter was that Gillian's hellion phase was bound to come to an end soon—according to friends, no one was more sure of that than Julia.

If she was conducting an extramarital affair, Mrs. Sayre had been extremely discreet about it. I still hadn't ruled out the possibility that she had left Giles Sayre for someone else, but it was no longer my pet theory.

I asked Gillian to tell me again what her mother had been wearing. A black silk skirt and jacket, she said. A white silk blouse, a pair of black leather pumps and a small black leather purse. Her only jewelry had been a simple gold chain necklace, a pair of diamond earrings, and her wedding ring.

"Not her wedding ring, really," Giles said. "On our fifteenth anniversary, we had new rings made." He held his up. "Hers is gold, like this one, and it has three rubies on it."

He drove me to the mall where she had last been seen. With his help, I got the Nordstrom manager to look up the time of the transaction. Julia had used a MasterCard to purchase a black slip at 4:18 P.M. the previous afternoon. We thanked the manager and left. Giles called the MasterCard customer service number on his cell phone as we walked from store to store in the mall, showing Julia's photo to clerk after clerk, none of whom had seen this lady yesterday. Eventually, he got his answer from the MasterCard customer service rep, and asked her to repeat the information to me. She confirmed that Julia Sayre hadn't used the credit card since making the Nordstrom purchase.

I called an overworked missing persons detective in the LPPD and told him I was writing a story about Julia Sayre's disappearance. He wouldn't comment for the story, but—off the record—told me he'd try to get some action on the case.

When Julia Sayre's Mercedes-Benz was first spotted on an upper floor of the Las Piernas Airport parking garage, the two patrolmen who found it thought the woman might have decided to escape her marriage after all. But then the detectives called to the scene made a discovery, a discovery that had my editor—overjoyed that we had beaten the competition to the story—praising my instincts, while it tied my stomach into knots.

Julia Sayre's left thumb was in the glove compartment.

2

▲ ▼ ▲ ▼

Four weeks ago, when the Kara Lane story first broke, I had expected another of Gillian's "try to find out" calls. Over the years following Julia's disappearance, I had heard from Gillian whenever certain events were reported in the *Express*. If a Jane Doe was found, Gillian calmly asked me to try to find out if the unidentified body might be her mother's, never failing to recite the details of her mother's height and coloring and clothing and jewelry. Was the victim a blue-eyed brunette? Was the victim wearing a gold ring with three rubies?

If a man was arrested for killing a woman, she wanted me to interview him, to try to find out if he had killed her mother, too. If a suspected serial killer was arrested in another state, she wanted me to try to find out if he had ever been in Las Piernas.

I quit the paper once, and went to work for a public relations firm. She tracked me down and called me there—O'Connor, my old mentor at the *Express*, was a soft touch for a missing persons case, and told her where to find me. When I told her that she should ask O'Connor to follow up on these stories, she quoted him as saying it would be good for me to remember what it was like to have a real job.

I could have refused her, of course, but even at an observer's distance, I had allowed myself to become too close to the Sayres' misery over those years.

I seldom saw Giles, and never away from his office; he apparently worked long hours to distract himself from his grief. His mother moved in with the family to help care for the children. Two months after Julia disappeared, Giles told me that he didn't know whether or not to hold a memorial service for her. "I don't even know what's involved in having her declared dead," he said. "My mother says I should wait, that people will think I was happy to be rid of her. Do you think anyone will think that?"

I told him that he should do what he needed to do for his family, and to hell with everybody else. It was advice he seemed unlikely to take—the opinions of others seemed to matter a great deal to him.

Jason got into trouble at home and in school on a regular basis. His grandmother confided to me that his grades had dropped, he had quit playing sports, and had become a loner, having little to do with his old friends.

Only Gillian seemed to continue on with her life. She gave her grandmother as much grief as she had given Julia. She dropped out of high school, moved out and got a small apartment on her own, supported herself by working at a boutique on Allen Street—Artsy-Fartsy Street, my friend Stuart Angert calls it. And spent four years quietly and persistently reminding the police and the press that someone ought to be looking for her missing mother, her determined stoicism shaming us into doing what little we could.

On the day the Kara Lane case first made headlines, Gillian waited for me outside the Wrigley Building, home of the *Express*. She seemed to me then as she had seemed from the first day I met her: no matter how likely it was that she would meet with disappointment, Gillian simply refused to acknowledge defeat. This affected me more than tears or hysterics. Nothing in her manner changed; she was often brusque, but she was never weak. Her clothing, hair, and makeup styles might be a little extreme, but her feelings—whatever they were—were not on display.

So I made calls, I followed up. There was never any progress. Until Kara Lane disappeared.

By then, I wasn't allowed to cover crime stories—a result of my marriage to Frank Harriman, a homicide detective. But my marriage is more than worth the hassles it causes me at the *Express* and Frank at the LPPD.

As it happened, Frank was part of the team that investigated the Lane case. I learned details about it that I couldn't tell the paper's crime reporter, let alone Gillian. But before long, almost all of those details became public knowledge.

Kara Lane was forty-three, dark-haired, blue-eyed, a divorced mother of two teenage daughters. She had gone to the grocery store at eight o'clock one evening, and when she had not returned by eleven, her daughters became concerned. Too young to drive, they called a neighbor. By midnight, after a search of local store parking lots, the neighbor called Kara's ex-husband. After another search of the stores, the ex-husband called the police. The search for Kara Lane began in earnest early the next morning.

Several factors caused the police to search for her more quickly than they had Julia Sayre: Kara was a diabetic who needed daily insulin injections—and she had not taken her medication with her; she had never before left her daughters alone at night; and during the morning briefing, Detective Frank Harriman noticed that in height, age, build, and hair color Kara Lane resembled Julia Sayre—a woman whose daughter pestered his reporter wife every now and then. He suggested to his partner, Pete Baird, that they take a look at the Las Piernas Airport parking lot.

Kara Lane's aging VW van was parked in exactly the same space where Julia Sayre's Mercedes had been left four years earlier. Not long after they called in their discovery, the van was carefully searched. Kara's left ring finger was found in the glove compartment.

At this point, the department called Dr. David Niles, a forensic anthropologist who owned two dogs trained for both search and rescue and cadaver work, and asked him to bring them to the airport. The results were remarkable—so remarkable that when Frank and Pete told me about it that evening, I was fairly sure they were exaggerating.

"One of his dogs—Bingle—is so smart," Pete said. "He can find anything. I mean, he makes these mutts of yours look retarded, Irene."

"Wait just a minute—" I said, looking over at Deke, mostly black Lab, and Dunk, mostly shepherd, who were sleeping nearby.

"Our dogs are smart," Frank said, trying to head off an argument, "but Bingle is—well, you'd have to see him to believe it. And he's highly trained—"

"And don't forget Bool," Pete said. "His bloodhound. He works with two dogs. If one acts like he's found something, he gets the other to confirm it."

"Bingle has even located bodies underwater," Frank said.

"How is that possible?" I asked. "You put him in a little scuba outfit?"

"Very funny," Pete said.

"The dog can do it," Frank said. "It's not as miraculous as it sounds. The bacteria in a decomposing body cause it to give off gases. The scent rises through the water, and the dogs smell it when it reaches the surface. They can take Bingle out in a boat and cross the surface of a lake, and he'll indicate when he smells a body below."

"All right," I said, "that makes sense. But—"

"Let us tell you what happened," Pete said.

The gist of the tale was that Bingle led a group of men at a fast clip over a weaving trail out of the parking structure and across the grounds of the airport. Then he headed toward an airplane hangar.

"He went bananas," Pete said, moving his hands in rapid dog-paddle fashion.

"He was pawing furiously at one of the back walls," Frank explained.

It took the police some time to get a warrant, and to locate the owner of the building, but they gained access. At first, nothing seemed amiss. The hangar was leased by Nicholas Parrish, a quiet man, the owner said; a man who paid his rent on time, never caused any problems. An airplane mechanic. The police ran Parrish's name through their computers—he had no outstanding warrants. In fact, he had no criminal record at all.

David Niles brought out Bool and let the bloodhound sniff an article of Kara Lane's clothing. Bool, who needed this "prescenting" in order to track, traced a path almost identical to the one Bingle had followed.

Frank suggested getting a crime scene unit to check the hangar with luminol, a chemical capable of detecting minute traces of blood, but the skeptics in the group were starting to grumble, especially Reed Collins and Vince Adams, the detectives in charge of the Lane case.

"Collins is starting to make remarks about wasting precious time and his partner is making noise about wild goose chases," Pete said, "when all of a sudden, Bingle lifts his head and sings." Pete crooned a single high note that brought both of our dogs to their feet, heads cocked. "David gives another command and the dog takes off again."

This time the dog headed across the Tarmac, to a field beyond the nearest runway. When he stopped, he pranced and bounced around, pawing furiously at the earth, crooning again—actions which Pete, getting into his story, performed for us. Quite a workout.

David moved ahead, to the place where Bingle had alerted, and called back, "I think he's found her."

The others soon caught up. They saw the shallow grave, the freshly turned earth, and a woman's shoe protruding from something shiny and green—plastic sheeting. Frank got on the radio, telling the officers in the hangar that they should secure the area, call out a crime scene unit, and put out an APB for Nicholas Parrish.

"The whole time he's on the radio, I'm moving a little closer," Pete said, "and I see what the dog was digging at, what he uncovered. It's her hand—you know, the left one, the one that's missing the finger."

I looked at Frank. "Gillian Sayre will—"

"You can't tell her yet," he said firmly. "Nobody. Not any of this. Not yet."

But by the next morning the Kara Lane case had made the front page, and Gillian was standing outside the newspaper, looking a little more anxious than usual. When I was within a few feet of her, she held up a creased copy of the *Express* and pointed to Parrish's photo. "He's the one who took my mother."

"It looks as if the cases have a lot in common," I agreed.

"No. I mean, I know he's the one. He used to live on our street—a long time ago."

"What? How long ago?"

"Before my mom disappeared."

"Have you told the police?"

She shook her head. I wasn't surprised. Whatever faith she might have once had in the police had been damaged when the LPPD delayed searching for her mother, and was utterly destroyed when they had failed to find her. Gillian and I shared a dislike of Bob Thompson, the Las Piernas Police Department homicide detective who handled her mother's case. Once or twice she had talked to other homicide detectives when a Jane Doe was found, but usually she relied on me to make contact with the police on her behalf.

"I thought maybe you could tell your husband," she said now.

"Yes, sure," I said, still reeling. "Parrish lived there alone?"

"No. I think his sister owned the house."

"You ever see anything strange going on there?"

"No, not really. They were quiet. She moved away—don't remember exactly when. I don't know where she lives now. She wasn't friendly."

"Was he?"

She shrugged. "He kind of kept to himself. I guess he was nice to everybody—you know, smiled and waved. But he used to stare at my mom."

Now, as I held fast to the armrests of my seat while the plane jolted in the choppy air above the southern Sierra Nevadas, I watched the killer awaken not far from me. It was not difficult for me to imagine Nicholas Parrish stalking his prey, staring at Julia Sayre as she left the house to run errands, or as she worked in her garden, or came home from the store. Staring at her, while she imagined herself safe from harm.

Staring at her, much in the same way he was staring at me now.

3

▲ ▼ ▲ ▼

MONDAY AFTERNOON, MAY 15

Southern Sierra Nevada Mountains

After a bouncy landing on a rough patch of ground that served as the airstrip, there was a wait before we were allowed to disembark. Bob Thompson addressed one of the guards as "Earl" and muttered some order to him. Earl was the first to exit; he returned shortly and, giving an "all clear," worked with the other three guards to remove Parrish from the plane. Thompson was next, followed by a quiet young man who seemed to be his assistant—though not his partner. Thompson and Phil Newly, Parrish's attorney, were the only members of the group that I had met before that day. A few years back, I had covered some crime stories, and had seen Newly around the courthouse.

Thompson and I had known each other for close to ten years. The contempt was both strong and mutual.

I figured that made me the show horse in the race to capture the hostility of the other passengers. Parrish was first by a length, followed by Newly. As a member of the press, I was a distant third.

Newly and Bill "Flash" Burden, an LPPD crime scene photographer, stepped off after the guards; then the pilot came back into the cabin and stood in the aisle. "Rest of you wait until they get Parrish settled," he said, then left the plane. Minutes passed.

"Do you know who's meeting us from the Forest Service?" I heard David Niles ask.

"J.C.," said Ben Sheridan, the other anthropologist. "Andy is coming up with him."

"Andy who?" I asked.

Sheridan eyed me coldly, then turned back to the window, frowning. After a moment's silence, David Niles said, "Andy Stewart, a botanist who works with us sometimes."

"Thank you, Dr. Niles."

"Call me David."

Sheridan sighed loudly. This only seemed to amuse David, but he didn't say more to me. I had known that we would be meeting a couple of people at this airstrip; men who were being flown in from another location, but Thompson had only said they were "part of Sheridan's team."

"Okay, folks," Earl called. I stood, but gestured to David to let Bingle—fidgety since the landing—lead the way. "Thanks," he said, then followed the dog. That left me with Ben Sheridan, who was still frowning as he gazed out the window.

"Listen," I began. "I don't want to—"

"I'm not leaving you here to snoop around on the plane," he interrupted. "Go on outside."

I felt a flare of temper, checked it, and left the plane without saying another word to him.

I stretched at the bottom of the steps, taking in the view before me. We were in a long meadow, near the center of a narrow valley that was already shadowed and cooling. The scent of pine from nearby woods mixed with the fragrance of late spring blossoms in the meadow, of grass and earth. When I saw the slender mown strip where we had landed, I felt new respect for the pilot.

A base camp would be set up here.

Bingle, once he had relieved himself, began cavorting wildly through the meadow, not so much running as bouncing through it, stopping now and then to try to lure his handler into playing with him. But David, Sheridan, and everyone who wasn't involved in guarding Parrish were busy unloading gear from the plane. I gathered my own, then moved to help the others. I had only taken a few steps when a voice from behind me asked, "Are you the reporter?"

I turned to see a lean, golden young man smiling at me. I guessed him to be in his mid-twenties. His hair was short and spiky. He was tanned and had the kind of calf muscles a person can only get by moving his feet over long distances, on a bike or running or hiking. He wore a closely trimmed beard and a single earring in his right ear.

"Yes," I said, setting down my backpack and extending a hand. "Irene Kelly."

"Andy Stewart," he said, with a firm handshake. "I'm the botanist for the team. J.C. and I got here at noon. We're all set up. Can I give you a hand with anything?"

"I can manage this, but it looks as if Dr. Sheridan still has some gear in there."

He grabbed another canvas bag and continued to chat with me, telling me that a Forest Service helicopter had brought them in earlier.

"Forgive me for asking, but why is a botanist needed for this search?"

"Well, whenever anybody like Mr. Parrish comes along and digs a hole, drops what will ultimately amount to a big chunk of fertilizer in it, and then covers it up again, nature doesn't let that pass unnoticed. The plants he dug up, the new ones that begin to grow, the surrounding soil—he's created a disturbance in the existing system. With enough practice, a botanist can learn to see the signs of that disturbance."

"So you're paid to look for changes in plant life?"

His face broke into a grin. "Paid? No, none of us are paid. Ben, David, and I do this forensic work voluntarily. I'm a grad student in biology; Ben and David teach in the anthropology department. David also pays for all of Bingle's training and equipment. Even J.C. doesn't get any special pay for coming along, although he's on the Forest Service payroll while he's here." He paused. "If you don't mind my asking the question you asked me—what's a reporter doing here?"

"Good question. There are any number of folks, here and at home, who'd tell you I have no business being here." I paused, trying to shut out the memory of the fight Frank and I had before I left.

"I don't want you up there with him, no matter how many guards he has on him."

"I don't want to be up there with him, either, but I can't get out of this one, Frank."

"Refuse the assignment. Goddamn it, Irene, those amputations were antemortem. You know what that means?"

"Stop it," I said.

"It means," he went on ruthlessly, "that those women were alive when he began mutilating them, Irene. Alive."

"But you're here anyway," Andy was saying.

"Yes. I know Julia Sayre's family—" I began.

"Sayre's the victim he claims he'll lead us to?"

"Yes."

I'm here to put an end to the last remnants of their hope, I thought. That small, impossible burden of hope that would ride in back of their minds like a stone in a shoe.

Years as a reporter had taught me that families would hold fiercely to whatever little hope they could find, whatever possibility they could imagine. If their son was on a plane that crashed, they wondered if perhaps he had missed the flight, pictured him giving his ticket to a friend.

The Sayres would have such hopes, I knew, although Gillian would never betray their existence to me.

Parrish's announcement would have nearly put an end to that sort of fantasy. What a blow it must have been to Gillian. Still, the Sayres would wonder if Parrish was bluffing, or mistaken about the identity of his victim.

And so now there was only this, this final identification. We would unbury Julia Sayre's remains and leave the last of her family's hope in their place.

"Good of you to go to this much trouble for them," Andy said, bringing me out of my reverie.

"No, it's not," I said. "I'm here because my boss insisted on it, and I wasn't exactly pleased with the assignment. I got caught in police politics. The Las Piernas Police got a black eye recently—"

"When they tried to hide mistakes made in an Internal Affairs investigation," he said, nodding. "But one of the reporters on the *Express* learned about it and made them look twice as bad."

"Yes. So to prove to the public that they're doing a great job, and everything's aboveboard, the brass decided to let a local reporter get in on a success story—the resolution of an old case that has been given big play in the paper. The *Express* was already leaning on them to let me come along. I never dreamed they'd say yes, or I would have tried to head those plans off before they got this far."

"I'd think this would be a reporter's dream."

"I'm not too fond of the mountains."

"Not fond of the mountains?" he said, aghast. This, clearly, he considered to be sacrilege.

I swallowed hard. "I used to love them. But—I had a bad experience in the mountains once."

"Backpacking?"

"No. In a cabin." My mouth was dry. I could feel my tongue slowing, clacking over the simple little word, *cabin*.

Andy seemed not to notice. "But you've been backpacking before," he said, puzzled.

"Yes. The gear give me away?"

"Yep. Not novice style—not like that lawyer's bullshit outfit. Most of yours is broken in—like your boots. The attorney's boots are brand new, and I'll bet you he's going to have blisters in no time. You've got a few new items, but they aren't just for show."

"It's been a long time since I've used my gear." I didn't want to think about why.

"Then separate this from whatever happened in that cabin," he said, with the easy logic of youth.

Before I could answer, a deep voice called from the other side of the meadow. "Your botanist is upsetting Ms. Kelly."

Parrish.

I felt my face color under the sudden attention that came from almost everyone else—from all but his guards, one of whom was telling him to shut up.

"Am I?" Andy asked me.

"No. No, you aren't. You're making me feel much more comfortable about being here."

He grinned again.

To some extent, I had told him the truth. At least he was speaking to me, being friendlier than the others. Maybe he was right about backpacking; maybe my fears wouldn't be triggered in the same way they might be if I were driving to the mountains, staying in a cabin.

"I used to know a little about wildflowers," I said, trying to keep my thoughts away from cabins and glove compartments and Nicholas Parrish. "Perhaps you can help me remember the names of some of the varieties in this meadow?"

4

▲ ▼ ▲ ▼

MONDAY AFTERNOON, MAY 15

Southern Sierra Nevada Mountains

We ended up postponing our botany lesson; there was simply too much to be done to set up camp before nightfall.

I pitched my tent and set my backpack in it, then looked to see if anyone else might need help. I saw Earl, the one guard whose name I had heard spoken, taking some medication. He was a man who appeared to be in his late forties; I thought his partner might be a little older.

"Are you feeling all right?" I asked.

"Me?" he asked, quickly stashing the pills away. "Oh, I'm fine." At my questioning look he added, "Just getting over an ear infection. If certain parties knew, they would have kept me off this assignment."

"I won't tell anyone."

He grinned. "Especially not Thompson."

"Right. I guess it's pretty clear that there's no love lost between us."

"Lady, there's no love lost between Thompson and *anybody*." He put out a hand. "Earl Allen, by the way. I noticed Detective Shit-Don't-Stink failed to introduce you to the peons."

"Nice to meet you, Earl. I'm Irene."

"Oh, we all know you. You're Harriman's wife."

"Yes."

"Good man, Frank. Any of these other jokers give you problems, you let me know."

"Thanks."

"Hey, Earl!" one of the other cops called out. He was the burliest of the crew, and seemed to be the oldest.

"My partner, Duke Fenly," Earl said, moving off. "Looks like he needs help with that tent."

"Duke and Earl? You're kidding."

"Naw—we're real aristocrats," Earl said over his shoulder. "That's why they put us in charge of all the royal assholes."

Even with Earl's help, the pair had trouble pitching their large tent, so I decided to help out. As we worked, Earl pointed out Merrick and Manton, two other guards, and an officer named Jim Houghton, who was putting up Thompson's tent.

"He's young to be a detective," I said.

Earl snorted. "He's no detective. He's a uniform, just like we are. Thompson's got no regular partner at the moment."

"Why not?" I asked.

"Off the record? 'Cause nobody can stand working with the s.o.b. So poor Houghton got drafted to be Thompson's *assistant*."

"His flunky," Duke growled. "But Houghton's quiet—doesn't let anything get to him. He'll be okay."

We had just brought the tent up on its poles when Thompson suddenly looked over from a discussion with Newly and shouted, "What the hell is wrong with you guys?"

Our hands stilled. Earl looked behind us, as if he couldn't believe Thompson was yelling at him.

"What's the problem, Detective Thompson?" Duke said icily.

"Get that goddamned reporter out of there!" Thompson said. "I don't want her touching anything that belongs to the LPPD!"

"Gee, Bob," Earl taunted, "that's gonna be awful tough on Harriman when she gets home."

The other cops laughed—even Houghton—which didn't help Thompson regain his temper. "That's his problem. Up here, I'm in charge. Got that?"

Duke and Earl didn't look entirely convinced, but I decided

to choose a better fight. I was tempted to loosen my grip on the tent and allow it to collapse, but again I saw Nick Parrish watching me. I looked away, seeking an ally. Andy was moving a wanigan—a chest full of cooking supplies—toward the cooking area. I was about to ask for his help, but before I could say anything to him, Ben Sheridan strolled over and took hold of the support I was clasping. "Go on," he said.

My own small tent was on the edge of the clearing, on the lee side of some trees. I studied the sky for a moment, and decided to put the rainfly on. Then I chose a moment when even Nick Parrish wasn't looking at me and backed myself inside the dome's opening. I stayed facing the opening as I stowed my gear, an awkward process at times, but I needed to see the darkening sky, feel the cool air. I refused to let myself think about staying inside this confined space. I put on another layer of clothing, then stepped outside. I took out my little white-gas stove, and began to prime it.

Phil Newly saw me and hurried over. Watching his tense, jerky pace, it occurred to me that this trip into the woods might relax him, but I quickly snapped my thoughts back into reality—this wasn't a vacation or some backpacking trip for a little R&R—we were on our way to unbury Nick Parrish's horrible handiwork.

And here was his defender, smiling down at me. Charismatic at will. Newly had brown hair, chiseled features, and a pair of intense, dark eyes that were said to be able to unhinge a prosecution witness long before he asked his first question on cross. But decked out in his brand-spanking-new designer outdoorwear, he looked decidedly dudely. And harmless.

"Irene," he chided, "you aren't going to deprive us of your company at dinner, are you?"

"Deprive is hardly the word your opposition would use." I'd been told to bring my own food supplies, although the others would be fed courtesy of the LPPD. Newly had bought steaks for this first night out.

"Hell," he said, "if I can face all the loathing they express for my profession, you can manage, too. Come on and join us."

"Thanks for the invitation, Phil, but if I don't eat this meal I'm planning to make, I have to pack it on my back tomorrow.

Besides, I don't think I want to watch Nick Parrish enjoying a steak dinner."

"I believe Earl will be serving a bologna sandwich to my client."

I smiled. "And you didn't object?"

"Not much." He hesitated a moment before adding, "I don't have to like my clients, Irene. I just have to provide them with the best legal defense work I can offer."

"But Parrish didn't seem to want much of a defense, did he?"

"I was opposed to this deal."

"They had a solid case against him."

"Irene, please—"

"Okay, okay. I'm not hopelessly naive about what can become of a solid case once you've had a crack at it."

He laughed. "I'll take that as a compliment. Now, say you'll join us."

"Sorry, Phil. The journalist in me says I'd write a better story if I tried to build a sense of camaraderie and all that, but I figure we'll have plenty of time to be in each other's faces over the next two or three days."

"All right, then, I won't pressure you. But don't stay away all evening—you'll just look as if you're pouting."

"You're right," I acknowledged, feeling a little disappointed that I'd have to lace up my gloves and go back into the ring. "See you later."

Wondering if, during the years I was away from it, any aspect of backpacking had improved more than freeze-dried food, I cleaned up and rejoined the group, which had gathered around a small campfire. Earl and Duke had taken Parrish into his tent and were on duty there; but one of the other cops, Manton, was friendly to me, as was Flash Burden, the photographer. With two exceptions—Bob Thompson and Ben Sheridan—there wasn't much after-dinner hostility at all.

Not long after I arrived, Thompson said he was going to bed. "I suggest the rest of you do the same." The others, however, ignored him.

Manton noticed my uneasy glances toward the tent where

Parrish had been taken and said, "Don't worry, we aren't gonna let him out of our sight. You'll be okay."

"Thanks," I said, but could not rid myself of the notion that Parrish was lying wide awake, listening to every word, every sound from beyond his tent.

A sharp sound made me glance over at Ben Sheridan, who was snapping twigs into smaller and smaller pieces. I wasn't the only one who was having trouble relaxing in the great outdoors.

The others soon distracted me, though, as they began to tease me about missing out on the steaks.

"Took less time to prepare the steaks than it took for old Dave there to make his dog's dinner," Merrick said, and launched into an exaggerated tale of David's elaborate preparation of Bingle's food.

"Hey, I've got to take good care of Bingle," David said. "*¿Estás bien, Bingle?*" Bingle, sitting between him and Ben, leaned over to kiss David on the ear.

"Goddamn," Manton said, "you let that dog kiss you after he's gone around licking dead bodies?"

"Bingle, he's slandering you!" David said, in a tone that caused the dog to bark. "Bingle only kisses the living. Of course, a guy with breath like yours might confuse him, Manton, so maybe he won't kiss you."

"What is that stuff you feed him?" Flash Burden asked.

"Oh, that's my own secret Super-Hero-In-Training formula."

"It produces its own acronym," Andy chimed in.

"Just don't step in it like you stepped on my punch line, kid," David said, but without malice.

Bingle lay quietly, ears forward, watching David. David, I noticed, spent a lot of time watching Bingle, too.

Andy asked about Bool, and David explained that he had injured one of his paws during the search for Kara Lane. "Bool gets involved in finding a scent, he doesn't exactly watch where he's going. He'll be okay, but he's not ready for a search like this one. I've got a friend who trains bloodhounds, he's keeping an eye on Bool while I'm here."

"This shepherd must be the smarter of the two," Manton said.

David smiled. "Bingle is certainly a highly educated dog. He's bilingual, too. *¿Correcto, Bingle?*" Bingle sat up again and gave a single sharp bark. "And besides his cadaver training, he's had voice training."

"Voice training?" Manton asked.

"*Cántame, Bingle,*" David said, and began singing "Home on the Range." Bingle chimed in with perfect pitch at the chorus. I'd swear we all heard that dog sing the lyrics. Nobody could keep a straight face. Almost nobody.

"Enough, David," Ben said sharply.

Silence.

Everyone shifted a little uncomfortably, except for David and Bingle. Both dog and man looked at Ben, Bingle cocking his head to one side, puzzled.

"Ah, the discouraging word," David said softly, without a trace of anger. He began quietly praising Bingle.

Ben stood and walked off.

5

▲ ▼ ▲ ▼

TUESDAY, MAY 16, 2:25 A.M.

Southern Sierra Nevada Mountains

Nothing can keep you up all night as effectively as calculating what sort of condition you'll be in the next day if you don't fall asleep soon. I heard soft snoring from most of the other tents, including a double set of saws from the one where Bingle was curled up next to David. I heard the pacing first of Manton and Merrick, and later of Duke and Earl.

My claustrophobia kicked in—not able to stay long in the tent, soon I was sitting in its opening, watching the stars, listening to the insects, wondering what animals were making the other noises I heard—occasional rustlings and snapping sounds. Our food had been hung up high in bear bags, a safe three hundred feet from camp, but I wasn't so sure we weren't the object of ursine scrutiny.

I thought a lot about Frank—wondered if he were also lying awake, if the pilot's radio message that we had arrived safely had reached him. I thought of my cousin Travis, who was staying with us. I thought about my dogs, my cat.

I tried hard to keep my thoughts away from memories of a particular time I had spent in the mountains, in a small room in a cabin, the captive of some rather brutal hosts. The nightmares induced by all that had happened there were fewer now, but I knew what might trigger them again—enclosed spaces, stress, new surroundings.

Think of something else.

I thought of Gillian Sayre. I thought of her mother. I stayed awake.

I was wondering if I should give in to the old memories of captivity, go ahead and think about them—dwell on them for God's sake, if that would relieve the tension—when there was a sudden brightness on my face. A flashlight, quickly lowered. Both the path of the beam of light and the sound of footsteps made it clear that someone was making his way toward me. As he drew closer, I saw that it was Ben Sheridan. I moved to my feet as he reached me.

"Why are you awake?" he whispered, his breath fogging in the cold air. "It's three in the morning."

"Just waiting for my big chance to look through all your gear and touch everything that belongs to the Las Piernas P.D.," I whispered back.

He was silent for a moment, then repeated, "Why are you awake?"

"Am I disturbing you?"

"No."

"Well, then, why are *you* awake?"

"Shhh. Not so loud. You'll wake the others."

I waited.

"I did sleep," he said.

"Not for long," I said.

"You haven't slept at all."

"Ben, if you've slept, then how could you possibly know I haven't?"

He started to move away again.

"I have problems with enclosed spaces," I said.

He halted, then said, "Claustrophobia? The tent bothers you?"

"Yes."

"Sleep outside."

"It's not just that." But I couldn't bring myself to say more.

We were interrupted then. Bingle had heard us, and he emerged from David's tent, shaking himself as if he had just stepped out of a bath. Tufts of fur around his ears spiked out from his head, making him look genuinely woozy. The effect was comical.

David soon followed him out of the tent. Before I could apologize, David was whispering drowsily, "Hi, Ben. Need to borrow Bingle?"

"She does," Ben said.

"What?" I asked, startled.

"Okay," David said, turning to Bingle. "*Duerme con ella,*" he commanded in Spanish, pointing at me. Sleep with her. Bingle happily trotted over—and flopped down next to me.

"Wait a minute—"

"Keep him warm and he'll be okay," David said, and went back into his tent.

I looked up at Ben in some exasperation.

"He'll wake you if you start to have a nightmare," Ben said, and started to walk off.

"Who said anything about nightmares?" I asked.

He looked over his shoulder, then said, "No one." He kept walking.

Bingle was watching me, a look of expectation on his face.

I sighed and got into my sleeping bag. Bingle did a brief inspection of the interior of the tent, then lay down next to me. He moved restlessly for a moment or two, until he seemed to find a position he liked—resting his head on my shoulder.

"Comfy?" I asked.

He snorted.

I buried a hand in his thick coat, and found myself smiling. A few minutes later, I was asleep.

I awakened briefly when Bingle left me the next morning, but slept in a little longer, until the sounds of the camp stirring to life were too much to snooze through.

Not long after breakfast, we left the base camp. Only the pilot stayed behind with the heaviest gear. Parrish claimed that Julia Sayre was buried at least a day's hike from the airstrip. Backpacks on, we began our journey into the forest.

Our progress was slow. Following the lead of a man who was handcuffed and heavily guarded—and perhaps savoring his last days outside of prison—was only part of the reason for our sluggish pace.

Ben and David had extra equipment to be carried, beyond the usual camping gear, and were heavily loaded down.

The group was large, and within it our level of experience varied from novice to expert. I suppose I fell somewhere in the middle; plenty of time spent hiking and backpacking, but nothing recent. J.C., the ranger, was undoubtedly the most seasoned backpacker, with Andy a close second; Flash, Houghton, David, and Ben only a little less so, but all were certainly at home in the outdoors. Bob Thompson and Phil Newly were the apparent novices. Duke was the oldest of the guards—he had shown me a photo of his new grandson, and a story about his high school days made me guess that he was in his early fifties. He was in better shape than Merrick or Manton, who were in their early thirties. Earl, somewhere in between in age, was also somewhere in between in fitness.

Flash Burden could have run circles around all of them. He was enthusiastically taking shots of wildflowers, double-checking with Andy before scribbling their names in his photographer's notebook. Andy only corrected him once or twice. They soon fell into easy talk about places they had gone hiking or rock climbing.

It was difficult to judge Parrish's experience on the trail. My suspicions were that in this forest, at least, he was absolutely at home. Perhaps in other forests as well. His boots, for example, were his own, and they were well made and broken in. He did not panic, as Phil Newly did, when a gopher snake hurried across the trail.

Bingle was not disturbed by wildlife, either. He didn't chase squirrels or other small animals, even when it was clear that he had noticed them. For the most part, he stayed near David, his behavior alternately regal and clownish.

At times, he walked near Ben. I learned from David that there was good reason for Bingle's attachment to Ben—for the last few months, Ben had been living at David's house. Although David was reluctant to supply details, apparently Ben had split up with a girlfriend, moved out, and was staying with David until the end of the semester. "He plans to find a place of his own then, even though I've told him he can stay on if he'd like. The dogs and I have enjoyed his company."

"Forgive me if I have a hard time understanding why," I said.

He smiled and said, "No, I guess Ben hasn't made a great impression on anybody on this trip. He's not at his best right now."

"Why?" I asked.

"Oh, all sorts of reasons," he said vaguely, and moved on.

We eventually stopped for lunch in a small clearing that didn't allow us to spread out as much as we had before. Nick Parrish used this opportunity to resume staring at me. Bingle, perhaps remembering who had shared a tent with him, took exception to this, standing rigid and growling at him.

"*Tranquilo, mi centinela,*" David said softly, and the dog subsided.

"What did you say to him?" Parrish asked.

David didn't answer.

"You appear to have a protector, Ms. Kelly," Parrish said. "For now, anyway."

"Leave her alone, Parrish," Earl said.

"But I think Ms. Kelly ought to be interviewing me, don't you?"

I was spared having to answer as the last member of the group hobbled into the clearing. Phil Newly moved gingerly toward a large flat rock, then sat down on it with a sigh. It was obvious that he was about to cripple himself with those new boots. For the last half mile or so, he had been walking as if every step were over hot glass.

I was searching through my pack for some of the moleskin I had brought, when Ben Sheridan walked up to him and said, "Take your boots off."

Newly blushed and said, "I beg your pardon?"

"Take your boots off! You've probably got blisters. You should have spoken up on the trail."

"I'll leave them on, thank you," Newly said, with as much dignity as he could muster.

"Don't make a bigger nuisance of yourself by being stubborn," Ben said. "You're endangering this whole trip by damaging your feet. Or perhaps that's what you have in mind?"

"Now see here—"

"Ignore his manners, Phil," I said. "He's right about the blisters. Dangerous if they become infected."

But he wasn't ready to give in, and instead took out a Global Positioning System device and began the process of taking a reading. Not hiding his exasperation, Ben walked off.

"You ever use one of these handheld GPS receivers?" Newly asked me.

"No," I said. "I manage okay with a compass, an altimeter, and a map." And a little help from J.C., I added silently. His familiarity with the area had helped me identify features of the terrain more than once.

"These are pretty amazing little gizmos."

He handed it to me and spent a few minutes showing me the basics of how it worked. As the display came up with a longitude and latitude reading, he said, "Of course, it won't work in narrow valleys or in dense forests, or other places where it might have a hard time picking up signals from the satellites. I noticed Detective Thompson is using one, too."

I handed it back to him. He tucked it away, started to stand up, and swore. "Excuse me," he said, sitting down again.

"Why don't you let me take a look at those blisters? If they aren't too bad, this moleskin will help."

But when he took the boots off, it was clear that he had already done some real damage. Over the years I've taken first aid classes, but I was relieved when J.C., much better trained and experienced, stepped in to do what he could for Newly.

We moved out again, Newly moving slowly but not giving up. When we stopped about an hour later to get our bearings, he didn't hesitate to take the boots and socks off again. I could see new blisters forming. I was starting to cut another set of moleskin pads for him when we heard Parrish call out, "I want to talk with my lawyer. Privately."

"What kind of idiots do you take us for?" Duke said. "You can't just go off somewhere in the woods with your lawyer."

Phil Newly sighed, and with a wince, stood on his bare feet. "I'll talk to him over here, in plain sight of all of you. Surround us, if you like, but give us a little room to confer." When Duke looked skeptical, he added, "I'm in no shape to 'go off somewhere in the woods' with anyone."

Duke looked over to Bob Thompson, who nodded. "But I want them surrounded," Thompson said. "And nobody else near them. Ms. Kelly, get the hell away from Mr. Newly."

No one had to coax me to move out of range of Parrish, who was smiling at me. "Ah," he said, feigning disappointment. "And I was hoping she'd play with my feet, too."

That earned him a sharp push from Earl.

Wary, none of the guards stood too far away from him. "Newly," Bob Thompson said, "you two will just have to whisper."

Parrish looked down at Newly's bare feet. "You're moving too slow, Counselor," he said, not trying to lower his voice.

"There's nothing I can do about that now," Newly said. "What do you want?"

"To move faster," Parrish said, and brought one of his sturdy boots down hard on Newly's bare left foot.

Newly gave a shout of pain, and Bingle began barking, but the guards had already moved in, shoving Parrish hard to the rocky ground and pinning him there. Houghton, gun out, covered them from a short distance away. Earl was on top, holding Parrish's face against the earth, distorting Parrish's smile of satisfaction.

J.C. hurried over to Newly, who looked as if he might faint. The ranger spent a moment examining the foot and said, "I think he broke some bones. It's swelling up fast."

He opened his first aid kit again and applied an instant cold pack to the foot. Soon it became clear that Newly would not only be unable to walk, he wouldn't be able to put his left boot back on.

This led to a heated discussion over whether to end the entire trip then and there.

Thompson was the main proponent of calling it quits. The others pointed out the time and expense already incurred. "If we have him up here without his lawyer—" Thompson began, but Parrish interrupted.

"I fire him, then."

"And I'll take you right back to Las Piernas anyway," Thompson said. "You think the D.A. won't go for the death penalty if he finds out how you screwed up this expensive search? Which may just be a wild goose chase, after all."

"I can promise you," Parrish said with a cold smile, "that this is no 'wild goose chase.' "

There was a long moment of silence before another round of arguments began. Newly agreed to allow Parrish to lead them to the grave out of his presence. "Leading you to her saves his life," he gritted out, his face pale and drawn.

Thompson finally relented, and decided to let J.C. and Houghton take Newly back to the plane. "Houghton, you fly back with him, take him to a hospital, then get in touch with the D.A. as soon as possible. Let him know exactly what happened here, and that Newly agreed to these arrangements."

J.C. and Houghton divided up the contents of Newly's pack, then supported Newly between them. Newly, still white with pain, tried to give me the GPS, saying, "Mark the position of anything I need to know about, will you?"

"I'm sorry, I can't," I said, not wanting to be even vaguely involved with Parrish's defense.

He managed a small smile and said, "You'll be using your compass, then?"

"Yes, and although I don't think any sane judge will let you get your hands on my notes, we both know Bob Thompson is using a GPS, too."

He nodded, but seemed too distracted by the pain in his foot to keep talking.

J.C. asked Andy to keep an eye on things while he was gone. "Leave trail signs for me," he said, "and don't let them destroy too many acres of forest, if you can help it."

We all watched the trio move slowly away from us.

I had a few chances to talk to Andy when he stopped every so often to mark a turning with a strip of cloth on a bush or small rocks in the shape of an arrow.

"Do you think J.C. will ever catch up to us again?" I asked.

"Absolutely," Andy said. "He's in great shape. He can cover

distances in a day that would have most of us looking as wiped out as Phil Newly was at lunch."

By late that afternoon, I began to wonder if we would make it to an area where we could set up camp, let alone to Julia Sayre's grave. We had wasted a lot of time, and the air was cooling rapidly. Clouds were gathering overhead—cirrus clouds. We might be in for a storm.

Thompson apparently had the same concerns. He stopped the procession. "We don't seem to be heading in the direction of the valley you indicated on the map," he complained to Parrish.

"I was wrong," Parrish said. "I know exactly where I'm going now."

Just then the breeze shifted a little. Bingle lifted his nose and made a chuffing sound, then began to whine, looking at David, ears pitched forward.

"Is he alerting?" Ben asked softly from behind me.

David was focused on the dog. "*¿Qué te pasa?*" he asked. "What's wrong?"

The dog started to move ahead, and David hurried to catch up with him. I followed, ignoring Thompson's "Get back here!"

The dog was moving rapidly now, and soon was out of sight. "Bingle! *¡Alto!*" David called, but Bingle had already stopped. He was ahead of us, barking, then whining in distress.

We reached it at the same time, both giving a cry of revulsion at the same moment. Bingle was at the base of a pine tree that at first seemed draped in some strange, gray moss. But it was not moss. The objects dangling from its branches were animals. Coyotes. A dozen or so carcasses, hanging upside down, in varying states of decay, nailed to the lower branches, as if someone had started to decorate a macabre Christmas tree.

I put my hand over my mouth, fighting off the urge to be sick.

David was quieting Bingle, praising the dog, but I could hear the shakiness in his voice.

We heard the sound of the others, pushing their way through the woods behind us.

Nicholas Parrish looked up at the tree and smiled. "I told you we were headed in the right direction."

6

▲ ▼ ▲ ▼

TUESDAY, LATE AFTERNOON, MAY 16

Southern Sierra Nevada Mountains

Flash took pictures. Merrick, arms held back by Manton, red-faced with anger, shouted at Parrish that he was "one sick fuck," while Manton did his best to keep his fellow guard from punching the prisoner. Parrish kept smiling.

I had watched the others arrive at the coyote tree; their faces had expressed first horror, then fury. Ben Sheridan, although briefly startled when he first saw the tree, now calmly studied it. He turned to Flash. "We'll need photographs of this, Mr. Burden."

Merrick, seeing Ben start to take notes, shouted, "That turn you on, Sheridan?"

"Shut up, Merrick," Bob Thompson said without heat, moving closer to the tree, studying it as well.

"From several angles, please, Mr. Burden," Ben said, then glancing at Merrick added, "if you videotape, please keep the sound off. David, perhaps it would be best to move Bingle away."

"There's a small clearing about fifty yards away—down that pathway, there," Parrish said, pointing. No onc thankcd him for his help.

I stayed for a while, but no one else was talking. I saw

Thompson take out his GPS. I used my compass to note the position of the tree.

I wondered if Thompson would ask for additional charges to be brought against Parrish for this—maybe J.C. could bring them on behalf of the Forest Service. I forced myself to count the coyotes—there were twelve of them. They appeared to have some sort of coating on them. Much as I tried to mentally brace myself, the sight made my stomach churn. I turned to Parrish. "Why?"

He grinned and said, "Feeling a kinship with them? Perhaps you'd like me to hang you here among them. Let them sway against you in the breeze."

I felt a sudden surge of anger, but just as quickly saw that he enjoyed my reaction—so I clenched my teeth against a retort.

Quietly, Thompson asked me to leave, and for once, I was happy to comply with his request.

When I caught up with Andy and David, they were playing tug-of-war with Bingle, using a cotton rope toy that had the worn look of a favorite plaything. I joined in the game. The dog would shake the rope fiercely and then proudly prance around the clearing whenever he took it away from one of us, high-stepping as he let the others know who had won the encounter, looking slyly at each of us to dare the next comer. It was almost enough to take our minds off what was happening by the tree, but not quite.

"David," Andy said, "you've been around this type of guy before. Why do you think Parrish did that?"

"There could be any number of explanations," David said, "but if you're trying to make any real sense of it, well, that's something for a forensic psychologist to tackle."

"He's insane," Andy said.

"Not by the legal definition," David said. "He was found competent to stand trial."

"According to Newly, Parrish was a severely abused child," I said.

"Oh?" David said. "Maybe he was, maybe he wasn't. His mother is dead and his sister has mysteriously disappeared, so we only have Parrish's word about the abuse. In fact, he's probably the only person on earth who knows where his sister is—either one of you believe she's still breathing?"

Silence.

"Did he kill his mother?" Andy asked.

"No," I said. "She died of natural causes. But one of the psychologists who interviewed him thought her death may have set him off."

David shook his head. "I guess psychologists have to try to understand him. Me, in most ways, I don't think I'll ever really understand a man like Nick Parrish. Other people survive abuse and go on to lead productive lives—they don't torture women and animals. Parrish is beyond explanation. Bingle's actions make more sense to me."

"So why is Ben back there studying that—that tree?" Andy asked.

"So that when the next Nick Parrish comes along, you catch him on his first coyote. Ben has done a lot more of this kind of work than I have. Maybe too much." He glanced over at me. "He's had a lot of tough cases lately. And a couple of back-to-back MFIs—he's on the DMORT team for the region."

"What's an MFI?" I asked.

"Sorry. Mass fatality incident—anything that takes the lives of a large number of people. Natural or otherwise—earthquakes, riots, bombings—"

"Airplane crashes?"

"Yes. Ben was called out to one of those in Oregon a few weeks ago."

"The commuter jet that crashed in the Cascades?"

"Yes. Eighty-seven dead. And we had just come home from working the flood up in Sacramento when the DMORT team got called to that one."

"What's a DMORT team?" I asked, pulling at the rope as Bingle nudged me with it.

"Disaster Mortuary Operational Response Team—it's a federal program. Let's suppose you're a coroner or a mortician in a rural area, coping with—oh, at the most, a few bodies a week. A plane crashes in the local woods, and suddenly you've got two hundred bodies to deal with. Usually, in a mass disaster, the local coroner and mortuary facilities can't handle it. If the coroner needs help with victim identification and mortuary services, the DMORT team can bring in a mobile morgue and the specialists to go with it. There are ten DMORTs, organized by region. Ben's on the one for this region."

"But this is different," Andy said. "Even working on criminal cases, I'll bet this is the first time he's seen something like that coyote tree."

David shrugged. "Maybe. You might be surprised at some of the things we've seen, Andy. Things that . . ." His voice trailed off. He shook his head, then called to Bingle. After a moment he said, "Ben wouldn't take the time back there if he didn't think he could learn something from it."

"Like what?" Andy asked.

"Maybe they're a way of keeping score," I said.

"The number of victims?" David asked. "Maybe. Or maybe the coyotes are part of some warm-up ritual, a preparation for a kill. Or maybe when he couldn't find the kind of victim he was looking for, he killed a coyote."

"But that would mean they've been there a long time," I said. "They would have been in worse shape."

David nodded. "Unless he's treated them with some sort of chemical to help preserve them—that's the sort of thing Ben is probably trying to determine."

Bingle's ears suddenly went up, his posture rigid. He sniffed the air, then moved into a protective position near David, hackles raised. "*Tranquilo*. I'm okay, Bingle," David said. The dog looked up at him, then sat at his feet.

Soon we saw what Bingle had heard and scented; the four guards and Parrish joined us, and not much later, Flash and Bob Thompson. Ben Sheridan came strolling along last of all, not greeting any of us, lost in thought.

Thompson looked at his watch and gave an exasperated sigh. "We've only got a couple of hours of daylight left. Can we make it to where the grave is before sunset?"

"Certainly," Parrish answered.

He led us down a steep path through dense woods, to a small pond. Thompson was marking it on his GPS when Parrish said, "No, no, not here." He moved off in another direction, back through the trees, crossing a stream, and after wandering through the forest, brought us to a long meadow.

"Not here, either," he said, and led us off again.

I asked Thompson what position he was reading on his GPS and doublechecked it against readings I had taken with my compass. I was about to tell him what I had learned, when David called to him.

"Bingle is showing some interest in that last meadow," he said. "It's worth spending more time there—"

"We've marked it on the GPS," Thompson interrupted. "I'm giving Parrish one more chance. We can go back to the meadow if he misses on this last try."

"Look at the map," I said, showing him the markings I had made. "He's taking us in circles. That ridge he's walking toward is the one with the coyote tree on it."

"Yes, he's had his little fun and games," Thompson said. "I've told him this next place had better be it, or the whole deal is off."

We crossed the ridge again, on a narrow path some distance from the coyote tree, and moving downhill again we found ourselves in another long, narrow meadow. It was nearly dark by then; the air was cold, but still.

"This place gives me the creeps," Manton said.

"Never mind that," Thompson said. He turned to David. "What does the dog say?"

"Conditions aren't good to work him," David answered. "If we get a breeze, I can tell you more."

"Parrish—exactly where in this meadow did you bury her?" Thompson asked.

"Exactly? I'm not sure. But that's why you brought the dog, right?"

Thompson's eyes narrowed. He looked ready to deliver Parrish a beating. He clenched his fists, then turned from Parrish, pacing two stiff steps away before saying, "Make camp here. We'll look for her in the morning."

And so we all went to work setting up tents. No one spoke much that night; there was none of the joking or camaraderie of the evening before. Bingle stayed with David, which was all right, I wasn't going to sleep. I'm sure I'm not the only one who lay awake that night, thinking of Julia Sayre being marched to this meadow, forced to dig her own grave. Not the only one, I'm sure, who thought it was worse somehow that Parrish had transformed this paradise into her hell.

And I'm sure I'm not the only one who wondered just how far away from us she lay.

7

▲▼▲▼

WEDNESDAY MORNING, MAY 17

Southern Sierra Nevada Mountains

Just after dawn the next morning, I went for a short walk, telling Manton, who was on watch with Merrick, which direction I planned to go. I hadn't hiked far when I found a shallow cave, not quite ten feet deep. If it had ever been the lair of an animal, it had long since been abandoned. There was nothing in the way of a cache of food or a nest, no scat, no bones of smaller prey, no bits of fur. In fact, the more I thought about it, the more it seemed to me that the cave looked a little too clean. No animal I could think of would leave so little evidence of its residence there.

I decided to ask J.C., the ranger, about it when he caught up to us again. It also occurred to me that Parrish could have made use of this place, and if so, the experts in our search group might be able to detect traces of his activities there.

I began to feel uneasy, and try as I might to chalk it up to another round of claustrophobia, I knew that wasn't the case. I hurried outside and went through the routine of using the compass and altimeter to calm myself down. I made a note of the cave's location and headed back to camp.

Although it was still early when I returned to the meadow, most of the others were up and about. Manton was studying a photograph of a blonde with shoulder-length hair, holding his thumb over part of the picture.

"Your wife?" I asked.

"Yes."

"She's pretty."

"Thanks."

I started to walk away, but as if it had just occurred to him, he said, "Hey, you're a woman . . ."

I turned back to him. What woman can resist responding to that observation? You always know what's coming next. Its equivalent is, "Hey, you speak Urdu, translate this." On behalf of your Urdu-speaking sisters, you listen.

"Tell me something," he continued. "You think her hair looks better like this?"

"Your thumb's in the way."

"No, that's where she cut her hair, just before I came up here. Pissed me off. We argued."

"Let me see," I said, and he handed it to me. I studied it for a moment. "She's pretty either way, don't you think?"

He took the photo back. "Yeah, I guess so. I guess I just need to get used to it." He yawned. "Nothing I can do about it now." He moved off to his tent.

Several yards away, Ben and Andy stood on top of a large, rounded boulder. Both were using field glasses; Andy pointed down the field, seeming to indicate a particular location, and Ben focused his binoculars in that direction. They then lowered their binoculars and made markings on a piece of paper. As I watched, this process was repeated several times.

I moved closer to them. Andy saw me and called out a greeting. "Come up here," he said. "I'll show you some of the signs we look for."

Ben was obviously displeased with this suggestion, and walked away before I reached the boulder.

"Here," Andy said, handing me his binoculars. "Look out over there, just to the right of that tree." He waited while I located the place he was indicating. "What do you see?" he asked.

I studied the meadow, which sloped gently upward from where we had camped. "Mostly grass and wildflowers," I said.

"Is the grass all the same height?"

I studied it again, more carefully this time, then said, "No! There's a patch of shorter growth."

"Right," he said. "It might be shorter because it's newer. We found several places like that in this meadow, and mapped them out. We'll need to take a closer look to get an idea of what caused the growth to be different there."

"Is that where David will search with Bingle?"

"Maybe. Usually he likes to start by giving Bingle a chance to sniff around on his own, without any guidance from us—see if he gives an alert."

"Like he did at the coyote tree?"

"No—not exactly. Bingle gives a very clear signal when he smells human blood or remains. He's trained to look specifically for human rather than animal remains. The way he reacted to the coyote tree—I think he was just upset."

"I don't blame him."

"Me, neither." He was quiet for a moment, then said, "Anyway, Ben and I will be checking out the places where the plant life is disturbed while David works with Bingle. Any number of natural factors can cause a change in plant life, of course, but I think one or two of the areas we want to look at are typical of burial places."

"Typical?" I asked. "What do you mean?"

"Studies have been done about how serial killers choose special burial places for their victims. Despite his claims to the contrary, we think Parrish knows exactly where to find the victim's grave. Ben thinks Parrish likes to stage things precisely—and dramatically. Detective Thompson and Ben agree that Parrish has probably revisited the burial site; he most likely chose a site that he could find again and again. Ben said it would help Parrish relive the pleasure of the kill."

"The pleasure . . ." I shook my head.

"I know," Andy said, grimacing. "Ben says we have to try to think of this the way Parrish would, if we want to find her."

"So what would we look for, then? Some sort of landmark?"

"Exactly. Anything that would help Parrish find the site again."

At that moment, Ben called to Andy, so I gave Andy's binoculars back to him and thanked him for the explanation. As I walked back toward the camp, I noticed that Bingle and David weren't in sight. Bob Thompson joined Ben and Andy.

I heard Bingle give a single, happy bark from somewhere in the woods. I looked for the dog and found him pacing back and forth before David, hardly sparing me a glance, focusing his attention on his owner, who was opening one of Bingle's equipment packs. David called a greeting to me, then commanded Bingle to sit. The dog immediately obeyed, but it seemed to be taking all his self-control to do so. His body was taut, his eyes watching David intently. His ears were pitched forward, his cheeks puffing slightly with excited breaths.

David smiled at me. "Don't you wish you felt this way about starting your workday?"

He pulled out a leather collar and Bingle's tail began swishing rapidly through the pine needles beneath it.

"For him, it's play. Just a big game. His favorite game." He replaced the bright-colored nylon collar Bingle had been wearing with the leather one.

"*¿Estás listo?*" he asked the dog. "Are you ready?"

Bingle got to his feet and barked.

"Can I join you?" I asked. "Or would it be too much of a distraction to Bingle?"

"No, he's used to other people being with us. When my group of handlers trains together, we always have at least two people out with the dog. On most searches, there are detectives or rescue personnel or other people around. Bingle has learned not to be distracted by them."

As we walked with the dog to the edge of the meadow, Bingle's attention was so focused on David, I was afraid the dog would walk into a tree.

"Great conditions," David said to me. "See how the grass in the meadow is moving?" He took out a small, rounded plastic object and squeezed it. A small cloud of fine powder puffed from it, and he studied its movement as it drifted by.

"Nice breeze, coming right at us," he said, pleased. "Moist air. Let's try to get some work in before it gets too warm. *¿Está bien, Bingle?*"

Bingle barked sharply in impatience.

"Yeah, yeah, yeah," David said.

"Rowl, rowl, rowl," the dog answered, in near-perfect imitation.

"*¡Busca al muerto, Bingle!*" David said, sweeping his hand out in a flat and low motion. Find the dead.

The dog took off in a weaving pattern, not running full bore but moving in his steady, long-legged pace, David not far behind him. I was a close third.

Sniffing the breeze, Bingle stopped every now and then, sometimes doubling back a short distance, but almost always moving forward. David spoke to him, encouraged him as he made his way through the meadow.

I kept watching, puzzled. This search method seemed to be all wrong, at least according to all the movies I had seen—which usually portrayed dogs tracking escaped convicts. How did he know what to look for? Or where? Bingle's nose was up in the air most of the time, not down on the ground. And he wasn't baying. He was zigzagging quietly through a field, obviously pleased to be at his work, but not giving any indication that he was close to finding anything.

After about twenty minutes, David gave Bingle a command to rest, and gave the dog some water. When I caught up with them, I took out my notebook and the one item of special outdoor journalism equipment I had packed—a waterproof pen. I asked David about Bingle's style of searching.

"The baying business is basically Hollywood, trying to combine a foxhunt with a manhunt, I suppose," he said. "Bingle barks more than the average search dog, mainly because I let him—some handlers consider it a sign of poor training to let a search dog bark. They only want the dog to bark when he finds a missing person alive. There's a lot of religion out there when it comes to handling dogs, if you know what I mean. I suppose if you had one that barked all the time, he might, oh, scare a lost child, for example. And if you've got a police dog trailing a killer in the woods, you don't always want the dog to alert the criminal to your presence with a lot of baying and barking.

"But Bingle isn't a police dog, and most of the people he looks for are dead. I guess I figure I know Bingle—and he's got a personality that needs to let out with a bark every now and then. He's a talker. None of the cadavers has complained about it yet. And if I ask him to work silently, he'll do it."

"Okay, so no baying. But how will he ever find Julia Sayre's scent? You never gave him any article of clothing to work with, or—"

"If you ever meet Bool, my foolish bloodhound, you'll see a tracking dog. I'm not saying that Bool never uses air scenting—he does, but primarily, he's tracking. He spends lots of time with his nose on the ground. He was born with a truly amazing sense of smell—probably better than Bingle's. Unlike Bingle, though, he's not what you'd call smart. I've got to keep him on a lead, or God knows, if the person he was trailing happened to have fallen off a cliff, he'd follow the scent right over the edge. He becomes nose-blind." He paused, smiling wistfully to himself.

I thought about the times my own dogs had relentlessly pursued some interesting scent, which usually resulted in holes in our backyard or knocked-over trash cans. "You're searching areas that might include crime scenes," I said. "I suppose the cops can't just let every clown who thinks Fido is pretty clever put his pet on a leash and come on down to snoop around."

"Right. Fido and his master are likely to destroy evidence—not to mention dozens of other legal and health problems. Search dogs are working dogs, and the handlers and their dogs all go through lots of training. It's ongoing, and requires years of work—but it's more than work. It's a bond, it's learning to read your dog, it's—well, it's hard to explain. Bool and Bingle work differently."

"Different in what ways?"

"Bool needs to be pre-scented—given something of the victim's to smell. He tracks that scent, nose to the ground. Bingle is primarily an air-scenting dog, and he is specifically cadaver trained."

"Which means?"

"Every individual human being gives off a unique scent—with the possible exception of identical twins. Otherwise, we each have our own. We give off this scent because every minute, every living person sheds an estimated forty thousand dead skin cells, called rafts, that carry bacteria and give off their own one-of-a-kind vapor."

"Even if you bathe and use deodorant?"

He smiled. "No getting away from it. You can mask it from your fellow humans, but not the dogs."

"Okay, but what if I'm not near the dog?"

"Let's go back to the rafts. Every minute, these tens of thousands of rafts come off us like a cloud, surrounding us and drifting away from us as we move, with the heaviest concentration very near us. As we move, it spreads into a wider and wider cone—that's known as a scent cone. As they drift, some of these rafts will catch on other objects, especially plants."

"And Bingle smells the rafts?"

"Yes. A dog's nose is literally a million times more sensitive than ours for some scents. And it's thought that their brains process scent information in a different manner than our brains do."

"So he can follow this cone of scent?"

"Yes. He's also trained to find the scent of human blood, body fluids, tissue, skeletal remains, and decomposing remains. And he can find any of these things in minute amounts."

"I know I'm going to hate myself for asking this, but how were you able to train him to find bodies—to teach him what a dead body smells like?"

"In this line of work, I have access to bones and other biological material from cadavers. But some trainers use a synthetic chemical that's made just for the purpose of training these dogs."

I couldn't hide a look of disbelief. "Fake cadaver smell?"

"Yes. Different formulas for different levels of decay."

"Not the kind of thing you'd want to accidentally spill on your carpet, I suppose."

He laughed. "No, but Bingle might not mind. Dogs aren't bothered by what we think of as horrible odors. To them, the worse it smells, the more interesting it is. And for Bingle, that smell is associated with praise—finding it brings a reward."

"But even decaying bodies must smell—well, unique, right? Because of the varying conditions they are left in, if nothing else—out in forests, in deserts, underwater—"

"Sure, to some extent. He's not trained for one smell alone, of course. Best of all, Bingle has a couple of years of experience, so he knows what it is he's looking for. Bingle's nose is sensitive enough to find a single drop of blood. You let him sniff a car, he can tell you if a body has been in its trunk."

"My husband and his partner made Bingle sound as if he were Super Dog."

"Oh no. He has his limitations. Conditions have to be good for him to search, and there are things that can throw him off. But his biggest limitation is talking to you right now."

"What do you mean?"

He smiled. "If I could understand everything he tries to say to me, we'd get better results. Lord, who knows what he could accomplish? More than once, I've looked back and realized that I just failed to read him; he was trying to show me where to find something, but I insisted that we do things my way. There are times when I can see he's frustrated, trying to get things across to his dumb handler."

"I don't know," I said, "you two seem to have a pretty good partnership."

"Well, partner," he said to Bingle, who immediately became alert, "ready to have another go at it?"

Bingle got quickly to his feet, but continued to watch David with anticipation.

"*¡Búscalos!*" David said, giving the same hand signal he had before. "Find 'em!" The dog immediately went back to work.

David worked him for another twenty minutes, and again provided water and rest. On the fourth round of work, the dog's weaving pattern suddenly narrowed. He was still moving side to side, but faster and faster. He stopped and looked back at David, his ears forward, the look intent.

"That's an alert," David said excitedly. "Whatcha got?" he said to Bingle. "Show me where it is. *Muéstrame dónde está. Sigue*—keep going."

Bingle moved off again, nearly in a straight line.

"How did you know it was an alert?" I asked.

"I know him," David said simply, hurrying after him. "When his ears are straight forward like that, it's as if he's checking in with me. I'm part of his pack. He's asking me,

'Can't you smell that?' " He kept watching the dog as he spoke, then said, "He's got something. Look—the scent has caught on the grass."

Bingle was rubbing his face against the grass, biting at it.

"*¡Búscalo, Bingle!*" David said. "Find it!"

The breeze came up again and the dog stopped, held his head high, and sniffed with a slight bobbing motion of his nose, as if trying to draw in more of a specific scent.

"Whatcha got?" David asked again. "Whatcha got, Bingle? Show me! *¡Muéstramelo! ¡Adelante!*"

Bingle sang a high little note, then rushed on ahead of us. He stopped about twenty yards away—I could see him circling anxiously in one area, heard him making chuffing noises. Suddenly, he sat down on his haunches, lifted his head back so that his nose was straight up in the air, and began crooning.

"That's his way of giving a hard alert," David said, rushing forward.

Bingle met him halfway, and nudged at a pouch on David's belt. "*¿Dónde está?* Where is it?" David said, and the dog loped back to where he had alerted and barked.

David reached the dog before I did. "Bingle," he suddenly said, "you beautiful son of a bitch!"

Bingle gave a loud bark of agreement.

8

▲▼▲▼

WEDNESDAY MORNING, MAY 17
Southern Sierra Nevada Mountains

If I hadn't talked to Andy before following Bingle, I might not have understood why David was now enthusiastically praising his dog, pulling out a floppy toss-toy that was apparently the dog's all-time favorite. On the ground where Bingle had indicated his find, I could clearly see the burial signs Andy had mentioned. There, in a long patch, the soil contrasted slightly in color with other nearby soil—it appeared to be less compact and there were more rocks and pebbles in it. The plants growing over it were not as tall or sturdy as their neighbors.

It was not a clearly defined grave-size rectangle with nice, neat edges. But it was not much bigger than a grave might be, and was obviously unlike the area immediately around it.

"Let's move back from this site," David said. "We don't want to disturb evidence."

We moved over to a level spot nearer to the tree, where David continued to play with Bingle and praise him. The other members of our group must have been watching us, because before David beckoned, Ben and Andy donned packs and headed our way, with Thompson and Flash Burden not far behind. Duke and Earl moved more slowly from the campsite, bringing

Parrish; Merrick and Manton managed to sleep through the commotion.

"A hard alert?" Ben called as he came within earshot.

David smiled. "Yes, and my dog doesn't lie."

"Where?"

But Andy had already noticed the plants near the place where Bingle had alerted. "Wow. Right there." Drawing closer, he pointed out several wildflowers and said, "You see? Most of them are shorter than others of the same species, growing right next to them. That might be happening because something's preventing their roots from developing—the roots may be running into some type of barrier underground."

David commanded Bingle to stay and we walked with the others to where Andy stood.

David conferred briefly with Bob Thompson and Ben, then said to me, "Would you mind keeping Bingle company while we check this out? You can watch from the shade over there—best spot in the house. You'll be able to see and hear everything."

"Look, I'm fond of the dog, but I have a job here, too. I don't want to be shut out—"

"This is a crime scene—" Bob Thompson began, but Ben interrupted.

"Oh, I think Ms. Kelly should be allowed to stand as close as possible," he said, and although he wasn't smiling, I could hear some amusement in his voice.

"Ben—" David protested, in a way that made me all the more unsure of Ben's motives for suddenly being so cooperative.

Ben ignored him. In quiet, considerate tones, he said to me, "Allow me to explain that we don't just bring out our shovels and dig, Ms. Kelly. We start slowly and carefully, systematically surveying the burial area, setting up a grid system and so on. Perhaps you wouldn't mind staying with Bingle while we do the preliminary work. I'll let you know when we're about to actually see the body—if there is a body here."

"She's there," I heard a voice say. I turned to see Parrish looking straight at me, smiling. "Yes," he drawled slowly, "her lovely body is right there."

"*Tranquilo,*" David said to Bingle, who was standing between us. The dog had not growled or barked at Parrish's approach, but I could see what had caused David to give the command to take it easy—Bingle's stance was rigid.

"I'll watch Bingle," I said.

Parrish laughed. "Better let him watch you."

"That's enough out of you," Earl said, pulling Parrish back from the group.

"*Ve con ella,*" David said to Bingle, and gave me a tennis ball. As he said this, he made a motion with his hand that evidently told Bingle that I was to receive all of his attention. Bingle stared at the ball with the kind of intense concentration that might have been used by a psychic to bend a fork. We played for a while, then sat together and watched as Flash videotaped and photographed the site, Thompson talked to Parrish, and David, Andy, and Ben hovered over maps and studied the ground, defining an outer perimeter several feet beyond the loosened soil.

Our place was, as David had said, the best spot in the house. We were only a few yards from the patch, we were in the shade, and the breeze had shifted toward us—both shade and breeze provided relief to Bingle, who lay panting softly, eyes closed in contentment.

Ben bent over a duffel bag, and handed out gloves. He next removed a set of metal rods, each about half an inch thick, bent at a right angle at one end—the handle. Working from different directions, the men each picked a spot, leaned on the probes—which did not go too far into the ground—then pulled them from the ground and moved them a little closer to the site of the alert. This process continued, until Ben's probe sank easily into the earth. "Here," he said. As he pulled it up, Bingle lifted his head, then came to his feet, ears pitched forward. The dog started to move toward Ben.

"Stay," I commanded. He ignored me, but David had heard me, and snapped the command again—in Spanish this time. Bingle obeyed, but protested with a sharp bark.

"He smells it," David said. Then, wrinkling his nose, added, "So do I."

David went back to the duffel bag and took a small jar from

it; he dipped a finger into it and then rubbed the substance just beneath his nose, making a small, shiny mustache of it. He offered the jar to Andy, who used it. He didn't offer it to Ben.

Ben was putting a little marker—a small yellow flag on a wire—near the spot where he had probed. They continued in this fashion until they had a few other places marked. The yellow flags formed a rough oval, about six feet long.

Bingle was agitated—fidgeting but obeying David's command to stay. Every now and then I would get a whiff of what he was reacting to—an unmistakable smell, a smell that is sweet and pungent all at once—a smell that you instantly know the meaning of, even if you have never smelled it before. Perhaps some primal memory repulses us from this scent, tells us that this is the smell of the death and decay of one of our own.

"I'll show you what we're doing," David said, coming over to calm Bingle. As he moved closer to me, I said, "Vicks VapoRub."

He moved his hand, just stopped short of touching his upper lip. "A menthol and camphor smell compound that's sort of similar to it, yes. I use it to mask the decomp odor. Do you need some?"

"Not yet."

"Don't wait too long," he said. "Once the smell is in your nose . . ." He paused, then said again, "Don't wait too long."

He began to show me the scene maps they were drawing, with nearby peaks as triangulation points to mark the position of the tree. The grid lines were shown, over which the position of the grave, the outer perimeter boundary, and a cluster of boulders were drawn.

"If we need to testify about any of this in court, we'll have a precise record of where we found any evidence or remains, how the remains were positioned—and so on."

Bob Thompson walked up to us. "What's taking so long? Parrish says she's there, about two feet down. He's already confessed. I just need a preliminary identification."

Behind me, I heard Ben ask, "And what if this is some other victim, Detective Thompson?"

Thompson hesitated, then said, "Fine, but let's not dawdle, all right? We aren't going to be able to stay up here forever."

Ben simply walked off. From one of his duffel bags, he pulled two rolls of screen, one about one-quarter-inch mesh, the other about half-inch. David helped him use these and two sets of support pieces to build two sieves.

Bingle occasionally called out to David, and in Spanish, David answered, "It's okay, Bingle. Stay with Irene." Invariably, I'd get a quick kiss from the dog in response.

Whenever I looked over at Parrish, he was watching me, a knowing smile on his face. I repressed the urge to quickly look away, to show how uneasy I was under his scrutiny. But I was always the first to break eye contact, and once, when an involuntary shiver went through me as I turned away, I heard him laugh softly.

With Andy's help, the anthropologists carefully scraped the surface level of the soil inside the markers away, and put it through the two sieves. They continued in this fashion, a few centimeters at a time—over Thompson's impatient protests. Although they didn't seem to be getting anywhere at first, before long I saw more clearly defined edges of the oval they had marked with the flags. The smell was getting stronger.

Ben took a moment to stretch. When he came over to say hello to Bingle, I said, "You wouldn't happen to have any of that smell compound with you?"

"I don't use it."

"But how can you stand—"

"For professionals who deal with it all the time—well, I suppose it's a matter of personal preference, but I don't recommend using any compound to cover up the smell. Try to deal with it the way nature designed you to deal with it."

"What do you mean?"

"Sooner or later, after your brain has received the message from your olfactory cells that something bad is out there—and received it again and again—the signal stops registering. There will be residual odor on your clothes and you'll smell it again later, when you aren't so near the grave."

"Charming."

"You'll smell it later no matter what you do now. But if you use something that will open up your nasal passages, it will continue to stimulate your olfactory cells—which will keep you smelling decomp throughout the day. It may also result in your brain connecting the good smell to the bad."

"You mean that every time I use anything with a menthol or camphor or eucalyptus odor—"

"Yes. Your brain might add decomp to the mix."

I looked over at David. He had used the smell compound, why shouldn't I?

"Of course," Ben said, "I don't expect you to be able to handle this situation at all, so do whatever you need to do."

That settled it, of course. David obviously thought I was a fool, but didn't say so—he just checked in with me every so often to see how I was bearing up. He offered the smell compound to the others; Ben and I were the only ones who didn't take him up on it. As he was passing it around, he pointedly skipped Parrish. Parrish just grinned and drew a deep breath.

"Move him back to the camp," Thompson ordered the guards.

The excavation went on, now even more slowly, as the sides of the grave were carefully uncovered. Ben focused on defining the grave's edges with painstaking care; David gently scraped away at the inside layers; Andy sifted for objects that might have been missed, bagged certain portions of the removed soil, labeled it, and made notes as needed.

From time to time the odor from the grave would suddenly seem worse. Ben would look over at me, smirking. I smiled back, taking satisfaction in knowing that whenever he looked over at me like that, he must have just gotten a beak full of it, too.

Flash continued to videotape the process, and to take still photographs at Ben's or David's request. Ben and David had a second camera, and took some photos on their own.

"Why are you photographing the edges of the grave?" I asked Ben.

He hesitated, then said, "Possible tool marks."

"From the shovel that was used to dig the grave?"

"Perhaps."

"If you know who did this, why do you need to gather evidence?" I asked.

"We don't necessarily know who made this grave," he said. "We have to treat this site as we would any other. Objectively."

"But Parrish has confessed—"

"Confessions can be recanted. Convictions are appealed. Deals fall apart, Ms. Kelly. We never know what we may need to prove, what evidence may become important. So we work carefully." He paused, then added, "The rules of evidence are much stricter in courtrooms than in newsrooms."

I turned away to keep him from seeing me grit my teeth.

After the first few layers of earth had been removed, a layer of large rocks appeared, scattered over the pit. When Thompson asked about them, Ben, not stopping his work, said, "My guess is that they were supposed to discourage carnivores from raiding the grave."

"Coyotes?" Thompson asked.

Sheridan looked up. "Yes, we know he's thought about coyotes."

Once the rocks were removed, the slow, scraping process began again. David was working on the portion near the center of the grave when he suddenly said, "Hold up."

Ben and Andy stopped what they were doing and began to focus on the area where David had been scraping soil away. They stepped back a little, and called Flash in to take a few photographs. After a moment, they called Thompson over.

I stood up and moved a little closer.

The object of all this scrutiny was a tuft of dark green plastic. Soon we would all come to realize what the forensic anthropologists already suspected.

This was a shroud.

9

▲▼▲▼

WEDNESDAY MORNING, MAY 17

Las Piernas

Frank Harriman hung up the phone and turned to his wife's cousin. "The lawyer's back—he's in the hospital." He drew a deep breath, let it out slowly. "Courtesy of his client."

"What happened?" Travis asked.

"Parrish stomped on Newly's foot. Caused multiple fractures. They had a tough time getting him back out—fainted a couple of times from the pain."

"She'll be all right," Travis said, knowing where Frank's concern lay, repeating a refrain that might have been wearying had Frank not needed to hear it.

"All the guards right there," Frank went on. "Watching him! And he still manages to injure his own lawyer." He paused, shook his head. "She shouldn't have gone up there."

"You couldn't have stopped her."

"She shouldn't have gone," he repeated, not listening, pacing now.

"Frank," Travis said.

But he was lost in unpleasant memories. He was thinking of the day they found Kara Lane's body, of what had been done to her. His pacing came to a halt when he thought—ever so briefly, but far, far too long—about the possibility of his wife being at Parrish's mercy, in as much pain, as much afraid, as much alone as Kara Lane had been in her last hours. He felt his stomach pitch.

"Frank," Travis said again.

He looked up.

"She's still surrounded by lots of other people. You know they'd kill him before they let him harm her."

He didn't answer. How could he explain this kind of foreboding? He knew it to be something more than simple fear for her welfare. It was the kind of uneasiness he sometimes got out on the job—instinct, gut feeling, the heebiejeebies—call it what you will. No cop worth a damn ignored it. Right now, it was irritating the hell out of him. He believed in it, trusted it, even though he couldn't have testified about it in a court of law . . .

"You've got to find something to do with yourself," Travis was saying. "You can't just sit here, getting more and more freaked out about this. Find something to occupy your time."

Lost in his thoughts about Parrish, for a moment Frank merely stared at Travis. The suggestion that he keep himself busy—which had at first seemed ridiculous—began to take hold, and now made perfect sense.

He reached for his car keys.

"Where are you going?" Travis asked.

"To visit Mr. Newly in his sickbed."

10

▲▼▲▼

WEDNESDAY AFTERNOON, MAY 17

Southern Sierra Nevada Mountains

J.C. caught up to us again when about half of the plastic had been uncovered. If he was weary from the additional hiking he had done or by difficulties in helping Phil Newly to the plane, he didn't show it.

Bingle noticed J.C.'s presence at the other end of the meadow before I did. Because I had been watching the dog, I caught the change in the focus of his attention before the others did. During the last few hours, I had been spending much of my time ensuring that Bingle didn't sneak closer to the open grave—after he made one nearly successful attempt, David taught me how to say "*¡Quédate!*"—which means "stay"—in a tone of voice that Bingle would obey.

"You can also say, *'No te muevas,'* " David said. "If you say it in a no-nonsense tone of voice—let him know you mean what you say—you'll get him to set aside his other impulses, even the ones that tell him he was on to something really great and now we're having all the fun. He'd like to join in, but his notions of amusement wouldn't be too helpful for our purposes."

I shuddered.

"I know, I know," David said. "But in order to do this kind of work, he has to be interested in that smell. He behaves himself for the most part, but the trouble is, Bingle tends to feel a little proprietary about his finds."

Now, as J.C. approached, Bingle's ears were pitched forward and he watched the ranger closely. Dogs—natural hunters—see motion better than detail, and Bingle's body posture said that he was on guard against this approaching figure. Eventually he must have managed to catch J.C.'s familiar scent—although how he could do so over the increasingly intense smell of the grave, I'll never know—because suddenly he let out a happy bark of welcome.

For a time, work stopped as we greeted J.C. and caught up with one another. He applied some smell compound as he listened to the story of Bingle's find, and praised the dog, who was happy to bask in his attention.

He had seen the coyote tree, and his disgust over it was plain; he was all for bringing charges against Parrish for it. "Not a big deal to someone going down on a double murder rap, I suppose, but still—" He shook his head, as if ridding himself of the memory of the tree. He bent down to pet Bingle. "So you've found Mrs. Sayre, eh, Bingle?"

"We don't know who or what this is yet, J.C.," Ben reminded him, handing him a pair of gloves. "We haven't even opened the plastic."

"Well," the ranger said, looking amused, "the plastic seems to rule out an American Indian burial site, and I can tell you that there aren't any legal cemeteries in this meadow, and no hunting allowed here, either. So whoever or whatever it is, it doesn't belong here."

"When will the plane be back?" I asked him.

"Tomorrow, weather permitting. Some rain in the forecast, so they might be delayed a day or so. Did you bring rain gear?"

I nodded.

"We'd better get back to work," Ben said. "The last thing I want to cope with is a flooded site."

J.C. had apparently done this work before, but even with his help, things could only progress at a certain pace. Eventually, the top surface of the plastic was uncovered. It was a dull, dark green. It appeared to be of a heavier gauge than the plastic used to make trash bags, more like the type used for ground cover by landscapers.

Thompson paced, muttering none-too-quietly about guys who think they're working on a pharaoh's tomb instead of a crime scene; about wishing to God he could bring in a backhoe; damning Parrish's hide for picking this place out beyond East Jesus to bury a body—and other unhelpful remarks that made life a little less pleasant for everyone within earshot.

Ben didn't gratify Thompson with a response. He walked over to him, though, while Andy, J.C., and David stood back from the grave to allow more photographs to be taken of the lumpy plastic.

"We want to dig down a little more on the sides," Ben told the detective, "just to see if we can find the edge of the plastic. We'd prefer to keep it intact. But if we can't find an edge, we'll go ahead and cut it open."

Thompson looked up into the sky and said, "Thank you, Lord!"

"We aren't being careful just to irritate you," Ben said. "My guess is that the plastic wrapping, the cool temperatures and altitude here, the lack of animal disturbance—"

"What is it you're trying to say?" Thompson snapped.

"In terms you'll understand?" Ben shot back.

Thompson's face was red, but he said, "As a matter of fact, yes—I'd like the nonegghead version."

Ben looked away from him for a moment, as if trying to regain his temper. "This body may be—let's see, in 'nonegghead' terms? It may be a little soupy. With this much odor, I don't believe we'll be looking at completely skeletonized remains—what we're smelling is not just the scent of bones. That's one reason why I'm not sure these remains are four years old—perhaps they are, perhaps they aren't. If they aren't—you may have a different victim here."

"Yes, you mentioned that possibility earlier, but—"

Ben raised a hand, and Thompson—with a visible effort—held his peace.

"There are lots of 'ifs' here, Detective—if the remains are human, if this is a homicide and if this is not Julia Sayre—if all those conditions are met, you will obviously have a new set of charges you can bring against Parrish."

Seeing he had Thompson's interest, he went on. "Obviously, you can bring new charges only if we can prove that he's the one who put this body here. We're going slowly, because trace evidence that will link Parrish—or anyone else—to this crime may have been left in the surrounding soil, and if so, we want to find it."

Ben paused and smiled, not very pleasantly, then added, "Just think, Detective Thompson, if this is a different victim, you'll go back to Las Piernas a hero."

"The D.A.'s deal with Parrish wasn't exactly popular, was it?" Thompson said. "We weren't too happy with it."

"The police weren't the only ones who were outraged that Parrish was protected from the death penalty. I think the D.A. has regretted it. That's partly why Ms. Kelly was allowed to join us, right?"

Thompson looked over at me and nodded. "Everybody knows he's hoping she'll make his decision look good. She's been writing about the Sayre case for a long time."

I knew he resented my stories about Julia Sayre. As far as Thompson was concerned, they were an ongoing, embarrassing announcement that he had failed to solve the case.

"With a new case to pursue," Ben said, "the D.A. could redeem himself with both groups—he'll claim he tried to find Julia Sayre, but won't fail to seek the death penalty for a third murder. And with what may be the resolution of another missing persons case, I'm sure the Las Piernas Police Department would be pleased with you."

Thompson glanced back toward the camp, where Parrish, surrounded by his guards, stood staring toward us. Parrish was too far away to see us very clearly, or to be clearly seen by us, but he seemed intensely interested in our activities. And even at this distance, the defiance in his stance was unmistakable.

When I looked back at Thompson, though, I saw that Ben's words had produced the opposite effect of the one he had intended. If Thompson was anxious to proceed before—when he'd thought only of being able to get back home with his mission accomplished—Ben's vision of his heroic return now only intensified his impatience to achieve it.

"Who else could have left the body here?" he said. "Parrish led us right to it!"

Ben sighed. "Believe me, Detective Thompson, I want to know what's underneath that plastic as badly as you do. But remember what I told you about the possible condition of the remains? Lifting the plastic out of the grave might cause the remains to shift, and perhaps to be damaged. We need to proceed with caution."

"Christ, Sheridan, you've been creeping along like a three-legged turtle! If what you've been doing up to now hasn't been 'proceeding with caution,' we'll all be skeletons by the time you're ready to get that body out of here!"

"If you'd like to continue without my help—"

"Don't be ridiculous!" Thompson said, but cooled off a little. "Look, I don't mean to push you—"

David laughed.

"I don't mean to push you into doing anything that will destroy evidence," Thompson went on, "but I also don't have the time or resources to allow you to make this into a museum-quality archeological dig." He glanced back toward the camp, and missed the derisive looks the others exchanged. He turned again to Ben. "Among other problems, I need to get Parrish back into a cell as soon as possible."

"If we're allowed to get back to work," Ben said meaningfully, "you'll get your answers sooner."

It was, in fact, not much later that Ben said, "We're not going to be able to unwrap the body without risking damage. We're ready to cut the plastic."

David, seeing me come to my feet, said, "I can get Bingle to stay there if you want to come closer—at least long enough for you to take a look."

"If this is not Julia Sayre," Ben objected, "there may be details here that we don't want released to the public."

Thompson said in exasperation, "Agree to keep it off the record, will you, Kelly? If it isn't Sayre, you can report that another victim has been found. The rest you keep out of the paper—write about it only after we release the information."

"The rest goes to the *Express* first," I said.

"All right, fine. Sheridan, get on with it."

Ben didn't try to hide his contempt for me, but being in this line of work, I had my disapproval vaccinations a long time ago and don't expect I'll ever be killed by a snub. The sooner he realized that all his wishing I would go to hell wasn't going to keep me from doing my job, the better for both of us.

"*Acuéstate,*" David commanded Bingle, and the dog lay down. "*Bien, Bingle. No te muevas.*"

David offered the jar of smell compound again, and a mask. I reluctantly took the mask after he told me that everyone who stood near the grave would have to wear one. I put mine over my head, but knowing how confining it would feel, didn't pull it up over my mouth and nose just yet.

Watching me, David said quietly, "This isn't going to be pretty. You've seen decayed remains before?"

"Yes," I said.

"This will probably be worse. Much worse. My guess is that it's going to be tough on these cops, because even though they see some horrible things, usually the bodies they find are—well, fresher. Seldom this far gone." He paused, then said, "If you're going to get sick, for God's sake, run as far away from the site as you can to do it."

Seeing my look of apprehension, he added, "Ben really hates the smell of barf."

I laughed, felt better for it, and told him I'd probably try to pick some other way to get back at Dr. Sheridan.

He smiled. "You'll be fine."

But when the plastic was cut, I-shaped, and then—with a crackling sound—pulled back, I wasn't so sure I would be fine. I held on by making myself think of the strange mass—the misshapen figure that was in some places bone, some places hair, or liquid, or leathery tissue—to think of this figure that lay before me as something to be studied, something that might tell a secret.

Even then, I could not manage to be a cold observer; perhaps those much touted tricks of divorcing one's mind from the victim's humanity worked for someone there, but not for me, and as I glanced at the faces of Ben and David, who had seen this sort of thing so often before, I realized that I didn't see coldness there at all—only quiet compassion. Perhaps they felt as I did: for all its distorted aspect, there was no doubt that this had been a human being, that this had been someone, and although her fate had been terrible, it would not remain hidden.

Ben caught me studying him, or so I thought, until I realized that the reverse was true he had quickly studied me, and the others as well.

"Mr. Burden, will you be able to continue?" he asked the photographer, whose face was drained of color.

"Mr. Burden?" Ben asked again.

Flash tore his wide-eyed gaze from the remains, and looked up at him. "Yes, sir," he said shakily.

"The camera?" Ben prompted gently.

Flash looked down at his right hand in surprise; at some point he had dropped the video camera away from his face, and was now holding it limply at his side.

"Yes, I'll start taping again," he said, a little more steadily. He pulled the camera up.

"J.C., you're taking the notes now?" Ben asked.

"Yes," the ranger said, his own voice unsteady.

"Let's get started, then." Ben gave the date and time, named the persons present and gave the coordinates for the grave. As he calmly recited this information, I found my own nerves steadying, felt the first shock of the sight before me receding. I tried again to study the remains.

The body was lying faceup. The underside was, from all I could see, a gooey mess. The upper portion was part mummy, part skeleton, part waxwork figure—this latter, I was told, was due to the formation of adipocere, a soaplike substance produced during one of the phases of decomposition.

"These observations are preliminary," Ben was saying, "and subject to verification in the lab. We have one, unknown adult female, of European descent. Age and stature yet to be determined. No clothing is apparent. Position is supine, with arms slightly outstretched. The individual's head is positioned west along an east-west line. Hair is dark brown." He paused, then said, "Focus on the left hand, please, Mr. Burden. . . . Subject is wearing a yellow metal band inset with three red stones on the fourth finger of the left hand . . . the left thumb, apparently severed antemortem through the shaft of the proximal phalanx, is not present."

"It's her," Bob Thompson said quietly, and walked away.

11

▲ ▼ ▲ ▼

WEDNESDAY AFTERNOON, MAY 17

Southern Sierra Nevada Mountains

Ben noted for the tape that Detective Thompson was no longer present, then made a few additional observations, most of which concerned "apparent antemortem trauma" and also some comments about damage that probably occurred perimortem—near the time of death—or postmortem. He paused, seemed to take a long moment to look at the body as a whole, then said, "Okay, that's it for now."

He asked Flash to take some still photos; he named specific shots he wanted. He asked David to tell Flash of any others he might need, and asked him to bag the hands and feet—to place plastic bags over them to help keep them intact. He asked me to follow him, and pulling his mask down, stepped back over to his stack of supplies. I was happy to pull my own mask down again, and wondered briefly if—having already guessed that I have problems with claustrophobia—he had suspected my dislike of having part of my face covered.

He didn't mention this though, and simply asked me to help him assemble the lightweight stretcher he had brought. He gave me a body bag to carry, and we took both bag and stretcher back to the site.

Thompson had returned by the time these tasks were completed, and Ben, after conferring with him for a moment, gave him a pair of gloves and a new mask.

"You, too, Ms. Kelly, if you don't mind," Ben said, motioning to my mask, giving me a pair of gloves as well.

I took the gloves with some trepidation. "What do you want me to do?"

"It's going to take all of us to lift her out of the grave and into the body bag," he said.

I felt my mouth go dry. "Is she that heavy?"

"Probably not, maybe a hundred-and-fifteen, hundred-and-twenty pounds. But I'm trying to minimize damage."

He knelt near the edge of the grave, leaned in and grasped one end of the plastic, near where the skull lay. He pulled slightly on the plastic, as if testing its strength. He then directed each of us to specific places near the edges of the grave; Bob Thompson and Andy were on her right side, David and J.C. on her left. Ben was at her head. I was at her feet. The stretcher and bag were near Bob and Andy.

Flash was back to operating the video camera. I hoped with all my might that he wouldn't be getting a shot of anything splashing out of the plastic and onto my boots.

Following the others' lead, I knelt down. David and Ben carefully folded the plastic back into its original position, covering her.

"Please try not to disturb the edges of the grave," Ben said. "Ready? Take hold."

The plastic felt cool and stiff beneath my gloved fingers. I told myself that I could cope with feeling the warm, close air of my breath in the mask. I told myself I would not fall into the grave. I moved back a few inches.

"I'll count to three," Ben continued. "When I say the number three, we're each going to lift very slowly, very carefully, very evenly. The remains are fragile. They may shift inside the plastic. We may find that the plastic won't be strong enough to hold them, and if not, we're going to have to set them down again. I know this is an awkward way to lift; try not to strain your backs. Anyone having trouble, speak up right away. We'll come straight up to just above ground level, then I'll give you instructions from there. Everything should be done as if you're moving in slow motion. Watch more than the section just in front of you—make sure we're moving together. Everyone ready?"

We nodded.

"Gently. One . . . two . . . three . . ."

There was a crackle as we began lifting.

"Easy . . . easy . . ."

Ben was watching me as we began to feel the weight. I tried not to let my uneasiness show. The remains weren't heavy, but knowing what we were holding was unnerving.

"Slowly. . . . What do you think, David?"

"It will hold," David said.

There was a sloshing sound. The plastic moved as if it were alive, rippling toward me.

"A little higher, Andy and J.C.," Ben said calmly. "Easy . . ."

We continued lifting, Ben guiding our way, watching one another, listening to the slight shiftings, the small rustling sounds of the plastic.

When it was above the burial pit, we slowly straightened our backs, so that we were sitting up over our knees, and the plastic was stretched a little tighter. Ben waited a moment, then he asked Bob Thompson and Andy to step away. The four of us edged the body away from the pit. Next, Ben and David briefly managed the body alone, placing it in the body bag. The bag was zipped up and locked with a crimped metal seal. The stretcher was already beneath the bag.

I turned to look back into the grave. "Oh, Jesus!"

The others hurried over, stood next to me, peering down.

Stained and moldy, but laid out in neat array, were articles of women's clothing: a black jacket and skirt, a once white blouse, black pumps and purse. Underwear. A bra. A slip. There were other objects as well—some candles, some wire, a knife. A gold necklace.

Some objects were loose, some encased in clear plastic bags.

The Polaroid photographs were in bags.

As much as I knew that they were photographs that never should have been taken, of things that never should have happened to anyone, I could not keep myself from staring at them, all the while not wanting them to be there.

They stared back.

She stared back.

I felt a strong hand on my shoulder, and someone said, "Come away. Come and sit next to Bingle. Come on. He's worried about you."

Ben, I realized. He pulled the mask off my face, kept talking to me. I don't know what he said. I let him lead me over to Bingle. The dog nuzzled me as I sat down next to him.

I held on to Bingle, and looked back toward the grave, toward the black body bag.

I thought of a girl who had once wished her mother dead, and knew that Julia Sayre must have wanted her daughter's wish to come true long before it did.

12

▲ ▼ ▲ ▼

WEDNESDAY NIGHT, MAY 17

Southern Sierra Nevada Mountains

I sat at the edge of my tent that evening, listening to laughter. The gathering around the campfire had been quiet and solemn at first. After a long day of laboring over the grave and its artifacts—photographing, mapping, collecting, and labeling its grim contents—the team of workers was tired and subdued.

Parrish, now being watched by Duke and Earl, was kept away from the rest of the group. He was taken to a tent after Merrick had another flare-up with him, this one undoubtedly resulting in Parrish receiving a bruise or two.

It had started when Parrish, handcuffed, had seen a moth fluttering not far from his face. He watched it intently, then snapped at it with his open mouth, and exaggerated the act of chewing and swallowing it. "Why the hell did you do that?" Merrick asked, disgusted.

Parrish stared at him, smiled, then glanced at the body bag. "It reminded me of someone."

Merrick tackled him to the ground before Manton could stop him. Later, even Merrick acknowledged that Parrish seemed pleased to have goaded him into that loss of self-control.

No one blamed Merrick for his edginess. While yesterday Parrish might have been guided to a place and told to take a seat, today he was shoved down, and roughly yanked up again when his guards were ready to go. We didn't protest at all. A line, it seemed, had been moved. Having just seen photos of Parrish pouring hot wax into one of his victim's ears, I was not willing to champion his civil liberties.

All day, Parrish had met with increasing hostility and disgust; while most of us kept our tempers in check, no one wanted to be anywhere near him.

I looked toward the body bag, which had been brought to the camp and now lay nearby. J.C. sat next to it, taking his turn watching over it. David had told me that from now until it reached the lab, the body would always be guarded—not just from Parrish, whose request to see it had been denied—but also from any animals that might be attracted by the smell. "And it's evidence, of course," he said, "so we have to be able to account for it during every moment that it's in our possession."

Still, its nearness was unnerving. Again and again, I found my eyes drawn to it. I tried to force my thoughts along other channels, but before many minutes passed, I was thinking about it and its contents.

Duke, who was whittling a little wooden horse for his grandson, would stop every so often, look toward the long black bag, then return to his carving with a vengeance.

The others, I noticed, often looked toward the body, too.

David started the clowning. It began during dinner, while Ben was on duty near the stretcher. David gave Bingle a command to do a headstand, which—without lifting his hind legs—the dog attempted. The dog not only looked ridiculous, with his head upside down on the ground and his forepaws flattened next to it, he "talked" the whole time he held this position, making a sort of half-howling, half-barking sound. He brought the house down.

David said, "*Bien*," and Bingle raised his head up, glancing around the laughing group with that grinning look that dogs sometimes get on their faces, wagging his tail, seeming for all the world to be enjoying the joke with the rest of us.

This set off a round of dog stories, and then a round of cop and forensic anthropologist stories, and next a round of bizarre homicide stories. The humor was often dark, and most of the tales would, I knew, never be repeated around those whom this group thought of as civilians.

I noticed that the stories and jokes never touched on this day's work or this victim—subjects that by some unspoken agreement were taboo—and that the most any of them got out of Ben was a soft smile.

I called it a night long before most of them were ready to do the same. Now I sat wondering if I would ever get the smell of decay off my hair and skin, wondering if another day or so spent in proximity with the body would permanently mark me with its scent of death.

I heard footsteps in the darkness and gave a start.

"Ms. Kelly."

I sighed in relief. "You scared the hell out of me, Dr. Sheridan."

"Oh." He paused. "I'm sorry."

It must have nearly killed him to say it.

He came a little closer. "Ms. Kelly, you're married to a homicide detective, right?"

"Yes. Frank Harriman. He's with the Las Piernas P.D."

"Then I suppose you understand . . . I suppose you've heard him tell stories or make jokes about things . . ."

"Dr. Sheridan, I've not only heard him make this sort of joke, I've joked with him. If you think I'll misjudge what's happening around that campfire, you misjudge me. But, come to think of it, that seems to be a specialty of yours."

There was a long silence.

"They're just releasing tension," I said. "I know that. Under the circumstances, it's probably one of the healthiest things they could do."

"Yes," he said quietly.

"I know you think that I'm one of a species other than your own—one of an unfeeling life form that crawled out of the sea a little later than the one that became forensic anthropologists—but miraculously, maybe sometime during the Paleozoic Age, reporters developed a sense of humor, too. Someday I'll have to sneak you into a newsroom, Ben Sheridan, so that you can hear our own brand of sick humor. We're getting pretty good at it; you should hear how quickly the jokes start whenever a particularly shocking story comes over the wire. And it works almost as well as it's working over by that campfire."

"Well, yes, I just—"

"You just thought I might write that these guys didn't show proper respect for Julia Sayre. Just thought I wouldn't understand that this really has nothing to do with her—that I lie in wait for anyone in this group to make a mistake or betray a little human weakness so that I can trumpet it to the world. That I don't understand the horror and the strain of . . ." I suddenly felt that horror, that strain, and stopped talking.

He didn't speak or move.

"I'm sorry. I didn't mean to lecture you," I said. "And I owe you my thanks."

"For what?" he asked, and I could hear the surprise.

"At the grave, when I—I kind of lost it there for a little while. I hadn't expected to see—what I saw."

"Your reaction was understandable, Ms. Kelly. And you don't owe me thanks—I owe you another apology. It was cruel of me to ask you to help."

"I'm not unwilling to help," I said. "I just wasn't ready for . . ."

"No one ever is," he said. "No one."

He started to walk off, then said, "David will want to keep Bingle with him tonight. Will you be all right?"

"Yes."

He looked up at the sky. "Better put the rainfly on your tent."

13

▲ ▼ ▲ ▼

WEDNESDAY AFTERNOON, MAY 17

Las Piernas

When Frank arrived at Phil Newly's hospital room, he found the lawyer looking disconcerted.

"Bad news about the foot, Mr. Newly?" he asked as he walked in.

Newly was frowning, but when he recognized Frank, he smiled broadly at him. Not exactly the reception Frank had expected. Outside of testifying against a couple of his clients, Frank had never spoken to Newly. There had been nothing personal, Frank knew, in Newly's attempts to discredit his testimony on those occasions. Newly was better than most on cross-examination, but his efforts against Frank's testimony had been unsuccessful. Each man had just been doing his job. He hoped Newly thought of it that way, too.

"Detective Harriman!" Newly said. "You cost me the Beringer case, and one other, as I recall." He didn't seem especially bothered by it. "You're also Irene Kelly's husband, right?"

"Yes, I am. That's why I'm here. I'm hoping you can tell me how she's doing."

There was the slightest hesitation before Newly said, "Fine.

She's fine—at least, she was when I left the group. Listen, Frank—may I call you Frank?"

He was surprised, but said, "Sure."

"Great. And please call me Phil." He smiled again, this time in a way that Frank was sure was calculated to be disarming. "Now that we're on such friendly terms," Newly went on, "may I ask a favor of you?"

"Nothing that will cause me to be busted down to traffic division?" Frank asked warily.

"No, nothing like that. I just need a ride home."

"You're going home already?"

"Yes, they only kept me overnight for observation. If I weren't a lawyer, they probably would have sent me home yesterday. Always afraid we'll sue, I suppose. Anyway, I'll have to wear this cast for a while, but there's no reason for me to take up a hospital bed."

He figured giving Newly a ride home would allow him the time he needed to talk to him, so he said, "Okay."

"Great! And—if you don't mind—my clothes—in the backpack there? Would you mind handing that to me?"

He supposed that Newly was probably perfectly capable of getting it himself, but he humored him.

The lawyer began emptying the pack out on the bed, which was soon covered with a camp stove, a cooking set, a flashlight, a poncho, a water bottle, matches, a roll of toilet paper, and all sorts of other gear, including an impressive array of clothing. It must have killed him to march around in the mountains with all of that on his back, Frank thought, making an effort to control his amusement.

Newly smiled up from the middle of the mess he had made. He held a pair of jeans in his hands. "Would you mind taking these to the nurses' station and asking them to cut off the bottom half of this pant leg? The left one. Otherwise, I'll never get these on over the cast. I'll start getting dressed while you do that."

Suppressing a desire to tell him what he could do with his pant leg, remembering that he needed the lawyer's help, Frank said, "All right."

* * *

"So your friend thinks I'm a tailor," the nurse said, but took the jeans from Frank. She was a young, slender redhead—a woman with an air of self-possession that he thought must serve her well in this job.

"Don't feel so sorry for yourself," he answered, which made her look up at him. "He thinks I'm his chauffeur and valet—but he knows he's not my friend."

She held her head to one side, studying him, and smiled. "No, I don't suppose you are his friend. What puts you in charge of his pants—dare I ask?"

"Just trying to get him out of here. I'm giving him a ride home."

"Thank you! We can't wait for that pain in the ass to leave."

"I can understand that," he said, smiling back at her.

She glanced at his left hand, saw the ring, and went back to cutting the pants.

He did his best to repack the backpack while Newly finished dressing. He had just fit the cookset in when he came across something that, at first glance, he thought was a cellular phone—but he quickly realized it couldn't be.

"Is this a GPS receiver?" he asked.

Newly looked up from his efforts to put a sock on his right foot—although not broken or in a cast, it was badly blistered. Seeing it, Frank didn't feel so bad about fetching the backpack.

"Yes," Newly answered, holding out a hand. "Here—I'll show you how it works."

He spent a few minutes proudly demonstrating the unit, then asked Frank to help him put one of his hiking boots—the only shoes he had with him—on his tender right foot.

The nurse Frank had met earlier brought a wheelchair in and offered to escort them down to the hospital lobby.

"Everybody knows that you don't let patients leave without wheeling them out of here," Newly said.

"Undoubtedly thanks to people in your profession," she said.

He laughed and cheerfully admitted that it just might be so. As she helped Newly out of the bed, Newly put an arm around her shoulder and winked broadly at Frank. Frank ignored it and answered the nurse's question about what he did for a living. This resulted in an animated conversation that lasted until they reached the lobby. He left them to get the car; by the time he brought it around to where they waited, Frank could see that in another few minutes, she might have gladly rolled Newly out into traffic.

Frank had already put the backpack on the backseat, and now he opened the car door as the nurse was bending to lower the wheelchair's footrest. Newly said, "Frank is married to a good-looking brunette, you know. But I'm available!"

"Phil," she said, helping him to stand up, "as surprising as that news is to me, I have to tell you this: There are lots of women who would pursue Frank even though he's married. But even though you're single—well, let's just say, I hope you're rich."

She was moving away before he shouted, "I am!"

She didn't look back.

"Well, how do you like that!" he said, laughing.

He joked about himself when recounting the tale of blistering his feet. "And the worst part," he said, "is the number of lectures I've endured from this foot specialist at the hospital."

He proceeded to give an imitation of the man; it made Frank laugh, and in this good humor he gave in to Newly's request that they stop off at a pharmacy not far from the lawyer's home. Newly insisted on trying to walk into the store on his own.

"Look," he said, "while I'm in there, could you rearrange my pack a little? I left the GPS on top, and I'm afraid it will fall out and break. Cost me about six hundred, you know, so I'd rather not smash it on my driveway."

Frank looked at him sharply, and saw, for the first time that day, the intelligent member of the Bar Association he had met in the courtroom—not the clowning klutz of the past hour or so.

Newly smiled and said, "Play around with the GPS if you like. This may take a while."

He was hobbling into the store before Frank could respond.

Frank knew a clear invitation when he heard one, and hesitated only long enough to try to figure out if Newly was setting him up somehow, or worse, setting the department up for problems by using him in some way. But he couldn't see how

Newly could use this against him, and if it meant he'd know where Irene was right now, he'd risk it.

He wasn't going to ignore his instincts; he was going up there. If she didn't need him, fine. She might even be angry with him. At that thought, he smiled to himself. It wouldn't be the first time.

But the next thought sobered him—it was one thing to imagine that he might hike up there for no real reason, that she was fine. It was another to think of her hurt or in danger. If she was in trouble and he stayed home, he'd never forgive himself.

By the time Newly came out, he had written down every set of coordinates that had been stored in the GPS unit's memory during the two days Newly was in the mountains, and the GPS unit had been returned to the backpack.

"Did you get everything you need?" he asked Newly.

"Yes. And you?"

He hesitated, then said, "Yes. Tell me why you're helping me."

"Oh, I could try to make this sound quite innocent, and say I'm returning a kindness; that your wife was very good to me while we were hiking. She even went so far as to doctor my smelly, blistered feet. But it wouldn't be the truth."

He fell silent, and Frank wondered if he was going to leave it at that. But then he said, "A policeman comes to my hospital room. A man not connected with the case. He tells me that he is concerned about his wife. I involve him in some foolish business so that I can consider my situation. I have no difficulty believing that he is there for the reason he says he is; he's willing to take on demeaning errands in order to talk to me. He's genuinely worried about her. I'm concerned about her, too."

"Why?" Frank asked. "Has something—"

"Nothing. Nothing to be alarmed over. Not yet."

Frank's hands tightened on the wheel. "Does Parrish have something planned?"

"Undoubtedly." At Frank's look of alarm, Newly quickly added, "I don't know what he has planned, and I don't know if it involves your wife, except—well, no, I don't have any idea of what he has in mind."

"You're his lawyer!"

"Yes, but he doesn't confide in me. Not at all—I'll swear that to you, if you'd like. If I didn't feel certain that he's about to do something that will endanger his chances of avoiding the death penalty, I wouldn't be talking to you right now."

They had reached Newly's street, and the lawyer gave Frank his address. It was all Frank could do to concentrate on the house numbers painted on the curbs. It was an expensive neighborhood. Not many criminal defense lawyers made it this big, he knew. He found Newly's sprawling Spanish-style home. He pulled into the driveway and turned off the engine.

"You think he has some plan for Irene," he said to the lawyer. "You started to say so earlier."

"Nick Parrish . . . studies her. Stares at her."

Frank swore.

"Yes," Newly said. "I agree."

"I need to know—I need to know everything you can tell me about where they were headed. Yes—I wrote down the coordinates. But where were they going from the last position?"

"I don't know."

"Newly—"

"I don't know! Punching me in the nose won't help you."

He relaxed his hands, made himself think. "The ranger who took you out—was he going to rejoin them?"

"Yes."

"How? Did they name a place?"

"No . . ." Newly grew thoughtful. "I was not very clear-headed at the time, but . . . oh! Now I remember! He said something to Andy, the botanist, about leaving trail signs. Does that help?"

"Yes," Frank said, almost laughing with relief. "Let me help you get settled in the house. I have a few more questions."

Newly sighed. "I thought you might. But I demand a price."

"Oh?" Frank said, wary again.

"I cannot tell you how anxious I am to throw these boots away. . . . I don't think I'll recover if I have to keep looking at them. Once we're inside, would you mind dropping them in the trash compactor for me?"

"With pleasure," Frank answered.

14

▲ ▼ ▲ ▼

WEDNESDAY NIGHT, MAY 17

Southern Sierra Nevada Mountains

He lay on his back, drawing in one deep breath after another.

He modestly acknowledged to himself that he had failed to envision how magnificent it would be. The excitement of it bordered deliciously on the unbearable. A weaker man would have been forced to seek some kind of release. Not him. No, not him.

Earlier, before they had opened the plastic, he had dared to touch himself, just once, but he knew better than to try that now.

Her death scent was on all of them, but especially on those who had stayed closest to the grave throughout the day. The guards had taken turns, had gone to see her. They couldn't resist, of course. Pilgrims drawn to a holy place, he thought, remembering his delight as each returned, bathed in her incense.

But that little tease had been nothing compared to the moment when they brought her back. The memories of their time together—he had almost grown dizzy under the spell of the recollection.

Sheridan and Niles positively reeked of her, of course. That was delightful. How he envied Sheridan. Yes, it really was something near to jealousy—he had touched her. Thinking of Sheridan's gloved hand on her hand—oh!

He was drawn tight as a bow now, thinking of that, and so he made himself move his thoughts to safer ground.

He thought of Merrick roughing him up. Childish! Nothing could have made him feel better. He'd met Merrick before, in one form or another. Bullies. Schoolyard bullies, like Harvey Heusman in seventh grade. He knew how to handle them. He'd done it before. Harvey had been one of his first victims. He wondered idly whether they had ever found him. It had been many years since he had visited Harvey's grave, and realizing this, he felt a moment's remorse—not for killing Harvey, of course, but for failing to keep his appointed rounds.

Like a favorite story that had been read and re-read again and again, recalling the killing of his childhood enemy had long ago lost its power to excite him, but that did not make him less fond of the memory. Visiting the older burial sites could make him quite nostalgic, and he was not one to ignore them. He was good about paying homage to—well, to himself, really! The thought amused him.

Ah, that little humorous moment was enough to ease the tension a bit.

He returned to his very detailed recollections of this afternoon, about to reach his favorite moment. Yes, here she was, pale and looking a little tired—she didn't sleep well. He would have liked to believe that he caused her late-night restlessness, but on the first evening he had heard the sounds of one of her nightmares, and knew some other terror visited her. That was all right. He'd focus her fear where it belonged, all in due time. For now, it was enough to see the dark circles beneath her blue eyes, her hair falling forward across her face as she looked down for a moment as she walked.

She was coming closer now, closer, and—oh yes! She had the scent. He had breathed in deeply as she walked by him, smelling her scent and the dead woman's scent together, mingled and lovely, lovely, lovely. Thinking of it made him tremble.

Oh, it was so right, so exquisite! Anticipation hummed

through him like an electric current. Everything was working so perfectly, and with everything working so perfectly, it was all that he could do to be still, to lie on his back in this tent, simply feeling his own blood moving through his veins, every nerve thrumming with the strength of his desire.

15

▲ ▼ ▲ ▼

THURSDAY, EARLY MORNING, MAY 18

Southern Sierra Nevada Mountains

The rain held off until just before dawn the next morning. The rainfall was not hard or steady—just a series of intermittent gentle showers for the most part—but the first of these awakened me as its chilly droplets struck my face. In my fitful sleep I had moved off my open sleeping bag, and so I came awake lying faceup, halfway outside the tent. The part of me that was still on the thin insulation mattress was fine, but the other thirty percent or so wasn't so comfy. Especially the part that was getting pelted by cold water.

I moved back inside only long enough to change and pack up my gear. When I emerged, I saw the others were already breaking camp. No one wanted to linger here. Although weather might delay the plane's arrival, last night it had been decided that we would hike back to the landing strip to wait for it.

Occasional but unpredictable gusts of wind made taking down my small tent a tricky business, and those who were managing the larger tent that had housed Parrish nearly lost control of it more than once.

I wondered if the trail would be muddy. Our progress had been slow before, and even though some of the weight of the food was gone from our packs, the body would be an awkward burden to steer through the terrain we had covered on the way in.

The rain briefly lessened the body's lingering odor, to which I had almost become accustomed, and brought the scent of dampened earth and woods to replace it. But when the first storm passed, and the air became still again, the scent returned. Perhaps it was the moisture in the air that seemed to increase the scent's power, or that short respite now resulted in a renewed awareness of it, but whatever the cause, its presence was soon unmistakable.

We set out just after a quick breakfast, which I made myself eat because I knew I'd need the energy for the hike, although my appetite was nearly zilch. I tried to cheer myself with the prospect of going home, of seeing Frank again, of being finished with this sad business. But I would not be finished with it, of course; the Sayres awaited me, and my editor expected a story.

As we began hiking, I saw that while the ground and grass were damp, there wasn't much mud yet. The wind had steadied, and was not much more than a strong breeze. J.C. was in the lead, assuring us that he could now take us on a much more direct route back to the plane. Bob Thompson and the guards followed with Parrish, who seemed lost in his own thoughts—I hoped they were distressing visions of spending the rest of his life in prison. Bingle walked with me, while David and Ben took the first turn with the stretcher.

We reached the ridge between the two meadows—not far from where the coyote tree stood—and stopped to rest so that Andy and J.C. could take over the task of bearing the stretcher. We only planned to stop for a few minutes. But here, just after David and Ben had gently laid down their burden, two things happened that changed the course of our journey.

The first was that Nicholas Parrish said to Thompson, "I thought you would have shown more initiative, Detective Thompson. To find only one body, when my lovely tree surely tells you there are more here."

After a moment's silence, Thompson said, "Are you volunteering information, Parrish?"

"Do I need to say more than I have? Not all of my works are

as enchanting as dear Julia—I do wish you'd let me have a peek at her. Her fragrance is so enticing!"

"Out of the question," Thompson said, then reconsidering, added, "if you show me the other graves, I might be able to work something out."

Parrish laughed. "You've made your forensic anthropologists frown at you, Detective."

"He's just stalling," Duke complained.

Thompson nodded. "We'll discuss your other victims when you're back in your cell, Parrish."

"Oh no," he said. "It's now or never."

Thompson began pacing.

"You can count, can't you?" Parrish said. "Count the coyotes."

"A dozen. I know, I know," Thompson said, still not decided. "If you knew there were more, why did you get rid of your lawyer? You know we can use everything you say to us against you."

"He was boring. As you are becoming boring. I will show you another grave, Detective Thompson," Parrish said, "but if we continue to hike, we hike away from it. We both know that I won't be allowed to accompany you on another expedition, so as I said—now or never!"

"It's a trick of some kind," Manton said. "If there were more bodies, he would have negotiated for whatever he could get while his lawyer was still here."

"Ms. Kelly," Parrish said. "Can you understand why I don't want my dear ones to be left behind?"

I thought I knew the answer, and why he asked it of the only member of the media he could appeal to at that moment. But I didn't especially want to be involved in this decision; I was there as an observer. And the things I had observed—after looking into Julia Sayre's grave—made me certain that I didn't want to aid Parrish in any way, shape, or form. The others were looking at me, waiting.

It was Ben Sheridan who answered, almost exactly as I would have. "Mr. Parrish takes pride in his work. He doesn't want it to remain hidden. That's why we're up here in the first place."

"Yes!" Parrish said warmly. "You surprise me! You understand perfectly!"

Thompson was besieged by arguments for and against, mostly against.

It was then that the second thing happened, the one that decided the issue.

The wind shifted.

Later, I would look back at that day and wonder what would have become of our group had the wind blown in some other direction. But it shifted—shifted toward us—a stiff breeze coming off the other meadow, up one sloping end of it, to the ridge where we stood, and beyond.

Bingle raised his nose and then pitched his ears forward. He looked back at David. I had seen that intent look the day before.

"*¿Qué pasa?*" David asked Bingle.

Bingle turned back into the breeze, lifted his nose in short quick motions, sniffing, eyes half-closed, then brought his ears up again and stared at David. This time, the dog's tail was wagging.

"What's going on?" Thompson asked.

"Bingle is alerting," Ben said.

Thompson turned back to Parrish with a gleam in his eye. "Maybe we won't need you to show it to us! Maybe the dog is going to take us straight to it!"

Parrish shrugged in indifference.

"I thought we needed to get to that airstrip," Manton said.

"Go ahead," Ben replied. "We're going to see what the dog is after."

"Maybe he's just smelling the body J.C. and Andy are carrying," Manton persisted.

"No," said David. "He's finding it on the wind. The wind is coming up the slope, off that meadow. The wind isn't in the right direction to carry scent off the body. And he's not excited about that find now. This is something new."

But Thompson's certainty had been shaken. "What if it's just a dead deer or something like that?"

"He won't alert to nonhuman remains," David answered, after commanding Bingle to sit quietly. The dog shifted on his front paws like a kid that needs to go to the bathroom, but obeyed. "He was interested in that meadow when we walked there two days ago. I'm going to check it out."

"I'll stay with you," Ben said, then turned to Thompson. "Go on to the plane. We'll catch up."

"Catch up?" Thompson said. "What if you find something? How are you going to get it out?"

"We'll mark it and come back later," Ben said.

But only yesterday Thompson's mind had been filled with visions of glory for bringing in a second body, and he wasn't going to be left out of a chance to make those visions a reality, especially not after Parrish himself had hinted that there were as many as eleven other burials. "No way," he said. "You stay, we all stay. We're in this together."

"Suit yourself," Ben said.

David had by this time put the leather working collar on Bingle. Bingle was staring at him intently, and began barking.

Andy and J.C., who had been standing near the stretcher, were deep in conversation. I saw Andy nodding. Just as David managed to quiet the dog, J.C. said to Thompson, "Let the two of us go on to the airstrip with the body."

"That's a lot of hiking for the two of you," Ben said.

"True," J.C. said, "but we can manage it. And I've got an idea. The plane should be back soon, if it isn't waiting for us there already—the weather hasn't been bad enough to keep it from landing. When we get to it, I'll radio the ranger station for a chopper. They can pick me up at the landing strip, and I'll show them where to find you. They won't have any trouble landing in this meadow. And leaving by chopper won't give your prisoner many opportunities to make a break for it—not as many as a walk through the forest might."

The idea of skipping the hike back to the airstrip obviously appealed to Thompson, but he hesitated. "You can get one in here before nightfall?"

"No problem. Without Parrish leading us on his goofy side routes, it shouldn't take us long to reach the airstrip. You can have him locked up before the end of the day."

Thompson looked over to see Parrish frowning. Caught at this, Parrish gave a sugary smile to the detective. Thompson hesitated.

"The guards are looking tired," J.C. said. "This hasn't been easy duty. This way, they won't have to backpack, watch the trail, and keep an eye on Parrish all at the same time."

"Okay," Thompson said.

Ben extracted a promise from Andy to stay with the body while J.C. came back for the others. "I don't want anyone claiming that the body or evidence was out of our control at any time."

David and Bingle went down into the meadow first, at a fairly fast pace. Ben and I followed not far behind them, carrying the excavation equipment. Flash carried some of this as well, along with his camera equipment. Thompson, Parrish, and the guards moved more slowly.

The wind died down, but David didn't seem to be bothered. He used the opportunity to rest the dog, set down his backpack and equipment, and pick out a place to wait for the chopper. "J.C. was pretty optimistic about the weather," he said, looking up at the sky. "I don't know. It's not bad right now, but I think we might get more rain yet."

"I thought the same thing," Ben said. "I have a feeling that we'll be spending the night here. On the other hand, J.C. knows these mountains better than we do. If the plane is waiting for him when they reach the airstrip, and the chopper gets up here fast enough, we may be okay. But I don't want to be rushed if Bingle finds something."

"I'll stay here with you even if Thompson and the others want to go back," David said. He paused, took out the squeeze bottle with the powder in it and tested the air. The powder drifted slowly off toward the ridge. "Look at that. A really fine breeze. This is better for working than that wind—it could have been blowing scent from a mile away." Bingle, standing a little apart from us, was alerting again.

"*¿Quieres trabajar?*" he called out. Do you want to go to work?

Bingle's tail wagged, and he gave a bark.

"Find us a good spot, Ben," David said, moving toward the dog. "Haven't heard any thunder yet, but if there is a storm, I sure as hell don't want to be standing out in the middle of a meadow like a lightning rod." To Bingle he said, "*¡Búscalo! ¡Busca al muerto!*"

Dog and handler began to move in a crisscross path down the meadow, much as they had done when I followed them the day before.

From our earlier hike through this area I remembered that the woods were denser here than those near the meadow where Julia Sayre had been buried. Farther in from this meadow, there was a stream; beyond that, a small pond.

Flash, Ben, and I set up one of the smaller tents in the woods, to give Duke and Earl a place to catch up on their sleep. If necessary, we would set up camp there. While sheltering under a single tree, or even a small stand of trees, would be extremely dangerous in a bad storm, a forest of this size would be safer than the meadow. We would no longer be the tallest objects.

It wasn't long before we heard Bingle crooning.

We hurried to the meadow, where David was praising the dog. "*¡Qué inteligente eres! ¡Qué guapo eres!*"

"Yes, he's handsome and intelligent," I said, "but what did he find?"

David commanded Bingle to stay, and walked with us to a place another few yards away. "A little newer, I suspect."

The plants here were shorter and sparser than growth nearby. This time, it was not so difficult to see the oval shape formed by the edges of the grave; the fill soil within the grave had settled, so that the surface of the grave was slightly concave. The edges of this depression had cracked, outlining it.

"Great!" Bob Thompson said. "You did it! We've got the bastard now!"

"Detective Thompson," Ben said coldly, "there is nothing to celebrate here—on any count. We don't yet have any idea who or what is buried here, let alone who's responsible for burying it."

Thompson's mood was not easily suppressed. Even though I disliked him, I recognized that he was not rejoicing over a victim's grave, but over the opportunity to see Nicholas Parrish face the death penalty.

Parrish, who must have known what this new find would

mean to his chances of avoiding that sentence, looked almost serenely at us. His eyes came to rest on me. He smiled.

"Soon, my love," he said, "soon."

Bingle's hackles went up, and he began barking at Parrish.

A warning we should have heeded.

16

▲▼▲▼

THURSDAY MORNING, MAY 18

Southern Sierra Nevada Mountains

Ben and David soon began the next phase of their work, and with the same painstaking care they had taken at Julia Sayre's grave. Duke and Earl decided to get a little shut-eye, but made Thompson promise to wake them if the anthropologists found anything.

Merrick and Manton took their prisoner some distance from the grave, where Thompson tried to question him, but Parrish was unwilling to say anything about this victim. That is not to say he was silent.

"Do you know why those coyotes died?" Parrish asked, staring at me again.

"No, tell me," Thompson coaxed.

"For disturbing the peace," he answered, not so much as glancing away from me. "Now, look at Dr. Sheridan and Dr. Niles. Are they any better than coyotes?"

"What do you mean?" Thompson asked.

"*Requiescat in pace.*"

"What does that mean?"

"Ask Ms. Kelly. She grew up hearing Latin—at least on Sundays."

Thompson turned to me.

"It means 'rest in peace,'" I said. "The R.I.P. on old gravestones."

"You see?" Parrish said. "Do you know the habits of coyotes, Ms. Kelly?"

I didn't answer.

"They rob graves. They will steal bones and gnaw on them."

"Coyotes aren't the only animals that will do that," Thompson said.

"I don't like coyotes," Parrish said, smiling.

I walked away, headed back toward the grave.

Bingle was pleased to see me, and David as well. "Would you mind dog-sitting again?" he asked. "He's especially restless for some reason."

I had already realized this. Bingle had been dividing his time between trying to sneak closer to David and turning to bark fiercely toward Parrish.

"Duke and Earl must be ready to kill me," David said. "They probably managed to fall asleep just in time to have him wake them with all his racket. I don't know what his problem is."

"With J.C. and Andy here yesterday, he could command more of your attention."

"He's had to sit quietly while I worked on other cases. He's not usually so unruly. And he seldom reacts to anyone the way he has to Nick Parrish."

"They should make him a judge," I said.

David laughed. He showed me that they had already reached a layer of large stones, and could see green plastic in some places. "If this grave wasn't made by Nick Parrish, he has an imitator," he said.

"David," Ben said, on a note of exasperation. He was in one of his crankier moods, and had been frowning throughout the time he had been working on the grave. He didn't scold me for getting too close to it, though. Progress, I supposed.

Bingle decided to bark at Parrish again.

"Maybe I should take Bingle for a walk," I said. "Get him away from Parrish for a while. God knows, I'd like to get away from him." And the smell of decomposition, I thought, but didn't say so.

"That would be great!" David said. He stopped working and went to get a leash from the dog equipment bag.

"A good idea, Ms. Kelly," Ben said, carefully scraping soil off the plastic. "I'd prefer to work without curiosity seekers this time."

"Curiosity seekers?" I said, outraged. "I'm a professional here on a job. If you could just get that idea through your thick skull—"

"What a profession. You profit from other people's suffering—"

"Excuse me, Saint Ben of the Bones, but—"

"—you'll peddle the details of another person's misery to anyone who's willing to drop a coin at a newsstand—"

"Ben," I heard a voice say behind me. "Please." David was back with the leash.

Ben looked away, but couldn't hide the effort required to keep his anger in check. He scowled at his gloved hands for a long moment, then went back to scraping soil.

David leashed Bingle and made sure that the dog would heel at my command, then he walked with us toward the forest. He seemed preoccupied.

"Bingle won't stay with me without a leash?" I asked.

"Hmm? Oh—no, sorry. He understands that when I give his lead to someone else, he has to stay with that person. Otherwise, I couldn't depend on him not to take a notion to come and see what I was up to. He might run off and leave you in the middle of the woods." He smiled. "I could probably make him find you, of course, but it's easier on everybody if we just give him the message ahead of time."

"I see—so the leash is to make sure I don't get lost."

He laughed. "Exactly."

I thought he would stop at the edge of the forest, but he continued a little way into it. "About Ben," he said suddenly. "He has this problem with reporters. I know he can be abrupt—"

"Abrupt?"

"Rude."

"Yes."

"Okay, rude," he admitted. "But you shouldn't take it personally. I know that outside of your profession, he thinks you're okay."

"I'll have to remember to congratulate myself!"

"I'm not doing a very good job with this, am I?"

"You're doing fine. Sorry. I shouldn't take my anger at him out on you. If you're going to tell me that he's good-hearted, I already know that."

"You do?" he asked, incredulous.

"Yes, and not just because Parrish is here to hold up for comparison. I think I first really noticed it when Ben asked you to have Bingle sleep with me—on a night when I think he had come to borrow the dog to ease his own nightmares."

David nodded.

"Besides, Judge Bingle likes Ben," I said.

David went down to eye level with Bingle, and caressed the dog's ruff and ears. Bingle lowered his head, butted it against David's chest, and held it there, making soft, low sounds of pleasure. "Bingle's a good judge," David said. "He likes you, too."

"The feeling is mutual. But I suspect you were going to try to make a few excuses for your other friend?"

"Not excuses, really. I just thought if you knew—he has his reasons for mistrusting the press."

"Such as?"

"Just this year, he—" He halted, shook his head, then thought for a moment before saying, "A couple of years ago, when he was working on a plane crash, a TV reporter overheard Ben talking to someone—using one of those spy-type microphones."

"A parabolic mike."

"Yes. She went on the air, and misquoted him. That happens to all of us, but this was misinformation that led the victims' families to hope that they'd be—that the remains would be relatively intact. Do you know what really happens—in a high-impact crash, I mean?"

"Yes," I said. "The physics aren't in anybody's favor."

"Right. Most of the time, we make identifications on fragments."

"So the families were upset with him?"

"Yes. I don't think the thing that bothered him most was that the families were angry with him. He just hated seeing them tormented. People who were grieving, already unable to really accept what had happened, and then this expectation—Ben said it amounted to a form of public torture. I think he was right."

"So this one incident has tarred all reporters with the same brush?"

"I wish I could tell you it was one incident. There have been photos taken in temporary morgues by hidden cameras. Misinformation about missing persons—you can't imagine how painful that is for the victims' families!"

"If you want me to say that I'm proud of everyone in my profession—"

"No, no, of course not. I can tell you about colleagues of ours who make us shake our heads. I'm just trying to help you understand Ben, I guess. Like I said, I don't want you to take it personally."

"I don't," I said. "But over the long run, Ben won't be doing you any favors if he's so openly hostile to the press."

"There's more to it than—well, I don't have any business talking about him in this way, I suppose. I should get back to help him out."

"Wait a minute, David—please."

He gave me a questioning look.

"I could take or leave most of the rest of these guys," I said, "but you and Andy have gone out of your way to be kind to me. I'm grateful for all the time you've spent talking to me about your work. So if you tell me that I need to give Ben Sheridan another chance—another dozen chances—I will."

He smiled at me. "Thanks. Ben has seen me through more than one rough patch. It's not hard for me to have a little patience with one of his." He gave Bingle's fur one last ruffle and said, "Take good care of her, Bingle."

"I'll take good care of him, too," I said.

"Oh, I know that!" he said, laughing as he walked away.

I took my time on the walk. Clouds continued to darken the sky and it rained a little, but not enough to discourage either of us. Bingle enjoyed flopping into a mud puddle before I could stop him, but otherwise, he was content to go wherever I wanted to wander. He was curious about any number of sights and scents and sounds along the way, and some of these, I allowed him to investigate. But if I wanted to keep moving, he never resisted or yanked on the leash or failed to display anything but the best manners.

At some point, I had to own up to the fact that I was escaping. I didn't really want to see another green plastic bag opened up, another set of decomposing remains. I most especially didn't want to see what might be at the bottom of that grave.

But as I had told Ben, I had a job to do, and all the arguments I presented to myself about why it was unnecessary for me to be at the site failed to ring true. I made my way back through the woods.

When we were within sight of the meadow, I halted, still not quite ready to leave the quiet of woods behind, to rejoin the men. Bingle lifted his nose, sniffing the air, but otherwise sat quietly beside me.

Flash was standing near the grave, running the video camera. Merrick and Manton were still guarding Parrish, but apparently Duke and Earl had been awakened by Thompson. Like David, the two guards and the detective wore masks and gloves, and knelt at the grave's edge. David talked to them, giving them instructions. Ben Sheridan was missing from the group.

I knew that I should move closer, should try to think like a reporter, should just get the story and worry about my reactions later. If Parrish stayed true to form, I'd soon be able to see photographs of the victim. That was the important thing here, I told myself—finding out who was in the grave. I should be like Manton, who was moving closer, trying to get a better look.

"On the count of three," I heard David say.

I was distracted from the proceedings by a distinctive splashing sound. I turned toward it just as Ben realized I was nearby.

"Oh, Christ!" he said, hurriedly tucking himself in and zipping his fly.

"One . . ." I heard David call.

"I—I'm sorry!" I said. "I didn't know you were here!"

Ben was beet red with embarrassment. "I suppose *that* will be in the paper?"

". . . Two . . ."

"Yes, of course it will," I said, my own embarrassment turning to anger. "The headline will read, 'Who Shrank the Forensic Anthropologist?' "

To my utter surprise, he started laughing.

"Three!" I heard David call.

The sound came at us like a prizefighter's punch—a thundering, out-of-nowhere explosion that shook the earth and nearly deafened us.

I stood frozen, unable to comprehend what had happened. A cloud of dust and debris suddenly billowed over the meadow as the echoes of the explosion continued to rattle and roar through the mountains, until soon the sound seemed to come from every side. There were other sounds, too—screams and the quick crack of shots fired. Bingle gave a yelping cry of distress and charged toward the dust cloud, pulling me off balance; I fell face first onto the ground; he dragged me forward a few feet, but still I held on tightly to the leash. If he had not further tangled it up in the brush between us, I doubt my weight alone would have been enough to stop his progress.

Ben ran ahead. I called to him, but he was already gone, soon halfway across the meadow, answering their screams with his own, even as one by one they grew silent. He was shouting David's name, shouting, "No!", shouting words I could not understand as he ran and then—and then Nicholas Parrish emerged from the dust, struggling to keep his balance as he used Merrick's corpse as an obscene shield. Parrish's still-chained hand raised a gun—the dead man's gun—and the dead man's arm rose with his, Ben too far into the meadow to take cover, suddenly not shouting, not making any sound, just falling.

He did not get up.

17

▲ ▼ ▲ ▼

THURSDAY, EARLY AFTERNOON, MAY 18

Southern Sierra Nevada Mountains

I stayed where I was. Bingle kept barking, revealing our location to Parrish. For one terrifying moment, fear paralyzed me—it was as if any Spanish words I knew had been taken from me, and I could not think of the command to quiet the dog.

"*¡Cállate!*" I finally remembered, and had no sooner said it than Bingle fell silent. Hoping to God Parrish didn't hear me, I whispered, "*Ven acá, Bingle. Ven acá.*"

Bingle obeyed, crouching low as he came back to me, panting fast and hard, his ears pressed flat, his tail curled between his legs. Afraid.

"*Muy bien,*" I whispered to him, my voice unsteady.

I moved closer to him, until I was lying next to him. He was trembling. So was I. I ran an unsteady hand over Bingle's coat.

"*Cálmate, tranquilo,*" I said into his ear.

I tried to watch Parrish, to stay aware of where he was. I saw him sink down into the grass, still holding the dead guard.

Long moments passed. We did not move from our hiding place. Soon I saw him stand again, free of his gruesome burden, calmly using a key to unlock the one handcuff still attached to his wrist. It dropped away from him and hit the ground.

The air was still thick with smoke and the smell of scattered flesh and blood. Now there was a silence, as unsettling as the screams had been. Impossible, I thought wildly, to conceal my trembling from him in that silence—my fear would be felt across the meadow, telegraphed to him through the ground itself.

The smoke began to clear. The wind picked up, and he laughed into it, raising his arms to the darkening sky, shaking his fists triumphantly, as if calling on the gods to behold his victory.

He stopped and stared into the woods. I felt certain he could see us. Suddenly he started to run—right toward us. I felt Bingle's hackles rise and whispered, "*Quieto*." The dog remained silent.

Parrish kept coming closer, heading for the trees, and my mouth went dry. I reached into my daypack and pulled out my knife and opened it. Not much of a weapon against a loaded gun, but even being shot to death would be better than meeting Julia Sayre's fate. But then I saw that Parrish was moving at an angle—veering away from us.

He was going to the camp.

I strained to hear his movements, fearing that at any moment he could double back behind me, attack from some unexpected direction. I would have to trust the dog to react to any approach by Parrish.

Before long Parrish was making plenty of noise in the camp, not bothering with any attempt at stealth.

It began to rain again.

I fought off a temptation to despair over this. Yes, the helicopter might have to wait for the weather to clear, but J.C. and Andy had probably made it out. You can make it out, too, I told myself. One way or another, someone will be coming back to this meadow. You just have to avoid him for a few hours. It's not even raining hard—the helicopter might be able to fly in this weather. I had no sooner thought this than I heard the distant rumble of thunder.

I was still shaking. I told myself it was the damp.

I had my poncho with me, and I decided to risk making noise to pull it on. The poncho's dark camouflage colors would blend better with the surrounding forest than the rest of my clothing.

The rain made it harder to hear Parrish, but from the sounds of pans clattering, I guessed that he was emptying the backpacks.

He could take what he wants, I thought. He could destroy the rest and leave me here in the woods, in the mountains to die with this dog.

Stop it.

My muscles were cramping, more from tension than the strain of staying still, and I was cold.

Too bad. It could be worse. These are signs of life, after all. You could have been lifting that body from that grave.

Knife in one hand, dog in the other.

Bingle's head came up. He was clearly listening to something. He had stopped trembling. I heard the sound of someone moving through the woods. Toward me.

"*Quieto,*" I whispered again to Bingle. He looked into my face, then lowered his head. He was still listening, though, ears flicking. I was praying.

The footsteps paused somewhere in front of me. Bingle tensed.

Don't growl, Bingle, please don't growl.

The footsteps moved on.

Eventually I could see him; he was moving toward the ridge. He was carrying a backpack—and Duke's rifle. He was hiking at a fast pace, not much less than a run. There was a little more distance between us now, and I was still hidden by the trees, so I moved to a more comfortable position. Bingle wanted to go out into the meadow; I did, too—harboring some slim-to-none hope that someone else might have survived, worried that someone might need my help. But we would easily be seen by Parrish if he turned back to survey his handiwork, and I was certain he would do so.

He didn't disappoint me. I lost sight of him for a time, then caught a glimpse of him raising his fists in victory again, at the top of the ridge. Despite my heartfelt wishes, no lightning struck him.

Soon he moved over the ridge and out of sight.

Bingle and I set out together, hurrying through the rain toward the grave. Nothing but carnage awaited us there. The grave itself was now a larger, deeper, blackened hole. Bingle did no more than to peer nervously into it, then shied away. What sort of explosive device Parrish had planted there, I had no idea, except that lifting the weight of the body was apparently all that was needed to trigger it.

A quick look around the site confirmed what I had already suspected. The others were dead; there wasn't much to find of those who had been bending over the grave. Bingle was whining now, anxiously moving from fragment to fragment. Later, perhaps, some forensic anthropologist would come to the scene, would study these fragments and be able to tell what had once been whom. I was only sure of one, a boot with the remnants of a foot in it, because Bingle began whining more loudly when he found it, then lay down next to it, head on paws, and wouldn't leave.

I didn't argue with him; I wasn't sure how much longer I would be able to stand there. Some part of my mind had shut down—I knew what I was seeing, but at the same time refused to know it. I dropped his leash and kept walking, careful where I stepped, but still feeling the soles of my boots grow slippery. I moved mechanically, waiting to see something that could be comprehended.

A short distance away, I almost found it. I came across the bodies of Manton and Merrick, who had not been killed by the blast. Parrish had fired several bullets into each of their faces.

I must have made a sound when I saw them, because Bingle came over to me. With horror, I realized that he was carrying David's boot.

"*¡Déjala!*" I said sharply. "Leave it!"

He looked up at me rebelliously and held on.

"*¡Déjala!*" I repeated.

Gently, he set it down, but hovered over it.

"*Bien, muy bien.*"

He watched me warily, as if I might want to take it from him. When he seemed ready to pick it up again, I said, "*¿Dónde está Ben, Bingle?*"

He looked up at me, cocking his head to one side.

"Where's Ben? Come on, show me. *¿Dónde está Ben, Bingle?*"

The question wasn't as easy to answer as it might seem. I wasn't sure where Ben had fallen. The grasses and flowers of the meadow were tall enough to hide his body.

The rain had slowed to a drizzle, but it would still make it hard for Bingle to pick up any scent in the air. It didn't deter him; he came with me when I started to weave a path between where Merrick and Manton lay and the place where Ben had run out of the forest.

We had only covered a few yards when Bingle took off, then ran back to me, barking.

"*Bien, bien—cállate, Bingle,*" I said, afraid that Parrish might hear him. "*¿Dónde está Ben?*" I asked again, and he took off once more—stopping every few feet this time, to look back at me.

I had no doubt that I was being asked to hurry up.

I praised him, even as I dreaded taking a closer look at another body.

Ben Sheridan's motionless form lay faceup near a large rock. His face was covered in blood. His left pant leg was also soaked in blood.

Bingle started licking him. There was no response.

Suddenly something David had said about Bingle came back to me. *Bingle won't lick a dead body.*

I knelt next to Ben, placed my fingers on his neck and felt for his pulse.

"Bingle," I said, struggling not to weep. "*¡Qué inteligente eres!*"

Ben Sheridan was alive.

I was determined he would stay that way, come hell or high water.

We got both.

18

▲ ▼ ▲ ▼

THURSDAY AFTERNOON, MAY 18

Southern Sierra Nevada Mountains

First things first. It's a bitch when you can't just call 911. When simply being conscious makes you the closest thing to a doctor in the house, rule number one is the toughest rule of all: don't panic.

Two problems made it hard not to panic. The first was that it looked as if the only thing between "Ben Sheridan" and "dead" were the words "not yet." The second was that Parrish could come back over that ridge at any moment, and if I hadn't managed to get Ben Sheridan out of the middle of the meadow by then, I was certain we would become two more ducks in his shooting gallery.

So I forgot about the smell of death all around me, forgot about the fact that I had just seen seven good men slaughtered mercilessly, forgot about the rain—and forced myself to concentrate on first things first.

First aid lessons came back to me.

I leaned my cheek close to his mouth. I felt his breath. One relief after another. He was breathing, he had a pulse.

I called his name several times. He didn't respond. Bingle barked at him. He moaned—softly, weakly. I waited. Nothing. I commanded Bingle to sit and stay. The dog obeyed. Ben stirred, almost as if he thought the command was for him. This brought to mind something a first aid instructor had once said to me—that consciousness wasn't an ON/OFF switch. An unconscious person may respond to pain, or to commands. So I gave it another try.

"Ben, open your eyes!"

Nothing.

Get on with it, I told myself. Check for bleeding.

The wound on his head had clotted; it didn't seem to be a deep cut, but there was a good-sized knot beneath it. The other obvious wound was the one on his leg.

I suddenly remembered a time when I had watched Pete, my husband's partner, work frantically to stop a victim's head from bleeding—only to later realize that her lungs had been filling with blood—a bullet had made a much smaller wound through her back.

I checked Ben as best I could for less apparent injuries. I wasn't able to discover any, but I did find a pair of unused latex gloves in one of his shirt pockets. I put them on, got my knife out again and cut the pant leg away.

Under other circumstances, the damage to his lower left leg might have horrified me. After all I had seen just a few minutes before, it had no power to shock me. It was a through-and-through bullet wound, a shot that had entered sideways, from the inside front of his leg between his knee and ankle, and exited on the other side—the messier side. It seemed to have broken at least one of his lower leg bones. The wound had bled profusely—at least, to my inexperienced eye, there seemed to be a lot of blood—but there was very little bleeding from it now.

The few first aid items I carried in my daypack were not intended for treating shooting victims, but there was enough clean gauze and tape to make a pressure bandage for the leg wound.

He moaned. I moved nearer his face and called his name again. Say the injured person's name often—I remembered that this was one of the rules. He opened his eyes, stared up at me.

"Ben? Can you understand me?"

He closed his eyes.

"Ben!"

He looked up at me. Bingle barked. Ben slowly turned his head toward the dog, groaned, and closed his eyes again. "Raining," he said thickly, hardly more than a whisper.

"No," I said. "It was raining, but it has stopped now."

He made no response.

"Ben! Ben!"

"Go away."

"Ben. Wake up!"

He didn't respond.

"Ben Sheridan, listen to me—I don't want to get shot just because I'm out here with you. So wake up!"

Nothing.

"Bingle needs you, all right? What would David say if he knew you didn't take care of his dog?"

"David," he said miserably, but opened his eyes.

"Are you hurt anywhere besides your head and leg?"

He frowned. "Don't know. Can't think." He lifted his head, tried to move. "Dizzy," he said, closing his eyes.

"Does your neck or back hurt?"

"No—my head. My leg—broken, I think."

I picked up his right hand. "Squeeze my hand."

He did. Weak, but a grasp. I tried the same thing with the left.

"You passed test number one with flying colors." I moved to his boots. "Try moving your right foot, Ben."

He moved it.

"Your left."

Nothing, but the attempt made him cry out.

"Can't," he whispered. "Can't."

"Don't worry about that now. We need to get out of this field, then you can sleep if you want to—but not now. Stay awake."

"Okay," he said, then added, "for Bingle."

"Suit yourself, asshole. just stay awake."

I saw a small, fleeting smile. I had to admire that—in the amount of pain he must have been in, I don't know many people who could have managed it.

"I can't leave you in this field," I said. "Parrish may be back."

He rolled to his right side, as if he was going to try to move to his feet, and promptly threw up.

"Christ," he said.

"It's probably because you hit your head," I said, taking my neckcloth off and wiping his face. I helped him rinse his mouth. "At the very least, you've probably got a concussion. And if you're going to be sick, it's much better for you to be lying on your side. Dangerous to be lying on your back."

I helped him lift his head a little, to offer him water. He seemed thirsty, but soon closed his eyes. "Go away."

"Stay awake, Ben."

"Go away."

"Bingle, remember?"

"Damned dog," he said, but opened his eyes again.

I tried to make him comfortable, to do what I could to keep him from going into shock. But nothing I needed was at hand, and more than anything, I wanted to get us the hell out of that meadow.

I kept looking back at the ridge. No sign of Parrish. Not yet.

"Bingle," I said, "*¡Cuídalo!*"

The dog moved closer to Ben.

"What?" Ben said groggily. "What did you say?"

"I said it to Bingle. I told him to watch over you. It was an experiment, really, but he seems to know the command."

"What?" Ben said again.

"Stay awake."

I hurried to make another search of the area near the grave, concentrating on objects, locking my mind away from thoughts of the dead scattered all around me.

In my haste, I didn't move as carefully as I had before, and something made a cracking sound beneath my right foot—a small piece of bone.

Steady—keep going. Just ignore it. It can't hurt you.

I kept moving, but now my fear of Parrish's return began to reassert itself. It found its way to my knees and ankles—my steps grew clumsy and slow.

Stop thinking about him! For God's sake, get a move on! You've got to help Ben.

I found one of the duffel bags that held the anthropologists' equipment, largely unscathed. The same was true of Bingle's equipment. I hoisted both bags and brought them closer to Ben. I praised Bingle, and could not help thinking that he seemed happy to have something to do.

I used the support pieces from the sieves that had been used to sift dirt and a roll of duct tape I found in the bag to splint Ben's left leg. I also took a few small items that looked as if they might be useful later on, including a small tarp, and put them in my daypack.

Ben had lost consciousness again, but when I shouted his name, he came around. He wouldn't talk to me, but when I asked him to help me move him to a half-sitting position, he did.

"Are you thirsty?"

He swallowed, nodded slightly.

I held my water bottle up to his mouth. He managed to drink a little more this time.

"I'm going to have to do something that is going to hurt like hell, Ben. But we have to get out of the meadow, and in among the trees. From there, I'm probably going to have to move you again, but I promise I won't do that more than I have to, okay? But I need you to help me as much as you can."

He did. I supplied most of the lifting power, but he managed to move to a standing position. We soon found that he was unable to put any weight on his left leg. He leaned heavily on me and tried hopping. He gave a shout of pain and passed out again. I barely managed to lower him to the ground without dropping him.

Don't panic, I told myself, but I envisioned Parrish sighting the rifle on my head as I pulled out the tarp. Could he hit me from this distance? I didn't think so, but I crouched lower in the tall grass.

Ben came to, and though his wakefulness was helpful while I was putting him on the tarp, knowing what lay ahead, I wished he had stayed unconscious.

I lifted the corner of the tarp near his head, and began dragging him over the bumpy ground.

"Bingle," he called, making a weak gesture with his hand.

The dog hesitated, looking back toward David's boot, then followed us.

I stood, nervously giving up concealment for speed, but it was still slow going. Ben made no protests, but he grimaced in pain. By the time we reached the trees, tears streaked their way through the dirt and bloodstains on his face. I stopped, and he wiped the tears away, embarrassed.

But my thoughts were elsewhere. Panting with exertion, I looked up at the ridge.

Where are you, Parrish?

Had he come back? For all I knew, he could be hiding in the trees ahead, waiting to attack us. I listened, and heard a hundred sounds that might have been made by him. I looked back at the meadow. Not an option.

Something hit the ground behind me and I jumped away with a yelp. I was moving to shield Ben when he said, "Pinecone. Fell from the tree."

"Oh. I thought it might be—"

"Watch Bingle," he gritted out, closing his eyes against a fresh wave of pain.

I studied the dog. He was calmly studying me. I realized what Ben meant, then. Parrish wasn't nearby. Bingle would have reacted.

I took Ben as far as I could into the forest, where eventually there were too many obstacles to allow me to continue dragging him. I brought him to his feet again. I moved in front of him, took his arms and pulled them over my shoulders, rolled him up on my back, and half-carried, half-dragged him through the woods. I'm not in bad shape, but carrying him was awkward and exhausting. The ground was too uneven to make this a smooth trip. Occasionally, despite Ben's efforts to hide his torment, sharp cries escaped him. Bingle began whining in sympathy.

When we came to ground with fewer rocks, bushes, and branches on it, I set him down. He had passed out again. I took a few minutes to catch my breath. Then I unfolded the tarp again, placed Ben on it, and pulled him deeper into the trees.

We reached the stream. I told Bingle to stay—the water was deep enough to make me worry that he wouldn't be able to swim it if he fell in. I scouted ahead and found a relatively narrow place to cross. There was no way to make it if I dragged Ben after me, though, so I cut the tarp and bundled it around his legs, taping it on to him like a bizarre form of waders, to help keep him dry if I fell. I managed to rouse him long enough to help me get him on my back again. Slowly and carefully, I stepped from flat rock to flat rock. I only lost my balance once, misstepping into chilly, knee-deep water midstream and nearly dumping him in.

We made it across. I had jostled Ben badly, though, and by the time I laid him down among the trees on the other side, he was unconscious again. This whole endeavor had cost us hours, and I wondered how much blood he'd lost. I moved him onto his side, into a position that would ensure that he could breathe and would not choke on his own vomit, should he get sick again. I cut the tarp-waders off, and was pleased to see that at least one of us had stayed fairly dry.

Bingle whimpered anxiously, perhaps afraid we were leaving him behind. I went back for him as soon as I could. It took much less time to cross without Ben on my back, and soon I had fitted Bingle in a harness and returned with him. He nimbly made it to the other bank without incident.

I did some quick scouting and found a place that seemed to be fairly safe, out of view of the meadow and stream. I dragged Ben there.

My next concern was keeping Ben from going into shock. In part, that would require warmth. I took off my jacket and what layers of warm clothing I thought I could safely spare. Then, remembering my first night in the mountains, said to Bingle, "*Duerme con él.*" Sleep with him.

He cocked his head at me, perhaps wondering what I could mean by that at this time of day—then, when I continued to look at him as if I expected to be obeyed, he slowly moved to lie down close to Ben.

I was tired, but I moved as quickly as I could back across the stream, through the woods to the camp we had set up that morning. I didn't want to leave Ben alone any longer than necessary, or to be caught at the campsite if Parrish returned.

The camp was some distance from where Ben lay. I didn't

know how well Parrish knew this area, but his awareness of the airstrip, his coyote tree, and the two burials were all indicators that he had been here again and again. The odds of successfully hiding from him for a long period of time weren't great, but I only needed to manage it until J.C. and Andy returned by helicopter. That could be soon, I told myself.

The camp was in shambles. Parrish had dumped the contents of the backpacks out onto the ground. Cookware, tent supports, clothing, sleeping bags, and other items were scattered over the site. Most were damp. For all the disarray, though, I felt some hope when I saw what was left.

I found my own pack, looked it over and could see no damage. I picked up most of my clothing, putting on a few items for warmth. I had a moment of almost losing whatever semblance of calm I had managed up to then when I realized that he had taken all but one pair of my underwear. Telling myself that it was a very small matter to become upset over, given his day's work, and congratulating myself because the pair he left was clean, I went back to the task at hand.

I started to gather whatever I could remember seeing Ben wear, then thought better of it. If Parrish returned here and saw that the only clothing that was missing was mine and Ben's, he might learn that Ben was alive.

This brought me to my next task, one of the most difficult to face. Bracing myself, telling myself this was not the same as going through a battlefield, stealing coins off the bodies of soldiers, I began to sort through the belongings of the dead.

I tried hard not to think of Earl wearing this shirt or David, this sweater. I would not think of what had happened in the meadow, or worse, who it had happened to. I came across the little wooden horse that Duke had whittled, felt tears welling up, and tucked the horse into my backpack, all the while telling myself I was a fool to add something so unnecessary to the pack.

Stay alive. Keep Ben and Bingle alive. First things first.

I took a duffel bag—the largest one I could find—instead of Ben's backpack, and began to gather clothing belonging to each of the dead men, mixing Ben's in with them.

I did not take much of the clothing, saving room for food.

But as I looked through the pile of belongings, I only found three packages of chicken noodle soup—which had been in Manton's daypack—and Bingle's dog food.

You have water and a filter, I told myself. You also have lots of water purification tablets. If you're rescued soon, you won't even have to worry about feeding the dog.

Although only one of the tents had been set up when Parrish went on his rampage, he had pulled the others from their nylon cases, scattering their supports, rainflies, and tie-downs. But I was able to find all parts for mine, and was pleased to discover that even the rainfly had not been damaged during his rampage.

To this collection I added two well-stocked first aid kits, three sleeping bags that were unharmed—including my own—my insulation pad and one other, my stove and cookset, a flashlight, three candles, a tarp, some rope, a shaving kit that had Ben's name on it, a plastic bucket, and a few other essentials.

I considered it a major stroke of luck when I found Earl's medications for his ear infection. One plastic cylinder held a decongestant, but the other might help me save Ben's life. The label said it was Keflex, an antibiotic.

Since Ben had lain in a damp meadow with open wounds for over an hour before I could reach him, infection was a major worry. But here, at least, was a weapon to fight it.

I put on my own pack and made a quick false trail to the upper portion of the stream, trying to make it look as if I were heading back to the airstrip. I returned in a less obvious manner, and did my best to obscure my tracks. I picked up the duffel bag, and loaded down, cautiously made my way back to Ben and Bingle.

A strong breeze kept my scent from Bingle, who growled as I approached. Until I called softly to him, I was half-afraid he'd start barking, or attack me outright.

Ben was awake.

"How are you doing?" I asked, setting down the duffel bag.

"The others . . . ?"

I shook my head.

He looked away.

I hurriedly unrolled one of the sleeping bags, put it over him. Carefully enunciating each word, like a man who had downed a pint of whiskey but was trying not to appear to be drunk, he said, "You should leave me here."

"Don't start that bullshit," I said.

"It's not. Makes sense."

"You took a hard blow to the head, I'm amazed you're not screaming in pain from that leg wound, and you've just suffered a terrible loss. I'm not going to listen to you tell me that you're the one who's making sense."

He sighed.

"Besides," I said, "when have I listened to you, anyway?"

"True," he said, and fell silent.

"Are you allergic to Keflex?"

He shook his head.

I read the label, which said to take one tablet four times a day. I gave him two of the pills, and helped him to drink more water.

"Thanks," he said.

"You're welcome."

"Whose medication?"

"They were Earl's." Before he could think too much about that, I added, "I'm going to set up the tent. Once we're situated, I'll try to do a better job of looking after your injuries. At least you'll be warmer and drier."

I went to work. I put the tent up, and after a look at the darkening sky, added the rainfly. Once I had managed to get Ben, Bingle, and necessary gear inside the tent, there wasn't much room to move around. Luckily, my claustrophobia didn't kick in—I was too distracted by something I had noticed when I moved Ben inside the tent to think of my own concerns: his leg was bleeding again.

I had more medical supplies to work with now, though, so I took off the makeshift splint and bandages and attempted to do a better job of it. Below the wound, his leg was a grayish color. At one point, he shouted in agony over some clumsiness on my part, and we both said, "Sorry!" in unison. I finished up and re-splinted it.

I checked the head wound as well, which had also reopened, but was not bleeding nearly as much as the leg had been. I now had a chance to wash the rest of his face, to remove the bloodstains and dirt that had caked onto it while he lay out in the field.

He was so pale, and his skin felt too cold. Although he was conscious, he was listless.

I loosened his clothing, elevated his feet, and in addition to the pad and sleeping bag beneath him, placed another bag on top of him.

"Talk to me, Ben."

He looked at me as if I had awakened him from a deep sleep.

"What's my name?" I asked.

After a long, frightening moment, I asked again.

"Irene," he answered.

"How many fingers am I holding up?"

Long pause. "Four."

The correct answer was two.

"What's your name?"

"Ben."

"What's the dog's name?"

"Bingle."

Bingle, who had been sniffing at the contents of the duffel bag, heard his name and moved closer to Ben; the dog was carrying something in his mouth. David's sweater. He set it down, rubbed his face on it, then lay on top of it, head on paws.

"David," Ben whispered, shutting his eyes tightly. I took his hand and held it while he quietly wept.

I know that people with head injuries are likely to become easily upset. But even if Ben had come back from that field unscathed, given the events of that day, I wouldn't have blamed him for crying all night.

Bingle worried over him and gently laid his head on Ben's chest. Ben began lightly stroking his fur, but wore down quickly and fell asleep not long after Bingle nuzzled his cheek. I let go of his hand.

I tried to feed Bingle, but he didn't even sniff at the dried dog food I put out for him. I didn't know David's elaborate preparation routine—but I don't think Bingle's refusal to eat was a matter of being finicky.

Ben awakened once, and I got him to drink more water.

I decided not to waste the rain and set up a makeshift system for trapping it, using a trash bag to catch and funnel it into the plastic bucket.

When I heard Ben stirring again, I made one of the packets of soup. He was more alert this time, and I was relieved to find that he was no longer seeing double. He was still pale, but not quite the chalk white of a few hours before, and his speech was clearer. All of these signs were so cheering that when I brought the soup to him, I didn't mind bearing with the slow process of his feeding himself. I ate some of the soup, too, but gave him the lion's share, convinced that if he went hungry he'd never recover, while I could forage for food if need be.

"Thank you," he said when he finished, then added, "I know you probably can't imagine a fate worse than being stuck here with me—"

"Funny, I was going to say the same thing to you. I know you don't trust me, and being this dependent on me must really be galling."

He shook his head. "You should leave me here tomorrow. Save yourself."

"Hmm. Well, your martyrdom *would* spare me a lot of trouble, but without anything to do all day, I'd likely fall into a decline."

He smiled a little at that.

"I don't want to be out there alone with Parrish, Ben."

He considered this for a moment, then said, "Shall we call a truce?"

"Yes—more than a truce. Allies."

"Allies, then," he said. He lay back, and fell asleep again before the rain started.

Bingle lay between us, his head on David's sweater, which he had definitely claimed as his. I hoped that he might be content with that, and not go looking for the boot in the morning.

There was no light in the tent; I was unwilling to use up my flashlight batteries, and lighting a candle inside a tent ranks among the more foolhardy things a person can do—even if you don't make a crematorium out of the tent, you're filling it with carbon monoxide. Besides, I had already decided that we would have a blackout come nightfall—Parrish might be watching for some beacon to our whereabouts.

I wondered where Frank was, what he was doing. Worrying, undoubtedly. The rain would make him worry more. Under some circumstances, that would have annoyed me; tonight, I took comfort—if anyone would force the powers that be to look for us as soon as possible, Frank would. The more I considered this, the more sure I was of it. Frank would come for us. He would not let us be abandoned to whatever plans Parrish had made. I felt myself grow calmer.

I tried hard to think of Parrish not as some mysterious bogeyman—the monster who tortured women, who booby-trapped graves—but as a flesh-and-blood enemy. He wasn't endowed with superhuman powers. It was raining on him, too.

I listened to Ben's and Bingle's breathing, to Ben's occasional moans and Bingle's occasional snores.

I'd have to make the best of my allies, I decided.

I might not capture or kill Parrish, but if the three of us could survive, I'd count it as a major victory.

The rain kept falling, drumming harder now. I was exhausted, but ghosts in the meadow and thoughts of our common enemy kept me awake long into the night.

Realizing that rest was armament, I finally fell asleep.

19

▲ ▼ ▲ ▼

THURSDAY AFTERNOON, MAY 18

The Mojave Desert

"Let me go in first," Jack Fremont said, as Travis brought the van to a halt at the foot of the gravel drive. Jack had warned him not to pull into the drive itself—the man they had come to see was serious about backing up his no trespassing signs.

Frank sat in the back of the van with the dogs.

"I know the delays are killing you," Jack said to him, "but once we get past Stinger's little welcoming rituals, he'll be able to save us a hell of a lot of time."

"Not if this weather holds," Frank said, taking an anxious look at the sky.

"Maybe not if it stays this bad," Jack agreed, "but you wouldn't make much progress on foot in this weather, either. Mud would slow you to a crawl."

"You sure you can trust this guy?" Frank asked, taking a wary look at the odd structure at the end of the drive. It was a homemade house if he'd ever seen one, a pile of cemented rocks and timber that looked more like a cross between a log cabin and a low-budget medieval castle than a home.

"I'd trust Stinger Dalton with my life—and have on several occasions. Just give me a minute to get him used to the idea of having company."

They watched Jack move down the driveway, hands held up as if he were at gunpoint.

"Oh, yeah, he trusts him with his life," Travis said. "Trusts him to try and take it, looks like."

Frank shook his head. "Roll the windows down a little, I want to hear this."

Frank had been willing to go it alone to find Irene if that was what it would take, but he had been relieved when Travis insisted on being included. Jack had come over not much later, and seeing them preparing their gear, offered to join them.

That had been an even greater relief, and not just because Jack was resourceful and a skilled outdoorsman. Jack said he would trust Stinger Dalton with his life, and Frank felt that same level of trust in Jack—a trust he seldom extended to others.

Jack lived next door, and his concern for Irene would be nearly as great as his own, Frank knew. Jack hadn't tried to talk him out of going up into the mountains. Without any hesitation, he had simply asked to be allowed to help.

Watching Jack walking through the rain, hands held high, Frank wondered if Jack was risking life and limb for Irene right this moment. But as if Jack could feel their concern, he looked over his shoulder at them and smiled.

Deke and Dunk lifted their noses to the open window, watching anxiously as Jack moved farther away from the van.

It had been Jack's idea to bring them along.

"They aren't trained to track," Frank had objected, "and I don't want to be worried about them. They won't be able to find this group any faster than we will."

"There's a male dog on this expedition she's on, right?"

"Right."

"Maybe they'll find this other dog, then. Besides, your dogs have been camping with me more than once. They'll behave."

"For you, they will," Travis said, speaking Frank's thoughts on the subject aloud.

But in the end, the dogs were allowed to join them. Frank had arranged for care of the cat. Finally, he had called Pete Baird and told him of his plans to find Irene. After listening to his partner's warnings about the inevitable problems at work, Frank had refused Pete's offer to join them.

"I'd love to have you with me, but one of us getting into this much trouble will be bad enough. I need you in there to beg for my reinstatement. Besides, if Irene comes home safe and sound before I do, you can tell her where I am. And I need someone to cover what's going on here—to try to contact me if anything comes up while I'm still within cell phone range."

"Anything else I can do for you before you're fired for interfering in Thompson's investigation?" Pete asked.

"Yes. If we're not back by Sunday at six, come looking for us."

So now Frank sat in the van, watching a man whom many people thought of as his most unlikely friend. Jack Fremont, tattooed and scar-faced, wearing black leather and sporting a gold hoop earring, his head completely shaved, looked made to order for the job he had once held—leader of a biker gang. That Jack had been born into wealth, and—after a number of years on the road—was now one of the wealthiest men in Las Piernas, surprised almost anyone who learned of it. It wasn't a fact he advertised. He fit better into the role he was playing now.

"Stinger Dalton, you crusty-assed old son of a bitch, put your guns away!" he called.

"Jack?" a low, gravelly voice called back. "By God, I don't believe my fuckin' eyes. I figured you were dead!"

"What? And you think I wouldn't have come haunting you before now?"

The front door opened, and a thin man with a shotgun stepped onto a ramshackle front porch. He was of medium height, and was wearing jeans, heavy boots, and a sleeveless blue T-shirt. He had long, gray hair that he wore in a single braid down his back. His arms were covered with tattoos. As he came into view, the dogs began whining.

"Hush," Frank said to them, trying to hear the conversation outside.

"What the fuck happened to your hair, dude? And who fucked up your face?"

"You ask me the same questions every time you see me. You

need someone to write you some new lines. Man, put the gun away. I want you to meet some friends of mine."

Dalton looked at the van with misgiving.

"I'd never bring trouble to your door, Stinger. You know that."

"No feds?"

"Shit, Stinger. We both know you aren't hiding from the feds."

"Any of 'em feds?" he repeated obstinately.

"No. One of 'em is a cop—"

"What!" Dalton brought the gun up.

Christ, Frank thought, why did you tell him?

"Now, Stinger, in a minute here, I'm gonna take offense," Jack said easily. "I'm trying to tell you that he's a cop, but he's not here on a beef or anything like that. He's my friend. You've heard me talk about Frank. Works homicide in Las Piernas. But he needs to do some business with you that's got nothing to do with him being a cop, except that maybe it will get his ass fired."

"I don't follow you," Dalton said, holding his position.

"The man's as good a friend to me now as you've been, Stinger. Remember me telling you about Irene's husband?"

At that, Dalton lowered the gun.

"Let us come in out of the rain, Stinger, and I'll explain. Unless you think I've turned into a liar, you've got no reason to keep me standing out here."

"Haven't seen you in a long time, Jack," Dalton said.

"Bullshit. I was out here just a month ago. By the way, keep in mind that this is the guy that lets me borrow his dogs."

"Your neighbor's dogs—"

"Oh, yeah—I almost forgot! I've brought a couple of dogs that would like to see you again."

Dalton's face broke into a grin. "Bring everybody in." He turned and went inside.

Jack motioned to Travis, who started the van.

"What do you think of him?" Travis asked, as they turned up the drive.

"I think Jack is pretty free about introducing my dogs and

talking about my wife to head cases. But if Jack says Stinger's a good friend of his, I'll try to reserve further judgment."

Travis said nothing, but Frank didn't miss his look of unholy amusement.

Deke and Dunk sprang from the van and charged toward Dalton, who was back out on the porch, without the gun. To Frank's amazement, though, they slowed as they neared him, and approached with ears back, tails wagging—suddenly well mannered. Dalton spent several minutes praising and petting them, to their obvious delight.

He stood up and extended a hand as Jack said, "Doug Dalton, this is my friend Travis Maguire, Irene's cousin."

"You don't look old enough to shave," Dalton said.

"He's traveled all over the state," Jack said, "working as a storyteller."

"Storyteller!" Dalton said, but catching Jack's eye, kept any further comment to himself. He turned to Frank. "You must be the cop." There was no rancor in it, though, and his handshake was firm, his smile welcoming.

"Stinger taught me all I know about dog training," Jack said. "He's met Deke and Dunk when we stopped by here on our way to go camping and fishing. He's also the best helicopter pilot I know of, and protected my butt on more than one occasion when we did a little riding together. Now he protects me from the fiercest opponent I've ever encountered."

Dalton smiled. "I'm his tax accountant."

"Tax accountant!" Travis said. "How many people come all the way out here for tax advice?"

"Besides the ones that live out here or who contact me by fax or modem?" Dalton asked. "Just a bunch of old bastards on Harleys."

Travis looked stunned.

"Not everyone on a hog is a hell-raiser these days, you know. Bunch of CEOs on 'em now. And as for hell-raising, a lot of us just got tired of that shit. Plenty of cops ride," he added, casting a glance at Frank.

"Sorry, not this one. But we're not here about—"

"My apologies about the welcome," Stinger said. "I just happen to appreciate privacy. Come on in."

Just before they walked through the door, though, Frank's cellular phone rang. He excused himself and stayed on the porch to answer it, uncertain about being able to pick up a signal inside Dalton's fortress.

When he rejoined the others, they were seated around a plain, thick oak table at the center of a large, open room. The few other furnishings were equally spartan.

Jack took one look at his face and said, "What's wrong?"

"That was Pete. The group up there is getting smaller—a little while ago, a botanist and a ranger hiked out with a body bag—Julia Sayre, as far as anyone can tell at this point. These two said the others in the group were going to work on finding a second grave. Seems Parrish hinted there might be as many as eleven others up there—"

"Eleven!" Jack said.

"Yes. Pete didn't have too many details, but I guess they had just come out of one meadow and were up on a ridge when Parrish started hinting about more bodies being up there. Thompson thought Parrish was playing games, until the cadaver dog reacted to a change in the wind.

"So the others went down to check out this second meadow, while the botanist and the ranger hiked out to the plane. The ranger radioed for a helicopter to pick him up so that he could show the chopper where to find the others—including Irene. But by the time the helicopter came to the landing strip for the ranger, the weather was bad. The chopper pilot said they'd have to go after the others later—they'd have problems just making it back to the ranger station.

"Storms are supposed to get worse during the next twenty-four hours. They won't send a chopper in today—the pilot of the plane said if these two guys had come out an hour later, they wouldn't have been able to take off at all."

"Fucking wussies," Dalton grumbled.

"I've told him the basics," Jack said, "as you can tell, he's already got some opinions on the matter."

"Fuckin'-A," Dalton said, crossing his arms over his thin

chest. "How long ago did these two leave the rest of the group?"

"This morning. The rain and hiking with the body slowed them down. My partner's going to try to talk to them, but it doesn't look likely. He learned as much as he could from the pilot of the plane."

When he didn't go on, Travis said, "You looked upset when you walked in here. I take it there was more to it than that?"

"I don't know," Frank said. "I don't know. Maybe it's nothing, but—more than a fourth of the people who started out on this project are no longer with the group. And Pete said the pilot told him that these two were real unhappy about taking off. The botanist had promised to stay with the body, but he still protested about leaving the others. The ranger was even more adamant. When the pilot asked the ranger what the big deal was, since the group had enough food to be out for another couple of days, the ranger said that he thought the guards were fatigued."

"Hmm," Jack said, frowning. He turned to Travis. "Why don't you take out those topo maps we marked up? It won't hurt anybody if some extra campers show up in the area, right?"

"Free country," Dalton said with a grin.

"Hell of a thing for a tax accountant to be saying," Jack muttered.

Travis unfolded the maps and on one of them, pointed out a location on a western ridge. "That's where the makeshift airstrip is." He moved his finger along a line that connected a series of dots. "That's the trail we think they were on when the lawyer was injured."

Dalton nodded. "How many days ago you say that was?"

"Tuesday," Frank answered. "Two days ago."

"Hmm." Dalton frowned over the map. "How many folks you say were on this star voyage?"

"Originally, or after the lawyer was taken home?"

"After."

"Twelve people and a German shepherd. The ranger was gone for a day or so, then rejoined them after getting the lawyer out."

"And the ranger and the botanist say the others were tired but doing okay as of this morning?"

"Yes."

"And the ranger hasn't been with them much, right? I mean, after this lawyer got stepped on, the ranger had to hike out and back in—had to find the others—and now he's hiked out again. Spent most of his time on the hoof."

"I think so—at least, that's the way it sounds to me."

"Tell me about the people in this group—you don't need to bother with the ranger, I don't think he figures into this part of the equation very much. Just tell me about the others."

"Including Parrish?"

"Especially Parrish."

Frank told him as much as he could, although he knew little of Ben Sheridan, David Niles, or Andy Stewart. From Dalton's questions, he soon figured out what the other man was interested in: How would this group work together? Who would make decisions? How fit were they? How experienced as hikers?

The main problem before them—where had the group gone after they left Newly?—started to feel more like the kind of problem he worked with every day. Human behavior. So if you were this person, thinking the way he does and in this situation, what would you do next? Instead of the unfocused, nagging anxiousness of the past few hours, Frank knew he had something to work with, something he could set his mind to.

"You think Parrish was bringing these women to this place alive?" Dalton was asking.

"Yes," Frank said. "He told us he flew Julia Sayre to the airstrip, made her hike for about a day, forced her dig her own grave, then tortured and killed her. Everything about it was planned. He had chosen her long before he made the kill. He isn't disorganized or opportunistic. You listen to him talk, it's all under control." He frowned. "Except . . ."

"Except this victim you caught him on."

"I wasn't the one who caught him. Not my case, but—"

"Was it difficult, catching him on that one?"

"No," Frank said, already seeing where this was going. "It wasn't as difficult as it should have been."

"Broke a pattern?"

"Stinger, with only one body and nothing more than Parrish's own version of the Sayre case," Jack said scornfully, "how the hell could the cops tell which of two cases set the pattern?"

But Frank was not so quick to answer, because he knew—he *knew* there had been other victims. He had said as much to his bosses when news of the deal with Parrish came down. Every other detective in the department had said as much. They had all known that the D.A. had made a wrong call.

"Mr. Dalton's right," Frank said. "Parrish broke a pattern." He drew a steadying breath. "He wanted us to catch him."

"Because—?" Dalton asked.

"Because he knows that he'll escape."

"He might want to," Jack said, watching Frank begin to pace, "but he couldn't know who would be going up into the mountains, or how heavily guarded he'd be."

Frank didn't answer. He was thinking of Parrish's two known victims. Dark hair, blue eyes. Near Irene's age.

"Never mind polishing that strip of floor, Frank," Dalton said. "Get over here and take a look at these maps. Mother Nature has given us a little time to figure out where our man made himself a couple of cemeteries. According to what this ranger and botanist said, we're looking for two meadows divided by a ridge. That could be several places, but not as many places as you'd think."

"No," Frank agreed. "Those two made it in less than a day, carrying a body and hiking in the rain."

"Julia Sayre a big woman?"

"No. And the remains might be nothing more than a skeleton or a partial skeleton after this much time."

"Right. So let's see what this ground looks like and start making circles. Come up with some likely places, then as soon as the weather clears, we'll take a pass over them. Save some time if we do a little thinking before we go."

After the first hour of looking at the maps, Frank felt less optimistic. There were so many places the group could have reached within the time allotted, and the likelihood of finding the right one seemed small. But as Dalton continued to study them, he found reasons to eliminate one or another, narrowing the field. "I'm not saying cross them off the list altogether," he said, standing up and stretching, "but they aren't where I'd look first."

When he walked away from the table, Frank said, "You aren't stopping now, are you?"

Dalton opened his mouth to make a rude reply, then closed it. He studied Frank for a moment, then said, "Do you some good to take a break from it, too. I figure I'll enjoy a little dog time. You all do what you want. I'm going to attend to my guests."

He moved to the floor and began to wrestle with Deke and Dunk, who entered into the spirit of the game immediately, complete with loud and dramatic barks and growls.

Jack gave an apologetic look to Frank and Travis. "Stinger has to do things in his own way," he said, trying to keep his voice low and yet still be heard over the ruckus. "No use trying to push him. But I'll go with you if you want to leave . . ."

Frank's need to reassure himself that Irene was safe tempted him to leave—tempted him until it was almost irresistible. Staying still was maddening. The urge to move, to act, to get as close to the mountains as possible nearly drove him to set aside all other considerations. But as he smoothed the uppermost topo map beneath his hands, spreading his fingers in an effort to release a fraction of the tension that invaded every muscle in his body, he saw circle after circle on the map, and realized that trying to find her without the help of the helicopter pilot would be all but impossible. There was simply too much ground to cover. And the storm would only make things worse.

"The weather is what's holding us up, not your friend," he said. "Stinger's not the problem."

"I like him," Travis said. "Did he fly helicopters in Vietnam?"

"Never heard of the place," Dalton said from the floor.

"He might be gray haired," Jack said, "but the crazy-assed wild man's ears are still sharp."

So is his mind, Frank thought, studying the map as Dalton's laughter mixed in with the barks and growls of the dogs. So is the crazy-assed wild man's mind.

20

▲▼▲▼

THURSDAY EVENING, MAY 18

A Cave in the Southern Sierra Nevada Mountains

His lair, as he thought of it, was warm and dry. He wouldn't have minded being out in the rain. He had many times suffered deprivations in pursuit of his goals; more than once, the mere observation of one of the objects of his affection had required a night spent in some inconvenient place during inclement weather. But at present, it was far more entertaining to be comfortable when she was not.

She would be alone in the dark, surrounded by death. She would have made the best of what was left of the camp, but there would be no food. This wouldn't really harm her—water was readily available—but psychologically, her hunger would be to his advantage.

She wouldn't know if he had made good his escape, or if he would return for her. He thought she probably knew of this cave. He had seen footprints and thought they were most likely hers—she had wandered off in this direction yesterday. But she would not know if he had stayed or fled.

At this stage of the game, hope would counteract some of her fears. She would think of the promised helicopter, coming to the meadow. While it was in some ways a nuisance, he was grateful that it tethered her to one location. She would not, in hysteria, go wandering off into the forest, simply trying to run from him or the scattered remains of her former protectors—he would have found her anyway, of course, but this made it so much easier.

He pictured her, huddled in her own tent—he knew that she would choose her own tent. The rain would drum loudly against it. She would be tired, but unable to sleep. Cold, hungry, afraid, alone.

Oh, she had the dog. But the dog would not be of much help to her. This dog was a spoiled and pampered dog, a dog whose master had been a silly man who sang songs and made up tricks for the dog. He had seen the attachment dog and master had to each other, the man's constant displays of affection—really, it was almost obscene! The man had spoken to the dog nearly incessantly. Where was the dog's dignity in that? And as for letting the beast slather his tongue all over his owner's face—he was disgusted by the mere thought of it. He was glad to have put an end to it.

With his master dead, the dog would become depressed. Dogs did become depressed, he knew. Even Julia Sayre's little dog had mourned her. He sighed, remembering how much he had enjoyed watching the little Pekingese staring from the second-story window, looking as if it would jump to its death, if it could only find a way to open the latch. He might have helped it, too, had he not been so entertained by its sorrow.

This German shepherd—though not a purebred shepherd, surely—would be no better off. No, this dog—he couldn't bring himself to say its ridiculous name!—would only make the night seem gloomier to a woman of her sympathetic nature.

He had so many plans for her. He was torn between considering these, and considering the successes of the day. He knew how to build his own anticipation, though, and so for the moment, the latter won out.

Things had indeed gone well today. Here he was, barely a scratch on him. He preferred to slowly savor murder, and was surprised that he could kill so efficiently and yet feel the sort of triumphant satisfaction that he had felt then. He had outsmarted them, of course, but it was so enjoyable to have such tangible proof of his abilities available to the world!

It was satisfying, but held none of the pleasures that previous killings had given him. It had all gone by a little too quickly. Especially Merrick and Manton—that really was a shame. Manton, standing closer to the explosion, had been stunned by it, but Merrick, although unable to comprehend what had happened at the grave, had reacted rather speedily to having his weapon taken. That was nearly admirable. He had been forced to kill him immediately.

Ah well, life would always have its minor disappointments. He would counter this with the knowledge that their bullet-riddled faces would shock and anger their comrades. And with the knowledge that Irene had been there to see it all, including his display of marksmanship in the killing of that pompous ass, Sheridan.

Sheridan, who had stared at his coyotes, who had presumed to know something about him. Sheridan, who had touched Julia!

He remembered that the man had actually had the nerve to go to Irene's tent late one night. He had heard their voices, but could not make out their conversation. He only knew that she had refused Sheridan, for he had walked away. She must have told him that she would rather sleep with the dog, because it was the dog who kept her company that night. Just as somewhere, out in those rainy woods, the dog was with her tonight.

It was at this point that he decided he had put off his treat long enough. He carefully withdrew them from his breast pocket. They weren't the lacy, frilly type. Nothing like that for her. Even before he had seen them, he knew that she would wear simple cotton briefs. He found them charmingly innocent, almost like a little girl's panties. Slowly, reverently, he brought them to his face.

Had he been a weaker man, he would have wept.

21

▲ ▼ ▲ ▼

THURSDAY EVENING, MAY 18

U.S. Forest Service Ranger Station and Helitack Unit Southern Sierra Nevada Mountains

The saboteur who watched the rangers' helicopters had never had such an important role to play. This provided a certain level of excitement, but not anxiety. Nicky's instructions had been explicit, the hours of training had been rigorous, and every contingency except failure had been considered. There was no thought of failure.

Nicky Parrish would not, the saboteur knew, consider for a moment that his trust—never given to anyone else before—was misplaced. Nor would Nicky be thinking of his helper—Nicky must concentrate on other matters. Nicky would simply know that his orders were being carried out—he would *know*. The way he always knew things. He would know that his little Moth had obeyed.

The intruder loved this nickname—this Nick name. The first time they had met, Nicky had said, "You are drawn to my light, aren't you, little moth? That's what I shall call you. From now on, you are my Moth."

No one who had met the Moth at work or socially would

have ever said, "Here is a servant." That was one part of the delight the Moth took in serving Nicky. Nicky had immediately discerned the Moth's desire to serve. The Moth was, in fact, the perfect servant, and to be the perfect servant, one must serve the perfect master.

And together, they were making history. Nicky, who had always acted alone, had deemed his servant worthy of this honor.

Just thinking of this heightened the Moth's sense of anticipation. Perhaps later, during one of their dormant times, the Moth would write a poem about it. But for now, there was work to do—and unmindful of the darkness and the danger, of the rain and the cold—the Moth waited and watched, and eventually saw that the perfect moment for action had arrived.

It was not difficult to cause problems, little hitches in other people's plans, if you knew what you were doing.

The Moth knew.

The people in the ranger station were careful with the forest, where they expected trouble, but not with the helicopters. Not on rainy nights, when the clouds were covering the mountains—nights when there was little to do. They did not look at these machines, nor walk out into the cold rain. All but one of them watched television—an old movie, made long before there were computers, served up by the ranger station's satellite dish.

Perhaps the world outdoors was no longer exciting to the helicopter crews and forest workers—perhaps the sky and the forest were their offices, and the television and all things interior were more interesting to them.

Or perhaps it was just the rain that lulled them.

They should be thankful for it, really. The Moth had trained for many possible scenarios, including ones in which the five people in the small building with the satellite dish on it must be killed. But the rain would allow them to live. The rain masked sounds, made visibility poor.

One man in the station looked out at the rain from time to time. Wishing it away. He was the one who had been with Nicky. It was a little puzzling that he should be here. But that was not important. Nicky, who knew everything, had said that a few of them might see God and live.

The Moth went to work. Within moments, the Alouette and the Bell 212 had small, disabling problems. They could be repaired.

Just not in time.

J.C. went back to the window and stared out into the darkness. He did not talk to the others; it only made the waiting worse. So he pretended to be watching the rain—pretended, because he didn't see the rain at all. He saw a horrible thing rise from a crude grave and beg for an embrace; he saw coyotes dancing on marionette strings held by a puppet master in a tree. He closed his eyes against these terrors, but to his dismay, he saw them more clearly.

How did David and Ben stand it? He had helped them before, but it had never been this bad. He had seen decayed remains before this, and had thought he would be prepared—but the bodies they had found before were suicides, or people who had wandered and died lost, or who had fallen while hiking alone. Not pleasant, and he had always felt sorry for them, but—but it was not like this.

He knew a hatred for Nicholas Parrish that he could taste in his mouth like bile.

Up there, in the meadow where they had found her, he hadn't felt this way; he had stayed cool, had kept it together. Even carrying her body through the rain with Andy, he had been all right. It didn't start to get to him until they were at the plane, after the pilot said they'd have to leave. And it wasn't until he was here, at his own station, safe and warm, that he started to come apart.

He would show the Helitack crew where to find the group in the second meadow, and then he would take a couple of weeks off. He had the time coming to him. Maybe he'd even see a shrink. The idea didn't bother him. If you needed help, get help.

David had told him that often enough. He had said that it would be weirder to do that kind of work and never be affected by it.

There were specialists who dealt with counseling people who had worked these cases. He'd ask David for the name of one of them.

He gave a sudden start—involuntarily brought his hand to his throat, as if holding a sound back—as if holding himself back. Out of the corner of his eye, he saw something moving in the darkness—or did he? Jesus, he was jumpy! Beneath his hand, his pulse raced. He tried to stare past the rain-splattered window. No, nothing out there.

Was there?

He couldn't keep standing here. His legs weren't going to hold him. God damn.

No, he couldn't live like this—cowering and jumping at shadows. He was going to face it—that was the only way for now. He was going to walk out there and look around—reassure himself. He turned away from the window. He put on his parka, and when his hands shook as he tried to fasten the snaps, he shoved them into his pockets until he opened the door. He stepped out into the rain, peered into the darkness.

Nothing.

The cool air felt good, calmed him, until—

There! In the trees!

But . . . no, nothing.

Nothing.

The door suddenly opened behind him and he heard himself make a small sound of fright.

"J.C.? What's the matter, man?"

One of the pilots.

"Just needed some air," he said, not too steadily.

"Come inside," the pilot coaxed.

J.C. stared out into the rain.

"Come on inside, man." The pilot paused, then added, "They'll be okay. Just camping out in the rain. We'll pick them up first thing tomorrow. Come on in—nothing you can do tonight."

He followed the pilot in, ignoring the uneasy glances the others exchanged. He made his way to his closet and took out another set of clothes. He went into the bathroom and stripped to take a shower. His third one tonight, and the others were probably already talking about it, but he didn't give a shit. He could still smell the stink of that body on him and he needed to get clean.

He scrubbed until his skin was raw, let the water beat down on him, rinsed his mouth, his nose. He stood there letting the sound and feel of the water drown out everything else, until it just got too cold to stand it any longer. He toweled off and changed clothes again, then stared at himself in the mirror. He didn't know the man who stared back at him, even though he recognized the face.

He didn't want to go to sleep. Not with this shit running around in his head. He was spooked when he was wide awake—what the fuck would happen in his dreams?

Yes, he would get help.

But until then, what the hell could he do?

22

▲ ▼ ▲ ▼

FRIDAY, MAY 19, 2:00 A.M.

Southern Sierra Nevada Mountains

"David, tell those two they can't work in here without masks," he said.

He had said something before that. The sound of his voice had awakened me before I could make out what it was.

"Ben?" I asked in the darkness.

"Oh, good—you're here," he said.

"Yes, I'm here," I said.

"Can't something be done about the heat in this place?"

"In the tent?"

"The air-conditioning—we'll lose the computers."

"Ben, it's Irene," I said, sitting up. "Wake up, Ben."

He didn't answer. I had just decided that my voice had stirred him from his nightmare, allowed him to sleep more peacefully, when he said, "Need a postmortem dental."

Bingle, I soon realized, was sitting up, too. I scooted closer to Ben, reached over to try to rouse him. He had moved around in his sleep, and had pushed the upper sleeping bag off. Patting carefully around the tent, my hand found his hand—hot and dry.

"Note the development of the muscle attachment areas on

this long bone," he said. "This fellow might have been a southpaw."

He was burning up. I risked using the flashlight, praying that Parrish wasn't outside watching for it, that the rain was keeping him in for the night. I took in Ben's glazed look, the sheen of perspiration that covered him. I found water and a neckerchief and the Keflex. Berating myself for not giving him more of the drug from the start, I managed to get his attention long enough to give him four of the pills now. How much would be dangerous?

I dampened the cloth and began the work of trying to cool him down.

"Camille?" he asked, frowning as he looked at me.

"Not even Garbo," I said. "No deathbeds in this tent, understand? You fight this, Ben. Stay with me."

"It's so hot," he said, pushing the sleeping bag lower. He remained restless, and his ramblings became less coherent. He would lie quietly, then suddenly shout something, often making me jump. Before long, he began thrashing around and I soon became worried that he'd reopen the bullet wound or worse if I didn't get the fever down.

I opened the tent and went outside long enough to gather some water from the rain catcher; it was nearly full. I managed to get him to drink some of it, and to give him some aspirin. I didn't have much faith that the aspirin would help at this point, but I wasn't going to pass up a chance that it might lower his fever.

Ben seemed calmer when he heard my voice, so I talked to him as I worked. I took the sleeping bag off him, and when I saw him tearing at his shirt, unbuttoned it and helped him take it off, running cool cloths over his skin. Eventually I cut his pants off, too, afraid that his occasional delirious efforts to pull them off would do more harm to his injured leg. Fortunately, he didn't seem to mind keeping his briefs on.

I kept on talking, kept changing the cloths. It seemed to me that he was feeling cooler, but I couldn't be certain—my hands were beginning to feel numb from the cold rainwater.

"Thirsty," I heard him say, in not much more than a whisper.

One look at his face told me that he was no longer out of his senses—but he was in pain.

I propped his head up, gave him more Keflex, and let him drink from the water bottle as long as he could.

"Thanks," he said, and closed his eyes.

"Do you want some more aspirin? I'm sorry, it's all I have."

"No. I'm beyond the reach of aspirin," he said.

I counted the Keflex tablets. There were ten left. I wondered if I had given him too many, or not enough. Or if it would do any good at all. Maybe I was trying to put out a four-alarm fire with a squirt gun.

I called Bingle to my side. He came, but he brought David's sweater with him. I turned out the light and lay down in my sleeping bag. I felt a rush of emotion, a sense of relief that made me want to cry. I stroked the dog's fur, tried to calm down enough to sleep.

Outside, the stream was running stronger, and its rushing sound overpowered the sounds I had listened for earlier in the night. I tried to listen for Ben's breathing, or Bingle's snore, but the stream and the rain were too loud. I didn't hear Ben crying out in delirium, though, or moving restlessly, so I thought he must have fallen asleep. I don't know how much time had passed when I heard him say, "What was that story you were telling me?"

"When?"

"Tonight."

I felt my face grow warm. "You knew what was happening? You could understand me?"

"Not always. It's a little jumbled."

"Parzival," I said.

"What?"

"The story was *Parzival the Grail Knight*. He's this kind-hearted young knight who often unwittingly causes harm where he means to do good—there are several versions of the tale, but I told you stories from the German poem, by Wolfram von Eschenbach."

"You told me a story in English," he said testily.

"Yes, of course—based on a translation—"

"Good grief. Don't tell me Brenda Starr is a scholar of medieval poetry?"

I didn't reply.

"Sorry," he said.

After a long silence he said, "Why do you prefer the German version?"

"It's the only one I know. That's the one Jack gave me, that's the one I read. Some scholar, huh?"

"Look, I said I was sorry."

"So you did."

After another silence, he tried again. "Who's Jack?"

"Our neighbor. He's—well, Jack isn't easy to explain. But he's big on mythology and folklore."

"Tell it to me again," he said. "I'll listen better this time."

"I won't be able to do it justice. There are lots of complicated relationships and battles and characters whose names I don't remember. I sort of faked my way through it tonight. You'd be better off reading it when we get back."

"I'll let you sleep, then," he said, and it wasn't until that moment that I heard what had probably been in his voice all along.

"Well, if you don't mind an inferior version of it . . ."

"I don't mind."

So I tried to distract him from his pain by telling him of young Parzival, raised in ignorance of knights and chivalry by an overly protective mother. Of course, the first time Parzival encountered knights, he could think of nothing he'd rather do than become one, and set off to offer his services to King Arthur. Although embarrassingly naive and untutored, he had a natural talent for the work.

Ben fell asleep just as Parzival was about to visit Wild Mountain and meet the Fisher King.

It was just after dawn by then, and although it was still fairly dark in the tent, there was enough light for me to see Ben Sheridan's pale and haggard features.

"What's wrong, Ben?" I whispered, my mind still half caught up in Parzival's tale.

It seemed to be a silly question, under the circumstances. Pain, weakness, severe injuries. Bad weather, hunger, a killer on the loose nearby. Easy to name what was wrong with him.

Or was it? I thought back to my last conversation with David, as I left for my walk with Bingle. David had hinted that Ben had troubles before we began our journey to these meadows. Whatever those troubles were, I supposed it would be a long time, if ever, before Ben Sheridan would confide in me.

When I woke up, Bingle was gone. Worried, I put on my boots and jacket. I had just stepped out into a misty morning when he returned, his fur damp and muddy, his mouth looking swollen.

Oh, hell, I thought, he's met up with a porcupine. But as he drew closer, I saw that he was gently carrying something in his mouth.

Please don't let it be something from the meadow, I prayed. He looked at me uncertainly, as if he expected me to do something. Not knowing what my part in this script was, I stayed still. He shifted his weight, looking anxious, then lay down at my feet. Very slowly and carefully, he opened his mouth, and, between my feet, deposited what he had been carrying.

Eggs.

Three small eggs.

Quail eggs. I hoped that he hadn't taken every egg from the nest. Perhaps I should have scolded him, but between my relief at not having someone's remains disgorged on my boots and my inability to guess if this was something he had been praised for doing in the past, I only managed a feeble, "*Gracias, Bingle.*"

He wagged his tail.

"I suppose you want one of these on your dog food."

He kept wagging his tail. On the fur on his chin, I saw something that looked suspiciously like egg yolk.

"Then again, I guess you've already had breakfast."

There was no way to put them back at this point, and as my stomach growled, I decided I wasn't going to waste the food. I carefully stowed them inside the tent. I had a wild vision of J.C. finding them there and refusing to allow me to leave on the helicopter as punishment for disturbing local fauna. Telling him the dog brought them to me probably wouldn't get me out of trouble.

Although the rain had let up, a heavy mist seemed to be settling in. Near the tent it was not terribly thick, but I doubted that visibility near the low, flat meadow would be good enough to allow a helicopter to land. I tried not to let this distress me, but the thought of not seeing the helicopter arrive that morning was upsetting. If Parrish didn't find me, I could manage, but what would become of Ben? The fever, the loss of blood, the possibility of infection—if Parrish never showed his face, Ben's life would still be in danger.

The rainwater bucket was full again. It felt good to have something going right. That feeling of confidence was not destined to last long.

Bingle joined me as I left for a walk to the stream. The rain in the container would help, but wouldn't be enough. I decided I would refill our water bottles, which shouldn't take long; my Sweet Water unit could filter a quart of stream water in a little over a minute.

I walked quickly. I didn't want to leave Ben alone for any extended period of time. The ground was soft and muddy, but not impossibly so. On the way, I found a long, broken branch that ended in a curving fork. I picked it up and tried leaning on it, placing the forked end under my arm. It easily withstood my weight, but was a little tall for me—which would make it about right for Ben. I took it with me, thinking I might be able to fashion it into a crutch. If we had to move again, a crutch would be useful.

I stepped through the trees toward a sound that grew louder and louder. To my shock, the stream was now a much higher, debris-filled torrent, wildly coursing through the forest, and moving far too rapidly to be entered at this point. It cut us off completely from the meadow.

The meadow where the helicopter, if it arrived, would be landing.

23

▲ ▼ ▲ ▼

FRIDAY MORNING, MAY 19

Southern Sierra Nevada Mountains

When I got back to the tent, Ben was still sleeping. I used a piece of string to make three measurements—from his armpit to his elbow, from his elbow to his palm, and from his armpit to the bottom of his foot. I went back outside and checked the full length against the branch. A little short, perhaps, but I thought it might do. I used rope to fasten a short, thick stick at the place where I thought his hand might rest. I was taping cloth padding there and in the fork when I heard Ben call my name.

I went into the tent. "Ben? How are you feeling?"

"Better."

"Good. Let me get some more Keflex for you."

"I'll take some a little later. I—I need to relieve myself. Would you please help me dress?" he asked.

"Oh. If you're in a hurry—"

"Not that much of a hurry."

The humiliation was obviously about to do him in, but we managed to find a shirt and a pair of shorts that would fit him from among those I had gathered from the camp.

"Did David train Bingle to steal eggs from birds' nests?" I asked, trying to distract him.

"What!?"

"Uh—that was a change of subject. This morning, Bingle brought me those quail eggs—the ones on my sleeping bag."

He looked over at them. "No, in fact, he's trained not to disturb wildlife. Very strange. He likes eggs, though." He smiled a little and added, "Maybe he's courting you."

"I don't think dogs carry out what most women would think of as courtships," I said, "although the average guy probably admires their direct approach."

I helped him to sit up.

His skin was a little too warm; the flush on his face was obviously not just from embarrassment.

"You seem to be a little feverish."

"Help me with the shirt, please," he said, ignoring my comment.

I got him started with it, but he batted my hands away when I tried to do the buttons.

"God damn," he said, lying back down, his hands shaking after the third button.

"You're not doing so bad, all things considered," I said, finishing up without further objection from him. "Need to rest, or you want to try a trip outside?"

"Rest—just a few minutes," he said, breathing as hard as if he had been running.

"Want an egg for breakfast? They're little but—"

"You should eat them. Or give them to Bingle."

"I think he's already eaten."

"You gave me the soup last night. You didn't have anything to eat, did you?"

"No, I ate some soup. But of the two of us—"

"You're doing all the physical labor. You need strength. Eat the eggs. Have some soup, too. It's all he left us, isn't it?"

"We're near a meadow. There are dandelions out there, and other things to eat. Besides, J.C. isn't going to forget about us. As soon as the weather clears, the helicopter will come."

"Eat the eggs before J.C. gets here."

"But—"

"While I rest. Please."

So while Bingle looked on, I scrambled the eggs, which combined to make a little less than one chicken egg's worth of breakfast. I put a small forkful into the furry thief's bowl of dog food and ate the rest.

I helped Ben get out of the tent—no easy task—and showed him the crutch. He put it under his arm and leaned on it. It fit better than I thought it would.

"I need two," he said.

I laughed.

"I mean, thanks. I didn't mean to—"

"It's okay. You do need two. I'll try to find another branch. In the meantime, lean on me."

Slowly, we made it from the tent to a tree. "Can you manage from here?" I asked. "Call me when you're finished—I won't watch."

"I—not so close to the camp," he said.

"Ben, under any other circumstances, I'd applaud your sensitivity. But you're running a fever and you look as if you're about to pass out. Bingle has marked all of these trees already, so show him who's alpha. Even injured, I'll bet you can hit higher."

"No," he said. "Not here."

"Jesus. You're not exactly in a position to argue, you know that?" But I helped him move farther into the woods.

It was while I was waiting for him to finish that I heard Bingle barking. "Shit! I'll be right back!"

I ran back to the camp. Bingle wasn't there, but his fierce, warning barks continued.

Oh God, oh God, oh God. Don't let him kill the dog. Don't let him kill Ben. Don't let him kill me.

I had no weapons other than my knife. I picked up a large stick, which even then I knew would probably be utterly useless, but it gave me some primitive sense of power—that cave dweller bashing power, I suppose.

More cautious now, I made my way toward the barking, which was coming from the woods nearer the stream. Exactly which direction, I couldn't tell, but the dog seemed to be in front of me. I moved from tree to tree, running in a crouched position, staying as close to the ground as I could.

"Bingle!" I said in a low voice, even before I saw him.

"*¡Bingle, ven acá! ¡Cállate!*" I didn't dare to shout it. But the dog must have heard me, because he stopped barking and began running toward me. I heard a shot, and Bingle yelped, but he kept running.

He soon reached me, panting and agitated. I dropped my bashing stick and ran my fingers over his fur, but I couldn't find any wounds. I whispered praise to him and tried to stop shaking. Where was Parrish?

I waited, whispering to Bingle to stay still, to stay quiet. He obeyed, anxiously watching me.

"Irene Kelly!" a voice called out.

I thought Bingle whimpered, then realized I was the one who had made the sound.

"Thanks to that ill-mannered mutt," Parrish shouted, "I know exactly where you are, Irene! I know, do you hear me? Yes, of course you do! I know exactly where you are!"

I held on to Bingle.

"I will find a way across, Irene!" he shouted. "I will find a way across! Did you think a little water would keep you safe? Think again!"

I didn't move. My heart was hammering in my chest.

I waited, but he didn't say anything more. If I had been alone, I probably would have just taken off with Bingle, but I had Ben to think of. As quickly and as quietly as I could, I ran back to the camp.

I hurriedly took up all the used bandages and anything that had blood on it—including the pants I had cut off Ben, and hid them beneath a pile of leaves, away from the camp. I returned to the tent and took up Ben's sleeping bags, his shaving kit, three water bottles, matches, a mess kit and the soup. I grabbed some bandages, the aspirin, and the Keflex. I left my sleeping bag, but took some clothing, mostly rain gear. I took Bingle's food and harness. I folded the tarp and was ready to leave, when I saw one last item. I grabbed David's sweater, which Bingle quickly took from me, and together we ran toward the place where I had left Ben.

He wasn't there.

"Ben?" I called softly. Had I mistaken the place?

"Over here," I heard him say.

"Where?" I asked, but Bingle, wagging his tail, moved to a fallen tree. If his mouth hadn't been full of sweater, he probably would have barked.

A pile of wet leaves moved, and Ben's head emerged. I breathed a sigh of relief.

"Are you okay?" I asked.

"A little damp, but okay."

"Thank God you hid. Listen, Bingle was barking—"

"At Parrish," Ben said.

"Did you hear him?"

"Parrish? Not really. Just a voice. Couldn't make out what he was saying. But Bingle's bark—it had to be Parrish. I managed to drag myself over here."

"He's going to try to cross the stream—the stream has been swollen by the rain, so luckily for us, crossing it won't be easy. Still, he might find a place where it narrows, so we may not have more than a few minutes."

"Then listen—"

"I'm going to draw him away from you," I said. "Even if he catches me, he'll probably—well, you'll still have some time."

"For God's sake—"

"I don't think he knows you're alive," I went on. "I tried to bring or bury anything that might let him know you were at the tent. I brought the sleeping bags and a tarp, and a little food and water. If you can hold out until the helicopter comes, maybe light a signal fire when you hear it—I don't know, that might not be safe, either—anyway, here's the water and the Keflex, I'll look for a place to hide you, and I'll be right back."

"Irene, listen to me—this is stupid. Run. Just run. I'm begging you, please. Please get the hell out of here. I can hide beneath this tree."

"If the dampness doesn't kill you, insects will eat you alive. I'll bet you've already got ant bites."

"Ant bites! Who gives a shit about ant bites!"

"Bingle," I said, "*cuídalo*."

"What did you just say to him?"

"He'll guard you while I'm gone."

"Oh, Christ."

"Be right back."

"Don't! Don't come back! Just run!"

I started praying to St. Jude, which is something an old-fashioned Catholic will do in times of trouble. While I was at it, I asked St. Anthony to find a hiding place for Ben. I also used the direct line.

I'm not sure who got through to the big guy first, but I hadn't gone far when I found a group of relatively dry boulders that were large enough to hide a man, and would not force Ben to suffer all the insect life in a fallen tree.

I dragged the gear there first, not listening to Ben's renewed arguments, which he should have known were useless.

By the time I came back for him, he had either realized that or worn himself out, because he didn't give me any more grief—nothing beyond muttering about hardheaded women, but the line forms to the left for people who've said something like that to me over the years.

I praised Bingle and told him to follow us, then helped Ben, carrying him on my back when we reached the boulders.

Once we had managed the hellish business getting him ensconced in his rocky fortress—his bad leg was jostled four or five times—I went around the outside, studying the boulders from every possible angle. I couldn't see him unless I climbed up over several layers of rock. Satisfied that it was the best we could do on short notice, I gave Bingle the sentinel's job again and crawled back into Ben's cubbyhole with him, bringing his crutch with me. I quickly helped him change into a dry shirt. The shorts had fared better. I put a sleeping bag around him. I made sure the water and other supplies were within reach.

"I'm going now," I said. "Will you be all right here?"

He nodded.

"If you see Frank Harriman before I do, tell him—say hello for me, okay?"

"Sure."

There was a sound from the forest then. It was repeated, again and again at regular intervals. I didn't recognize it, but Ben did.

"An ax. He's cutting down a tree. He's probably making a bridge across the water."

"I'd better get ready to lure him right back over it, then. You sure you'll be all right here?"

"Yes."

"You'll be able to get out again if you need to?"

"Yes, I can pull myself out over the rocks if I have to. You're taking Bingle, aren't you?"

"Yes. Parrish will wonder why I don't have him with me if he's not at my side. But if—if necessary, I'll try to send him back to you."

"I don't know much Spanish," he said. "Come back for me yourself."

I laughed and started to leave, then bent back down and hugged him. He seemed a little surprised at first, but then he hugged back. "Be safe," he said.

"You, too."

I stood up and had climbed about halfway out when he said, "Thank you."

"You keep fighting, Ben Sheridan, or I'll really be pissed off at you."

"Take care, Lois Lane."

"Sure thing, Quincy."

"Oh God, don't make me a pathologist!"

I reached the top of the rock pile, saw him below me, suddenly looking vulnerable and alone. I almost considered staying with him, but I knew that we'd be fish in a barrel for Parrish if he found us.

Maybe he saw my indecision, because he said, "Shove old Nicky off a cliff and come back and tell me the rest of Parzival."

"Sure. I'll try not to make you wait to hear the ending."

I took one last look at him, hoped it wasn't really a last look, waved, and began my journey back to the stream, listening to Parrish's ax ringing out its challenge, its siren call, its alarm.

24

▲ ▼ ▲ ▼

FRIDAY MORNING, MAY 19

Southern Sierra Nevada Mountains

He was strong.

I suppose I had known that before, but watching him swing that ax at the tree on the opposite bank disheartened me, made me wonder what on earth had led me to believe I could defeat him.

He was swinging hard, angrily. The tree was not huge—a pine tree that was tall enough to span the stream and thick enough to support his weight when he walked on it.

I forced myself to think in terms of escaping him, drawing him away from Ben. My first frantic thoughts included improbable methods of killing him: throwing a large rock at him while he was chopping down the tree, beaning him while his hands were occupied; swinging across the stream from a vine, Tarzan-style, plunging my knife into him while the ax was stuck in the wood; whittling a javelin and spearing him while he was halfway across the river.

All impractical. I have a decent pitching arm, but this was no straight shot, and if I missed him, he'd shoot me; there were no convenient Tarzan-strength vines; even if I had the time to whittle a javelin, chances of learning to throw one accurately for a one-chance, winner-takes-all shot were nil.

I did find another stick that could be used as a club, and a few baseball-sized rocks. If he had somehow seen me watching him, and came after me before I crossed to the other side, I'd use whatever was at hand to stop him.

There was a slow creaking sound, then a thunderous crack. The tree began to give way, its upper branches catching and snapping like gunfire as they struck the branches of other trees on the way down. It hit the ground on my side of the stream with a loud bang that shook the earth beneath me.

Bingle flattened himself to the ground and put his ears back, but stayed next to me. I peered cautiously from my hiding place.

Nick Parrish stood surveying his handiwork. He could easily cross over now; the lowest branches of the tree would present an obstacle or two at this end, but he had chosen his crossing place and bridge material well.

Would he plan on my being this close? Would he know that I might have moved toward the sound of him felling a tree? I didn't think so. He would expect me to run. He expected fear.

He was looking at the ax now, and as he did, I tried not to think of him using it on me. He expects fear, I told myself again. Don't give it to him.

So I tried to think about the ax being in my own hands, which suddenly made me wonder—whose ax was it? I couldn't remember anyone hiking with one, or using one in the past few days. Did he have other tools and weapons cached nearby?

He carried the ax with him as he began to walk along the tree trunk. He used it as a kind of balance. He moved cautiously. Closer and closer.

He had his hands full, the gun holstered. The temptation to try pitching one of the rocks at him was strong. The stream wasn't very far below him, only about four feet. It was running swift and cold, but I wasn't sure how deep. He wasn't looking toward me now; he was getting closer to the branches, which would partially obscure him. I might not have a better chance. But if I missed? Perhaps I could still evade him.

I had picked up one of the rocks and was weighing it in my hand when he lost his balance. He had almost reached my side of the stream when one of the branches supporting the fallen trunk gave way beneath his added weight, The whole trunk suddenly dropped a few inches, and Parrish lunged forward. He let go of the ax and grasped wildly at the branches nearest him.

The ax fell into the rushing water below, but the branch he had grabbed held. He pulled himself upright, looking shaken. My enjoyment of that was brief.

Whispering to Bingle to remain quiet, I watched as Parrish quickly made his way to safety, and onto the bank. I moved behind a fallen tree, no longer risking watching him, listening as he moved through the woods. He came closer to where I crouched. I took my club in hand. He paused not far from me, and for a moment I was sure he had seen me, and that he was merely deciding how best to take me captive. But he moved on, heading downstream, toward the place where he had heard Bingle barking.

I made myself wait a little longer, then stood and stretched. Bingle stretched his back legs, then followed me to Parrish's bridge. I snapped the leash onto his harness, hoping he wouldn't balk at crossing the noisy current. If he fell in, I wasn't sure I'd be strong enough to keep him from being swept downstream.

I needn't have worried. He didn't resist my efforts to help him scramble up onto the tree, and once we were clear of the branches, he began to move so quickly and easily that I had to concentrate on keeping up with him, rather than on thoughts of falling into the water.

"*Bien*," I whispered, when we reached the muddy bank on the other side. "I think you've crossed streams this way before, Bingle."

I removed his leash, then took a moment to examine the fallen tree, to look for something that I might later use as a lever to move it, but found nothing. I realized that this part of the stream was not far from the group camp. Thinking that I might scrounge some useful items from it again, I went back to it. I had to call to Bingle a couple of times to keep him from going back to the meadow.

Among the sodden ruins of the camp, I saw a length of rope that might come in handy, but not much else. I figured that it would take Parrish a little while to find where I had stayed last night, and to rummage through the tent—but I didn't want to give him enough time to find Ben. I hurried back to the stream, and continued along the bank, until I was near where Parrish had stood when he called to me.

I moved a little way into the woods, found two small trees and stretched a length of the rope between them at about ankle height. I covered it with leaves. I hurriedly sharpened three sticks with my knife and planted them in the soft ground a few feet beyond the rope, sharp-end up, at roughly forty-five-degree angles, so that they formed a row pointing back toward the rope. These I also covered with leaves. A little farther away, within easy sight of the first trees, I tied another length of rope between two other trees, this time at a height of almost a foot off the ground.

I quickly worked out a route through the woods, occasionally piling stones up as markers.

"Okay, Bingle," I said, snapping the leash back on. "Let's put on a show."

I moved back toward the stream, but stayed out of sight, in the trees. "*Cántame, Bingle.*" Sing to me.

He looked at me, looked back at the meadow, and whimpered.

I swallowed hard. "*Cántame, Bingle.*"

He lay down, and would not look at me. I tried holding his face, and still he kept his eyes averted.

"Okay, so that belongs to David," I said. "I apologize. Will you speak for me? *Háblame, Bingle. Por favor, háblame.*"

He looked up at me.

"*¡Háblame!*"

He was watching me, looking undecided.

"*¡Háblame!*" I tried again.

He barked.

"*¡Muy bien! ¡Háblame!*"

He entered the spirit of things then. He barked and barked, and I praised him in Spanish, until finally I saw movement through the trees on the other bank. Loudly in English, I called, "Stop barking! Please, Bingle!" In Spanish, I continued to enthusiastically command just the opposite.

Not wanting to overdo it, I finally said, "*¡Cálmate, cállate!*"

He fell silent. I quietly petted him and praised him in Spanish. We walked back toward the starting line of the obstacle course I had set for Parrish.

Bingle had become aware of Parrish's presence some time before, probably catching his scent on the breeze that came our way every few minutes. At the same time, if it's true that animals can smell fear, I was overloading the poor dog's snoot.

Parrish reached his little bridge, and couldn't resist taunting me. "I'll find you, you know!"

What the hell? I thought. Do not go gentle into that good night.

"Hey, Nick!" I shouted. "Who'd you pimp for after your mother died?"

There was a gratifying silence before he shouted, "You'll pay for that!"

"Taking up Mama's slogan, Nicky?"

That put him into a hurry.

"*¡Apúrate!*" I said to Bingle, and we gave ourselves a head start. We made a lot of noise as we ran; Bingle kept up with me at an easy lope, enjoying the hell out of himself. I was having a harder time of it, slogging through the mud. Over our own noise, I soon heard Parrish crashing through the woods behind me.

I came to the first set of trees, veered around them, and positioned myself not far from the trees with the more visible rope. As soon as Parrish came into sight, I made a show of hurrying over that rope, Bingle leaping behind me. I heard Parrish shout, "Nice try!" just before he tripped on the other, hidden rope.

I heard him scream.

I kept running, calling Bingle to follow me. We ran for a long way, keeping to the trees, until finally I was sure Parrish was no longer following me.

I rested, feeling sick and shaky. I held on to Bingle. He gave no sign of scenting or hearing Parrish.

I waited as long as I could stand it. If one of those stakes had killed him, I wanted to get back to Ben.

At the very least, I knew I had wounded him. If he was only wounded, I wanted to know where he was. I had a job to finish.

* * *

I almost ran into him.

Bingle realized that he was near before I did, but not quite soon enough. He had kept downwind of us, and although Bingle had growled a moment before, I still gave a cry of surprise when Parrish stepped out from behind a tree.

His shirt was covered in blood, and he had tied a makeshift bandage around his left shoulder. In his right hand, he held a gun.

Bingle barked at him.

Parrish smiled. “I think I will begin by shooting that dog.”

25

▲ ▼ ▲ ▼

FRIDAY MORNING, MAY 19

Southern Sierra Nevada Mountains

"How unsporting of you," I said.

"Unsporting?" he said, looking faintly amused.

"I mean, shooting a dog that's leashed and standing just ten or fifteen feet away from you? Wow—what a great hunter you've turned out to be."

"Do you think this sort of nonsense will spare you anything at all? Am I supposed to be impressed?"

I hoped he was. I was proud of myself just because I hadn't wet my pants yet. Bracing for the sound of gunfire, I stooped down near Bingle, sheltering his head. Not really much of a risk. Parrish might shoot me, but I knew it wouldn't fit his fantasies. He would want my suffering to be much more prolonged. I almost wanted him to shoot me.

"Stand up!" he shouted.

I unsnapped Bingle's leash.

"Give the dog a head start," I said, staying low.

"You're going to tell him to bite me," he said, leveling the gun at me.

"No, you'd just kill him. I'll tell him to cross the stream."

"You expect me to believe he understands such a command?"

"You've seen how well trained he is. Give him the command yourself—say it in Spanish, he'll obey you."

"I don't speak the languages of inferior peoples."

"Prince of the polyglots," I murmured.

"What?"

"I said, I doubt you're such a great shot. I'll give him the command. Let him cross the stream. See if you can shoot him at that distance. Even if you can't hit him, you'll scare him off."

"Can't hit him?" He laughed. "All right, Irene, you seem to need a lesson in respect. Perhaps this will provide a demonstration of sorts. But I'll warn you that if you plan to have him attack me, I can easily squeeze off a shot before he gets near me."

"We'll see," I said. "Let me calm him down."

"Bingle," I said in a low voice. "*Bingle, ¿dónde está Ben? Búscalo, Bingle.*"

Bingle stopped growling, looked at me, and cocked his head. He whined.

"*Eres un perro maravilloso, Bingle. ¿Dónde está Ben? Es muy importante, Bingle. ¡Búscalo!*"

He looked across the stream, back at me, then at Parrish. He looked at me and whined again.

"*Bien, Bingle. ¿Listo? ¡Búscalo! Cuídalo. Por favor, Bingle. Ben, Bingle. Ben. ¡Apúrate, búscalo! ¡Cuídalo! ¡Vete!*"

He moved off, stopped, and looked back at me. "*¡Bien! ¡Sigue, adelante!*"

I tried to keep my voice full of enthusiasm, thankful that Ben's name wasn't something like "Charles" or "Jim," which would have been more noticeable among the Spanish words.

Bingle started moving again. Parrish said, "Follow him to the stream."

He was never far behind me, and I had no doubt that the gun was trained on me, not the dog. Seeing us follow, Bingle was less reluctant, and began to make quick progress toward the felled tree.

"*¡Adelante!*" I said, wondering if he could manage getting up onto the tree.

I needn't have worried; he was fit and agile, and was soon making his way across. But when I didn't follow, he stopped.

"*¡Lárgate!*" I said. Scram!

He didn't budge.

"I've had enough of this ridiculous mutt," Parrish said, stepping out from behind me and aiming the gun at the dog.

"I knew you couldn't do it," I said quickly. "I knew you'd take an easy shot!"

"Hurry up then!"

"*¡Lárgate!*" I said again, in the sternest voice I could manage.

Bingle quickly moved away. When he was partly hidden by the branches, I yelled, "*¡Apúrate, Bingle! ¡Vete!*"

He obeyed. He ran away from the stream, into the trees. But he was not out of sight yet. Parrish was taking careful aim when I slammed into him, knocking us both into the mud. Parrish fired the gun as he fell, screaming as he hit his shoulder.

"*¡Vete!, Bingle! ¡Vete!*" I shouted again, even as I got to my feet. He was obeying, running through the trees. I tried to do the same.

I didn't get far. Parrish rolled and grabbed my ankle, pulling me down, hard. I kicked and clawed, but he scrambled up on top of me, shoving my face deep into the mud, holding me there until my lungs were screaming for air. I struggled, tried to buck him off, tried to push up, but he was stronger. For a moment I wondered if this was where it would end, if I would simply be suffocated on this muddy bank, if Parrish's plans for me were not so elaborate after all.

He yanked my head up by the hair. I gasped for air. He shoved my face down again.

By the fourth time, all I wanted was air. That's all. Air. Just air. Just to be let up again. I was half out of my mind, panicked.

By the tenth, he could have taken anything he wanted.

He knew that, of course.

He went for twelve.

I think it was twelve. I had lost track. The world, all life, everything of importance had come down to taking the next breath.

"Wipe your face off!" he said angrily, dragging me up. He pushed me forward, seated me clumsily against the stump of the felled tree. He crouched in front of me and said it again. It took me a while to understand him. I was gasping. There still wasn't enough air. The sky didn't hold enough of the stuff.

"Wipe your face off or I'll shove it back down into that muck," he said. "Only I'll piss in it first!"

I reached up with shaking hands and wiped my face. The slime wouldn't all come off, of course. He reached over with one finger, drew something on each of my cheeks.

"There. Now I've branded you. You bear my initials."

I felt a sudden dampness on my cheeks. I was crying.

They awakened something, those tears. A little spark of anger. At myself. But it was enough.

He was pleased by the tears, I could see. I wiped them away. His initials, too.

"Oh, you are going to be such a delight to conquer, Irene."

I didn't answer.

He didn't say anything, and suddenly I realized he was listening to something. There was, I thought, a faint, rhythmic rumbling in the distance. A helicopter?

We waited, each with a different sense of anticipation. I knew he had other weapons. Would he shoot whoever landed in the meadow? Would they see the destruction, be cautious about approaching? Could I warn them not to land less than a SWAT team here?

But the sound stayed distant, then stopped altogether.

He smiled.

Be angry, I told myself. But it was so hard to find anger, buried so far beneath my fear.

"You suggested a hunt for the dog. You're something of a bitch yourself, you know. Did you have sex with the dog last night? Is that why you tried to save his life?"

He treated me to a long series of not very inventive questions about Bingle's sexual prowess. I said nothing to him, but the fear receded a little, replaced by disgust.

"Well, it doesn't matter now. You're going to be the hunted, and I'm going to track you. No matter how fast you run, or how far you go, I'll find you. I have a marvelous sense of smell, you know."

He reached into one of his pockets, smiling as he removed something white from them.

My underwear.

He took a deep breath, and his expression was that of a man intoxicated by a heady perfume.

"Look!" he said, pointing to his crotch. "You've given me a hard-on."

Without dropping my eyes, I said, "Even Bingle can't find something that small."

He slapped me. It made my lip bleed. He laughed and pressed the crotch of my underwear to it.

"There!" he said, holding it to his nose again. "Now it will be even easier to find you. Get to your feet."

I stood up.

"Start running, Irene. I'll give you a head start. But just remember, no matter how far you go, no matter how safe you feel you are, no matter how well you believe you are hidden or protected—I will find you. I want you to understand what you've only begun to learn—I'm your master. You should be pleased—you will learn to be pleased. I will touch you as no one has ever touched you before."

He tucked the panties back into his pocket and patted it. "I have your scent now. I'm a very quiet hunter, Irene. Do you think you can evade me? I'll come upon you when you least expect it."

He stood. "Come along, let's get started."

I didn't move.

"Stand up!"

I stood.

"Let me make something clear," he said in exasperated tones. "I will either begin with you now, and in a way that will make you think those pictures of Julia Sayre were taken at a picnic, or you will start running on the count of three. Oh—and one other thing—remember this name: Nina Poolman. Someone will want to know it someday. Now . . . one . . ."

If he said three, I didn't hear it. I was already running through the woods.

26

▲▼▲▼

FRIDAY, NOON, MAY 19

A Private Heliport Near Bakersfield

Frank knew that the helicopter belonged to Jack, and its care and custody were Dalton's, but he had pictured a small commuter craft, and was shocked to discover that the "company helicopter" was a giant Sikorsky S-58T.

"What does Fremont Enterprises do with a helicopter this size?" he asked Jack.

"It's a shit hauler," Stinger said, then laughed at Frank's dismay.

"We have a contract with the Forest Service to haul waste from remote locations," Jack said, cuffing Stinger.

"Six tons a year off Mount Whitney alone," Stinger said with pride.

"We use the helicopter for other purposes, too," Jack went on. "We plant fish—we have a government contract to deliver live fish from hatcheries to mountain lakes. We transport fire crews. We've helped with flood evacuations. We've done lifting at construction sites, carried cargo loads. And Stinger gets involved in search and rescue from time to time."

Travis eagerly began asking questions, and Stinger didn't have to be coaxed into boasting about the Sikorsky. It was fifteen feet high, he told them, and—not counting its rotor blades—about forty-five feet long. It had been fitted with turbine engines and auxiliary fuel tanks. It could hold eighteen passengers, but Stinger had altered the interior so that now—in addition to a crew of two in the cockpit—the cargo area had seats for ten passengers and carried two stretchers.

Frank tried not to think about needing stretchers.

Stinger assigned seats. Travis and Jack climbed into the cargo area with the two dogs, who were safely strapped in special harnesses.

Stinger asked Frank to ride with him in the cockpit, high above the cargo area. "You'll be able to recognize these people we're looking for," he explained.

Frank crawled up the outside of the tall craft using only handholds and toeholds, then struggled to fit his 6'4" frame in through the cockpit window, feet-first. He supposed this standard way of entering the cockpit might come more easily with practice, but his first try was damned awkward—and Stinger enjoyed ribbing him about it.

With effort, Frank held on to his temper. He told himself that he should have tried to get a full-night's sleep last night, as the others had. Even as the others had headed off to bed, he'd known he'd need the rest, should have taken the room Stinger offered. But he had stayed up, staring at maps, pacing, and checking weather reports on the Internet using Stinger's computer.

Sometime near dawn, exhaustion must have finally outrun his worries, because he awoke with a start from a vivid nightmare of hearing Irene shouting for help, while he ran, calling to her, unable to find her. But when Stinger roused him by gently shaking his shoulder, Frank realized that all the shouting had been his own—in his fitful sleep. He had dozed off facedown on the map-covered table. Chagrined, he had waited for one of Stinger's typical smart-ass comments, but all the other man had said was, "Coffee's ready."

Stinger gave him a miked headset, then turned and leaned over to hand two other sets down a ladder, to Jack and Travis. The cargo area could not be seen from Frank's seat. Stinger went through a series of take-off procedures with Pappy, the elderly man who served as his ground crew, then said, "Everybody hear me okay?"

There was a chorus of replies.

"Okay then, just one question."

"Yes?" Jack asked.

"Everybody made out a will?"

"Yes," Travis answered, which allowed Jack a laugh on Stinger.

"That's the copilot's seat," Stinger told Frank. "I'm sure I don't need to tell you not to touch the sticks or the pedals—or anything else, for that matter."

"One person can fly this thing?"

"You'd better hope so," Stinger said.

"Stinger—" Jack's exasperated voice came over the headphones.

"It's okay," Frank said. "He's right, it was a dumb question."

"Naw," Stinger said. He hit some switches and there was a "whump" and then the whine of the turbines began to build. Frank saw a little puff of smoke from the exhaust. "Don't let that worry you," Stinger said, working the controls. The blades of the rotors swoop-swoop-swooped, faster and faster—within twenty seconds, both the main and tail rotors were spinning at a steady speed.

Everything around them was a roar.

Travis's voice came over the headphones. "The dogs are scared."

"They're always like that at first," Frank heard Jack say. "They'll settle down in a minute."

"You mean my dogs have ridden in this thing before?" Frank asked.

"Oh, yeah." Stinger laughed, managing pedals and sticks all at once.

They lifted off, and Frank was caught up for a time in simply taking in the sensation of flight, in the way that only a helicopter could provide it—close enough to the earth to observe it in detail, high enough to feel free of it.

They climbed, and then moved forward, and climbed again. He had grown up in Bakersfield, and now, below him, he saw familiar landmarks passing quickly. He stayed silent as Stinger acted as tour guide for Travis and Jack.

Frank thought of what it must be costing Jack to do this. The fuel cost alone would be outrageous—Stinger had said the helicopter used one hundred gallons an hour. All the trouble and expense his friend was going to on their behalf—how could he ever repay him? He knew Jack wouldn't expect anything in return for his help, but still . . .

Stinger piloted with the ease of long experience, and of a man who knew his territory. Frank began to realize that another pilot might not have been able to lead them so readily to the mountain airstrip; when Stinger pointed it out as they passed over it, it seemed to Frank to be little more than a roughly mown narrow swath in a meadow.

There was patchy mist and fog below them; the mountain air currents, temperatures and shapes of the valleys affected this—in some places fog lay thick and still; in others, it was no more than softly moving mist; in still others, there was none to be seen.

They were moving closer to her, Frank told himself. He could find her on foot from the airstrip if he had to.

Maybe she would be just fine. Maybe he was asking Jack to spend a ton of money for nothing.

Irene would be furious with him if she was okay. She had accused him more than once of being overprotective. And the rangers might have already gone in and picked up the whole group—she could be on her way home . . .

"Wonder what that lawyer is up to?" Stinger asked, snapping him out of his reverie.

Frank had tried to call Newly several times before they left Stinger's home. He had wanted to verify the GPS coordinates; the ones Frank had written down showed that the group had hiked in circles and doubled back on itself more than once. But Newly hadn't answered the phone.

"He may be knocked out on pain medication," Frank said.

"Hmm. Could be," Stinger answered. "Kinda odd, though, giving you access to that GPS. Doesn't make a lot of sense. Oh, well. We'll be able to check out some of these places we marked on our maps, anyway—maybe we'll get lucky."

"Any chance the rangers have already been in to pick them up?"

"I can radio them at their heliport. Only one problem, though."

"What's that?"

Stinger smiled. "Well, *technically*, this is wilderness area we're flying over. And the law says we shouldn't even be here in the first place, not in an aircraft, not in a truck—you know, emergencies and special situations only. Las Piernas cops must have had to have all kinds of special permission to be using that airstrip, which is really only there in case the Forest Service needs to land firefighters up here. Your department know somebody up here? We might need somebody on our side if we get caught."

"One of the rangers—he's had the help of the forensic anthropologists we work with," Frank answered, wondering if he'd just be fired, or fired and arrested. "They aren't department employees. The forensic anthropologists, I mean."

"Hope that ranger got along okay with Irene. Anyways, if I call the ranger station, I'm basically asking them to bust us."

"But you seem to know the area so well," Travis said, reminding Frank that their conversation had been overheard in the cabin. "Isn't there some legitimate reason we could be up here?"

"We'll think of something," Jack said.

"What the hell," Frank said. "We'll either get away with this, or it's too late to worry about it."

Stinger laughed. "I'm beginning to see how you and old Jack got to be friends."

They flew to the last place Newly had recorded on the GPS, then began circling from there, flying over the meadows they had marked as the most likely candidates. Most of the meadows were shrouded in fog; low and flat, the moist, cool air collected in them.

"Too bad I don't have infrared on this thing," Stinger said. "This fog should burn off in a while; we may just want to set down and wait."

They found three meadows that had fairly good ground visibility, which Stinger had explained was more important to flying the helicopter safely than most other weather factors. They had already taken a quick look over the third meadow when Jack said he thought he had seen something odd near a tree.

Stinger turned the helicopter and made a lower, slower pass.

"Good eye, Jack," Frank said suddenly. "Look at the ground. Somebody has camped here."

"Yep," Stinger said, hovering over the spot. "Although it's hard to know how long ago."

"Let's go back to that tree," Frank said, pointing toward the other end of the meadow. "The place where Jack thought he saw something. Some serial killers like to pick out spots they can find again—many of them revisit burials. It does sound as if Parrish brought the group to Sayre's grave—so he had some way of finding her."

It took only a few seconds to travel the distance to the tree.

"Look out there!" Travis said. "Someone was digging."

"Looks like you're right, Frank," Jack added.

They could all see it now, the dark oval, the markers, the loosened soil.

"I'm going to set her down," Stinger said.

"No—not here," Frank said. "They moved on from here, remember? We need to look for that ridge—the ridge that divides this meadow from another one."

They moved around the edges of the meadow, and saw only one place that seemed to fit the description they had—a third-hand description that had gone from the ranger to the pilot to Pete, Frank reminded himself. They flew up over the ridge, but the meadow on the other side was a pool of fog.

"Okay," Stinger said. "Let's go back to the ridge. I saw a place where I can set this baby down."

At the last minute, Frank did end up closing his eyes, and was thankful that Stinger was too caught up carrying off the tricky landing to notice his momentary loss of nerve.

"Jesus, Stinger," Jack said.

"You think I was gonna trim the trees, Chicken Little?"

"No, I thought they were going to trim us. I'm not as tired of life as you seem to be."

The dogs might have been veteran helicopter riders, but Frank noticed that they both seemed happy to be on the ground.

They stayed close to him; every few moments they would venture a few feet away, peer out uneasily into the fog, sniff the air, and come back to him. He had been discussing a plan of action with the others, and only now did he notice that Dunk's hackles were raised and that the dog was growling softly.

"Hey!" he called to the others, and they looked over at him from near the cargo door. He motioned them to silence.

Both dogs were standing with stiff legs and tails now, ears pitched forward, listening. Everyone was watching them except Stinger. He had hurried into the cabin of the helicopter.

When he came back out, he had a shotgun. "There's another one in there if anyone wants one," he whispered. "You probably have a fine enough handgun in that shoulder holster, Frank, but I'm gettin' old, so I like something that doesn't require such nice aim."

Stinger looked at Travis, who shook his head, and at Jack, who smiled.

"Still a knife man?" Stinger whispered.

Jack nodded.

Stinger shook his head.

"Could just be a squirrel or something," Frank whispered, but opened his jacket.

They heard twigs snapping, the sound of footsteps.

Dunk started barking; Deke joined him.

"Hush!" Jack said, and was obeyed instantly.

Good thing Jack gave the command, Frank thought, unsnapping his holster. The dogs were notoriously unruly around their true owners.

The footsteps came closer.

By silent consensus, the group moved to take cover, Jack putting Travis behind him. Frank called softly to the dogs, but they ignored him.

He was thinking of moving out to grab them, when he saw the vague form of a man—or a woman—he couldn't be sure—coming closer. Stinger chambered a round. "Could be one of our own!" Frank warned.

"Who's there?" the misty figure called out. A man. Frank didn't know the voice. Stinger was looking at him, read that lack of recognition, and raised the shotgun.

"I don't know all of them!" Frank said desperately. "For God's sake, calm down."

"Who are you?" Frank called back.

The man halted, then suddenly turned and ran away.

"Stop!" Frank called out. "Stop!"

The man kept moving—they could hear him crashing through the brush.

Frank turned to Stinger. "You and Travis, stay here!" he ordered. "Jack, come with me."

He didn't wait to see if he was being obeyed. He moved after the noise, once glancing back to see Jack behind him. The dogs took up the chase, and moved ahead of him, but stayed within sight.

There was a strange thudding sound, and then the man screamed—a scream of pure, unadulterated terror. Frank ran faster.

A few moments later, the man came into view. The dogs had halted, ears back, tails tucked down. The man was still screaming, and batting wildly at something, like a child whose face had been caught in a large spiderweb—batting at strange shapes dangling from a tree.

Christ! he thought, they looked like dogs—no, no, not dogs. Coyotes. They were jerking and swaying, bouncing off the man and swinging back, until the man suddenly dropped to his knees, huddling beneath them, curled up in a protective ball.

For a moment, Jack and Frank stood frozen in place, horrified by the sight of a dozen dead coyotes swaying and thudding into one another, some breaking as they collided.

It was Dunk who moved ahead, while Deke stayed back with Frank—Dunk who whined and cautiously sniffed at the huddled man.

The figure raised his head, and Frank saw the haggard face of a young man—a terror-stricken man, but one who had not just this moment become afraid. He wasn't looking at Frank or Jack, but at the dog.

"Bingle?" he asked, as if experiencing a miracle.

Frank relaxed a little, but still approached cautiously.

"That's Dunk," he said easily, moving a little closer. "But I know Bingle. I've worked with him. I'm Frank—what's your name?"

The man glanced up at Frank, seemed to catch sight of the coyotes, and quickly looked away, back at Dunk. He reached out and touched the dog, began to stroke his fur. Dunk leaned in for more; the young man held on to him.

"Jay. Jay Carter," he said, his voice shaking. "J.C."

"J.C.," Frank said. "Is that what your friends call you?"

J.C. nodded.

Frank moved closer still and reached out a hand. "J.C., why don't we move a little ways away from here? Give me your hand, J.C., and we'll get away from them, okay? Come on."

J.C. took his hand, let himself be led away from the tree, keeping his face averted as they passed it. He was watching Dunk and Deke, who were sniffing his shoes.

"They smell them," J.C. said.

"The coyotes?" Frank asked.

J.C. shook his head, didn't answer. His face drained of color, and he swayed on his feet. Frank put an arm around his shoulders, and with Jack's help, led him to a fallen tree.

"Here, have some water," Frank said, but J.C. fumbled for his own water bottle, then drank deeply.

"I'll let Stinger and Travis know we're okay," Jack said. "And I'll bring back some hot coffee and blankets."

"Thanks," Frank said.

Jack hesitated. "Should I take the dogs?"

"No!" J.C. said.

"Okay," Frank said easily. "We'll keep them here."

It wasn't until Jack left that Frank had the time to notice something about the man that he had missed before.

"You're with the Forest Service . . ."

"Yes, I'm a ranger," J.C. answered dully. He put the water bottle away, then moved from the tree to be closer to the dogs. He hugged them, buried his face in their fur. Frank wondered if the dogs would resist a stranger confining their movements, but they seemed more inclined to nuzzle and fuss over him than to try to escape him.

"And you know Bingle?" he asked.

"I knew Bingle," J.C. said softly, and tears began rolling down his face.

Frank felt his stomach clench. "You know David Niles, then? Ben Sheridan?"

"They're dead," he whispered.

"What are you saying?" Frank asked, unable to keep himself from shouting it. "Who do you mean?"

"They're all dead," he said.

"No . . ."

"I left them here."

"No!"

"Yes . . . I . . . left them," he said jerkily. "I promised them . . . promised them I would be back. But I was late . . . and he . . . he killed them."

"Irene—" Frank half-asked, half-called out.

"All of them! He killed all of them! I don't know how—a gun—in their faces! And an explosion, I think. They're in little pieces! They're—they're on my boots! I couldn't help it, I stepped on them. I didn't mean to. I didn't mean to be late!"

"You're crazy!" Frank said, angry and wanting to slap him, wanting to make him say it was a lie, that he had made it up.

J.C. looked up at him. He said calmly, "Yes, I know."

And then, as if earlier introductions had only now registered with him, J.C. said, "Oh, Jesus. You're her husband. I'm so—oh, God, I'm so sorry!"

Frank took a deep breath, and somehow found his self-control. His own voice was quiet again when he asked, "J.C., when's the last time you had any sleep?"

He was petting the dogs again. "I don't remember."

"It's Friday. You hiked out with Newly on Tuesday, right?"

"Yes, I think so. I don't know. It was a long time ago."

"You hiked back that same day?"

"No, I slept a little that night, hiked back the next day."

"Wednesday. What happened that day?"

"They were already unburying her." He shut his eyes.

"Julia Sayre?"

He nodded, looked back at Frank. "I haven't slept much since then."

"The rest of the group hiked into the meadow on the other side of this ridge?"

"Yes."

"You came looking for them today, J.C.?"

"The helicopters won't work."

"What helicopters?"

"Ours, at the ranger station. I was already late. I promised I would come back."

"And you kept your promise. You did the best you could. But Parrish—listen to me, J.C. This is really important. Could you actually identify bodies?"

"Merrick. Manton." His face twisted up. "I—I saw parts of the others."

"You must have been really upset, anyone would be."

"Yes."

"Did you run from there, then? It—it sounds horrible. I think anyone would run. Did you?"

He nodded, and, too tired not to be literal, said, "I walked, too. I got a little mixed up, I think. I was going back to the ranger station. I wanted to get help. Then—then I realized it was too late. And I heard a dog—I thought it was Bingle, because I hadn't seen him—I wasn't sure, but I hadn't seen him, and he might have been a little bit away from everyone, with Irene, like before. And then—then I thought *he* was out there, and—the coyotes—and—"

"Shhh, shhh. It's okay."

A little bit away, with Irene. Frank held on to it.

They heard the sound of the others moving through the trees. J.C. looked up at Jack as if seeing him for the first time, and then at Travis, but when he saw Stinger, his eyes widened. "Stinger? They sent for you after all?"

"You know each other?" Frank asked.

But Stinger was down on his knees, eye-level with J.C. and wrapping a blanket around him, hugging him hard, then holding him by the shoulders, looking into his face. "My God, J.C.," he said, "next time you play piñata with a bunch of dead coyotes, use something besides your face for a stick—you're looking as fucked up as I am."

J.C. laughed, then said miserably, "I was too late, Stinger."

Stinger hugged him again and said, "Poor old J.C.—Fremont, get with the fucking program. Let's have some of that coffee. Can't you see this man is in need of it? And Harriman, where the hell do you think you're going?"

"To find my wife."

"Shit—"

Frank cut him off, telling the others, in a few short sentences, what J.C. had found. Jack and Travis registered shock, then, sharing Frank's anxiety, were all for going down to the meadow right away.

"Hold on, hold on!" Stinger said, but this time it was J.C. who interrupted him.

"I'll show you, if you—if you really want to see where they are."

"Thanks," Frank said, "but Stinger's right. You need to rest a little, get some warm liquids into your system."

J.C. reached into his daypack, and pulled out a small black rectangular device. This time, Frank knew it wasn't a phone.

"A GPS device—did you—?"

"It was foggy and I wanted to make sure I could get back," he said, handing it to Frank. "Yes, I marked it. I knew—I know I'm kind of—well, I'm half out of my head. You're right. I'm crazy."

"No, I was wrong," Frank said, feeling ashamed. "And it was wrong to say it."

J.C. didn't say anything.

Frank hesitated, then asked, "J.C., just one more question. You think this is something that just happened a little while ago?"

J.C. shook his head. "It had rained on them. And—Merrick and Manton were cold. I—I couldn't touch the others. There wasn't enough—there wasn't any chance they were alive."

"Drink a cup of coffee, J.C.," Stinger said. "Then we'll walk back to the helicopter and outfit these hotheads here. They haven't figured out yet how they're going to signal me if they find his wife down there."

"You aren't coming with us?" Frank asked.

"Think on it a minute. You got a man who knows aircraft running around out here. I don't exactly want to walk off and leave my girl at his disposal. If it starts to clear down there, I'll fly in a little closer to you."

"What if he finds you first?" Travis asked.

Stinger smiled. "He won't be needing that lawyer."

27

▲ ▼ ▲ ▼

FRIDAY AFTERNOON, MAY 19

Southern Sierra Nevada Mountains

He handed the GPS unit to Travis not long after they had hiked down into the meadow. He heard the sound of vultures fighting, began to smell the decay. He asked Jack to stay with Travis and the dogs, near the trees, while he walked into the fog to have a look.

Jack understood—he knew Frank didn't want Travis to see what was undoubtedly waiting out there in the mist, to have to live with some of the memories J.C. was living with. He also knew that Frank depended on him to protect Travis, just in case Parrish was still around. In addition to his knives, he was carrying one of Stinger's shotguns now. Like Frank, Jack and Travis were also supplied with flares and radios.

"Don't panic if you hear gunfire," Frank said. "I may have to fire a couple of shots to clear the buzzards off."

The gunshots worked for a little while—although they didn't seem to bother the insects much. He knew the vultures would be back—probably before he walked away. He couldn't think about that now.

He told himself, as he looked through the field of remains, to treat this as if it were a job. He told himself that she wasn't here in this mess, that he wasn't looking at anything that had been part of her.

He managed fairly well by telling himself that, until he found Merrick and Manton. J.C. must have recognized their clothing—there was nothing recognizable left in their faces. Frank looked in their pockets. He had known both of them, and while neither were his close friends, he had worked with them at various times. He made himself move away from them, but he could feel himself losing a battle not to become overwhelmed by what he was seeing.

He checked in with Jack and Travis, just to hear living voices, just to reassure himself that there was more to the world than fog and stench, soft tissue and bone, buzzards and insects.

A light breeze had picked up. He could see Jack and Travis now, which was more than he had been able to do a little while ago. The fog might lift enough to bring Stinger down here after all.

He figured the dogs would give them plenty of warning if Parrish was still around. He doubted Parrish was anywhere near them now; Parrish would have made his escape as soon as possible. And Irene was probably his hostage. Or worse.

He wanted very much to be wrong about that; it was another possibility he didn't want to think about. But that thought returned to him again and again.

Before they left the ridge, he had asked Stinger to go ahead and call the ranger station—there was too much at stake here to try to go it alone. They had to get a search started for Parrish. If Frank was going to be in trouble for coming up here, so be it. That was less than nothing, if Parrish had her. Or if she were here among these bits of flesh and bone.

Be logical, he warned himself. *Think of it as if it were any other crime scene. Do your job.*

And so he asked himself the standard questions.

What had happened here? A group had been gathered around the grave, working on it. There had been some sort of explosion.

How did that happen? Parrish didn't have any weapons on him coming in—of that, he was certain. He'd have to let a bomb expert come up with the particulars, but most likely, the device was already in place, triggered by something the excavation team had done—a booby trap. Parrish must have planned that he would lead them to this particular grave all along. He had led them to Julia Sayre, though. So he gave them one, then enticed them with a second.

Treat it as you would any other crime scene, Frank told himself, wishing he had the time and resources that would have been available if that were true. Dental records and a forensic odontologist, for starters. He'd have to make do with rough guesswork for now. And so he asked himself the question he most wanted to answer:

Who are the victims?

The people closest to the impact would have been working on or near the grave. The two anthropologists, Sheridan and Niles.

From fragments of camera equipment, he had already decided that the photographer, Bill Burden, had been one of the victims. God, what a waste! Flash was a great guy, good man to have working on your team. So young . . . but he couldn't think about that now.

Thompson? Very likely. Frank knew him, knew Thompson wouldn't be far away from the dig.

Duke and Earl? He couldn't be sure. Merrick and Manton were killed by gunshots and not the explosion, which suggested they had been guarding Parrish. Frank had already theorized that Parrish had taken a weapon from one of them in the moments of confusion that must have followed the explosion. Everyone was tired, they had just been through the same routine in the other meadow. Who expected a grave to be rigged with explosives?

Everyone was tired . . . Merrick and Manton were on duty, which meant Duke and Earl were off. They might have been asleep somewhere. Could they have escaped? If they did, they probably pursued Parrish. They would have seen it as their responsibility to catch him. They might be chasing him now. Maybe that was what had happened—maybe they were already on his trail.

He needed a body count of the people killed in the explosion itself. But how? He began looking at the more identifiable pieces of remains, quickly assessing them, not doing more than making a rough inventory.

Boots. The boots seemed to have survived the explosion. He started counting them, looking at them. He found nine boots—men's boots. Maybe the vultures had carried the tenth one away. Five men, plus the two guards. He was thinking about this when he found part of a woman's shoe, and nearly came apart, then realized that it was a dress shoe, not a hiking boot. It was stained and stank to high heaven. Irene was not carrying dress shoes. It must have been the buried victim's shoe.

"Frank?" the radio crackled.

"Yeah, Jack."

"You hear a dog bark?"

"No—but I've been kind of distracted. You hear one?"

"I thought I did. And your dogs are acting kind of interested in something on the other side of the stream. The ranger said Irene might be with the dog, right?"

He wanted to believe that, instead of what he did believe, so he said, "Yes. Let me know if you hear it again. Listen, there has to be a camp somewhere around here. Let me know if you see one. They were carrying a lot of gear; some of it is here, but they had tents and packs—there isn't even a fragment of something like that out here. They probably set up camp in the woods within sight of the grave. Think you and Travis could look for it?"

"Sure."

"Just look from a distance, don't touch anything, don't go in, try not to do much walking around—just call me." He described Irene's gear. "Look for that especially, okay?"

"Okay. You doing all right out there?"

After the slightest hesitation, he answered, "Yeah. Travis, you listening in here?"

"Yes."

"I want to warn both of you, I can't account for everybody here at this site. That's probably good news, but you may find additional bodies in the camp. If there are any bodies, you won't even have to see them—you'll be able to smell them. And this guy booby-traps things, so like I said, if you find the camp, just call me."

He switched the radio to Stinger's channel. "Stinger, you there?"

"I'm here. Breeze is picking up. I might be able to come in if this keeps up for another hour or so."

"J.C. doing okay?"

"He's sleeping. I think he's had about all he can take."

"You reach the ranger station?"

"Yep. The Forest Service can't help us out as soon as they'd like, though. Seems somebody messed with the nearest helicopters. They were glad to know that we'd found J.C.; they've been worried about him. He took one of their vehicles to get himself up as close as he could to this place, so they don't have a hell of a lot of transportation options. Guess there's a fire road or two that will get them kind of close, though. And they're calling for reinforcements. We ought to have everybody but the goddamned U.S. Marines here eventually, and I wouldn't rule them out."

Frank didn't like the sound of that; the problems in coordinating efforts could end up outnumbering the help. But he couldn't search for Parrish alone. "I need you to contact the Las Piernas Police Department, too. Try to be diplomatic if you can."

Stinger laughed.

"Hey, asshole," Frank said, "I'm standing here with the bodies of at least seven people I've worked with."

There was a silence, then Stinger said, "That's more like it. Trouble with you, Harriman, you're a little too polite. You know, a little wooden-assed."

"Look—"

"Okay, okay, I'll take care of it. You find your wife—I'll try to negotiate things so that you don't get fired."

"Who gives a shit about—wait—you've just given me an idea. Listen—your guy on the ground can patch you through on a phone call, right?"

"Sure."

Frank gave him a number. "That should get you through to Tom Cassidy. He's a hostage negotiator. Tell him what's happened. Tell him—tell him I might need his help. He'll understand."

Frank went back to looking at the ground. He came across the tenth boot; it seemed to have been carried to a spot some distance from the others; oddly, it was nearer Merrick and Manton. He saw a dog's footprints, filled in with rainwater, and with them, a set of boot prints that were slightly smaller than the boots he'd been looking at.

A woman's boot? He tried to recall if any of the men on the trip were small in stature. No, they were all average height—in fact, most of them were fairly tall.

Were these smaller boot prints Irene's?

If she was with the dog—didn't J.C. say that she had been with the dog? It made sense; Thompson wouldn't want her working on the excavation, and she wouldn't have minded keeping the dog company while waiting for the results of the dig. She liked dogs.

He figured Parrish would have killed the dog at the first opportunity, but maybe Parrish liked dogs, too. Then he remembered the coyote tree and rejected that idea.

He decided to follow the tracks, thinking that at least he might find out where Parrish had marched her and the dog before killing Bingle.

But there were no footprints for Parrish with those of Irene and the dog.

Hope began to rise up in him. Could she have escaped him somehow? "Irene!" he called out, thinking maybe she could hear him.

The radio crackled, reminding him that he was a long way from being able to feel anything like relief.

He found a place where the grass had been mashed flat, and what might have been blood, but it was hard to say; the rain had washed over the whole area. He was too interested in the next set of marks—someone dragging something—someone? He was still following this set of tracks when Travis's voice came over the radio.

"We found the camp, Frank. It's been tossed. Everything is soaked. But no smell of bodies, and we don't see Irene's gear here."

"Okay. I—look, I think I'm seeing her tracks. Do you still have J.C.'s GPS receiver?"

"Yes, should I mark this place?"

"Yes, then come out to the edge of the woods where I can see you. I want to see if there is any relationship between these tracks and where you are."

But when Travis and Jack appeared with the dogs, Frank noticed that the tracks he was following angled off, away from the camp. What did that mean? If the boot tracks were Irene's—who was the other person? Parrish? Was he wounded? Was she?

No, hers—if they were hers—were the boot prints, deep, but distorted by something that had come by later, flattening a wide swath of grass. But he remembered seeing marks like these at other crime scenes, wherever a killer had dragged a body . . .

Oh God, no.

He began running alongside the path of the flattened grass. But when he had followed it through the trees, he came to a place where two people had stood—or so it seemed. There were three boots, and a mark he couldn't make out. And the dog's tracks. Nothing was being dragged. And then only two prints, but much deeper than before. The smaller boots, but—carrying something? Someone?

Two people had survived. Maybe Parrish had been wounded by the guards, but forced Irene to . . . what? Drag him behind her? He couldn't picture it. More likely he had tied her up and dragged her along.

The tracks grew harder to follow, and eventually, he lost them. Looking for them, he came across a different set of prints.

Something wasn't adding up. He counted again. J.C. and Andy had gone to the airstrip—that left Parrish, Thompson, Duke, Earl, Merrick, Manton, Flash, Sheridan, Niles, and Irene. Ten people. If the marks on the grass were made by Parrish and Irene, that left eight. Merrick and Manton shot, that left six.

Six pairs of booted feet. But there were only ten boots scattered by the explosion, not twelve. If someone else survived, who? And where was he?

Most likely, he figured, it was Duke or Earl. They were both veterans, they knew their stuff. Neither one of them would put

Irene in danger, but either one would be able to keep track of Irene and Parrish, figure out where the bastard was taking her, keep the pressure on so that Parrish wouldn't have time for . . . for other things. He began to feel a little better about Irene's chances of surviving.

"Bring the dogs," Frank said over the radio. "Let's see if they can find Bingle."

The dogs took them to the stream. They moved along one bank, where Bingle's paw prints could still be seen now and then. But Deke and Dunk seemed distracted, often taking more interest in the local wildlife than in trailing another dog, Deke at one point nearly pulling Travis down into the mud when she decided to chase a squirrel. Jack scolded, and they settled down a little.

Frank, who was wondering if he had just spent twenty precious minutes setting up a squirrel hunt, looked upstream. He came to a halt. "Holy shit—a bridge."

The others saw it too then—a felled tree, lying across the water. They hurried to it.

"Cut recently," Jack said, "and I mean, very recently. Everything around here has been soaked with rain. But this pine is fairly dry—and fresh enough to smell the cut."

Frank looked at the ground. The signs were confusing—two sets of boot prints, both people able to stand, and the dog nearby. There were other signs of disturbance—in one place handprints in the mud. Hers? He couldn't be sure.

Maybe Duke or Earl had made a move here—and failed. Maybe the sixth man lost his life here, and his body was downstream.

But someone had found the strength and time to fell a good-sized tree.

"Let's see what's over on the other bank," he said.

There were more confused prints, but the dogs seemed excited again, whining. Jack found Bingle's prints again, and they followed them until Travis suddenly shouted, "Her tent!"

It was there, set up in the woods. She had even made something to catch rain. "Irene!" Frank called. "Irene!"

There was no answer.

They looked in the tent; there were signs she had slept here, but Frank soon noticed that there was a mixture of clothing in the tent. The dogs were very interested in one side of it, and looking closer, Frank saw a small amount of blood there.

"She got across that stream and camped here," Jack said.

Frank picked up one of her shirts; no gash or sign of a wound or bleeding on it, or her bedroll. If she wasn't the wounded one, maybe Parrish didn't have her. Maybe she was with the other survivor. "Let's see if that dog left any other tracks."

As it happened, they didn't need to look for tracks.

Deke, catching Bingle's scent, began barking. Dunk took up the cry.

Near a group of boulders, Jack was the first one to see a large German shepherd emerge. The dog apparently decided that they were all close enough, because he began barking ferociously. Deke and Dunk immediately flattened themselves onto the ground, tails wagging nervously, as if bowing in supplication and begging his pardon.

"That sweater he's got on has them in awe," Travis said.

"No," Jack said, "he's born to rule. Deke and Dunk are just acknowledging that fact—although I'm sure they'll test it later on."

Telling Deke and Dunk—quite unnecessarily—to stay, the three men tried to approach the other dog, but Bingle bared his teeth at them, and continued to growl and bark.

Frank tried to recall the day he had spent working with David Niles and the dog, and suddenly remembered that the dog was given commands in Spanish.

"*¡Bingle, cállate!*" he said firmly.

The dog stopped barking and looked at him, cocking his head to one side. "*¡Bien, Bingle, muy bien!*"

From somewhere nearby—none of them could figure out where, at first—a faint voice said, "Bingle, it's okay. *Está bien, Bingle.*"

"Who's there?" Frank called.

"Ben Sheridan."

"Ben! It's Frank Harriman. Where are you?"

"Here. Down in the rocks—I'm injured or I'd crawl up to

you. Bingle can show you where I am. How do I say, 'Come here'?"

"*Ven acá*," Travis answered, reminding Frank that Irene's cousin was the most fluent speaker of Spanish among them,

The dog was looking at Travis, apparently hesitating over this new set of orders, when Ben repeated them. He hurried to obey the more familiar voice, and the men almost missed seeing the place he had scrambled down.

Peering down into the rocks, Frank said, "We'll get you out as soon as we can—"

"Never mind that—did you find Irene?"

Frank swallowed hard. "She's not with you?"

"Oh, God!" Ben said. "You've got to find her! Never mind me!"

"Tell me what happened!"

"Parrish—"

"We know he killed the others—did anyone else escape?"

"No," Ben said weakly. "Except—Andy and J.C. weren't with us, thank God. Parrish came after us this morning, chopping down a tree. She hid me in here and tried to lure him away from me. I—I didn't want her to! But I can't walk and—"

"We know how hardheaded she can be," Jack said. "Where did she go?"

"Back across the stream, I think. I heard gunfire, and then Bingle came to me, but maybe he was just shooting at the dog—I thought I heard her yelling to him after the gunfire."

"Go on, Frank," Jack said. "Travis and I can take care of Dr. Sheridan here. I'll call Stinger, see if he can get up in the air and start looking now. Fog has cleared off."

"You speak Spanish, right?" Ben asked Frank.

"Yes."

"Take Bingle. He's had a rough couple of days, but he's trained in search and rescue."

"I once saw David work with him," Frank said. "But I'm not sure Bingle will want to listen to me."

"He won't ever work as well with anyone as he did with David. David—" He seemed unable to continue for a moment. "Please take Bingle with you—it's worth a try. I think the command is, 'Find 'em,' and ask him 'Where is Irene?' Praise him a lot, make it a game. He won't need a leash. I think he's attached to her; I think he's wanted to look for her anyway—he's been acting very worried."

"Ask Stinger to get that helicopter up as soon as he can," Frank said, and called to Bingle.

The dog hesitated, looking back at Ben.

"How do I say, 'Go with him'?" Ben asked.

"*Ve con él,*" Travis said.

Ben repeated the phrase to Bingle as a command, indicating Frank. He repeated it three times, and finally, Bingle scrambled back up to where Frank waited.

Frank saw that the dog was now focused on him, seeming almost impatient. He tried to recall everything he had seen David do with the dog.

"Travis, you have hold of Deke and Dunk?" he asked.

"All set," Travis said.

"Bingle," Frank said. "*¿Estás listo?*"

Bingle barked, and wagged his tail.

Frank held out the shirt he had found in the tent, hoping that Irene had worn it recently.

The dog sniffed at it.

"*¿Dónde está Irene? ¡Dónde está Irene? ¡Búscala!*"

Bingle barked and bounded toward the stream.

28

▲ ▼ ▲ ▼

FRIDAY MORNING, MAY 19

Southern Sierra Nevada Mountains

There was no thought, at first, of anything but flight.

I ran blindly, into the fog, through the trees. The fog and the forest were at once my shield and my obstacle; together they hid me from him, but because of them I could not simply run, flat out, as fast as I could go.

At home, I ran almost every day on the beach, but there were few flat and forgiving stretches here. The altitude, the mud, and the unevenness of the terrain were only part of the problem—I wasn't exactly starting out peppy and refreshed. Despite my weariness, though, I ran hard—for a time, the threat of being at Nick Parrish's mercy was enough to sustain me.

At first, he called my name and shouted things at me, doing his best to frighten and upset me.

"Can't you run any faster than that?"

"You're running slower! I'm going to catch you!"

"I'm getting closer, Irene!"

Glancing over my shoulder, I tripped on a root and stumbled; I scraped the palms of my hands and fingers as I caught at a branch to prevent a fall. I clumsily regained my balance before hitting the ground. It taught me a quick lesson; I moved a little more carefully after that.

Even in the places where the ground was drier, the pine needles were slippery beneath my feet. My daypack was bouncing against my back. My hiking boots didn't give as my running shoes would, and made the ground feel different beneath my feet, so I ran awkwardly; before long, the boots seemed to be made of lead, my legs felt heavy and dull.

I began to feel light-headed. All the same, though at first he had been quite close to me, eventually it seemed to me that I was widening the distance between us. His voice came less often, the words were less distinct. Soon he stopped shouting altogether.

I ran—muscles unwilling, aching, breath coming in sharp-edged pulls that seemed to stab at my ribs when they reached my lungs. My calves were cramping. My mouth felt as if it were full of half-dried glue, my fingers tingled.

I slowed, but kept running—plodding, really. I could not see or hear him. It made me uneasy. Where was he? Had he pulled ahead of me? Or had I managed to evade him? Had the injury to his shoulder weakened him at last? I was sure I heard him nearby—then realized I was hearing the noises I was making as I ran.

I slipped again, recovered my balance, took my pack off and cradled it in front of me, as if it were a football. It stopped bruising my back, but the next slip jammed every object in the pack into my ribs.

I kept running. I was having trouble thinking clearly, and I had no sense at all of direction. Had I gone in a circle? I was no longer sure I was running away from Parrish—I became convinced that I was heading right at him. I heard the stream and tried to follow it, all the while becoming more and more certain that he was near, very near.

My hair was wet from the mud and fog, and kept slapping my face as I ran; I tried to keep it out of my eyes. I kept running.

I ran until I fell—hard.

I wasn't sure exactly what had happened—my legs just seemed to give out. I scraped my knees, forearms, and face as I hit. I wanted to get up, but nothing was cooperating; there was no strength in my limbs; everything trembled or ached, and I felt sick to my stomach. It was as if I had instantly caught a bad case of the flu.

I was lying in a thicket; I could hear the stream nearby. I fumbled for my water bottle, and was surprised by the realization that I still had it—and my daypack. Hands shaking, I managed to open it and drink. I emptied the bottle, but I was still thirsty.

I had to accept that not even panic would keep me going. I crawled to the stream. I found a large, flat rock, not more than a few inches above the water. I lay down on it. The world seemed to spin drunkenly; I was drenched in sweat and my breath was coming in painful and far too loud gasps; my pulse was pounding, my head throbbing along with it. Nick Parrish could have fired a cannon at me and I wouldn't have heard it.

The stream was moving too fast here to step into safely, but I bent my face close to it, scooped its chilled water into my mouth; I drank and drank. I was too thirsty to spend time filtering water—if I suffered for it with a case of the trots in two weeks, I'd thank God for the privilege.

The spray that came from the stream as it hit the rocks in its path felt good; I began splashing water over my face and arms, my legs. I bathed my scrapes in it, easing some of the aches. I dipped my head into it, felt the icy water rush over the top of my forehead and scalp, rinsing the mud from my hair. Cooler, I made the effort to use the filter to fill my water bottle and I drank again. I lay there. For what seemed to me to be a long time, I was unable to do anything more. I was still terrified of Parrish, but there was a barrier of exhaustion and dehydration between my fear and my willingness to do anything about it.

Eventually, I tried to get up and walk; every muscle and joint protested. I moved anyway. Not fast, not steadily, but I moved, wobbling away from the bank of the stream. I wanted to be able to hear Parrish's approach.

But I had so little energy, I did not get very far. I came across a cluster of boulders beneath some trees near the stream, not unlike the place where Ben was hidden. I had not heard Parrish for some time now, and the thought of Ben made me wonder if Parrish had gone to hunt Bingle, and might perhaps find Ben as well. Even if Parrish wasn't looking for him, how long could he last, hidden in the rocks? Would anyone be able to find him if something happened to me?

Something crashed through the trees to the left of me; I made a faltering attempt to spin toward it, my heart pounding.

A deer.

A little later, I thought I heard the sound of a helicopter again, but it was still foggy—if one passed overhead, I didn't see it. I told myself to stay calm, that once the fog burned off, J.C. would be able to take the crew to our meadow.

But what would prevent Parrish from simply shooting the helicopter crew?

From the air, they might be able to see the grave, and the bodies in the field. That sight would make them cautious.

I prayed they would be cautious.

I waited.

I felt myself jerk awake, and the realization that I had fallen asleep frightened me. I needed to be on guard—but for a moment I was so disoriented I couldn't remember why. I had awakened from a dream of gunshots, and of Frank shouting my name. I listened, and heard nothing but the stream, and birds calling to one another in the trees.

I turned my mind to my immediate problems.

If Nick Parrish came near again, and I needed to run, I couldn't afford to be dehydrated. I stood and stretched my sore muscles, drank the water I had filtered and took what seemed to be a lifetime to make the short walk to the stream for a refill.

Food would help, too. I found a few edible shoots near the stream; I wasn't sure of most of the other plants, and while I might take a risk with *giardia*, I wasn't going to try to kill myself on the spot. It's much easier to be poisoned by flora than fauna.

I stumbled back to my hiding place, unable to move with anything close to coordination.

I still had my knife.

I had no sooner remembered this than another thought intruded: Why did I still have my knife?

Why had Parrish left me with a weapon, however small? Why had he let me keep my water bottle and filter and the other contents of my daypack?

Perhaps he hadn't expected me to have time left to use them; maybe he wanted more of a challenge.

Why had he let me run away? I ran way off my pace, and still I had eluded him. Or had he allowed me to elude him?

He had felled a tree, which might have drained him of energy. He had a shoulder wound—maybe it had started bleeding again when he ran after me.

On the other hand, he had eaten food; he had probably slept. He had not dragged anyone to safety, had not spent the night taking care of an injured man. He was not afraid. He had not been nearly suffocated in the mud.

I weighed these factors, unable to decide if he had allowed me to escape from him, or if I had—at least temporarily—defeated him. The more I thought it over, the more confused I felt; I seemed incapable of holding on to any train of thought for long. One idea drifted past another, and I found myself staring blankly into space, or snapping my head back up, just before nodding off again.

I tried to recall what kind of shape he had been in just before I started running away from him. He had been giving me instructions . . . something about a woman named . . . named what? Nina Poolman. I was supposed to remember her name. But why?

I was tired, and I wanted to sleep, but thinking of Nick Parrish kept me awake, if not at my sharpest.

Faintly, I heard a man's voice calling something.

I could almost believe it was my name, but I wasn't sure.

The fog was rapidly lifting; out in the open, I might be seen more easily now. I slowly crawled back into the narrow space within the cluster of boulders.

Minutes later, I heard someone or something crashing through the brush, downstream from where I hid. Was it Parrish? Another deer? A bear? I didn't dare rise from where I crouched.

I waited. The sound kept moving away. Probably an animal, I told myself. I couldn't convince myself.

I fell asleep again; I don't know for how long. In the distance, upstream, I could just make out the sound of a dog barking. I was nearly certain it was Bingle, but the barking had a quality to it that made me fear for both Ben and the dog. It could only mean that Parrish was near them.

I did not want to hide helplessly, listening to whatever horrible things Parrish might do to them, even as faint sounds from a distance.

I slowly left my hiding place. I found a long, sturdy stick, and sharpened it. As I looked at the finished product, I had to resist an urge to leave it behind, if for no other reason than to save myself from serving up embarrassment as a side dish to my own death.

There was no possibility of taking off at a run, but I tried to stretch as I moved along the bank of the stream, using my homemade spear as a walking stick, leaning against it through dizzy spells, doing my best to rid myself of the soreness that made my movements stiff and slow.

Again and again, I heard movement in the brush near the stream; each time I hid as best I could, waited, saw nothing.

As I walked, once more I found myself growing lightheaded, feeling confused. The dizzy spells came more often. I stopped to drink again. I was exhausted and scared—of what possible use could I be to Ben and Bingle?

I had no sooner asked myself this question than I heard loud movement through the woods—much louder than before—followed by urgent barking. But if Bingle was here, what had happened to Ben?

I found myself filled with despair. Ben's survival had never been assured, but his death was a blow I wasn't ready for. With an effort, I regained my self-control. "Pay the bastard back!" I told myself, gripping my spear.

I was wondering if the dog was going to lead Parrish right to me, when I heard the helicopter. I couldn't see it, but it sounded as big as God.

I was going to get to it first, I decided—I might be too late to save Ben, but maybe I could warn the pilot off before Parrish started shooting at it. I began moving toward the sound—which was difficult, because it seemed to be coming from everywhere at once. I could hear nothing else. I took my knife out.

I saw movement to one side of me, and then Bingle loping toward me, and someone moving in the woods behind him.

Frantic, at first I stumbled away, but there was no time to run, so I crouched behind a fallen tree, spear in one hand, knife in the other.

Hoping that someone might be near enough to hear me over the helicopter, I screamed at the top of my lungs.

Bingle stopped in his tracks, looking puzzled.

Behind him, a vision appeared. Frank, coming through the woods.

For a few moments, I could only stare at him, wondering how Parrish had managed the disguise.

A great wind came up, blowing leaves and tree limbs and frightening birds and small animals. And me, a little.

The wind passed by, but the noise of the helicopter was still all-encompassing.

Frank slowed what had been a running approach, maybe because I was holding a sharp wooden stick and a knife in a threatening manner.

"Irene?"

I couldn't hear him over the roar, but I could see him form the word. Best of all, I could see those gray-green eyes of his—his eyes, not Parrish's. I dropped my weapons, got to my feet, and held out my arms.

He took me in his, and then I could hear him say my name. He said it over and over.

I probably should have told him not to fuss over me, and said that there were important things that needed to be done—but I was fresh out of wise and brave, and for a little while, all I could do was weep, and say his name to him, and tell Bingle that he was marvelous, too.

29

▲▼▲▼

FRIDAY, LATE EVENING, MAY 19

St. Anne's Hospital, Las Piernas

The doctors said they might not be able to save Ben's leg, that they might have to amputate it below the knee.

This possibility was not a surprise to Ben. He had spoken of it in the helicopter.

Although he had been weak and feverish, and obviously in pain, he had been able to converse. Bingle had refused to be tethered out of reach of him, and sat quietly nearby, watching him intently.

Stinger Dalton had offered to take Ben to the closest hospital—"Or wherever you want to go," he said, kneeling near the litter. "You'll be out of pain sooner, but sometimes proximity ain't the first consideration, if you know what I mean."

"Yes, I do," Ben said. I held his hot, dry hand in one of my own. He looked at me, then back at Dalton. "Take me to St. Anne's," he said. "I know one of the orthopedic surgeons there. If he has to amputate, at least he'll know what he's doing."

He saw my look of horror.

"If they take part of the leg," he said, "it wasn't because you did anything wrong. Understand?"

"But—"

"Understand?"

I stared at the amateurish bandage and makeshift splint. "I should have given you all of the Keflex," I said weakly.

"Listen to me. The bullet did the damage, not you."

"Maybe they won't—"

"Don't," he said, closing his eyes. "Don't."

Not this, I begged God. Nothing more. Hadn't he already been through enough?

"Do you want us to contact anyone?" Frank asked him. "Someone to meet you at the hospital?"

Ben didn't answer right away.

"A family member or a friend?" Frank asked.

"No," he said, not opening his eyes. "No one, thanks."

This answer to Frank's question made me worry about Ben as nothing else had. It was one thing to face the loss of a limb, another to face it without the support of family or friends.

Frank had his arm around me; I leaned my head against his shoulder. He felt solid and sturdy and safe. Ben was alive. Bingle was alive. I was alive.

I was alive, and fighting to feel something other than the numbness that kept creeping over me. Numbness and thirst. I kept drinking water, but I couldn't seem to get enough of it.

As the helicopter had taken off, Ben squeezed my hand. I realized he was trying to say something to me over the roar of the engine and rotors. He looked awful. I loosened my seat belt and bent closer.

"The story."

I looked at him in confusion.

"The knight."

So I began shouting my half-assed version of a medieval German poet's tale to him, but I didn't get much further in the story before Ben's grip slackened and his head lolled to one side. I froze mid-shout.

Frank hurriedly moved to Ben's side, checking his pulse and breathing.

"He's alive," he reassured me. "His pulse is okay. He's just passed out. I'm sure he's been in a lot of pain. Dalton will get us back to Las Piernas in no time."

J.C. stared at me as if fearing the next act in my bizarre program of in-flight entertainment. Bingle, Deke, and Dunk looked as if they were hating every moment of this ride, storytelling or no. Jack smiled and shouted, "You remember Parzival!"

Dalton managed to get us out of the meadow before law enforcement or the Forest Service came in. He radioed the ranger station to say that we had a medical emergency and could be met in Las Piernas at St. Anne's. He supplied a succinct description of the situation in the meadow, and warned that Parrish was heavily armed.

As the helicopter landed at St. Anne's, we were greeted by a team of doctors and nurses, and Tom Cassidy. Frank had asked him to meet us. Cassidy is a master at staying calm in the midst of high pressure, chaotic situations—he's in charge of the Las Piernas Police Department's Critical Incident Team. The big Texan's work ranges from negotiating a hostage's freedom to talking a potential jumper off a ledge, and his skills were being put to the test that day.

"Everybody's mad as hellfire at me," Cassidy drawled, grinning with pride, "but y'all will have a little time to yourselves and the doctors."

Jack and Travis and Stinger took a dog each—Stinger the only one who could get Bingle to leave Ben—and met with Travis's lawyer, who had helped us on previous occasions. Between his efforts and those of Cassidy, it looked as if no one was going to face charges, or receive department reprimands, or lose a job or a pilot's license.

J.C. and Frank were the first to spend time answering questions from the D.A. and the police. I got my turn, as Cassidy stood unofficial guard over me. I found myself answering as if from a distance, perhaps not always coherently. I tired quickly, and Cassidy shooed the others away.

He had to leave soon after—he was busy coordinating crisis efforts that extended further than I could have imagined at that moment.

* * *

I asked the doctor who was looking at my various scrapes and bruises about Ben. He hesitated, then said, "He's been taken into surgery. The leg is severely damaged and infected. We're going to give him antibiotics, but—"

"What sort of antibiotics?" I asked.

"A combination of cephalosporin—you might have taken it at one time or another as Keflex—"

"Keflex," I interrupted, turning pale. "Keflex? That might make a difference?"

"Yes, at a high dosage," he said, studying me. "Are you feeling faint?"

"A little," I admitted.

I wanted to go home, but the doctor asked me to stick around for a few hours because I was suffering from dehydration. I was placed in a bed, given an IV and a light meal, and fell quickly asleep.

I awakened a couple of hours later to see Mark Baker and John Walters standing near my bed. Mark is an old friend and the crime reporter for the *Express*. John's the managing editor.

A nurse tried to usher them out, but I told her it was all right, that I'd talk to them for a while.

After a few expressions of concern, which for all my exhaustion, I didn't take too seriously, John said, "You know why we're here."

"You want the story."

"You see?" he said to Mark, "I told you she's a pro." He turned back to me. "I figured you wouldn't mind Mark writing it up—this first one, anyway—you'll definitely get on the byline, but Mark's already been doing a lot of work on it, so—"

"I don't mind," I said dully.

"You come in tomorrow—catch up on your sleep, but come in by, say, eleven."

"I'm not sure—"

"I am," John said forcefully. "You don't need me to tell you how big this story is—and you were right in the middle of it. Your buddy Cassidy has already cordoned off your street, which hasn't stopped five big TV crews setting up their trailers at the end of the block. Your neighbors are complaining about helicopter news crews buzzing the area. You *will* come in tomorrow."

I didn't bother arguing with him. I understood that nothing—my sanity least of all—was more important to him than that story. That's the problem with the news. It won't wait.

So Mark wrote notes and asked questions, but soon my mind was wandering. Mark kept glancing at John.

"You aren't making a hell of a lot of sense," John finally complained.

"No. Shouldn't Morry be here?" I asked. Morry was acting news editor.

"While you were gone, he left the paper. So I'm wearing both hats for the moment."

Under other circumstances, this announcement would have startled me, and led to dozens of questions of my own. But I just yawned and said, "Oh."

The two men exchanged looks again.

Mark started to ask about the men who had died. But every time I said much more than their names, I seemed to forget what I was talking about. Again and again, I heard the explosion, saw bits of flesh and bone scattered everywhere, smelled blood and smoke and earth.

As vivid as these images were to me, I couldn't speak of them to Mark and John. It was as if there were some blockade between my mind and my mouth simply could not form the words to carry such things. And soon, my mind learned to jump from the image Mark wanted to talk about to something else, such as what the sky had looked like when I sat among the boulders, how my homemade spear had felt in my hand, how cool the water in the stream was.

Mark asked, "How did Parrish get the gun away from his guards?"

"Merrick and Manton," I said.

"Yes, did you see him shoot them?"

There was a silence.

"Do you think I'll get *giardia*?" I asked.

"This isn't like you, Kelly," John said, disapproving.

"No," I agreed. "I'm usually very careful about filtering the water."

"That's not what I mean. You're not yourself."

I was silent for a while, then I said, "I know. I'm not sure I'll ever be 'myself' again."

"Of course not," he said gruffly. "You've been through a terrible experience. But you've got to move on."

Mark shook his head in disbelief.

"She does!" John protested.

"Give her twenty-four hours to wallow in self-pity," Mark chided him. "I'm sure she'll be recovered in time to save Sunday's A-one. You know—up by the bootstraps and all that. She'll be bubbling over with the need to tell somebody all her deepest darkests by dawn tomorrow."

"I can't—I don't ever want talk about it," I said. "I think he wants me to, so I won't."

"Well, of course Mark wants you to talk about it!" John said. "But why should you—"

"Not Mark. Parrish."

The answer startled him.

He studied me, looked at his watch and said, "Get some sleep. That's all you need. A little sleep. I've got enough from you now to take care of tomorrow's paper. We'll see you tomorrow afternoon." He studied me a little longer and said, "I'll ask Lydia to come in, too."

I've known Lydia Ames, who works on the city desk, since grade school.

"Thanks," I said, and burst into tears.

"Oh, Christ!" John said.

Frank came into the room just then, and saw me crying. At his look of rage, both Mark and John held up their hands in surrender. It was enough to make me dry up.

"She's all yours," John grumbled, and they left.

Frank came close to the bed, and took my hand, the right one, which was IV-free. He gently brushed his thumb over my knuckles. But I could feel a tension in him that kept it from being a lover's gesture. And those gray-green eyes were troubled.

"What is it?" I said, sitting up. "What's wrong?"

He blew out a breath and said, "Ben. They had to amputate."

"No . . . oh Jesus, no."

"They said he came through the surgery fine."

"I don't want to hear about the fucking surgery!" I shouted.

He put his arms around me, which started the tears again. He let me cry hard and loud, listened to me berating God, and myself.

"I didn't know," I said. "I didn't know what to do, how to help him—"

"You saved his life."

I wondered if Ben felt very grateful to me for that right now. Aloud I said, "I have to see him."

"He's sleeping. He probably won't be allowed to have visitors before tomorrow."

I lay back against the pillows, miserable. Frank started talking to me about Cody and the dogs and everyday things, and I calmed down. Exhaustion began to conquer me again. "Don't leave me alone in here," I said sleepily.

He turned out the overhead light, stretched out on the other bed, and continued to talk to me for about another minute and a half before he fell asleep—too far away from me, but I didn't begrudge him the rest.

Over the next two hours, I drifted back and forth across the borders of sleep. I was dreaming of marching bloody boots when the phone rang. Frank awakened, and was up on his feet and at my bedside before I had turned the light on and found the right end of the receiver.

"Irene? It's Gillian."

"Hello, Gillian," I said, around a hard knot in my throat.

"Did I wake you up?"

"No, no, it's okay." And for the life of me, I couldn't think of what to say next.

"I wondered if I could talk to you—not tonight, but maybe tomorrow? Will you still be there?"

"No, I won't be here. I'm going home in a little while," I said, suddenly knowing that I wouldn't be able to spend the night in that hospital bed, that I needed familiar surroundings. "But I'll be going into the office tomorrow afternoon. Do you want to meet me there?"

"Sure. What time?"

"About four?"

"Okay."

A silence stretched, and I said, "I'm sorry, Gillian."

"It's all right," she said, although she didn't sound as if that were true. "Thanks for going up there. I—I heard about what happened on the news. Is the man—Ben Sheridan, is that his name?"

"Yes." The knot froze solid.

"Is he going to be okay?"

No, he's not. But I thought of her four-year wait ending as it had, and said, "Yes, he'll be okay."

After another silence, she said, "Well, I'll see you tomorrow then."

I had signed all the papers for my release and was changing into some clean clothes that Travis had thoughtfully brought by, when I remembered something. I got my maps out and showed Frank where the too-clean cave was located. "It might be nothing," I said, but somehow the act of giving him this information soothed me a little.

He thanked me, then said, "I talked to a nurse while you were filling out paperwork. It didn't seem likely to me that you'd be able to leave here without looking in on Ben. He's asleep, but she said if you kept it brief and promised not to disturb him, it would be okay."

I looked up at him, wondering how it was that he so often seemed to anticipate what my needs might be.

"You didn't abandon him in the mountains," he said. "We won't abandon him now."

"Thank you," I said. When I was fairly sure I could speak again without crying, I added, "Where would you like to celebrate our one-hundredth anniversary?"

My first shock came when, expecting a flat place under the blanket, I saw what appeared to be two feet at the end of Ben's bed. "A temporary prosthesis," the nurse whispered, reading my look.

I discovered that the only things that mattered to me at that moment were that he was still alive, that he was sleeping peacefully, that his face was not drawn tight with pain, that he was safe and in more capable hands than my own—but mainly, that he was still real in a world that seemed less and less so. I thanked the nurse and left quietly. I asked Frank to take me home, where, despite all the commotion above and around us, I slept dreamlessly in his arms.

30

▲ ▼ ▲ ▼

SATURDAY MORNING, MAY 20

Newsroom of the Las Piernas News Express

Our ill-fated expedition into the mountains supplied most of the material for Saturday's A section, which read largely like a giant obit page.

Most Saturday mornings, the newsroom would be fairly quiet, but when I came in at nine-thirty, there was more activity than usual. By then, members of the public who owned televisions or radios, or who purchased newspapers, knew that despite an extensive search effort, Nick Parrish was still at large and that no one could find Phil Newly. The public knew that after recovering Julia Sayre's remains, unauthorized (a word used often by people who had been safely at home) efforts to recover another set of remains led to a trap set by Parrish and tragically resulted in the deaths of six members of the Las Piernas Police Department and an instructor of anthropology at Las Piernas College.

Oh, David.

An associate professor of anthropology was in critical condition at St. Anne's Hospital. A reporter for the *Express* had sustained minor injuries. Others with the group, including a search dog, were unharmed.

I thought of Bingle—staying with us until other arrangements could be made—lying listlessly near David's sweater. I thought of the look I had seen on J.C.'s face. I hadn't seen Andy yet, but I was fairly sure he wasn't doing much better. "Unharmed."

Frank was sitting a few feet away from me, reading a paperback. He'd look up every so often, I'd smile at him, and look back at the blank computer screen. Or down at my fingers. My hands kept shaking, but I kept my fingers on the keyboard, hoping for a miracle.

John hadn't been happy about allowing Frank to hang out in the newsroom, but with Parrish on the loose and my nerves shot to hell, I wasn't quite ready to go anywhere without Frank yet. Besides, we were currently down to one car, so if he wanted me to come in, Frank was going to bring me anyway.

Lydia was there, giving up her Saturday plans with her boyfriend, but you would think sitting in the newsroom for the sixth day in a row—spending time with an uncommunicative friend—was just about as good as it could get for her. When I complained that she shouldn't have let John bully her, she told me he hadn't, and I couldn't bully her, either.

By eleven o'clock, I had been sitting at my keyboard for over an hour. I had come in early because, I told Frank, I wanted to get this part over with. But I wasn't getting anything over with at all—ninety minutes and all I had to show for it was a blinking cursor on an empty screen.

Lydia walked over to me. Frank watched, then went back to his book.

She made a gesture, moving her hand back and forth, indicating me, then herself. Lydia's parents were Italian immigrants. I've seen her mother make the same gesture. There's no need for pretense between us, the gesture says.

"We've known each other since third grade, right?" Lydia said.

"Right. But you only say that to me if you're about to be brutally honest."

She laughed, I didn't.

"I can't take any brutality right now, Lydia. Even in the name of honesty."

"Okay, I'll try to be gentle."

That time, I did laugh. Frank was watching us now.

"You were in this situation," she said, "in which everything went out of control."

I heard a soft rattling sound, looked down at my trembling hands, and lifted my fingers from the keyboard.

"You did everything you could," Lydia went on, "and things still went bad."

"Straight to hell," I agreed.

"If you don't want to write about what happened," she said, "I'll stick up for you with John. We'll both walk out of here, if that's what it takes."

"Because newspaper jobs are in such plentiful supply right now," I said.

"Because nothing is worth that much."

I couldn't say anything.

"You don't want to write about it, because you think Nick Parrish was seeking attention all along."

"Yes."

"Irene, you idiot, make him the smallest part of the story."

I looked up at her.

"You know what Tom Cassidy's team is doing right now?" she asked.

"Holding CNN and Channel Five away from my front door."

"Yes, that's true. But you know how there's a sense of family in any police department, so he's also got crisis counseling crews that are trying to help the LPPD cope with the deaths of six of its men."

I looked over at Frank, who nodded.

"He's coordinating another group at the university," she said, "in case any of Ben's and David's colleagues or graduate students need to talk about what has happened."

"How do you know about all of this?"

"A fine city desk I'd be running if I didn't."

"What happened to Morry, by the way?"

"He moved to Buffalo. Got a job with the *Buffalo News*."

"What?"

She shrugged. "His mom lives in Kenmore—the suburb, not the brand name."

"He left without notice?"

She smiled. "My only regret is that you weren't here to see easygoing Morry tell Wrigley to shove it."

I laughed. "I can't believe it!"

She made an *x* over her heart. "Swear to it. After Wrigley stormed out of the room, I gave Morry a kiss for it. He turned red and kept blushing for about four hours, but he was grinning the whole time. We gave him a big send-off at Banyon's."

I shook my head. "Sorry I missed that. I would have liked to say good-bye."

"Sometimes you get to say good-bye, sometimes you don't. It's why you have to be good to people."

I was silent.

"Nick Parrish is going to get his glory," she said, "even if the *Express* never prints his name again. He'll get it from all those folks who have their satellite dishes pointed over your rooftop. He'll get it from every other paper in the country."

I knew what she was saying was true. After a moment, I said, "He chased me. Or let me believe he was chasing me."

"I figured that was why you met me with a knife and spear," Frank said.

I realized that I hadn't told him much about what had happened up there. He hadn't pressed me for details, and he probably had lots of questions. Even if he had talked to the detectives who interviewed me, given the state I was in at the time, I doubted he had a very clear picture. I resolved to have a long talk with him that evening, but for now, I said, "I was going to go after Parrish at that point. I didn't want him to kill whoever was arriving on the helicopter."

"What?"

"My thinking was a little muddled then—but now—I don't think Parrish ever intended to catch me," I said. "I didn't realize it then—I was too out of it to put my thoughts together. Now it hits me, you know—that it was too easy. Getting away from him. Like when you're little and the older kids tell you they want to play hide-and-go-seek, but then they go off somewhere together while you stay hiding. You've been ditched."

"So Parrish wanted you to escape," Lydia said.

"Yes, I think he wanted a reporter to survive, wanted someone to go out there and add to the legend. You know, tell the story as someone who feared his power."

Was that all there was to it? I wanted it to be true, but I couldn't quite believe my own sales pitch. He had said he would find me again. Julia Sayre and Kara Lane both had dark hair and blue eyes. Maybe Parrish had more than one purpose in mind after he learned I would be the reporter.

"And he singled you out," Lydia said, startling me until I realized she was referring to my last spoken comment.

"Yes."

"If you're right about that," she said, "and he's expecting something special from you, disappoint him. You're the only one who can really do that."

It took me about another half hour to get started. But once I was started, everything else ceased to exist. After one mention of him by name, if I had to refer to Parrish, I called him "the prisoner." I found I didn't have to write about him all that much.

I wrote about the last days of Merrick, Manton, Duke, and Earl, of Bob Thompson and Flash Burden, of David. I wrote about Earl's sense of humor, of Duke whittling a toy horse for his grandson—and remembered that I must take that carving to his family. I wrote about Flash taking photographs of wildflowers, of Merrick playing with Bingle, of Manton trying to get used to his wife's new haircut by studying a photo. I tried to convey a sense of them that would make them more than names on a list of victims. Perhaps John or some copy editor would cut it up, or use a "search and replace" command to change "prisoner" to "Nicholas Parrish."

It didn't matter. I could only do what I could.

I wrote about finding Julia Sayre, then stopped to search our files for Nina Poolman.

A photo of a dark-haired, blue-eyed, forty-two-year-old woman appeared on the screen. Missing. Three years ago.

Nothing saying she was ever found.

I sat staring at her photograph, knowing that Parrish would expect me to write that he had told me her name.

"Frank?" I said.

"Yeah?"

"The victim in the second grave—do you think any of the teeth survived the explosion intact?"

"I'm not sure. Teeth are pretty tough though, so maybe. Why?"

"If they did, and you can get a hold of this woman's dental records, I think you can close a case."

In the story, I wrote the truth—no positive identification of the victim in the second grave had been made.

I filed the story, stood up, and said to Lydia, "Tell John that if I open the paper tomorrow and see Nick Parrish's name all over that story, I will not be back in. Ever. Which might not be such a big loss to either one of us."

"Will do," she said. "Are you okay?"

I shook my head, drew a breath. "Tell John I've got more to write, but—"

"You'll be happy to take it elsewhere," she interrupted. "I think he'll get the picture."

I e-mailed a brief note to Mark, thanking him for sticking up for me the day before, and logged off.

The phone rang.

"Kelly," I answered.

"There's a . . . a person here to see you," the security guard at the front desk said.

"A person?"

"She says she has an appointment with you. Gillian Sayre."

Four o'clock.

"I'll be right down," I said.

"Want me to go with you?" Frank asked.

I shook my head. "This one I think I need to handle on my own."

31

▲ ▼ ▲ ▼

SATURDAY, LATE AFTERNOON, MAY 20

Las Piernas News Express

"You look tired," I said, as I gestured her into a small meeting room off the lobby.

"I didn't sleep much last night," she said.

Of course not, I thought, wondering if I could avoid making any other clumsy remarks over the next few minutes.

The room was quiet, save for the combined overhead hum of fluorescent lights and air-conditioning. If there's a gray rainbow somewhere, the decor of that room—carpet, walls, chairs, and table—had tried to capture it. One color, assorted shades. It fit my mood.

When we were seated, Gillian said, "Do they know where Parrish is yet?"

"No. But I don't think he'll be able to stay hidden for long. I'm sorry he got away."

"I guess he had it all planned. From what they're saying on television, you were lucky to get out of there alive."

With an unexpected rush of relief, I realized that I *did* feel lucky, damned lucky! Lucky that I wasn't one of the ones who had been standing next to the grave, lucky that Parrish had let me go, lucky to have been spared.

These thoughts no sooner crossed my mind than I was horrified by them, ashamed to find myself rejoicing at all, no matter how silently, ashamed to be feeling good in any way about anything having to do with the last few days.

And worse, to think such thoughts while I sat next to a young woman whose mother had been murdered, tortured hideously by the man who had let me go. Christ, what a jerk I was to be calling that luck! Gillian must have wondered why—why her mother was dead and I was still alive. I had no children waiting for me to return. I looked down at the table, unable to meet her eyes.

She was silent for a moment, then said, "I was hoping you could tell me about finding my mother."

Instantly, I was staring at an uncovered, decaying corpse. Its smell filled the room.

"Irene?"

The tabletop came back into view. The room smelled of lemon furniture polish, and nothing worse. I drew a deep breath, then told Gillian a highly sanitized version of events up to the moment Bingle found the grave. I could not bring myself to talk about the coyote tree or the process of uncovering the grave itself.

She listened quietly, without comment, then said, "Was she . . . was the body . . . you know . . . just bones?"

Oh, Christ.

"No," I said unsteadily. I swallowed hard and forged ahead. "Apparently, she was buried not long after she died."

"But I've heard that animals sometimes—"

"No," I interrupted sharply. Forcing myself to speak in more even tones, I said, "No animals damaged the body."

"I know it sounds gross and weird to even be asking," she said, "but they haven't released her body to us yet, so—so I can't really deal with it. Do you know what I mean? I keep thinking about her being up there, and wondering what he did to her, but no one will tell me. Do you know?"

The Polaroids in the bag.

The hot wax. Julia's face twisted in torment, her mouth open on a scream.

I couldn't breathe. "Excuse me," I managed to say. "It's stuffy in here. I just need to open the door."

"I need someone to be honest with me," she said to my back, as I stood at the door, leaning on its frame, trying to get enough air. Her voice was as close to pleading as I had ever heard it. "I have to know. All along, you've been honest with me. You know the truth, don't you?"

I knew exactly. But damned if I was going to tell a child—even one who was now an adult child—what I had seen in those photos. I'd lie. She might think she wanted the truth, but she wasn't ready for it. No one was ready for that kind of truth.

It would be inhumane to hit her with all the brutal facts of the matter. That wasn't my job. Not even as a reporter. Newspapers of good repute didn't publish gruesome accident photos, or recount every gory detail of a murderer's work. One showed a certain amount of respect for the dead and their families.

Respect for the dead.

Julia Sayre—would you want me to tell her? This daughter of yours, who for four years has crucified herself over a flip remark? "I wish you were dead." Any details I gave her would only add to her guilt.

I turned to face her, saw her waiting for my answer.

Could I lie to her?

"The police and forensic scientists will know more about what happened to her after they've had a chance to study her remains," I began.

"But you saw the body," she insisted.

"It was wrapped in plastic," I said.

"Oh." She thought for a moment, then said, "But plastic—could you see—?"

"Nothing. It was dark green—completely opaque."

Her brows drew together. "But they must have opened it, looked inside. Otherwise, how would they be able to say that the body was my mother's?"

"They did open it, but . . . but they didn't really want a reporter near the grave itself," I said quickly.

A false picture of events, my conscience argued.

True as far as it goes, I argued back, but knew I was on shaky ground.

"The anthropologists made their determinations," I said,

"then they lifted the body, plastic and all, and put it inside a body bag."

That much, she seemed to handle okay. But again she asked, "How did they know it was my mother?"

"They aren't positive yet," I said. Seeing her growing skepticism, I added, "But there were other things that make it seem very likely that it was her. Other than the body itself."

Splitting hairs, that nagging voice warned.

"Like what?"

"In the grave, they found a ring that matches the one she wore, and clothing that matched your description of what she had on the day she disappeared."

She sat brooding for a moment, then said calmly, "Well, I guess I'll just have to be patient, then."

"Gillian, I know the past four years have been very hard on you and your family—"

"No, you don't really know, do you?" She said it calmly.

"No," I admitted.

"I've waited four years. I can wait a few more days, or weeks, or however long it takes the cops to give me some answers. Two years ago, a cop tried to tell me to give up, to quit bugging him, to face facts, he said. He said that they'd probably never find her—it was Thompson, the guy who died up there. He was wrong, wasn't he? So, you see, I can wait."

She started to leave, then turned back toward me. "I'm not angry with you, you know. I'm glad you're writing about this. That's the main thing. Maybe people will realize that when someone goes missing, it's important to find out what happened. My mother's death was important. You have to make everybody know that."

I slowly made my way upstairs. Frank looked up from his book and said, "Jack just called. They're starting to allow Ben to have visitors. Do you want to go over there?"

Ben. That's who I needed to concentrate on now. The living, not the dead. "Yes, I just need to clear off my desk."

He gently lifted my chin and studied my face. "Don't push yourself too hard right now, okay?"

"I'm fine," I said, pulling back.

I'm lucky.

32

▲ ▼ ▲ ▼

SATURDAY, EARLY EVENING, MAY 20

Las Piernas

The walk to the hospital wasn't a long one, but it did me some good; my muscles had grown a little stiff and sore, and I was glad for the chance to stretch. We walked in companionable silence, but caused a commotion when we neared the hospital lobby, for which I was sorry.

There was a group of reporters standing just outside the hospital, smoking. One of the smokers recognized me, and she tried to quickly make her way over to us before the others saw our arrival. No luck. Rarely can one reporter move off from a group of other reporters without being seen. Anyone who has ever dropped a bag of popcorn near a flock of pigeons might have some idea of what this is like—you are not going to feed just one bird.

We made it into the lobby slightly ahead of our unwelcome entourage, only to run into a slightly larger group—restless people who had grown tired of waiting in the large room the hospital had set up for the press, and who were no doubt devising plans to get up to Ben's room or, failing that, a chance to talk to his nurses, an orderly, or anyone who might have glimpsed him after his arrival there.

With no respect for nearby patients or their families, they started shouting questions at me, hurrying nearer.

Frank shielded me from the pushier ones, and fortunately, he was recognized by the officers who were providing the first line of security. We got through with only a little jostling, then made it into an elevator without much more trouble.

On Ben's floor, there were guards posted outside the elevator, and along the hallways. I had seen them the night before, but I didn't feel especially comforted by their vigilance. I realized that in some part of my mind I was now convinced that no guards would ever be able to stop Parrish—he was some combination of Houdini and the Terminator. He had escaped, and would be back. Not everyone in local law enforcement believed that Parrish would return to Las Piernas—most seemed to think that he would seek refuge where he was less well known—but there seemed to be universal agreement that Ben needed protection from the press.

Jack sat on one of a group of chairs near the nurses' station, reading a travel magazine. He looked up as we arrived, tossed the magazine down on the low glass table in front of him and invited us to have a seat. "There are a couple of doctors in with him now," he said.

There were a water fountain and some foam cups nearby. Frank, keeping in mind the orders I received from the doctors about fluid intake, filled a couple of cups and brought them back. "See if you can drink me under the table," he said.

We heard the bell of the elevator and saw a young woman step out. She looked as if she was in her early twenties. She was of medium height, slender and tanned, and wore wire-rimmed glasses. Her eyes were dark brown, and she had short, straight blond hair. She was wearing jeans and carried a blue canvas daypack on her back. She spoke to the officer at the elevator, apparently identifying herself to him. She turned and studied us for a moment, frowning, then went to the nurses' desk. There was a solemnity in her that made me wonder if one of her relatives was being cared for on this floor. Then I heard her clearly say the name "Ben Sheridan."

The three of us glanced at one another, then watched as the nurse nodded toward us.

The woman hesitated, then walked over to where we sat. "The nurse tells me you're waiting to see Dr. Sheridan."

"Yes," Frank said. "Would you like to wait with us?"

She blushed and said, "Thank you. I'm Ellen Raice. I'm one of Dr. Sheridan's teaching assistants."

We introduced ourselves and she said, "Oh. You were there—I mean, you rescued—"

"We were there," I said, looking down at my hands.

We fell into an awkward silence. She looked from the floor to the ceiling to the table, hummed to herself, drummed her hands on her thighs for a few minutes, then stood up and got a cup of water.

When she came back, Jack and Frank began to make small talk with her; she told them that she had known Ben for six years.

"I took a physical anthropology class from him—physical, not cultural—you know the difference? I took the class just to meet a general ed requirement," she said, tearing little chunks off the lip of the now-empty foam cup. "Before the first midterm, I changed my major. A lot of his students end up doing that—maybe not so quickly," she added, blushing, then rushed on. "He's a fantastic teacher. The two best teachers in the whole department are Ben and David Niles—" She stopped, drew in a sharp breath, set the cup down, and pressed her fingers to her eyes. She murmured, "Excuse me," and stood up and paced.

She apparently won her struggle not to cry. When she decided to sit down again, Jack asked, "Do you know who Ben's other friends are?"

She frowned, then said, "He has some friends at other universities. He doesn't seem to have a lot of time for a social life. He—everybody thought he was going to get married, but it didn't work out—I don't think Camille really understood, you know."

"Camille?" I repeated, remembering that Ben had spoken this name during his delirium. "Her name was Camille?"

"Yes, they lived together," she said, smiling, and seeming relieved that I had finally decided to enter the conversation.

"What didn't Camille understand?" I asked.

"About his work. The amount of time he devotes to it. And—and it gives some people the creeps, I guess. Too bad, really, because . . ." Her voice trailed off, then she said, "I probably shouldn't be talking about his personal life this way."

"I'm not trying to make you tell his secrets," I said. "I'm just concerned about him."

"Of course you are!" she said. "Even though you're a reporter . . . I mean . . ."

She went back to tearing at the cup.

"How long ago did he split up with his fiancée?" I asked.

"Camille? I don't know that it was ever actually an official engagement," she said.

I waited.

"It's been a while now," she said, scooping up the cup fragments and standing up again. "Back at the beginning of last semester—so this past January."

Jack, Frank, and I exchanged looks. "But that's only a few months ago," I said.

She shrugged, then said, "Yes, I guess it is only a few months." She walked to the trash can. When she came back, she stayed standing, staring at the door to Ben's room. She took off her daypack, opened it and took out a thick stack of bluebooks. She held them out to me and said, "Would you please do me a favor and give these to Ben?"

"What are they?"

"Final exams."

"I don't think he's in any condition—"

"Of course not. But—he should decide what he wants to do. I think I'm going to go. Please tell him I came by."

"Wait!" Frank said, as she set them on the table. "Don't you want to see him?"

"Yes," she said, "but while I was sitting here, I think I realized that Ben won't want to see me." She frowned again. "Maybe I should put it this way—he won't want me to see him. Not until he's had a little time to get used to the idea of—he's had a transtibial amputation, right?"

At our puzzled looks, she clarified, "Below the knee."

We nodded in unison, all fairly dumbfounded.

"Well," she went on, "I don't know everything there is to

know about Ben, but I do know that he's not crazy about appearing vulnerable, and that he would really hate it if anybody pitied him, but it would make him stark, raving batshit to see someone he teaches pitying him."

More softly, she added, "I feel so sad about David and everything else that happened, and I'm afraid that Ben might mistake that for pity, and the truth is, I'm not sure what I will feel if I actually see Ben lying there hurt, or missing his foot, and so—so I think if you give him these papers to grade, it will help him—because, you know, he can do this without a foot—but I'd better not be here."

And before any of us could recover from hearing this speech, she was gone.

"Because he can do that without a foot?" I asked blankly.

Jack started shaking with silent laughter, and Frank held up a hand to hide a grin, then made a little snorting sound. When I scowled at them, and said I was sure she meant well, Jack laughed harder, wheezing with it, really—and in the way hilarity will strike when you least want it to, we all lost it then.

At that moment, Ben's doctors—a man and a woman—came down the hall to talk to us. We sobered instantly.

"No," the woman said, "don't worry." She was tall, dark-haired, smartly dressed. Both doctors appeared to be in their early fifties. "Laughter helps to let a little of the tension out," she said with a reassuring smile.

They introduced themselves as Greg Riley, Ben's surgeon, and Jo Robinson, a clinical psychologist.

"Have a seat," Dr. Riley said. "Let's talk for a minute."

When we were seated, Dr. Robinson said, "Ben has given us permission to discuss his case with you, but Ms. Kelly, knowing what you do for a living, of course I have to tell you that—"

"I'm not here as a reporter," I said. "Nothing you say to me will end up in the newspaper."

Riley nodded. "I appreciate that. The hospital administrators are going to have my hide if I don't get downstairs and help them conduct a press conference, so I'm going to leave a little of the job I'd normally do to Jo. She's heard everything I've had to say to Ben, and if you have any other questions, call my office—I'm in the book. I'd give you a card, but I don't have one on me at the moment."

For all their efforts to put us at ease, I realized I had tensed up from the moment I saw them. I had to own up to a fear of seeing Ben awake and in this altered state, of reacting in the wrong way, of doing or saying something that would hurt him. What if Ellen Raice had been the smartest one of us all?

Dr. Riley laid out a set of statistics in what was obviously a speech he had given to other patients' family and friends on other occasions. Most of them went right past me. "It has been estimated that every week, about three thousand people in this country undergo an amputation," he was saying now. "But as high as that number is, awareness about limb loss is shamefully low. As far as Ben Sheridan is concerned, of course, there's only been one such surgery. And he's right, because each case is unique."

After a pause, he said, "Let's just talk about Ben's case."

He started by listing the things Ben had going for him. Ben was young, healthy, and intelligent. He had knowledge of anatomy—even of amputation. He was in experienced hands, at a hospital that had an excellent record of success with cases like Ben's. "And because he works for the college, he has good insurance coverage—insurance coverage, I am sorry to say, makes a great deal of difference in what we can do in terms of prosthetics, physical therapy, and other aspects of post-operative care and rehabilitation. Ben is already benefiting from that, because we were able to immediately fit him with a prosthesis."

"Immediately?" Jack asked. Not wanting to get the nurse who had let me see Ben in trouble, I kept my mouth shut.

"Yes. As soon as the sutures were closed, a prosthetist was able to fit him with the first one he'll wear."

"Psychologically," Jo Robinson said, "this approach makes some difference. He awakened from surgery and saw two feet at the end of the bed; even though he knows one is a prosthesis, he has a chance to make a more gradual adjustment to the change in his body image. And later, it will help him to develop his walking pattern."

"So he will be able to walk again?" I asked.

Dr. Riley looked at me and smiled. "Ms. Kelly, with this

type of amputation and the prosthesis we have in mind, he should be able to run, jump, swim, ridc a bicycle, play soccer—you name it. So, barring any unforeseen complications, there are few if any activities Ben was doing before the surgery that he won't be able to do again."

I thought of Ben's work and had my doubts. "Hiking over uneven ground?"

"An amputee recently climbed Mount Everest," Dr. Riley said. "If Ben puts his mind to returning to an activity, or taking on new ones, I wouldn't bet against him. I'm not saying he will be able to achieve all of this immediately—he has to heal from the surgery, and adjust to this change in his body. There will be pain, and a period of adapting to the use of the prosthesis. I don't want you to think I am minimizing any of that. I'll leave the rest to Jo, but as I say, if any of you have questions later, feel free to contact me."

"Perhaps it would be best if we went in to see Ben before he falls asleep again," Jo said as Dr. Riley left. "Then we can talk later, if you'd like."

I picked up the stack of blue books and we followed her down the hall.

He had dozed off, but as we came in, he awakened, and mustered a smile for us. "I see you found Nellie Bly and Company for me," he said to Jo.

"How are you feeling?" I asked.

"I'm so loaded up with morphine, I'm not feeling much," he said drowsily. "How about you? You weren't looking so good yesterday."

"I'm okay now."

"Frank and Jack—I didn't get a chance to properly thank you."

They both disclaimed any need for thanks.

"How's Bingle?" Ben asked.

I started to give a cheery little answer, then changed my mind. "To be honest, I think he's depressed. Jack got in touch with the man who's keeping Bool, and we thought a visit might perk him up a little, but then we were afraid that if they were separated again, it would be hard on him. The man who's keeping Bool doesn't mind having another bloodhound around, but he thinks Bingle is . . ."

"Obstreperous?"

I nodded. "His exact word for it, in fact."

"Yes, that handler's favorite word for Bingle."

"But Bingle's not ill-mannered! He's just—spirited."

Jack laughed. "Ben, he's got Frank and Irene's dogs bowing and scraping to him."

"I'll bet he does."

"The cat hasn't been converted yet," Frank said. "I'm afraid Bingle was a little taken aback at Cody's unwillingness to be chased."

"Good for Cody," Ben said. He smiled, but he seemed to be wearing down. "Irene, you've done so much for me already, but—"

"Name it."

"I rode with David to the airport; my car is still in the driveway—an old Jeep Cherokee. Under the left rear bumper, there's a spare house key in a magnetic holder."

Frank rolled his eyes at this; since he had made me take a similar key holder off my own car, I knew he thought of them as one of those "first things a thief will look for" items. I was grateful that he didn't say anything to Ben.

"If you would please use it to go into David's house," Ben went on, "there are some of Bingle's toys in the garage. David keeps—David kept a separate little toy chest for each dog—not that he spoiled them, you understand. You'll also see a cabinet with his food in it, and instructions for feeding him—David put them there for me."

"Anything else you need? Can I get anything for you?"

"Maybe later." He hesitated, then added, "For now"—he gestured toward the prosthesis—"they're waiting on me hand and foot."

Frank, Jack, and Jo Robinson groaned.

"Hey," Ben said, "it wasn't so bad, considering it was my first post-op amputee joke."

We were halfway down the hall when I realized I still had the bluebooks in hand. "I'll be right back," I said.

Just as I walked back into his room, I heard Ben moan. It

wasn't loud, and it wasn't—as I briefly suspected—because I had returned. When he realized I was in the room, he looked embarrassed.

"Not enough morphine after all?"

"I thought I was alone," he snapped.

"Ah, now there's the Ben Sheridan I've come to know and love. I think I would have left here wondering what they had done with him."

To my shock, he began crying.

"Ben . . ."

"I don't know what the fuck they did with him either," he said, wiping at his face. He drew in a halting breath and said, "Shit. Ignore this little display, please. It must be the drugs."

"Or maybe it's that part of your body has been taken from you."

"Not now, okay?" he said angrily. "Christ. Not now."

"Okay." It wasn't hard to capitulate.

"Why did you come back?"

"Ellen Raice."

That brought him back under control. "What?"

"She came by. I won't even try to repeat everything she said."

"She told you to, you know—say 'get well soon,' " he said, imitating her voice and mannerisms perfectly. It made me laugh. He smiled and said, "Not very kind of me, was that?"

"No, but that's the great thing, Ben, you don't have to pretend to be kind around me. I know you're an asshole, remember?"

"Too true, I'm afraid. Now I just realized what you have there. She brought the damned final essays in, didn't she?"

"Well," I said, not able to resist, "as she put it, it's something you can do without a foot."

His jaw dropped, then he gave a shout of laughter. "I wish I thought you were making that up."

I shook my head. "Shall I take them back to the college for you?"

He hesitated, then said, "Oh, what the hell. She's right. Maybe I'll actually be able to bear reading them. I'll end up devising excuses to be loaded up with morphine at the end of every semester."

I set them on the nightstand next to his bed.

"I'll see you tomorrow, Ben," I said, heading for the door.

"Irene—wait."

"Need something else?"

"You might—you might think about talking to Jo Robinson—no, don't make a face. I mean it. What happened up there—no one expects you to be a little tin soldier, marching on with life. Not after something like that."

"I'll be okay."

He acted as if he was going to say more, then seemed to change his mind. "Yeah. Well, see you tomorrow."

"Are you going to be all right? I mean, here alone?"

"Yes. Actually, I think I need a little time to myself."

"Call if you need to talk before tomorrow."

I caught up to the others in the waiting area. "Sorry about that. I forgot to give him the bluebooks—although I suppose Dr. Robinson would say there are no accidents."

"No, and I've never been to Vienna, either," she said lightly. "I'm sorry we won't have a chance to talk, I have an appointment this evening. Your husband and Mr. Fremont can fill you in on what I've said about Ben." She handed me a business card. "Call me if you have any questions."

I thanked her, stuffed the card into my purse without looking at it, and turned to Frank. "Think there's a way to take a few things from David's house without getting into trouble?"

But although I didn't want to admit it, I was already in trouble. Plenty of trouble.

33

▲ ▼ ▲ ▼

SATURDAY EVENING, MAY 20
Las Piernas

The first time I saw Nicholas Parrish in Las Piernas was early that evening.

Jack, Frank, and I left the hospital, then met up again at our local grocery store to buy the ingredients for dinner. I wasn't much help; I was too lost in thought. At some point, I realized that I wasn't letting Frank out of my sight—I was cowering. Despising that fact, I made myself move away from him. "I'm going to get some bottled water from the other aisle," I said, and when Frank started to move off with me, added, "I'll be right back." I ignored the glance Frank and Jack exchanged.

I had just bent to pick up a six-pack of spring water when I saw Parrish out of the corner of my eye, moving past the far end of the aisle. He was wearing a dark green shirt and some sort of baseball cap. I caught no more than a glimpse of him, but I let out a sharp cry and ran in the opposite direction.

Frank had apparently heard me—I nearly bowled him over as I turned the corner.

"He's here!" I shouted. "He's here in the store!"

Frank knew I didn't mean Elvis—and opened his jacket to have better access to his gun.

I hurriedly described the shirt and cap.

"Stay here!" he said, leaving me with the cart, while he and Jack moved in opposite directions, cautiously peering down each aisle, and yet keeping me within sight. Other shoppers were beginning to give us curious stares; a woman became alarmed when Frank sharply ordered her to "Keep back!"

I saw Frank tense, then relax. "Excuse me, sir," he said. "Could I ask you to come this way for a moment?"

He guided a man who wore a cap and a dark green shirt into view. He was about Parrish's height and build, had Parrish's hair color, and looked nothing at all like him otherwise. "Is this the man you saw?" Frank asked.

I nodded.

"Thank you," he said to the man, who looked at me as if he suspected I was out on a weekend pass.

"What's this all about?" he asked warily.

"Nothing," I said, my mouth dry. "Forgive me, I thought you were someone else."

I took that first Monday morning off—much to John's annoyance—and went with Frank and Bingle to David's house. As we drew closer to David's neighborhood—one of Las Piernas's older neighborhoods, with small but well-maintained homes on large lots—Bingle began sticking his nose out the windows, sniffing and snorting; by the time we turned onto his street, he was whining and pacing anxiously in the backseat, his tail wagging rapidly.

When we pulled up in front of the house, he began barking—sharp, short barks.

"*Tranquilo*," I said.

I saw an old woman part the curtains in the front window of the house across the street.

Bingle behaved himself as we walked to the front door, but it obviously required effort. Once we stepped inside, Frank unsnapped the leash, and the dog bounded through the house.

The big living room had little furniture—a sofa and chair, a television and VCR, and a bookcase. This latter held a number of videotapes, books about dogs and anthropology, and titles by Twain, Thurber, and Wodehouse.

Bingle distracted me from taking in much more of the decor.

He was hurrying from room to room at an anxious trot, whimpering. Several times he came back, looked up at me, and whined. I began following him.

"What's he up to?" Frank asked.

I felt my throat tighten. "I think he's looking for David."

In one bedroom, Bingle jumped up on the unmade bed, and rubbed his face against the sheets and pillows; in the closet, he put his nose into each of the shoes and then rolled in a pile of laundry; in the bathroom, he sniffed at hairbrushes, a toothbrush, drains, and the toilet seat.

I tried talking to him, but he just hurried out into another bedroom, one with a single dresser and a neatly made bed. He took a quick look around, nuzzled the pillow and whined, then went out into the kitchen, where Frank had started gathering his food, feeding instructions, and dog toys. Bingle ignored him.

Bingle moved to a door off the kitchen and scratched at it. I opened it; it led to the garage. There were stacks of cardboard boxes here; he gave them a cursory sniff and made his way to a back door, frantically pawing at it. He started barking.

I opened it, and followed him out into a large fenced yard, with two dog runs. Bingle looked into one of these and barked again. The one marked "Boolean."

There was no lock on it. I unlatched its gate, which creaked as I opened it. Bingle went inside, sniffed around, and again looked back at me. It was as if he were willing me to answer some question. I knelt down, and answered the one I thought he might be asking.

"They're gone, Bingle," I said, wishing I had never brought him here.

He sat down, studied me silently for a moment, then raised his head back and howled—not the high, crooning note he had playfully sung for David, but a low, primal and plaintive lament, a sound to beckon ghosts.

Three nights later, I sneaked Bingle into the hospital. I know an ornery nun on the staff at St. Anne's, and with her help and the cooperation of a couple of guards, we arrived on Ben's floor not long before the end of that evening's visiting hours. I had given the dog the command to be silent, but he already seemed to sense that he was part of a clandestine operation. He was at his most charming with Sister Theresa and the guards. He padded along quietly at my side. While I could see that his nose was working overtime, he didn't insist on checking out any of what must have been a multitude of intriguing scents.

Ben was expecting us; the visit was his suggestion, although I don't think he thought I'd be able to pull it off. Bingle wasn't eating. "I regret bringing him to David's now," I told Ben, "but I think part of what's depressing him is that everyone who is familiar to him is gone from his life now—David, Bool, and as far as he knows, you."

Ben's doubts that Bingle missed him were put to rest by the dog's reaction to seeing him. Bingle's ears came up, and his tail wagged furiously. He approached the bed quickly, but carefully, and after giving a little "rowl" of excitement, gently nuzzled and kissed Ben.

Bingle's presence wasn't such bad medicine for Ben, either. They both looked the happiest I had seen them in days.

It was during this reunion that the door to Ben's room opened and a nearly illegally gorgeous blonde walked in. She was tall and thin, had large, long-lashed, sea green eyes, high cheekbones, a lovely nose, and any number of other features that made me wonder how many women had to take an extra ration of ugly so that God could make this one turn out so beautiful. She was wearing a conservatively cut beige business suit and carried flowers—a cheery bouquet in an elegant ceramic vase—a personal touch, I thought, not your standard issue green glass from the florist.

"I seem to have come at a bad time," she said.

"How did you manage to get past the guards?" Ben snapped.

Was the man crazy? I knew how she got past them.

"A really bad time," she said, and started to back out.

"No, wait," Ben said, but I noticed he was holding fast to Bingle. "Sorry, I didn't mean to be rude. Come in, Camille."

So this was the ex-girlfriend.

She glanced at the end of the bed and her eyes widened in surprise.

"Can you spot the fake?" he asked.

She blushed but said, "I didn't think they'd fit you with a prosthesis so quickly."

"It's just temporary," he said. "Let me introduce you to my friends. You've met Bingle."

The dog wagged his tail; she nodded nervously.

"Irene Kelly, Sister Theresa, this is Camille Graham."

"Hello," she said. We said hello back.

Nobody said anything else for a moment.

"You can put the flowers on that dresser if you like," Ben said, then unbending a little, added, "if they're for me."

She smiled. "Yes, I thought—"

"Thanks," he said.

She set them down, then stayed near the dresser. She glanced at me and Sister Theresa.

"Maybe we should be going," I said.

"No, stay," Ben said quickly. "Please. I've missed Bingle."

Camille folded her arms. There was a brief silence, then he said, "So how have you been?"

"Okay," she said.

"Still seeing—"

"No. But I think you know that."

"Yes. David told me. Sorry things didn't work out."

She shrugged. "How long will you be here?"

"In the hospital? About two more weeks."

"Only two more weeks? Two weeks after . . ."

"Yes. I'll probably be in a wheelchair at first, but I'm already getting up on my feet—or should I say foot?"

"Ben—"

"By the middle of summer," he went on, determinedly ignoring her pitying look, "I'll have my prosthesis. Then it will be feet."

"If you need a place to stay—"

"I won't."

"Where will you live?"

He hesitated, then said, "David's lawyer came by yesterday. It seems I've inherited a house."

"But who will take care of you?"

He petted Bingle. "I'll be fine."

She glanced at Sister Theresa, turned red, but said to him, "If you want to move back in—"

"Absolutely not."

"I didn't mean—"

"I know you didn't," he said.

A silence stretched. I wanted out of there, and thought Sister Theresa might be feeling uncomfortable, too. But a quick look at her made me realize that she was enjoying the hell out of herself.

"Your work," Camille said. "You obviously can't continue—"

"And why not?"

"Be realistic, Ben. What are your plans?"

"Realistically? To go back to the work I've always done."

"But—"

"You think I won't be capable of doing it?"

"No," she said with resignation. "You can do whatever you set your mind to, Ben."

"You just don't approve of my choices."

"True, I've never liked your work, but after what's happened, I would think you'd consider changing your career."

"If anything," he said fiercely, "I'm more determined to do whatever I can to stop people like Nick Parrish. Irene—other than those of our own group, how many bodies have the searchers found up there now?"

"Ben!" Camille said angrily.

"Irene?"

"Ten women—last count," I answered. "They think there are more."

"They'll be working up there for months, Camille. Because of one man. And every family who has a missing daughter will want to know if she's one of them."

"We've been over all of this before," Camille said. "I don't know why I came by." She moved toward the door. "Silly to think you might need my help."

"I'm not a charity case," he said, his anger returning in force. "And I'd have to lose more than a leg to—"

"Don't," she said quickly. "I get the message."

She opened the door, stopped, and said, "I was sorry to hear about David."

He was silent.

"Take care, Ben," she said.

"You too, Camille. Thanks for coming by. I mean that."

She turned back toward him.

He smiled. "Really. I know your intentions were good. You've just forgotten what a"—he glanced at Sister Theresa—"what an old bear I am."

"No, I haven't," she said. "It's one of the things I like about you."

He laughed.

As if she couldn't resist saying it one more time, she added, "Please think about finding some other kind of work."

His smile faded. "Maybe you should do the same."

She left.

There was a collective release of breath as the door closed behind her.

Bingle imitated it with a loud sigh of his own.

"Sorry," Ben said to the dog, "that probably ruined your visit."

"I have the feeling he thinks he's spending the night," I said.

"Much as I'd like it, Bingle, I think we'll have to take a rain check."

Just before we left, I asked, "Ben, how will you manage after you're released?"

"I haven't thought that far ahead yet. Probably hire someone to help out."

On an associate professor's salary? I thought. He must have seen my doubts, because he said, "I've got to take it one step at a time." He grinned and added, "Having only one foot—"

"Oh, for God's sake—"

He laughed.

"I'm serious."

"Too serious. Take care of Bingle—that's plenty for the time being."

We slipped Bingle back out and I said good night to Sister Theresa and our co-conspirator guards. As I walked across the darkened parking lot, I saw other visitors leaving. I was unlocking the door to the Volvo, trying to manage leash and keys and purse when I saw Nick Parrish. He was sitting in the next car over, watching me. I dropped the keys and opened my mouth to scream, stumbling backward and tangling myself in Bingle's leash. Parrish would catch me!

That's when I saw that I was wrong. It was not Parrish. Just a man, waiting in a car.

I got into the Volvo with Bingle. I rolled the windows down and petted the dog while I waited to stop shaking. Bingle sat patiently, not fussing or barking. Twenty minutes later, I had calmed down enough to start the car.

"You need to stop thinking about Parrish," I told myself. "You need to find some distractions."

I pursued that idea with a vengeance.

34

▲ ▼ ▲ ▼

THURSDAY NIGHT, MAY 25

Las Piernas

It was late when I came home that evening, but I found that Frank, Jack, Stinger, and Travis had waited for me.

"You didn't eat dinner?" I asked.

But there was only one dinner anyone was concerned with, and I wondered if Bingle had ever before received applause for chowing down.

"It worked!" Travis said. "Was Ben happy to see him?"

"Oh, yes." As we sat down to our own dinner, I told them what had happened at the hospital, with the exception of my scare in the parking lot. Stinger asked me if I thought Camille Graham might go for a more mature type of gentleman, prompting Jack to ask him where he was going to find one.

"She sounds nice," Travis said, and blushed when that made the other men laugh.

"I think she is," I said. "But Ben seems to be a long way from accepting any offers of friendship from her—which is too bad. I think it might have been good for him to let her help him out. Without David, I don't know how he'll manage."

"Maybe he should stay with me," Jack said.

"You aren't really set up for houseguests," Stinger said. "I speak from personal experience. A few more nights on that couch of yours, and I'll need surgery myself."

"That can be remedied," Jack said.

"Damn straight," Stinger said. "I'm going back home."

Travis cleared his throat and said, "I'm going with him."

"What?" Frank and I said in unison.

"Travis here has a notion he'd like to learn how to fly a helicopter," Stinger said. "And I said that seeing as he has already made out his will, I'll teach him."

"I won't let another twenty-odd years go by before I come back," Travis said quickly, knowing my first concern. Until recently, family misunderstandings had separated me from my cousin, and I wasn't willing to lose track of him again. "I'm just going to spend a little time trying something new," he said. "I think I'll probably set up a place of my own when I do come back, though."

The men were looking at me, waiting for a response. "If it's what you want to do," I said, "that's great. Just don't become a stranger."

He became animated, telling me about how much he had enjoyed riding up in the cockpit of the helicopter with Stinger, about Stinger's desert retreat, about the work Stinger did with the helicopters.

"Any word on Parrish's whereabouts?" Jack asked Frank.

Frank shook his head. "We're getting reports from all over the place, some in town, some as far away as Australia. Not too uncommon to have this kind of stuff going on when there's a serial killer on the loose. People feel afraid, they start seeing him everywhere."

And how, I thought.

As soon as dinner was over, I told them I was going to bed early, that it had been a long day, and I was tired. It was the truth—perhaps not the whole truth, but the truth.

But when I lay down, I couldn't sleep. I was tense, and felt an unhappiness, the cause of which I couldn't name.

On the contrary, I had nothing to be unhappy about, I told myself. I was home safe and whole, unlike everyone else who had traveled to the mountains with me a week ago. I could not rid myself of visions of their faces, and found myself thinking especially of Bob Thompson, whom I didn't even like, which for some reason made it seem worse to me, trying to remember him kindly when I felt so little kindness toward him.

Bingle came in, and put his head on the bed next to me. I petted him until I heard him flop to the floor in a heap and sigh. Cody came in and pointedly ignored him, but curled up in the crook of my knees and purred.

I don't remember dozing off, but that night I dreamed I was standing in a field of pieces of men—not the mess of reality, but nice neat whole body parts: heads and torsos and feet and hands and arms and legs—all bloodless and clean, more like disassembled mannequins than men. It was up to me to reassemble them, and I felt that it was urgent that I should do so, but the mixture of parts wasn't right, and I kept making mistakes. I'd put the wrong foot on a leg and couldn't get it off again, the wrong neck on a head. And then I began to smell the stench of the real meadow, the death smell, growing stronger and stronger—the parts were going bad, because I wasn't assembling them fast enough. Some of the heads were angry with me; they were dying because of me, they said, and started yelling my name, making an angry, protesting chant of it.

After a time, I realized that it was Frank, not yelling, just gently saying my name, holding me, stroking my back. I was shaking, and for the longest damned time, I couldn't stop.

"Do you smell it?" I asked.

"What?"

When I didn't answer, his hands went still for a moment, and then he said, "The field?"

"Yes. You do? I think maybe it's on my clothes or something I brought back—or maybe Bingle—"

"Irene . . . no, I don't smell it."

I looked into his eyes, saw that he was serious, and said, "I have to get out of the house."

"Okay," he said, having plenty of experience with my claustrophobia.

We got dressed, gathered all three dogs, and went down to the end of the street. It was after midnight, and the cops who had been assigned to keep watch at the top of the stairs leading to the beach weren't too crazy about our plans, but let us go past them.

The moon was up, and although it wasn't full, it was bright enough to light our way. I took in great breaths of the salt air, and other scents receded. The sight of the endless silver stretch of moonlit water, the sounds of the advance and retreat of the waves, the soft give of the sand beneath my feet, all were so different from the mountain meadow of my dream. The terrifying images gave way, and I began to relax.

More aware, then, of Frank's big warm hand holding mine, I said, "Sorry, you probably need some sleep, and here I am dragging you down to the beach."

"I've had my share of bad nights, too. You can't go through this stuff and expect that now that you're home, you'll just pick up where you left off."

"No." After a moment, I said, "This time—I don't know how to come back from there, Frank. It's with me. It frightens me."

He put his arm around my shoulders and said, "Maybe you should talk to somebody."

I didn't answer. Two nights ago, I had told him everything that had happened in the mountains. He had listened patiently, and although he had been upset by how Parrish had terrorized me, and probably didn't approve of my trying to draw Parrish away from Ben, he didn't criticize me or blame me for what happened. The perfect listener, as far as I was concerned. So I knew that when he now said "talk to somebody," he meant a therapist.

"Just a thought," he said after a while. "I'm not trying to push you."

"I know you aren't," I said, but felt relieved.

"And you can always talk to me."

I pulled him closer to me. "Yes, I know. Thanks." We walked a little farther, and I said, "I guess that's why I don't worry about needing a therapist. I've got a great husband, I'm surrounded by family and friends—I have a support group. Ben—I get the distinct impression that he's not so lucky."

"The other day at the hospital, that's what Jo Robinson said. She was going to try to contact Ben's sister and some of his friends, but in the meantime, she thought Ben could use whatever emotional support we could offer—although she's concerned that you won't take care of yourself."

"Where does his sister live?" I asked, choosing to steer the conversation away from Jo Robinson and her concerns.

"In Iowa."

The dogs came by and shook water on us, making us swear and laugh all at once. For a time, we simply walked and watched them.

Bingle was enjoying himself immensely; today he had definitely been the happiest I had seen him since we brought him home. It occurred to me that with his level of training, David must have spent many more hours working with him than we did with our dogs. How often each day was this dog used to being walked? Would he lose skills if we didn't work with him?

The three dogs were getting along well together, engaging in harmless but rowdy play—dodging one another's charges, tumbling dramatically in the sand, chasing one another into the water, then running up onto the beach.

Frank said, "I've been thinking about the front steps."

I stopped walking. "The front steps?"

"I think I can get Pete and Jack to help me build a ramp. We'll need to make some changes in the bathroom, too, maybe get one of those handheld shower goodies, and a seat. Dr. Riley can probably give us a list of things that we wouldn't even think about on our own."

"Frank—" I swallowed hard. "You've had to live with my twenty-five-year-old cousin . . ."

"Like most guys his age, Travis has had better things to do than hang around the house. You know I haven't minded having him stay with us. I like him."

"But Ben—he's going to have problems, Frank. In fact, he had problems before all of this happened. This is not a great time in Ben Sheridan's life."

"Do you dislike him?"

"Last week, the answer would have been 'yes.' "

"Now?"

"I guess I see things differently. The situation forced me to spend some time with him when he should have been at his worst. Instead it seemed to bring out the best in him."

We turned around and headed back. Frank said, "I found you up there before Parrish did because Ben—even though he was obviously half out of his mind with pain—came up with the idea of sending Bingle with me to look for you."

"You would have found me anyway."

"Maybe," he said. "But who knows? With Parrish on the loose, it's not a chance I would have wanted to take. The other thing is—you know the old bit about saving someone's life?"

"And then becoming responsible for it? You aren't going to convince me that you're suggesting Ben should stay with us because of that."

"No, but there's some link between the two of you now, just because you survived this together."

"A link? Frank, maybe I should make something clear—"

"No need to," he said firmly. "I don't suspect that at all."

"Why not?" I asked, and he laughed.

"Don't worry—I have no doubt that you're attractive to other men."

"So you think Ben is gay?"

"No, I think Miss Ellen Raice would have blurted that out to us right off the bat."

"True."

He smiled. "And you didn't just invent Camille Graham to be cruel to Stinger, did you?"

"No. So what is it?"

"I trust you," he said. Then with a mischievous look, he added, "Besides, there are certain advantages to marrying girls like you, who never quite get over being Catholic—I would have seen the guilt from a mile away."

I opened my mouth to protest, shut it, then muttered, "You're right," which made him laugh again.

So we decided that it would be good for Ben to stay with us. It was not so easy to convince Ben.

Frank proceeded to make the changes to the house anyway, saying that it would make it easier for Ben to visit. We both kept hoping that Ben would change his mind.

The sister in Iowa called Ben once, said she was sorry to

hear about his trouble, but there was nothing she could do about it. She couldn't afford a trip out to California, and since she was seeing a man who might pop the question at any moment, strategically, this was not a good time for her to leave Iowa. He told me the phone call was more than he had expected from her.

He was moved to another section of the hospital, and began grueling physical therapy sessions. During those two weeks, he got many calls from friends across the country, but he always told them not to bother coming out to see him.

Those were busy weeks for me, just as I had hoped they'd be. Other members of the news staff, sick of hearing from John about my productivity, started hinting to me that I could slow down anytime.

No, I couldn't.

I was on the run, after all—as surely as I had been in the mountains. Parrish seemed to be everywhere. Seated at other tables in restaurants, walking past me on a crowded sidewalk, going down the stadium stairs at a ball game. He came out of a bookstore as I walked in, stood in the shadows at a bar when I had a drink after work with friends, stood on the pier, staring at me, when I ran on the beach. He was at the back of the bus when I rode it, he drove past me when I walked. I once saw him get into an elevator ahead of me—I took the stairs, four flights up.

I don't do well with elevators anyway.

Although each time was as terrifying as the first, I learned not to screech or run or point—and eventually, not to tell anyone what had made me suddenly turn pale, not to tell anyone anything about it at all. This, even though I knew that Frank wouldn't belittle me if I told him of every incident. What did that matter? I was too ashamed not to belittle myself.

When I wasn't working, I was visiting Ben or making preparations for his release from the hospital. I went back to David's house without Bingle, cleaning it up just in case we lost our argument with Ben. I asked Ben if he wanted me to do anything with David's belongings; he said no. "Except—could you bring some of those training tapes in? I think Sister Theresa is going to get a VCR in here for me."

"Bribing nuns?"

"You should talk, dog smuggler."

"What training tapes?"

"The ones of Bingle and the SAR group. The group videotapes some of the training exercises so that they can study the way the dogs work, the way the handlers work with them. David used to watch the tapes all the time. They'll be on the bookcase."

"So you're going to take up SAR and cadaver dog work?"

He glanced down at his left leg, then with a determined look, said, "Yes. If Bingle decides he doesn't want to work with me, fine. But David put a lot of time into training him, and the least I can do for David and Bingle is to give it a try. And no one can better teach me how to work with Bingle than David."

At first, watching the tapes upset Ben, as they did me. This was David at his best, his happiest, and the tapes served as a reminder of who it was we had lost. Seeing Bingle work with him, it was clear that they communicated superbly, that he made the best of the dog's intelligence and abilities.

Since David's death, I thought, Bingle must have believed himself to be in the company of dullards.

At one point, Ben paused the tape. I heard him choke back a sob.

"Do you want to wait and watch these when you're feeling better?" I asked.

He shook his head. "There's no feeling better about David's death; only getting used to it."

He hit the play button again. He was watching a tape made in the summer. At the end of it, there was some footage of a hilarious swimming party that had included the dogs. I was laughing with Ben at Bingle's antics in the pool when I saw something that made me draw in a sharp breath.

Ben heard it and paused the tape again. "What's wrong?"

"I'm sorry—I didn't know."

He looked at the screen, and saw what had startled me. "His back, you mean? The scars?"

"Yes."

"The worst were from a radiator."

"An accident?" I asked hopefully, knowing it wasn't so.

"No. David was abused."

I couldn't speak.

"He must have been very comfortable with the people in this group," Ben went on. "He didn't usually take his shirt off around others, and unless he came across someone else who was abused, he certainly didn't speak of his childhood." He paused. "Please don't mention this to anyone else."

I promised I wouldn't. "I begin to understand why he didn't think Parrish's childhood excused him."

"Yes," Ben said. "We used to argue about that. David was an obvious example of the fact that not all abused children go on to become twisted souls, that many overcome the horrors of their childhood. But I used to tell him that not everyone was made up of the same stuff he was, not everyone was as strong. Not everyone could overcome what he did."

I thought of Nicholas Parrish. "Perhaps there are a few who don't want to overcome it."

"Maybe."

He hit the play button again, and went back to watching David.

35

▲ ▼ ▲ ▼

TUESDAY, EARLY AFTERNOON, MAY 30
Las Piernas

The Moth stood still, watching, listening.

The door at the back of the garage was well concealed. There was a high fence, and a row of trees to shade the dog runs. The dog runs were empty, but clean.

A neighbor's dog was barking, but no one seemed to pay any attention to it. On a weekday, at this time of day, most of the residents were at work, and their children in school.

There was an old woman across the street who might have chanced to look out her window at the dead man's home, but if she had, she would be hard put to describe the person she had seen going into the backyard. A repairman, she probably would have guessed, judging by the large toolbox (mostly empty), the dark coveralls and boots, the leather work gloves, the billed cap pulled low over the Moth's face. She might have noticed a limp.

The Moth stooped to open the toolbox, then paused for a moment to handle a set of trophies there—drain plugs.

Not everyone would have thought of these fuel-coated bits of metal as treasures, and Nicky would probably be angry to know the Moth kept them. But Nicky wasn't here, was he?

In their intended place, these little darlings belonged beneath helicopters. By taking them, the Moth had ensured that the Forest Service Helitack units nearest to the meadow stayed on the ground.

The newspaper had even included a separate article about the cleverness of the ploy—an article the Moth had read every morning, almost as if it were a morning prayer—it was not a prayer, of course, but a wonderful tribute, even if Nicky had been given the credit.

Nicky *had* taught the Moth this method of disabling a helicopter, after all, and other methods as well. Still, the Moth had made choices. The Moth had succeeded.

The Moth was proud of this accomplishment not only because it had worked perfectly, but also because it was really a very considerate sort of sabotage, which gave it a subtlety the Moth liked. The removal of a drain plug could keep a helicopter on the ground without destroying it.

The renewed barking of the neighbor's dog reminded the Moth of the business at hand. The drain plugs were returned to the toolbox. The Moth removed a pry bar and, within seconds, entered the garage.

The Moth propped the toolbox against the door from the inside, to hold it closed, then flipped the light switch and listened to the soft "chink-chink-chink" and then hum of the chain of fluorescent lights overhead.

The garage was clean and orderly. A group of cardboard boxes was stacked along one wall, labeled with the names of rooms—KITCHEN, BEDROOM, BATHROOM, GARAGE and—the largest number of boxes, STUDY. Curious, the Moth inspected them more closely. The top of each box had a small address label on it, of the type that is sometimes mailed with a request for a donation. These had American flags on them. There were two names on the labels: Ben Sheridan and Camille Graham. The address wasn't this one.

Ben Sheridan. The Moth knew that Nicky was angry about Ben Sheridan. He thought he had killed Ben Sheridan, but he had only wounded him.

Only wounded for *now*, thought the Moth. Sooner or later he would have to leave that hospital. And poor Nicky, who couldn't go to a hospital! The Moth had wanted to comfort him, but wisely refrained. Nicky had been too angry to accept any coddling. Actually, the Moth thought, you really couldn't coddle Nicky. He didn't need anyone. Not even his Moth.

Frowning, the Moth picked at the address label on one of the boxes marked STUDY. It came off easily. The Moth carefully pocketed it. Using a utility knife to cut the tape which sealed it, the Moth opened the box and studied its contents. Books. Not even the books the Moth had hoped for—ones about forensic anthropology, which might have photos of dead bodies in them—but stupid, stupid books, by Jane Austen and James Baldwin and Charles Dickens and Graham Greene and Flannery O'Connor. Poetry by Auden, Dickinson, Eliot, Housman, Hughes, Neruda, Poe.

Tired old books that any kid in high school might be made to read! Why, any public library had these books in it—why buy them? And what did any of them really have to say about life in these times? Nothing! Had the writers ever met the likes of Nicky and the Moth? No, never!

Disgusted, the Moth folded the box closed and proceeded into the house.

The door between the house and the garage was not locked. The Moth stepped into the kitchen, then stood motionless.

Someone had already been here. The Moth could tell that the house had been opened, aired out. The Moth drew in a deep breath, tried to allow the scent of the house to tell the story, as Nicky might have done.

There was still the smell of dogs. If you allowed dogs to live indoors, even house-trained dogs, there would be their doggy scent. Trying not to allow that to interfere, the Moth continued through the house. In the kitchen there was the scent of cleaning products—chlorine and something with lemon in it. The Moth opened the refrigerator. The shelves were pristine; there was no milk or meat or any other thing that might rot. There were only a few jars and an open yellow box of baking soda.

The trash had been taken out; there was a new white plastic bag in the kitchen trash can—the only object in it was a crumpled paper towel, smelling of window cleaner.

As the Moth walked slowly through the house, it became clear that someone had been here in the time since the owner died. Who? Did the dead man have a maid? No—no, he only taught at the college. He had no money to hire someone to clean his house.

The Moth knew this, and all sorts of other things about the dead man, things most people didn't know. The dead man's mother had died when he was two; his alcoholic father had abused him terribly throughout his childhood—if there had been larger pieces of him left behind in the Meadow, investigators might have seen the scars.

The dead man's father had always marked him in places that could be covered by his clothes. These facts might have shocked another person, but they had quite a different effect on the Moth. The Moth knew all about hidden scars.

Like many abused children, David Niles was a good student, a child who tried to please. His father died when he was a teenager. He had been sent to live with his mother's sister, an old maid who raised dogs in New Mexico. He loved dogs. He loved his aunt. She put him through college, where he met Ben Sheridan, who was a year or two ahead of him.

The Moth knew that it was Ben Sheridan's enthusiasm for physical anthropology that led David Niles to change his major. Niles's graduate studies were interrupted when he took care of his aunt before her death. She had already found homes for her dogs when she became too ill to care for them. No one would take care of her except her nephew. After her death, he went back and finished his doctorate, then—with Ben Sheridan's help—obtained a part-time teaching position at Las Piernas College. Just before he died, he had been promoted to a full-time position.

The Moth also knew that David Niles—no, the Moth decided, call him the dead man—had inherited a little money from his aunt, and had used that to buy this house, build the dog runs, and cover the expenses of buying, training, outfitting, feeding, and otherwise caring for two large search dogs.

The Moth knew a great deal about every member of the group that went up to the mountains with Nicky, but knew more about this dead man than the others. This one had been the Moth's special project, which was how it came about that this search of the dead man's home was necessary.

In the living room, the Moth detected an odor of lemon furniture polish and, in the carpet, the scent of the dogs.

Not nearly as well as Nicky would have done. Nicky could distinguish scent better than any human alive. The Moth firmly believed this to be true.

Nicky would have been angry to know that the Moth had overlooked one small, small detail. But the Moth was about to take care of it, and Nicky need never know.

The Moth thought about the drain plugs in the toolbox and wondered why keeping secrets from Nicky was so exciting.

Before long, though, the Moth was feeling not excitement, but panic. What the Moth sought should have been in the living room, but it wasn't. And suddenly, what seemed like a very small detail loomed very large.

Why, of all things, should this be missing?

Did the police know? Had they already made the connection?

There was a knock at the door. The Moth froze, then moved as quietly as possible to one of the bedrooms, and hid in the closet. Would the Moth have to kill the person at the door? Nicky would be furious—the Moth wasn't here at Nicky's bidding. Nicky would have planned for this, would have foreseen this! What if the person at the door went around to the garage and found the toolbox?

Long moments passed, in which the Moth thought of the toolbox and the drain plugs, and felt sick, absolutely sick.

The doorbell rang.

The Moth curled up into a little ball.

There was a long silence, then the Moth found the courage to stand up and leave the closet.

The Moth made a quick search of the two bedrooms and of the bathroom, as silly a place as it would be to hide what the Moth wanted.

The neighbor's dog began barking again. Losing any remaining courage, the Moth left the house, picked up the toolbox in the garage, and hurried away from the dead man's house.

Driving away, the Moth didn't take time to look at the old woman's house, to see if she was spying at her window. The

Moth's thoughts were consumed by a single idea, a notion that was becoming something of a Moth mantra:

Don't tell Nicky!
Don't tell Nicky!
Don't tell Nicky!

36

▲ ▼ ▲ ▼

WEDNESDAY MORNING, MAY 31

Las Piernas

Ellen Raice called me at work to tell me that someone had broken into Ben's office by prying off a basement window latch.

"Was anything taken?"

"Not that I can see. If I hadn't tried to lock the window, I might not have even noticed that someone had been in here. But when I saw that, I looked around, and I could see that things had been moved, you know, looked through. Especially on some of the shelves, and in the desk drawers."

"Campus police know about this?"

"Yes. But I don't believe the officer understands the implication."

"That this is connected with Nicholas Parrish."

"I knew you'd understand! Will you talk to your husband about it?"

I called Frank. A detective and a crime lab technician were sent out to the college, and a patrol car to David's house—there had been a break-in there, too. At the house, it was apparent that someone had jimmied the back door of the garage. I let Ben know what was going on, and told him I would go to the house to see if I noticed anything missing.

Frank met me there. It was the sort of case that might have

otherwise merited a patrol car—if that—but because Nick Parrish might be connected to the break-in, the mobile crime lab was already at work when I arrived.

"Any fingerprints?" I asked Frank.

"No, but they're hoping they've picked up some tool marks on the door here and the latch of the window at the campus."

"Not likely that Ben would suffer a break-in at both the office and at home on the same day, is it?"

"No, especially unlikely that he'd have two break-ins and nothing stolen from either place. There were valuables here and in the office that weren't touched."

"What could Ben have that Parrish wants?"

"We don't know that this was Parrish."

I stared at him.

"Yes, I'm with you—but we have to stay open to other possibilities," he said. "You mentioned this ex-girlfriend of his."

"Camille. And don't even pretend you've forgotten her name."

He laughed. "Okay, Camille. There was some rancor between them, right?"

"Some," I admitted. "But I have a hard time picturing this woman in her silk power suit breaking in through a basement window."

"Just the same, I think I'll call Ben and ask for the name of the place where she works. I'd like to have a talk with her."

"I'll bet you would."

The detective handling the case approached us just then. "Neighbor across the street says she saw a repairman of some sort over here earlier. Either of you know if Dr. Sheridan had arranged for any repairs?"

"No," I said. "He hasn't."

"The neighbor said the repairman came directly into the backyard. She knows Dr. Sheridan is in the hospital, so she got suspicious and came over and knocked and rang the bell. There wasn't any answer."

"What time was that?" Frank asked.

"Early afternoon. She was watching a soap opera that comes on at one o'clock. She came over on a commercial break, so she didn't stay around too long."

"Any description of this repairman?"

"Not much of one, unless you call 'a white guy wearing a cap' a description. She has no idea regarding height or weight—changed her mind about three times on that one." He paused, then said, "At first, before she figured out that he would have used the front door, she thought Sheridan might be home from the hospital. She said this repairman limped."

Frank raised his eyebrows.

"Yeah," the detective said. "Exactly what I was thinking. Flights from San Francisco on the hour."

"Who's in San Francisco?" I asked.

"Phil Newly—north of there, really, but not too far from the city. He's visiting his sister."

"Lady across the street said she thought it looked like a fake limp, but then, she can't remember which leg the guy was limping on."

"There's someone else we may want to talk to," Frank told him.

"It's not Camille," Ben insisted. "Impossible. She'd never do anything like that. Besides, I have nothing she'd want."

"Just the same, I'd like to follow up on this," Frank said.

Ben grudgingly gave him Camille's work and home addresses. "If, for some unimaginable reason, she did this, I'm not pressing charges."

"You parted amicably?" Frank asked.

After a long silence, Ben said, "No."

"Thanks for being honest about it," Frank said. "As you say, it probably wasn't her."

Frank called me at the paper to tell me that Camille Graham hadn't been into work that day. "In fact," he said, "she's quit working there. We caught up with her at home, where she claims she's been holed up for the last few days with a summer cold. She did seem to be a little congested."

"You saw her?"

"Yes," he said, amused. "She's a looker, but I prefer brunettes."

"Even though classes are over for the term, can you imagine

a woman who looks like Camille crossing a campus undetected? Don't young frat boys have radar for such women?"

"Why, Irene! I think that might have been a sexist remark," he said.

"You know what I'm trying to say, Susan B. Anthony."

"Anything is possible—of anyone. That's all I'm asking you to keep in mind."

We were getting nearer the day when Ben would be released from the hospital, and he was still claiming that he didn't want to impose on us, but he wasn't protesting quite so much. He was having problems with both phantom limb sensation and phantom limb pain, and was feeling discouraged.

Dr. Riley had warned him that both were common phenomena, especially in the period of time just after surgery.

The phantom limb sensation made Ben "feel" the missing lower portion of his left leg, including his left ankle, foot, and toes, as if they were still there. One morning, half asleep, absolutely convinced that his left foot was still there, he fell trying to get out of bed. Although he bruised his hip and shoulder, fortunately, he didn't do further damage to his leg. On another occasion, his left toes itched maddeningly. I even tried scratching the prosthetic foot to relieve it—to no avail. He had to live with the itch for three torturous hours before the sensation went away on its own.

This "presence" of the missing limb was a weird sensation, Ben said, but not necessarily bad. Phantom limb pain was another matter. Not long after surgery, Ben's left foot and ankle cramped. Because they weren't there, though, he couldn't figure out what the hell to do to relieve it.

Sometimes, one of the nurses came in and massaged his "residual limb," as they referred to what remained of his lower left leg. It was very sensitive to touch, and still swollen from the surgery, but the massage seemed to help.

He told me that he felt phantom pain more often late at night, when he was alone, and in specific regions of the missing limb—sometimes it came as a sharp, stabbing pain in his calf, other times he felt as if he had been given an electric shock through his heel. Occasionally, only strong, painkilling drugs would bring relief—which, he told me, made him wonder if he was doomed to become a morphine addict.

Those were his worst days at the hospital. On the whole, though, he seemed to have a determined outlook.

"I want to be able to manage on my own," he said, whenever the subject of staying with us arose.

"We want the same thing," I said. "You aren't invited to move in forever. I don't even know if you should still be there after six months."

He laughed.

"We'll stand by you either way. You know that?"

"Yes," he said.

"The difference is, this way you don't have to clean up the house before we come over."

"I'll think about it," he said.

It was the day we got the news about Oregon that he made up his mind to stay with us—not because of his own fear of Nicholas Parrish, he told me, but because of mine.

37

▲ ▼ ▲ ▼

THURSDAY AFTERNOON, JUNE 1
Eastern Oregon

The receptionist, Parrish decided, would have to go.

Whenever she thought he wasn't looking, she stared at him.

Idiot. He was always looking.

She was afraid of him, he knew. He had lost his temper with her once, the first time he was here. She had been living strictly on his sufferance ever since.

A nurse opened a door and smiled at him. "Mr. Kent?"

Fat cow. What the hell was there to smile about? Maybe she'd go, too. Maybe there wouldn't be a woman alive in the state of Oregon by the time he left it. Entirely possible, he thought. He was smiling by the time the woman was taking his blood pressure.

She finally left him alone to wait for the sorry excuse of a doctor to get around to seeing him. Doddering old fart probably wouldn't have made it in a big city, Parrish thought. He passed the time waiting for the fool to appear by fantasizing a story about the physician's past, one in which he had performed back-alley abortions, lost his license, and run away to this little burg—where no one knew enough to question his phony diplomas and licenses. Parrish convinced himself so thoroughly, he was carefully studying the engraved parchment on the wall when the doctor walked in.

"Ancient, but real, just like me," the doctor said. "Let's have a look at that shoulder, Mr. Kent."

Oh, let's.

"It seems to be healing nicely now," the doctor said. "Scar tissue can't be helped, but you were lucky not to face worse. Well, I won't lecture you about ignoring puncture wounds—you've heard it all from me before."

Yes, indeed he had. He studied the doctor, considered adding him to his list—but suddenly the old man was regarding him with an unwavering stare. Parrish looked away and said, "In the future, I won't delay getting treatment."

Screw the old bastard, he thought, glancing up at him surreptitiously. God was going to call the stupid quack's number any day now, anyway. No use wasting the effort on him.

He wondered, briefly, if any of them had recognized him. But although only two weeks had passed, he was no longer the hot topic of news. He would be on the front page again, of course, but for now he looked nothing like the photographs, which no one would have seen for over a week now. He had dyed his hair blond and was wearing tinted contact lenses. Probably not even necessary in this little backwater.

That night, as he worked, he thought of Irene Kelly, who had made his shoulder stiff and sore. He did not like scars. He did not like pain. He chuckled a little at this thought. *Not my own*, he added silently, and pleased to find his sense of humor returning, went back to the matter at hand.

The next morning, he drove slowly past the clinic, smiling as he saw close to a dozen people waiting outside its door, their expressions varying from anger to puzzlement. One of them, hands cupped and pressed to the glass, was trying to see in.

"Some-bod-y's laaa-te to worr-rrk!" Parrish sang, a little child's taunting song. "The patients grow impatient!"

He found this remark such a heartening indicator that his

true, clever self was making a comeback that he laughed all the way to the highway, ignoring—whenever he braked or took a curve—the occasional thump in the trunk made by shifting dead weight.

38

▲ ▼ ▲ ▼

MONDAY AFTERNOON, SEPTEMBER 11

Las Piernas

I looked out the window of Jo Robinson's second-story office, idly wondering what other troubled souls might have shared this view, watching the rain plaster red and gold leaves to the black asphalt of the parking lot below. Autumn. I had almost managed to hold out until autumn.

"So Ben spent the summer with you and Frank," she prompted. I had been trying to tell her what had happened since the last time I had seen her, outside Ben's hospital room.

"Yes," I answered her, still watching the rain. If it hadn't ever rained again, I thought, I might have been all right.

What a lie.

"Ben and Bingle have moved back to David's house. He's doing fine there. Bingle, too."

"And you?"

I didn't answer.

"Why are you here?" she asked.

" 'To know, love, and serve God so that I may be happy in the next life,' " I replied.

She waited.

I glanced back at her. "Sorry—knee-jerk *Baltimore Catechism* response to that question. But you know why I'm here."

"You tell me."

"I'm here because I broke something at work."

"Really? I'd think a hardware store could be of more use to you, then."

"You'd think so, wouldn't you?"

"Tell me what happened."

So I told her how, coming into work one day, I had been told to report to Winston Wrigley III's "God office," which is how the staff refers to the glass enclosure near the newsroom. Wrigley deigns to visit the God office when he wants to view his minions in action, or, more accurately, to spy on whatever young, new female employee he has added to the roster.

There hadn't been any new additions lately—sexual harassment laws were severely cramping WWIII's style—so his current visit had the rumor-fueled newsroom aflame with gossip. These flames were fanned by the fact that he had two elegantly dressed couples with him, who joined him around the conference table at one end of the room. Before John Walters summoned me, I had heard that the paper was being sold to a big chain, that there were going to be layoffs, and that John was going to be fired for letting Morry mouth off to Wrigley before Morry left for Buffalo.

I didn't have a chance to hear any of the rumors that circulated after I got called in, but later Lydia told me that one of the best was that I was going to be asked to replace John after he was fired for letting Morry vent.

As I approached the God office, I was already tired and tense; I hadn't slept well lately, and the previous three nights, hardly at all.

Until three days earlier, the Oregon killings had provided the last solid leads on Nick Parrish's whereabouts. In June, the discovery of the bodies—one a legless torso—of two clinic workers had launched Parrish back into the headlines. The search for him intensified, but the rest of the summer had passed without any sign of him. I began to hope that he had been hit by a car.

But three days before I was summoned into Wrigley's glass domain, the LPPD had received a report that Nick Parrish had been sighted not far from Las Piernas.

* * *

Despite the fact that these sightings of Parrish were usually unfounded, the police checked out all leads. But this call led to the discovery of a woman's body in a trash container.

I've since wondered how things might have gone if Frank had been the one to give me the news. But on the day she was found, Frank was in court, giving testimony on another case. So I learned about Parrish's newest victim at work, on a day when there wasn't any way to contact my husband.

By the time Mark Baker arrived in the newsroom to file the story, there was already a buzz among the other reporters about it. I had already heard that Parrish had left another body somewhere. That news alone made me feel as if someone were sandpapering the ends of my nerves.

Mark had been in to talk to John, and John beckoned me in to join them. Looking grim, John said, "You should probably know about this before the others start asking you about it."

"Asking me about it?"

So Mark gave me the details. "This Jane Doe's fingers and toes were severed and missing. She was a blue-eyed brunette. Her name is not yet known, but your name was carved into her chest."

I felt my stomach lurch; I quickly excused myself, ran into the bathroom, and got sick.

I washed up, then, looking into the mirror with a measure of detachment, studied my tense, too thin face and the dark circles under my eyes. Detachment was becoming one of my favorite emotional states. It was constantly being disturbed, though—this time, when the door opened, causing me to jump.

It was Lydia. She asked if I was all right.

"No," I said.

"Maybe it isn't him," Lydia said. "It could be a copycat."

"What a relief that would be," I replied, and later wondered how much more of my sarcasm she could take.

"This happened three days before you were asked to see Mr. Wrigley?" Jo Robinson asked.

"Yes."

"Go on."

I turned back to the window.

When I entered the God office, Wrigley was smiling and holding an unlit cigar. (California's anti-smoking laws were second only to sexual harassment suits in making his life miserable.) I grew more wary; Wrigley's halo is always perched on his horns. He introduced the two couples with him as friends of the family who were visiting the area, who had stopped by the office today especially to meet me.

"To meet me?" I asked. "I don't understand."

"You're the one who escaped from Nick Parrish, right?" one of the men asked.

I looked at Wrigley. He's known me for many years, which is why he stopped smiling. His guests didn't seem to notice.

"Oh! It must have been so horrible!" one woman said, but she made the word "horrible" sound a lot like the word "thrilling."

"What is he really like?" she went on. "They say he's probably killed more women than Ted Bundy did. They say he's just as handsome as Bundy."

"He's not handsome," I managed to say. "Excuse me, I have to get back to work."

"Not especially handsome," the other woman corrected, "but charming. They say that's how he lures women."

"Don't run off," one of the men said, seeing me edge toward the door. "After all, you're here with the boss, right, Win?"

Win? I had never heard anyone call him that before.

"Right," Wrigley said. "Irene wasn't taken in by his charms," he added, trying to recover. "She's a professional, through and through. Why, she nearly killed him!"

This elicited gasps from the female members of his audience.

"And she was the only one up there who had the sense not to get herself killed or wounded!" he said, warming to his subject. "She saved the life of this one idiot who ran into the field after the shooting started—can you imagine anyone doing anything so stupid?"

"Mr. Wrigley—" I began angrily, but he must not have heard

me over the combination of exclamations of disbelief and laughter.

"He's crippled now, but really, it's his own damned fault. Irene has been taking care of him. In fact—"

"Yo, Win!" I shouted at the top of my lungs.

All laughter and conversation ceased.

"Yo, Win," I said quietly. "Go fuck yourself."

I walked out. But as I did, I heard them start to laugh again—nervously, at first, and then one of the men made some crack I couldn't hear, and they all laughed loudly.

"What happened then?" Jo Robinson prompted.

But I was frozen, watching a man walk across the parking lot.

It's him.

Panic replaced the blood in my veins, pumped through me, tensed every muscle in my body.

He's found out that I'm here alone. When I leave here, he'll . . .

In the next moment, I saw it wasn't him.

Just like every other time, it wasn't him.

"Irene?" Jo Robinson's voice, breaking through to me. Had she noticed?

"I was near Stuart Angert's desk," I said, forcing my mind back to the events of that day. "I seemed to go into this—this altered state. I heard this rushing in my ears, and then, after that, nothing. It was almost like being underwater, without the water—no sound, not even the sound of my own thoughts. I didn't see anyone, feel anything.

"But I saw Stuart's computer monitor, and I pulled the connections out of the back of it. Lydia tells me Stuart asked me what I was doing, but I didn't hear, didn't notice him. I pulled it off his desk with both hands—it's a big monitor, but I didn't notice its weight, either. I hurled it through one of the glass windows of the God office. I heard the glass breaking—that was the first thing I heard."

"And after that?"

"They stopped laughing."

She waited, and when I turned back to the window, she said,

"Do you remember what happened after they stopped laughing?"

"I was forced to take a leave of absence and told I couldn't come back until I had sought counseling."

"I meant, immediately after you broke the glass panel."

I frowned, then said, "Not really. There was a lot of shouting and—I'm embarrassed to admit this, because I should have been making a speech or something at that point, you know, a grand exit—but instead, I sort of fainted."

"Sort of fainted?"

I came back to one of the chairs near her, and sat down in it. I looked down at my hands, clasped in front of me. "I didn't really pass out, but all of a sudden I couldn't stand up, and the next thing I knew, Stuart and—I don't really remember, but a lot of people were around me, shielding me from Wrigley and his friends, or so it seemed to me, and Wrigley and one of the women were yelling and John was yelling back and Lydia and Mark and Stuart—Stuart, of all people! He never yells at anyone. Stuart was yelling. And the woman was saying, 'I want her fired!' as if she were anybody at the paper. It was close to a damned riot."

She poured me a glass of water.

"Thanks," I said, accepting it. "I still can't . . ."

"Can't what?"

"I often feel thirsty," I muttered, and drank before she could ask anything more.

"Pretty crazy, huh?" I said. She refilled the water for me.

"Being thirsty?"

"No, you know, smashing things at work. Launching expensive electronic equipment through glass walls in rooms where people are seated."

"Do you think you're crazy?"

"No—yes—I don't know."

"A, B, C, or all of the above?" she asked.

"I feel," I said, my voice shaking, "out of control. It scares me."

She waited a moment before asking, "Aside from this incident at work, what's making you conclude that you're out of control?"

"I don't know. I guess it's that . . . I can't concentrate. I don't sleep much. Maybe that's what causes the lack of concentration."

"Did you have trouble concentrating before you went to the mountains?"

"Not really."

"Trouble sleeping?"

I hesitated. "Sometimes. Not often."

She waited.

"When I'm under a lot of stress, I sometimes have nightmares." In a few words, I told her about my time of being held captive in a small, dark room in a cabin, of the fear and injuries I suffered there, of the occasional bouts with nightmares and claustrophobia I have suffered since. Only a few people know the details of that time. I don't usually talk about it very freely, but I found myself thinking that maybe if I could interest her in that, she would not ask about more recent events.

She asked a few questions about my life in general. Again, I considered this safer ground, and was fairly relaxed, even when describing situations that had been traumatic at the time they occurred.

"You've been through a lot lately," she said.

I shrugged. "Other people have been through worse."

"But you survived. All of that, and what happened in May in the—"

"I don't want to talk about the mountains," I said quickly. "I'm tired of talking about what happened there."

"Okay," she said. "I won't ask you to talk about those events just now."

I felt a vast sense of relief.

"In the time since you've been back in Las Piernas, and except for Ben, have you spoken to any of the other people who were in the group?"

"I thought you weren't going to ask—"

"Since you've been back," she said calmly.

"They died," I said, unable to keep the edginess out of my voice. "All except Ben and Bingle."

"Everyone?"

"Yes. Unless you mean—the original group that hiked in?"

"That's who I mean."

"J.C. came by to see Ben several times. And so did Andy."

"To see Ben," she repeated. "Did you talk to them?"

I lifted a shoulder. "They were there to cheer him up."

"So . . . ?"

"So I didn't talk to them."

After a moment, she said, "There were two others, weren't there?"

I thought, then said, "There was a cop, Houghton. He was Thompson's assistant, you might say. Frank told me he resigned on May nineteenth."

"The day you returned from the mountains. When everyone learned what had happened there."

"Yes. Maybe he felt bad about not being there. But it wasn't his fault."

"Maybe. Or he might have felt lucky," she said. "Sometimes, in battle, for example, a soldier will see the man next to him die, and feel lucky that it wasn't him. But even though that's a natural reaction, later, he might feel bad about having felt it."

I didn't say anything.

"Let's see," she said, "there was one more, person up there, right? The lawyer."

"You mean, Phil Newly?"

"Yes."

"Yes. Disappeared for a while."

"Why do you think he disappeared?" she asked.

"He said his sister was taking care of him while he recovered from his injuries. Parrish broke Phil's foot."

"So, there are four other people who went up into the mountains with you, but you haven't talked to any of them since then?"

"Right." I thought for a moment and said, "You think they might be having a hard time, too?"

"Do you?"

I hesitated only slightly before saying, "Yes."

"How could you find out?"

"Talk to them."

"Let's make that your first homework assignment."

"Homework!"

"Did you think therapy was going to be easy?" She laughed.

"No," I answered honestly.

"Just those four people. A phone call, a visit—just contact them. Okay? Now, let's talk about sleep and nutrition . . ."

39

▲ ▼ ▲ ▼

MONDAY AFTERNOON, SEPTEMBER 11

Las Piernas

Parrish was humming to himself as he worked. Being in a garage workshop was not quite as wonderful as having his own hangar to himself. The neighbors were a little closer, more caution was required.

But it was just so darned great to have his hands on some real tools again! He revved up the circular saw and listened to the high-pitched sound of the motor, smiled at how little resistance it met until it got to the bone.

He wondered if Ben Sheridan had been in the hands of so fine a surgeon—he doubted it was possible—and began to sing "Dem Bones." There was a little burning smell as the saw did its work. He took a deep breath, and sang another chorus. When the saw zinged to a finish, he was at one of the "connected to" phrases. He stopped singing and smiled.

"Not anymore!" he said aloud, and had to put the saw down until he could stop laughing.

He methodically continued his work, but was disturbed to note that he was subject to a certain degree of distraction. He kept thinking about Ben Sheridan.

Ben Sheridan had tricked him!

No, no, such a thing wasn't really possible. A trick implied cunning, and Sheridan had been acting in a ridiculously sentimental fashion when he charged into that meadow.

By pure luck, the man had escaped being killed by the bullet—little higher, Parrish thought, touching the bone he was working on—a shot in the femur, through the femoral artery and—glub, glub, glub—in no time at all, the man would have bled to death. Actually, he thought, if he had hit an artery, maybe it would have sprayed blood all over the place. The image was exciting to him, and he stayed with it for a moment, savoring it, pleasantly surprised by it.

He was constantly evolving, he knew, into a more perfect, higher being. He must embrace these changes in himself.

After all, Sheridan was on his mind almost as much as Irene. He had even thought of using the knife on him! His knife, which had never been used on male flesh.

Except for one of his early kills—the childhood bully Merrick had caused him to remember—he didn't bother much with killing males. They were obstacles: accidental witnesses and the like. For men, he used guns. He shot them, got it over with. But maybe he was missing out on something.

He smiled, doing a little detail work around the knee joint of bone, thinking of the pain Ben Sheridan must have suffered. Did he scream, he wondered? Did he cry? Perhaps he would cause Ben Sheridan to weep, and lick the tears from his face.

He felt an impulse to even the man out, to take part of the other leg. Sheridan was so asymmetrical now. It was displeasing to him to see such a thing; it disturbed his sense of orderliness.

"I'm a sawbones, after all!" he said aloud, and snorted with laughter.

He made plans. She was a tricky one, this Irene. She was no longer working. Did his little engraved announcement—oh, that was a good one!—of his arrival in town frighten her away? Had she quit or had she been fired?

When he had called to see if she had received his other little message to her, he was transferred to her voice mail. But a recording said the voice mailbox was full, and the imbecile at the switchboard claimed she didn't know when Ms. Kelly would be in. He considered and rejected killing the switchboard operator. He hardly had time to kill every ignorant nobody on this earth, now did he?

He must concentrate on more important matters. He went back to making plans for Irene Kelly.

But while making these plans produced rather lovely sensations, thinking of her brought him to an entirely different state, made him taut with desire. He was a patient man, but he knew that he would not deny himself much longer.

He finished working on the bone, and laid it gently aside. The bone scent was so stimulating!

He must bring himself under control—there was a great deal of work to be done.

He bent to pick up the other leg, and put it on the workbench. As he did so, he said in a little puppet voice, "Hey, pal, thanks for the leg up," and enjoyed a good bit of amusement over that. Unable to resist another moment of fun, he held it as if it were a rattle and said, "Shake a leg!"

He recovered his composure and went back to work, fastening the leg between two vises.

For short while, he distracted himself with thoughts of the Moth. The Moth was hiding something from him. Did the little fool think he didn't see that? He was beginning to tire of the Moth. One or two more tasks to fulfill.

He turned the saw on again. This workshop wasn't nearly as large as the one he would be moving into. Neither one was as big as his hangar, but he supposed it would be quite some time before he would be able to work on airplanes again.

The sacrifices he was willing to make were phenomenal.

He thought of all of the unworthy hands that were now disturbing the remains from the meadows. That this defilement should be the price of his fame angered him.

And close to anger was passion.

The little bone-burning smell came to him.

He was almost there . . . almost, almost there.

Simply volatile.

40

▲▼▲▼

TUESDAY AFTERNOON, SEPTEMBER 12

Las Piernas

Standing outside Phil Newly's door, I seriously considered bailing on my assignment from Jo Robinson.

Some perverse impulse made me decide to tackle the toughest visit first. I had already had some contact with Andy and J.C., but I had avoided Phil Newly. I hadn't had much contact with Houghton before he left the group, and because he no longer worked for the LPPD, it was going to take me a while to track him down. But I didn't have any ambivalent feelings about Houghton. My feelings about Newly were mixed.

He had been associated with Parrish, in a role that made him Parrish's champion. At the same time, Phil had made it clear that he didn't like Parrish personally. After all, Parrish had attacked him.

Although I wasn't proud of myself for thinking it, it had crossed my mind more than once that Phil Newly was fortunate to have his foot broken; a painful injury, but unlike Ben, he still had two feet. Because of that broken foot, he hadn't faced the same terrors; he had escaped before the worst of the journey began. He hadn't even seen the coyote tree. Afterward, he had cleverly dodged all efforts of the media to interview him; once it was clear to everyone that he had not been present at the excavation of either of the graves, there was little interest in him.

The police didn't seem to suspect him in the break-ins at David's house and Ben's office. They said his alibi had checked out. Still, while his sister backed up his claim that he had never left her San Francisco home during the day of the break-ins, a devoted sister might say anything to protect her brother.

But I couldn't think of anything he might have wanted at the house or university, let alone any reason for him to risk a lucrative law career to become a burglar. In fact, although I didn't know Phil well, I had never had any reason to believe he was dishonest.

I also felt grateful to him—Frank had told me about the ways in which Phil cooperated with him while I was in the mountains; he contended that without Phil's help, it would have taken him much longer to find me.

My mixed feelings stayed mixed.

I rang the doorbell.

I could hear someone approaching on the other side of the door, then there was silence.

I had called his office; I reached a recording that said the offices were closed and that he was not accepting any new clients. A little checking around led to the discovery that he had referred all of his current cases to other lawyers, and had told those attorneys that he was retiring from the practice of law.

It was already old news that a judge, considering the injury done to Newly by his client, had released him from the burden of defending Nick Parrish; a new attorney would be assigned if and when Mr. Parrish was ever back in custody. But no one had expected that Newly would end his lucrative law practice so suddenly and completely.

I didn't have Newly's home phone number, but Frank had dropped him off at this address.

Just as I was wondering if I'd get credit from Jo Robinson if Phil refused to see me, he opened the door.

"Irene," he said, "what a pleasant surprise."

It must have been etiquette lessons instilled from childhood that made him use the word "pleasant." He looked distinctly unhappy to see me. He peered nervously out at the street, and beckoned me in. I found myself almost reluctant to cross his threshold, but stepped inside.

Perhaps he noticed my reticence, because he put a determined smile on his face and said, "Come in, come in. I've thought so often of you. Is that your van out front? Frank picked me up at the hospital in a Volvo. And you used to drive—don't tell me, now—yes! A Karmann Ghia."

"Right, but the Karmann Ghia is no more," I said. "The van belongs to my cousin. He's letting me borrow it while he's out of town. I'm still in the process of shopping for a car of my own."

As soon as I said it, I realized that I had lied. I should have been looking for another car, but like a number of other things in my life, car shopping had been put off for another time.

Newly's house was spacious. If I had lived alone in it, as he did, I might have felt a little overwhelmed by its size. But as we ventured farther into it, I began to have the impression that he didn't spend much time in most of the rooms. There were no footprints on most of the carefully vacuumed carpets.

He took me to what was obviously his favorite room; a combination den and library. A few bookshelves stood along the walls, as did a stereo and a big-screen television. Across from the TV, two overstuffed chairs were positioned near a low table. Most of the books in the room were paperbacks, although one section held a lot of hardcover books. Popular fiction, for the most part. Not a weighty law tome in sight.

"Have a seat," he said, indicating one of the big chairs. "Can I get you something to drink?"

"Thanks. A glass of water would be great," I said.

"Water? Nothing stronger?"

It was two in the afternoon, but it could have been last call, and I would have answered as I did. "Just water, thanks."

He left the room to get it, and I began to look at the objects on the low table. They included his GPS receiver, a fancy mechanical pencil, a ruler, some loose papers on which some numbers had been scribbled, a handheld calculator, and beneath several small piles of books, a topo map.

When I realized what type of map it was, I looked away

from it, then, angry with myself, forced myself to pick up one of the stacks of books and read the map's legend.

Southern Sierra. The section where we had looked for Julia Sayre's grave.

I heard Phil returning, and set the books back down. It was then that I noticed the title of the hardcover on the bottom of the stack: *Mindhunter*, by John Douglas. I had heard of this book, a nonfiction work about serial killers, written by an FBI criminal profiler. There were other books in the stack by Douglas and several by Robert Ressler, another pioneering FBI profiler—if I remembered correctly, Ressler was said to have coined the term "serial killer."

I only had time to glance at the titles of the other books stacked on the table, but that was enough to see that they all had two things in common: they were true-crime stories, and their subject was serial killers.

"I find myself caught up in a strange fascination these days," Phil said, handing me a tall tumbler of ice water, then twisting open a bottle of beer as he sat in the other chair.

"Oh?"

"You're a reporter, Irene," he chided. "If you haven't taken a look at everything on this table, I'll be disappointed in you."

"Not a really good look," I said. "And technically speaking, I'm not sure I'm a reporter at the moment."

"What do you mean? Aren't you here to interview me about my most infamous client?"

"No." I explained what had happened at work.

To my surprise, he laughed and said, "If only you had aimed more carefully at your boss! But nevertheless—oh, that's great!"

"Not really." I explained that the consequences were that I was forced to take a leave of absence and seek counseling.

"Hmm. I know that at times labor law and criminal law might seem to be natural extensions of one another, but I really can't help you—"

"I'm not here to see you as a lawyer, Phil. I understand that you're closing your practice, anyway."

"That's right," he said, then took a long pull from the beer bottle.

"A little young for retirement, aren't you?"

"I've made the money I need to make. I'll probably sell this place, go to live near my sister, up north. She invited me to come up there after I broke my foot, and while I was there, I had a little time to think. As much as I love the law, I believe I'm through associating my name with those of people like Nicky Parrish."

"Nicky?"

He smiled. "The diminutive helps me to see him on a proper scale."

"I've had trouble with that lately, too. I have to tell myself that he's not invincible."

This gradually led to a discussion about our lives since that journey to the mountains; I was surprised to learn that Phil felt that his life had gone out of control since then, too. "It's the guilt," he said. "It eats at me."

"Guilt? What do you have to feel guilty about?"

"I allowed him to talk me into pursuing that deal with the D.A.! If I had taken charge of the case as I should have done, as I would have done with anyone else—"

"He would have fired you," I said.

"That's what I tell myself, but instead look what happened! When I think of those men—when I think of their families, and you—and Ben Sheridan! My God, Ben!"

"Ben's doing very well," I said.

"I heard through the grapevine that he's staying with you and Frank."

"He was. But now he's in his own place and back at work."

"Already? He's made remarkable progress, then!"

I gave him the sunny version of Ben's recovery. By unspoken agreement, that was the one that Ben, Frank, Jack, and I gave out to other people. It was so obviously the one Ben wanted other people to believe.

I understood that attitude; Ben was not big on thinking of himself as a victim. "Please leave all pity shipments unopened and mark them, 'Return to Sender,' " he once told me.

"So he's already up and walking?" Phil Newly asked me now.

"From the day after the surgery, they had him standing. As

soon as he had healed enough from the surgery to do so, he worked on learning to walk again. It hasn't always been easy, and there have been problems here and there, but for the most part, he's been making steady progress. Lately, he's been justifiably pleased with himself. And he has this remarkable new foot. It's a Flex-Foot Re-Flex VSP."

"A what?"

"A Flex-Foot. It's his prosthesis. Designed by an amputee. Ben loves it. He's managed to get around much better since he got it. It's this high-tech foot that's made from a carbon fiber composite—same stuff that's used on jets, so it's lightweight, but strong." I picked up his mechanical pencil and made a rough sketch on a scrap of paper.

"It looks a little like—well, a piece from a charcoal-colored ski," I said. "Flat and narrow like a ski, but much shorter—the length of a foot and part of a shin, in sort of a curved L-shape . . ." I looked up from my artwork and saw that I was losing him. "Sorry, Phil—I've become more interested in all of this lately."

"I can understand why. So Ben is living alone now?"

"Yes, David left his house to Ben. I'm a little frightened for him, I have to admit. Not because of the injury—Ben will swear to you that he's in better shape now than he was before the amputation—but because there was a break-in there a few months ago."

The color drained from Phil Newly's face.

41

▲ ▼ ▲ ▼

TUESDAY AFTERNOON, SEPTEMBER 12

Las Piernas

"Are you all right?" I asked.

"Sorry," he said, shuddering. "I seem to always let myself think the worst these days. Undoubtedly someone read in the paper that David had died and decided to take advantage of that. It's a sad commentary on life in these times, but it happens."

"Phil—don't give me the 'life in these times' bit. I can't take it from someone in your line of work."

He smiled, then said, "I understand you've made use of a defense attorney or two in your day."

I laughed. "Yes, it's true what they say. You stop making lawyer jokes the moment you're taken into custody."

"Was anything stolen at David's house?"

"No. Although now that you mention it, the break-ins occurred not too long after David's name appeared in the first stories about—about Parrish's escape."

"Break-ins? Plural?"

"They hit Ben's office, too."

"Hmmm. How about the other homes? Anyone else have similar trouble?"

"No, not that I know of, but—I haven't contacted their families, so I don't know."

"The families!" he said. "They must hate me."

"I hope any hatred they feel is centered on Nick Parrish," I said.

He fell into a brooding silence, then said, "He's my obsession, you know."

"Parrish?"

"Yes. That's why I have all of these books. It's not healthy, I know, but I keep trying to understand, to see if there was something I should have spotted early on, if there had been some warning that things would end as they did, something I failed to recognize."

I tried to tell him it was useless to blame himself, but soon realized that I wasn't going to be able to talk him out of this way of thinking.

"Here—" he said at one point, pulling the topo map out, heedlessly spilling the stacks of books. "Look—I can't even figure out where—where it happened."

Again I forced myself to look at his map. I hadn't even studied the one I had used in the mountains. This one encompassed a larger area than mine, and so the scale was smaller. It gave a greater overview of the area, but in less detail.

Newly had marked the clearing where his foot had been broken. "That's the last place I recorded on my GPS unit," he said, pointing. He moved his finger a short distance to another mark. "Here's where the landing strip was." He moved it once more, to a symbol some distance from the other two. "And this is J.C.'s ranger station."

It was odd to me, looking at the map now. Despite my initial misgivings, it was simply the earth's fingerprint, whorls and contour lines and colors, shapes that—once you got the hang of reading topo maps—transformed themselves into a landscape of ridges and valleys, cliffs and slopes, lakes and rivers.

A view so far above the burial ground could not harm me or upset me much. I had not seen the area from this perspective. "It happened in this section—here," I said, using the pencil to point out the ridge between the two meadows. "The coyote tree was on this ridge." I moved the pencil a slight distance. "Julia

Sayre was buried in a meadow on this side of it. You can't really see the detail of the meadow on this map. The other side of the ridge is where he set his trap."

Places. Just places, I told myself.

Phil Newly was staring at the map in silence.

"How many other bodies did they find there?" he asked at last.

"You mean—"

"Not members of our group, but buried. Women Parrish had buried there."

"In the one meadow, including the one he booby-trapped, ten. The others were all much farther down the meadow from the ridge. And Julia Sayre was the only woman buried in the other meadow."

"The only one?" he asked.

"Yes. She was apparently special to him in some way. I've heard that he was more . . . that the things he did to her were more . . ."

As I sought for a phrase, he said, "I think I know what you mean."

"Yes. Although there are signs in the victims in the other meadow that he was progressing—if you can call it progress—toward more and more sadistic treatment of his victims."

"None of the others had explosives rigged to them?"

It was more difficult for me to recite facts when the word "explosives" came into play, but I managed it. "No. The new search teams proceeded very carefully all the same. They had bomb squad experts check out each potential site. It took a lot of extra time, but no other explosives were found."

"Did search dogs find these other bodies?"

"Some of them. They were using lots of different methods by then—aerial photography, ground penetrating radar, you name it. Bingle had shown strong interest in that meadow, but the rigged grave was the first one he came to."

"Why?"

"I think Ben found the answer to that. The question bothered him, too. So he studied the plastic that had been wrapped around Julia Sayre's body, and some of the remaining fragments of plastic from the second body—"

"Nina Poolman?"

"Yes, both identifications were confirmed later."

"So what was of interest to Ben?"

"There were two different types of holes in the plastic. Some of the punctures had been made by the probes the anthropologists used, but the others were made by some other object. The diameters and other characteristics of the punctures were different."

"I don't understand," he said.

"We think he planned to be caught."

"Sooner or later, I suppose—"

"No, I mean *planned*. He allowed himself to be caught so that the world would know what a genius he is. At some point before he killed Kara Lane, he must have gone up into the mountains and punctured holes in those plastic coverings, which led to further decay of the bodies. The bodies would have been protected by the plastic until then."

"And the decay gave off scent through these holes."

"Right. So those were the graves that were easiest for Bingle to find."

"My God. These other women—do the police know who they were?"

"He buried most of them with some form of identification—usually a driver's license—but it will take a while to verify that they are indeed those women. They've ordered dental records and so on."

"They can't just tell—"

"No," I said quickly, shutting out the image of Julia Sayre's body.

"I'm sorry," Phil said. "I didn't mean to upset you."

"I'm okay," I said, then added, "Ben told me that driver's licenses are notoriously inaccurate sources of identification information in any case—men often report themselves to be taller than they really are when they apply for a license, women report themselves to be shorter and thinner. And sometimes hair color or weight changes after the license is issued."

"But if the identifications match?"

"I don't have information on all of the women. A lot of other law enforcement agencies have become involved in this since we went up there, and so it's not just a matter of going to the paper's usual sources for information. But one of our reporters learned that nine of the women had criminal records—for prostitution."

"And prostitutes are always the easiest prey for a man like Parrish," he said grimly. "Did these women all come from Las Piernas?"

"Most, but not all. They're from a number of cities in Southern California, but all of the cities have one thing in common."

"An airport?"

I nodded. "Apparently Parrish had been using the meadow for years. There are a lot of questions that will only be answered after all of the forensic specialists have had a chance to do their work."

"Eleven. Eleven women!"

"The police think there's a twelfth one somewhere nearby, because there were a dozen coyotes on the tree. I think it might have been for Kara Lane."

"The woman whose murder led to his capture? The one whose body was found near the airport. Yes, I suppose so."

"Just a theory."

"And now he has killed a woman here, and these two women in Oregon!" he said.

"Yes. The nurse and the receptionist."

"Did they ever find . . . ?"

"The receptionist's legs? No."

After a long silence, he said, "He's just getting started, isn't he?"

"Maybe."

He seemed more depressed than when I first arrived. I couldn't bring myself to leave him in that frame of mind.

"Frank asked me to thank you for helping him to find me. You have my thanks, too, Phil. You took a risk doing that, and for no other reason than kindness."

He looked at me with an expression so haunted, I reached out and put a hand on his shoulder.

"Do you really think of me that way—as someone who helped you?" he asked.

"Yes, I'm grateful to you. Not just for helping me to get out of there—you also probably saved Ben's life. If he had spent many more hours up in those mountains without medical attention, the infection could have killed him. And the arrival of the helicopter probably frightened Parrish off before he had time to hunt me down in the forest. If you hadn't helped Frank, he wouldn't have found us so quickly."

He looked back down at the map and said, "Thank you. I don't know that I did so much, really—Frank and his friends made the real difference. He was so anxious about you that day, so determined to find you, that he risked trouble with his department by coming to see me. It would have been inhumane not to help in some small way."

We talked a little more, but I still felt worried about him, so as I was leaving, I asked for his phone number. "I'd like to stay in touch, if you don't mind," I said. "Frank will want to talk to you, too."

"I'd like to talk to him again. Especially now that we won't be opponents in court."

He wrote out the number and handed it to me. "Thanks for coming by, Irene."

"I should have done it months ago," I said. "It was . . . helpful to me to see you today."

"For me, too," he said. "Come by anytime." He smiled and added, "I'm no longer such an expensive person to talk to—no billable hours."

Outside his house, as I was getting into the van, I saw a green Honda Accord drive off. I could have sworn that Nick Parrish was driving it. I took a deep breath, started the van, and pulled away from the curb.

When I got home, for the first time since I had returned from the mountains, I took out my larger-scale topo map. Even though the features of the terrain were shown in finer detail than on Newly's map, I wasn't as upset by this view of the area as I had thought I would be. It made me a little nervous to see where I had marked off the cave, the coyote tree, the graves. But again, it was from a distance.

Considering distance, I realized I couldn't see the ranger station on my map. I felt a knot tightening in my stomach. Distance. How did Parrish cover that distance?

It was a question I normally would have asked myself months ago, I realized. But for the last few months I had made a conscious effort to avoid all thought, all reference to what had happened during the week of May fourteenth. I helped Ben, I worked long hours, and exercised three large dogs. I did my best to end the day too exhausted to worry or dream. I tried to forget that I had ever boarded that plane.

Oh, it worked like a charm. I saw Nick Parrish leaping out at me everywhere I went. I had horrific nightmares about the meadow. I threw computers through glass walls.

And I didn't ask questions I should have asked.

So I called Ben Sheridan. When I got him on the line, I asked him for J.C.'s phone number.

"I'll give it to you," he said, "but J.C.'s right here."

"Can I talk to him?"

"Sure."

I exchanged greetings with J.C., then asked, "How long did it take you to get to the meadow from the ranger station?"

"Driving?"

"You could drive the whole distance?"

"No. I took a dirt road—a mud road, at that point—part of the way, and hiked the rest. Let's see, I left about an hour after dawn and got to the meadow in the early afternoon. It was foggy when I left; I drove as fast as I dared under those conditions, which was not all that fast." He paused, then said, "I wasn't really thinking very clearly that morning, Irene, so it's hard for me to judge time. It seemed like forever. Once I reached the end of the road, I think I hiked for about four hours, but again, I'm not sure. Why do you ask?"

"I've just started wondering about a few things. You and Ben have dinner plans?"

"Not yet."

"If Ben can stand our company again, why don't you come over for dinner? I have a theory to talk over with you. Tell Ben to bring Bingle, too."

They agreed to come over at seven. I called Frank.

"Hi," he said. "Must be ESP. I just talked to a friend of yours. Gillian Sayre called."

A wave of guilt hit me. I hadn't contacted her since the day she came by the *Express*, asking about her mother's remains. "Gillian? Why were you talking to her?"

"She was trying to reach you at the paper, but I guess your voice mailbox is full and the *Express* isn't telling anyone anything about your leave of absence. She even waited outside the building for you, but when she didn't see you for a couple of days, she decided to give me a call."

"Oh."

"I told her you were just taking a much-needed vacation."

"Thanks, Frank. I know I should have called her before now, but . . ."

"She wasn't calling to nag you. She saw the articles about the Jane Doe in the trash bin and was worried about you. And she said she never had a chance to thank you for talking to her on the day after you got back."

"I'll call her," I said again. "I haven't even tried to get in touch with her or Giles since those first days back."

Frank knows me too well not to have heard my reluctance. "Take it easy on yourself," he said. "You've had a lot to cope with. This might not be the best time to talk to the Sayres."

"Maybe you're right. I just don't know. I don't want to cower."

He laughed. "Like you cowered before Wrigley?"

"Look what that got me."

"Yeah—a few days off for yourself, instead of running your ass ragged for the paper. Wrigley's had the work of three reporters out of you lately, and he knows it. By the way—how'd things go with Newly today?"

"Fine," I said, "which reminds me why I called." I warned him that I had destroyed his chances of a peaceful evening at home.

"I get the sense that this is a meeting, not a dinner. What's on the agenda?"

"I think someone helped Parrish, Frank. I'm almost sure of it."

"So are we. He couldn't have managed to get out of that area unless someone gave him a ride. Idiotic thing for the driver to do, but that was undoubtedly before Parrish's name and description were all over the news."

"No, I don't mean that a stranger gave him a lift. Why would he plan everything else out and leave something like that to chance?"

There was a silence, then he said, "I'm sure they've considered that."

"I know you aren't allowed to work on any cases that have even the vaguest connection to me—"

"Which is every case in those two meadows," he said.

"Yes, but you talk to the other guys, right? The ones who are working on them?"

"As much as possible. To be honest, our resources are strained at the moment. All of Bob Thompson's cases had to be picked up by other people; since I can't work on the mountain cases that are connected to Las Piernas—and those are plentiful—guess who gets most of Thompson's other cases?"

"You."

"We're all running around ass-deep in alligators, as Tom Cassidy might say, and I don't hear as much about the Parrish cases as I'd like to. But let's talk about your theories tonight—if I can't get anyone to buy them, Ben might be able to—he's consulting on some of them."

So I was able to talk to Frank, Ben, and J.C. that night, which is why I had my husband and two friends with me when I received a gift from my not-so-secret admirer.

42

▲ ▼ ▲ ▼

TUESDAY, LATE AFTERNOON, SEPTEMBER 12

Las Piernas

In preparation for the evening's gathering, I drove downtown to a map store. I purchased several topo maps of the area Parrish had used as a burial ground. Coming out of the store, just as I reached the van, I saw the green Honda again. It was speeding away.

I don't know what made me feel so sure that it was the same car I had seen outside Phil Newly's house. I couldn't make out the license plate or clearly see the driver, but as the car turned left onto Elm, a one-way street clogged with traffic, I decided to settle the matter by following him.

I might have lost him already, of course. He could have turned down an alley and doubled back, or reached another intersection and turned, or pulled into a garage and parked.

I had to know. I had to at least try to find that car.

As I drove, I became convinced that I could smell bones; that the scent of bones was somewhere in the van, that if I looked in the rearview mirror I would see skeletons stacked like cordwood behind me, drying marrow their last perfume.

I watched the road, but I broke out in a cold sweat.

Find the Honda. Don't think about . . . but I smelled bones.

Stop the van. Call Jo Robinson. Tell her to reserve a room with rubber walls for you.

How could there be bones in the van? I asked myself, gripping the wheel. There couldn't be, could there?

It was possible, an inner voice argued.

I might not have locked the van; in fact, the more I thought about it, the more certain I became that I had not locked the van when I bought the maps, that Parrish had been inside it, that he had put the bones of some of his victims in the van.

Up ahead, I saw a flash of dark green and drove faster.

Bones.

I felt ill. I rolled down all the windows. There was not enough air.

I forced myself to look in the rearview mirror.

I saw the camper fixtures—cabinets, the small sink, stove and refrigerator, a fold-up table and seats that could be made into beds. I stared and stared, but there were no bones.

It was a huge relief and no relief at all.

I looked back at the road just as an old man with a hat on pulled his Dodge Dart out into my lane without looking; I swerved and narrowly missed him. He had the nerve to honk at me.

What the hell did I think I was doing? Even if it was Parrish in the Honda, what was I going to do? I wasn't armed.

I'll see if it's him. If it is, I'll get the license plate number.

Fine.

There! In the far left lane, stopped at a light and two cars back from the intersection, a dark green Honda Accord waited. I couldn't see the driver. The light turned green, but I was delayed by a driver trying to turn left. The Honda was getting away!

Finally the car turned and I sped to the next intersection. I put the van in park, opened the door, and stood on the door frame, trying to get a look at the green Honda's driver. A man—a man who could be Parrish. I couldn't see the Honda's plates.

The driver of the car behind me honked and flipped me the bird. The light had changed. More horns honked. I got back inside the van and moved forward, signaling a lane change, trying to get over to the left lane, desperate to keep track of the Honda.

But the driver in the lane next to mine was the fellow who had given me the finger. Still angry at me, he refused to let me pass. Red-faced, he shook his fist at me, and promptly rear-ended the car in front of him, which then came into my lane. I slammed on the brakes.

I was boxed in.

Through my open windows, I heard the red-faced finger flipper shouting that it was my fault. When I looked for the Honda again, it was gone.

Ignoring Red Face, I asked the guy who had been rear-ended if he was okay. He was. He turned to Red Face, told him to shut the hell up, and to my surprise, was obeyed.

The story provided amusement over dinner—that is, the part of the story I told, which was very little of it, after all, and had nothing to do with Hondas or bones.

The subtle scent of bones had plagued me even after I reached home. I took a long, hot shower, and my thoughts returned again and again to the events of the afternoon.

There could be bones in one of the cabinets inside the van. There were many little cubbyholes and crannies to search, I thought.

But what if I searched and there weren't any bones?

If you're scared and there's nothing to be scared of and you prove to yourself that there's nothing to be scared of and you're *still* scared . . . Added to vanishing Hondas and false Parrishes, ghostly bone scent became too much to contemplate. If there were no bones, I really was crazy.

The longer the warm water washed over me, the more it seemed to me that a search itself would be the act of a truly crazy woman. I made a vow to ignore the scent.

So somehow I made the story of buying maps and the red-faced man and a rear-end collision funny, and if my own laughter was a little brittle, no one but Frank seemed to notice.

When I saw that Frank also noticed the trembling of my hands when I spread out the topo maps, I hoped that he ascribed it to the area shown on the maps, and not what happened when I had purchased them.

I focused on the maps. It required concentration. My mind cleared.

Beginning with the largest-scale map, we tried to find the fastest and easiest routes a man could take from the cave—where evidence of Parrish's stay had since been found—to the ranger station and Helitack unit.

There were other ways to get in and out of the ranger station without using the dirt road, but J.C. had definitely chosen the quickest method of reaching us.

"The road you took looks closer to the meadow than the airstrip," I said.

"It is, but the hike in and out is rough and steep." He showed us the route he had taken. "It would be extremely difficult to carry a body out over it, and I'm not sure every hiker in that group could have managed that trail."

"We had lots of different levels of experience," I agreed. "If he hadn't set the trap, your idea of sending a helicopter to the meadow would have been the best one."

He made a harsh, low sound, as if I had hit him.

"What's wrong?"

"Instead," he said bitterly, "my brilliant idea got David and Flash and the others killed."

"What?!" Ben and I said in unison.

He told us his version of how decisions had been made on the ridge near the coyote tree. He felt sure that everyone would have continued safely to the plane if he had not suggested using the helicopter.

Ben and I countered with our claims that other factors, and not his offer of the helicopter, had led to the decision to look for the second grave.

He seemed unconvinced, until Frank said, "By the time you were all standing on that ridge, I think Parrish had Bob Thompson's number. If not everyone else's as well."

Seeing he had our undivided attention, he went on. "I can't get over the feeling that Parrish planned even more thoroughly than we've said he did—that he anticipated the reactions of certain key people in this scenario he devised. I think he knew he could get someone to take him up there, sooner or later."

"You mean that he intentionally allowed himself to be caught?" I said. "Yes, I think everyone agrees that he left Kara Lane's body where it would be found."

"Exactly. The trap was already waiting by the time he was taken into custody. He might not have known who would be on the trip up there, but once he started spending time with all of you, he studied you, figured out how to push your buttons. I suppose I shouldn't speak ill of Bob, but it was never hard to figure out where he was coming from."

"Ambitious," Ben said.

"Right."

"J.C.," I said, "have you ever stopped to think that you saved Andy's life?"

"Saved Andy's life?" he repeated blankly.

"Yes. Parrish undoubtedly wanted all of us to be down there. I think he planned to have me survive to—to chronicle his greatness." For a moment, I couldn't say more; there was an invisible nine-hundred-pound weight on my chest. Frank reached over and took my hand; I held tightly to it. "By separating from us," I went on, "you saved two lives, J.C.—yours and Andy's. It undoubtedly upset Parrish to have you spoil any part of his perfect little plan."

J.C. was quiet, staring at the maps. After a time, he said, "I hadn't thought of it that way."

"You probably had him worried that you'd have a helicopter in there taking him back to prison before old slow-digging Ben here uncovered the body. You nearly ruined his whole setup. The rain was the only thing that allowed him to get away with it—otherwise, your helicopter would have picked us up."

"Yeah, maybe," J.C. said quietly.

"So let's look at these maps and try to see if Parrish had time to disable those helicopters," Ben said.

There was one other unpaved road that ended within a few miles of the far end of the meadow, but this road came into the forest from a different direction. J.C. would have had a much longer drive from the ranger station just to get to the road itself; from there he would have been doubling back in the same general direction he came from, and once he parked the truck, the hike from that road to the meadow would have been worse than the one he made from the other road. It would have been almost entirely uphill and over steep terrain.

"You were in the Forest Service truck," Frank said. "Parrish was on foot. It's ludicrous to think he would have hiked that longer, steeper route to and from the ranger station."

J.C., much more familiar with the area than the rest of us, said, "I agree. And I think Irene is right about his having a partner. It's not impossible that he sabotaged the helicopters alone, but think about it—he would have been hiking in a downpour, after dark. He would have been risking some really nasty falls."

"Parrish is an experienced hiker," Ben said. "But he isn't in the kind of shape you're in, J.C.—you can cover ground faster than any of us, including Andy. He'd have had to hike quite a distance overnight in the rain, disable the helicopter, hike back, and then have the energy to chop down a tree that next day."

"That reminds me," I said. "Was anyone in our group carrying an ax up there?"

"Yes," Ben said. "There was one in the camping gear the police brought."

"Oh."

"You seem disappointed," Frank said.

"I hadn't seen anyone use it," I said. "If it wasn't in our group's gear, that would argue for an accomplice—someone who brought the ax to Parrish."

"Who would help a man like Parrish?" J.C. asked.

"His lawyer," Ben said.

"His lawyer was injured," Frank said.

"Unable to drive?" Ben countered.

Frank shook his head. "No, he could walk if he needed to. But Phil had nothing to gain and everything to lose if his client escaped."

"Did Parrish call anyone while he was in custody?" I asked.

"No," Frank said. "If we're right about this, though, he didn't need to make calls. He provided the destination for the group, so his partner—or partners—would know where he was going. And the date of departure was well publicized."

"Don't serial killers usually work alone?" J.C. asked.

"Usually, but not always," Frank said. "The Hillside Strangler—Kenneth Bianchi—and his cousin, Angelo Buono, tortured and killed together. In Houston, Dean Allen Coryll killed at least twenty-seven young men with the help of two friends—they knowingly brought his victims to him."

"Killers don't have to be loners," Ben agreed. "And apparently some women are excited by the idea of being with a killer. There's even a matchmaking Web site now where women can 'meet' the prison inmate of their dreams."

"But that's different, isn't it?" I said. "A woman who marries her prison pen pal *after* he's caught isn't necessarily in the same league as someone who'd help him torture and murder his victims."

"No," Frank said, "but there are plenty of examples of couples who've worked together before capture. Paul Bernardo and Karla Homolka teamed up for torture, rape and murder—the first time, she helped him rape and kill her own sister. In Nebraska, Caril Fugate went along with her boyfriend for a monthlong killing spree that started with her parents and her two-year-old sister."

"Charles Starkweather, right?" Ben said. "They made a movie about them."

"Yes. There are others. Coleman and West, the Gallegos, the Neelleys—"

"Why do they do it?" I asked.

"The age-old question, right? Sexual obsession, greed, power—you name it. Sometimes these women are dominated by violent male partners, other times, they clearly participate willingly. It's not just women—in addition to husband-and-wife teams, there are male partnerships, groups, and families that are serial killers."

There was silence around the table, then Ben said, "We're back to the question J.C. asked. Who would help a man like Nick Parrish?"

They threw out suggestions: debating the possibility of Phil Newly again; wondering if Parrish had a contact who also had an airplane or a helicopter; arguing over whether he was more likely to have a girlfriend or a boyfriend; speculating over the likelihood of a relative who was his Angelo Buono.

While this went on, I studied the small-scale topo map.

"We don't have enough information to know who his partner is," I said, which earned me a you're-no-fun-at-all look from every single one of them. "Maybe the FBI guys can help out with their profilers. I don't know. But I think I do know where his partner met Nick Parrish that day—it was at that other road."

They focused their attention on the map.

"Yes," Frank said. "It wasn't a good route to get to the ranger station, but he wouldn't have wanted to go anywhere near there once his partner had disabled the helicopters."

"And it's a downhill hike from the meadow," J.C. said. "The airstrip would be the most convenient way out, but he probably expected that law enforcement might be using it by the time he hiked to it."

"Right," Ben said, sighing. "I wish we had come up with this sooner. The mud would have been perfect for casting any footprints or tire marks on the road and near the helicopters."

J.C. shook his head. "If they didn't take any casts at the time, they're probably gone. Summer months are the busiest for Helitack. Our helicopters are primarily used for firefighting. There have been all kinds of people around there."

They decided to call the lead investigator on the team that was coordinating the mountain cases. I went out to get some fresh air in the backyard, where Bingle was engaging in playful antics with Deke and Dunk.

Ben joined me after a while. Bingle checked in with him, then went back to the other dogs. "I think Bingle misses them," he said. "Do you want to let them run on the beach together?"

I hesitated. I knew Ben could manage in lots of environments, but he hadn't conquered walking in soft, deep sand with a prosthesis yet. His prosthetist had told him that many amputees found walking on a soft beach difficult. Ben was still working on it.

"Yes, I miss walking on the beach," he said, reading my thoughts. "I miss lots of things. But the list is getting shorter, and the items that stay on the list, well, I'll learn to live without them. But there's no reason Bingle should have to forego his pleasures because of me."

Frank stepped out as he was saying this, and hearing it, said, "Tell you what—if you don't mind a public struggle to the boardwalk, we'll get you over to it. It's not far from the stairs at the end of the street, and it runs parallel to the water until you get to the pier. You and Irene can stroll along there while J.C. and I herd these four-legged hooligans."

He thought about it for a moment, but apparently the desire to be closer to the water won out over potential embarrassment, because he agreed to the plan.

He went down the long set of stairs from the cliffs to the sand on his own. From there, the four of us put our arms across one another's shoulders, in a line, so that no one person was left out—or singled out. J.C. started singing some silly camping song that made us laugh, so most people probably thought we were well into an evening party. Between Frank and J.C., Ben was able to get to the boardwalk without a fall.

Bingle kept running back and forth between us and the other dogs, but if Deke and Dunk followed him at high speed toward Ben, he herded them away from his new handler. "He won't allow other dogs to bump into me," Ben explained. "A service I sometimes miss when he's not around. But I'm learning to keep my balance a little better these days."

"How's the Spanish coming along?"

"I'm getting better at the dog commands," he said. "The rest still needs lots of work."

"Why did David train Bingle in Spanish?"

"Two reasons. Bingle was originally owned by an old man who spoke only Spanish, and David had learned Spanish after we did some earthquake recovery work in South America. We'd been frustrated by the language barrier, and he thought it would be useful to be able to speak it for cases here in Southern California, too. Anyway, this old man loved the dog, but he was having trouble keeping up with Bingle. He told David that 'Bocazo'—that was his name for Bingle—deserved someone who was more energetic for a partner."

"*Bocazo?*" I laughed. "That's Spanish for 'big mouth.' "

Ben smiled. "He established his rep early on, I guess."

"So what was the second reason?"

"It wasn't something people expected. I mean, here's this Anglo college professor speaking Spanish. When he was doing search and rescue work or cadaver searches, it often won them over. They would be in these horrible situations—waiting for him to search a building that had collapsed in an earthquake in South America, for example—and even though Spanish has many dialects, they understood what he was saying to the dog, and so it took one level of anxiousness away. The two of them made great ambassadors for the rest of us."

"It certainly helped that Parrish didn't know Spanish."

"Why?"

I realized that I had never told him what happened after I left him to cross the stream.

When I first came home from the mountains, I had told Frank everything that had happened there, but no one else, and I had steadfastly avoided the subject since. Now I wondered if Frank, who had often urged me to talk things over with Ben, had gone ahead with the dogs and J.C., hoping I would do exactly that.

So make the effort, I told myself. It's the perfect time to talk it out.

"Parrish didn't understand Spanish, so when I told Bingle to go to you, to guard you, Parrish thought I was just commanding him to go away."

A single sentence. I felt as if I couldn't breathe.

"I don't understand," Ben said, stopping and staring at me. "Your story in the paper—you didn't mention being so close to him again. You made it sound as if he tripped over that trap you made for him and ran off wounded. That you ran and hid after that, and just waited for the rescue."

Panic struck. In my mind, Parrish was holding my face down in the mud; for a few seconds, it might as well have been happening again.

"Irene!" Ben said sharply. "Irene, what is it?"

"Another time, okay?" I said. I realized I had tears on my face, although I couldn't remember when I had started crying.

There had been this easiness with tears between us for some time now. Frank and Jack and I had been allowed to see his. I don't think many other people did.

When he had stayed with us, lots of people got to see "how brave Ben is"—although he absolutely despised any comments of this sort. Ben showed the world a determined face. It wasn't an act—it just wasn't the whole story.

There had been a nearly constant stream of visitors at first friends from the university, colleagues who worked with him on the DMORT team and others. There was also a demanding schedule of recovery and rehab appointments, both at home and in other offices—doctors, nurses, his physical therapist, his prosthetist, Jo Robinson. There was work to be done learning how to balance and walk, to desensitize the residual limb, to strengthen Ben's upper body, and more.

Ellen Raice came by with projects and questions, sometimes bringing bones that had been brought to the lab for help with identification or other determinations. Ben seemed glad to have the work and distraction.

Sometimes Ben had been abrupt with Ellen or other visitors, who knowingly smiled at me as they left, saying, "He seems to be having a bad day." But they didn't know the meaning of a bad day with Ben.

At first, almost every day was a bad day at some point. Even Ellen didn't get to see that side of Ben. Ben tired of appointments and exercises that seemed designed to torture him. Ben in agonizing pain, taking bruising falls. The irascible, impatient Ben. Ben discouraged and grieving. Ben who wondered if women would be repulsed by him, who feared that his sex life was at an end at thirty-two, that he was doomed to a life of loneliness. Ben trying to get used to what he saw when he looked in a full-length mirror.

During that summer, whatever waking hours I could spend away from work, I spent with Ben. Frank and Jack covered the hours I couldn't. He allowed the three of us to see him at his most vulnerable, but we were also first on hand for the victories. He was one of the most blessedly stubborn people I knew, and if he had setbacks, he didn't let them stop him.

It was that stubborn determination that I saw on his face now, as I tried to regain my composure.

"I think," he said, "that I just might die happy if I can kill Nick Parrish with my bare hands before I go."

"It wouldn't be worth it," I said. "Besides, if you go, who . . ."

"Who will you have to talk to about it?" he finished.

I nodded. "I've told Frank. I've told him everything, but you—you were there."

"And yet, you haven't really talked to me, have you? Shielding the poor cripple?"

"Screw you, Ben," I said wearily. "You know that's a crock."

"Sorry. Just what you needed, right? More abuse. You're right. A crock. God, no wonder you don't talk to me—I should start a company, 'Cranky Assholes, Inc.' "

"I know the CEO's position is taken, but could I at least have a vice presidency? I'm good at throwing things. Any glass-paneled offices?"

"What are you talking about?"

"Oh," I said guiltily, "I guess I haven't filled you in on my news."

"It seems to me that there's a hell of a lot you haven't filled me in on. What is this, Irene? I move out, and you think I stop caring about you and Frank and Jack?"

"You wanted to be out on your own. Why should I burden you with—"

"Burden me! *You* burden *me!* Christ, that's a laugh."

I didn't say anything.

"Tell me what happened at work," he said.

I told him about my monitor shot put into Wrigley's office. I did so with trepidation, figuring that he was bound to start feeling a little wary about being left out on the beach with a madwoman. But that wasn't how he reacted at all.

"My God," he said, looking at me with such concern, my tears threatened again. "You've really been having a rough time of it, haven't you?"

"A little," I said.

He laughed.

"Yes, a rough time," I admitted.

"I feel like such a selfish bastard!"

"Don't," I said fiercely.

He didn't say more, but I could see that he was angry. At himself, at me—I wasn't sure who else was on the list.

By then Frank and J.C. had rejoined us. Frank took one look at me and put an arm around me. I returned the favor. Ben steadfastly ignored me, and sensing the tension between us, Frank let Ben and J.C. move ahead with the dogs.

"You okay?" he asked me.

I nodded. "Long day, that's all."

He gave a little snort of disbelief but didn't push me to unburden my soul right at that moment. I was grateful.

At the end of the boardwalk, we again helped Ben across the sand to the stairs, but this time, he seemed embarrassed. We let the dogs go up first, then J.C. and Ben. When we reached the top of the stairs, J.C. and Ben were watching Bingle, who was lifting his head, making chuffing noises. The other dogs tried to follow his lead. He looked back at Ben, ears swiveled forward, and barked.

"Jesus," Ben said, "he's alerting."

"Talk to him," I said, tightening my hold on Frank.

I was impressed. Ben flawlessly spoke a series of encouragements in Spanish. Then, giving a hand signal, he said, "*¡Búscalo!*" Bingle focused on Ben much as I had seen him focus on David, and then hurried down the street, head high and sniffing, moving in a fairly straight line.

Within a few houses of our own, Bingle started barking again. He waited for Ben, then, crooning, he veered close to the van, then passed it by and hurried toward our porch.

"Oh no," I said. "Please no."

J.C. was saying, "It looks as if someone sent you roses."

"Late in the day for a flower delivery," Frank said.

But there was indeed a long golden box with a red bow on it, waiting on the steps.

"Everybody get back," Frank said suddenly. "Ben, call the dog—!"

But Bingle had already pawed at the box, and it rolled down the steps and spilled open—ten, long-stem roses tumbled out, as did two long, dark bones.

We all stood frozen—until Frank shouted at our dogs, who

obviously thought Bingle had made a capital find and were venturing closer to see if he'd share it with them. Hearing the unexpected sharp note in Frank's voice, they immediately came to his side.

Ben called to Bingle and remembered to praise him in Spanish, then without needing to step nearer to the bones said to us, "Femurs."

"Leg bones?" I asked weakly, but I already knew the answer. I suddenly didn't feel as if I could rely on my own.

43

▲ ▼ ▲ ▼

WEDNESDAY MORNING, SEPTEMBER 13

Las Piernas

"The bones were those of the receptionist?" Jo Robinson asked during my appointment the next morning.

"It seems likely, but the bones were . . . altered. Parts of her legs are still missing, and these bones weren't even whole femurs. Someone had cut them. Ben knows someone who specializes in identifying toolmarks on bones who'll be studying them, but for now, Ben thinks it might have been a power saw. They're going to run DNA tests to be sure the bones belong to the receptionist. Those tests take a while."

"You seem quite calm about this now."

"It's an act."

She smiled.

"I guess you knew that."

She kept smiling, but said, "I'm not a mind reader. So tell me, what's your real reaction?"

"At first, fear. But now I'm just angry. No, that's not true. I'm both angry and afraid."

"What do you suppose he was trying to do?"

"To scare me. To let me know that he knows where I live, to tell me that he's around. He succeeded—I am afraid. More afraid."

I considered telling her more, but I wanted to go back to work, and I was convinced she'd never give me the release if I told her everything. If I could go back to work and stay busy, I wouldn't have so much time to dwell on memories of people in little pieces in a meadow or photographs in graves.

"I think most people would be afraid if they found leg bones in a box on their front porch," she was saying. "What are you doing in response?"

"Doing?"

"About your personal safety."

"Oh. That's the other problem. Frank has worked it out so that I'm never alone. If he can't be with me, then someone else is. Our friend Jack is in your waiting room as we speak."

"Does that seem unreasonable under the circumstances?"

"No, but I saw Parrish take out seven men in about three minutes flat, so I'm not comforted, either."

"Is that what bothers you about it?"

I didn't have to think long about that question. "No. It bothers me because it's confining."

I have to admit that she was very slick. She managed to get me to talk about my fear of confined places, and somehow that led to talking about being in a tent, which led to talking about the expedition and what had happened on it.

Jack had a long wait.

After a while, she asked, "Before you left for this journey, you were uneasy being in the mountains. You struggle with claustrophobia, yet you agreed to be part of a group that would be sleeping inside tents for several days. Detective—Thompson, was it?"

"Yes."

"Detective Thompson had been unpleasant to you on a number of other occasions, yet you decided to become a member of the expedition he was leading."

"Yes."

"Why?"

"I didn't have any say over who would lead it."

"Why did you agree to go on this journey to the mountains?"

I shrugged. "What can I say? I'm a glutton for punishment."

She waited.

"I went for work," I said testily. "It was a good opportunity for the paper."

She kept waiting.

"My hour was up a long time ago," I said, picking up my purse.

"Why did you go?" she persisted.

"Julia Sayre!" I snapped.

She didn't respond.

I set my purse down. "No, not Julia, really. Her daughter, and her husband and son. For years, they've wondered what happened to her. I was trying to help them resolve their questions about her disappearance."

"A good purpose."

"At a damned high cost."

"Yes, but you didn't set that price, did you?"

"No."

"In fact, it cost you much more than you bargained for."

I shook my head. "Other people paid much more."

"What can you do about that?"

"Nothing."

"Have you talked to any of the families of the men who went up there with you?"

"God, no." I felt myself color. "No. I feel terrible about that, but when I think of facing those people . . ."

"What will happen?"

"I don't know. They might ask—just after I came back, Gillian asked about her mother. I couldn't tell her. I can't—I can't talk about what I saw. Not to the families. Not yet."

She poured a glass of water, gave it to me. She waited for me to calm down a little.

"You talked to Gillian before her mother's body was released to the family?"

"Yes."

"But by now, the families have already been through funerals, right?"

I nodded.

"I doubt they'll have questions of that type, but if they ask," she said, "and you politely tell them that you'd rather not talk about that just now—?"

"They'll still be angry, even if the subject never comes up. They must hate me."

"Because you survived?"

"Yes. And because media attention was probably one of the reasons Parrish killed all of those men. You're looking at the only reporter that went up there."

"Did you go up there to glorify Parrish?"

"No. I suppose any attention from the media could be construed as glorifying him, but that wasn't my plan."

"So you think the families will be angry with you because he tried to use you for a purpose other than your own?"

"Yes."

"Really?"

"People aren't always reasonable. They'll see me as a reporter. Some days, I think it would be easier to tell people that I'm an IRS auditor."

"Do you have any evidence that this particular group of people—the families of the victims—will be unfair to you?"

"No," I admitted.

"Perhaps you should find out how they feel. Visit one or two of them. You have a little carving to give to Duke's grandson?"

"Yes," I said, awash with guilt over not having brought it to Duke's widow.

As I started to leave Jo Robinson's office, I said, "I want to go back to work."

"I think you will be able to do that fairly soon."

"I mean, this week."

"Soon," she said. "Try something entirely new—be patient with yourself."

She held the power to keep me from my job at the *Express* for as long as she liked. I was more than a little angry about that, and she undoubtedly read that in my face. She continued to calmly regard me.

I wondered if a woman reporter who had thrown a large object through the glass wall of her editor-in-chief's office could get a job an another paper. I wondered if I should go back to my friend and former boss at the PR firm I'd left a few years ago to ask if my old job was still open. I knew he'd hire me, but the thought of being forced to write cheerful, upbeat copy for the rest of my life truly depressed me.

Instead, I did my homework assignment.

Two days later, I completed the last of my visits to the widows and families of the officers who had died in the mountains. I was exhausted. No one had asked about remains. None of them had failed to welcome me; all had thanked me for taking the time to come by. There had been plenty of tears at each stop along the way.

Duke's widow thanked me profusely for the little wooden horse, and would hear no apology for my delay in getting it to her. It was the same with each of them—lots of remembrances, a few regrets, but no recriminations. All anger, all blame was focused on Nicholas Parrish.

The last visit had been to the parents of Flash Burden, the youngest of the men who had died in the mountains. They had gathered their son's belongings from his apartment, and today, from cardboard box after cardboard box, they showed me trophies he had won—mostly for photography, but another boxful from amateur hockey. They proudly took me into a room which served as a gallery for photographs he had taken. These included stunning shots of wildlife, but also glimpses of city life that showed him to be a keen observer with a sense of humor. Frank had told me that he had liked Flash, and had liked working with him, but thought he was wasting his skills on police work. Seeing these photographs, I had to agree, and found myself wishing that Flash had never come along with us to the mountains.

As I was thinking this, his mother said, "These weren't his favorites, of course. He was happiest if one of his photographs helped solve a crime or convict a criminal."

I regretted none of these visits, but emotionally, each was a run through a gantlet flanked by grief and remorse, by terrifying memories and lost chances. Each renewed my anger toward Parrish, but also made me aware of how much I feared him. When I said good-bye to the Burdens and walked back out to the van, I was a little unsteady on my feet, and hoped Jack wouldn't notice.

I found him cleaning out the van's refrigerator.

"The secret life of millionaires," I said.

He took one look at my face and put an arm around my shoulders.

"Sorry to make you wait out here so long," I said, when I could talk. "You must wish you hadn't agreed to do this."

"Tough assignment, huh?"

I wasn't ready to talk about it, so I changed the subject. "What possessed you to start cleaning the refrigerator?"

He wrinkled his nose. "There's some kind of weird smell in the van."

My eyes widened. "You smell it, too?"

"Not very strong, and not all the time, but yeah—something strange. I don't mind it much, but . . . hey, why are you crying?"

So I told him about smelling bones after my visit to the map store. That led to telling him about imagining that I was seeing Parrish. "Christ, I've even made up a car for him to ride around in!"

He handed me a packet of Kleenex. I used every last one of them. When I had calmed down a little, he said, "Have you told Frank?"

I shook my head. "He worries enough as it is. He doesn't need to walk around wondering if the bughouse will take Visa."

"For what it's worth, I don't think you're crazy."

I didn't reply.

"What do bones smell like?" he asked.

"Sort of a subtle, dry, sweet smell. I can only smell it if the bones are what Ben calls 'greasy.' "

"You know about it from the burials up in the mountains?"

"No. Those weren't just skeletons—there was adipocere and other tissue, and a really overpowering smell of decay. But I've visited Ben at his lab at the university on a day when they were working with bones."

"I've been smelling something that's kind of a sweet, waxy smell. Do bones smell like that?"

"Could be described that way, I guess."

"So let's search the van."

I hesitated, looking back at the Burdens' house. "Let's drive away from here to do it, okay? I don't want to upset them if we do find something."

He climbed into the driver's seat, a big grin on his face. When I took the passenger seat, I asked, "What's so funny?"

"Not funny—just pleased that I've finally convinced you that this could be a product of something other than your imagination, or you wouldn't want to move down the street."

"Don't be so sure," I warned. I looked in the mirror on the visor. The most horrifying thing in that van had to be my face—eyes swollen and nose a lá Rudolph. Still looking in the mirror, I opened the glove compartment and reached for my sunglasses.

My hand went into a pile of small objects before the smell hit me.

I screamed.

Jack slammed on the brakes.

Little bones spilled out of the glove compartment, onto my skirt, my feet, everywhere.

44

▲ ▼ ▲ ▼

WEDNESDAY EVENING, SEPTEMBER 13

Las Piernas

"The glove compartment," I said. "I should have known."

I was at home, sitting on the couch, being held by my husband. He was stroking my hair. Maybe I wouldn't go back to work, I thought. Maybe I'd just stay home and sleep and wait for Frank to come home and stroke my hair. I sighed. Not likely.

I had opened the van door and leapt out into the street, a shower of small, straight bones falling all around me. After he managed to calm my hysterics a bit, Jack had used his cellular phone to call Frank.

The van was impounded to collect the fingerprints Nick Parrish blatantly left in it, and also to collect the remaining small bones of Jane Doe's toes and fingers.

Ben showed up at the police department, with Jo Robinson in tow. I don't know who had called him, but he had called Jo. My resentment didn't last long.

I ended up talking to her about vanishing Parrishes, and I learned that people who had been attacked often had this experience of "seeing" their attacker, especially in times of stress or in public places.

When I was no longer shaking, she set up an appointment with me for the next day. For the first time, I looked forward to it.

The police checked out records of stolen dark green Honda Accords, hoping to establish Jane Doe's identity.

When Frank couldn't leave right away, Ben agreed to take Jack and me home.

Wondering how I was going to break the news about the van to Travis, I asked Ben why it should take so long to collect ten fingers and ten toes. "Ten? On each foot, it takes fourteen phalanges to make toes—and just the toes, mind you, not the whole foot. On each hand, fourteen to make fingers. That's fifty-six bones if we find them in whole pieces."

Trying to tease me into a better mood, Ben noted that he himself was able to get by with forty-two, which did indeed snap me out of thinking about the little bones of Jane Doe's fingers, wondering what work those fingers might have done, and if they had ever stroked a cat or touched a lover or held something as fragile as they were.

On Ben's behalf and hers, I let my anger toward Nick Parrish burn away a little more of my fear of him.

But as the evening wore on, even anger gave way to weariness. I was asleep when Frank came home, but woke up to talk to him while he made a late dinner for himself. Afterward, we spent time curled up on the couch.

"You know you can talk to me," he said,

"Yes."

"Sorry. No more reprimands."

"I deserve a reprimand for that."

"No," he said, pulling me closer. "No."

In another regard altogether, it actually ended up being yes.

We did sleep then, a solid, deep, and renewing sleep that lasted through the night.

"You're looking well today," Jo Robinson said.

"Slept better," I said, detecting a certain knowing quality in her smile.

At the end of this session, she said, "Your visits to the families of the men who were killed seem to have gone well. Better than you expected?"

"Much better."

"Have you tried calling Officer Houghton?"

"Jim Houghton is the one survivor I can't seem to track down. He quit police work altogether, and moved out of state. But a friend of mine who's an investigator is going to try to find him."

"You've made a good effort. I hope it works out. In the meantime, though, perhaps you should try to talk to the Sayres again."

I won a struggle with an impulse to object. "Will you let me go back to work if I do?"

"Hmm. You want to make a deal, is that it?"

"Yes."

"Sorry, doesn't work that way."

I studied my hands.

"However," she said, "aside from any deal you have in mind, I was going to suggest a gradual return to work."

"Gradual? What does that mean?"

"Part-time."

"I'm not sure the *Express* will go for that."

"Leave that to me. Between now and next time, I want you to think about Parzival."

"Parzival?"

"Yes. Why do you suppose you chose the story of Parzival?"

"Ben asked for that one. I'd been telling it in installments."

"No, I meant, why did you choose it the first time?"

"In the mountains?"

"Yes."

"I don't know. Because I had I read it recently, I suppose."

She waited, but this time she waited in vain.

"Give it some thought," she said.

"Okay," I said, standing up.

"Not so fast—about the Sayres . . ."

I tried calling Gillian first, since she had been trying to contact me, but she hadn't left a number when she talked to Frank, and the one I had for her was disconnected. I didn't have any luck with the boutique she had worked in, either.

"The media, man," the owner said.

"The media?"

"Yeah, she didn't come into work after all those dudes got whacked in the mountains—you know, the guys that were looking for her old lady? So finally she calls me and says she ain't comin' in and she's gonna look for new digs, 'cause the media is, you know, making her crazy. They were always tryin' to interview her and shit, you know?"

Yeah, I knew.

I called Mark Baker at the *Express* and asked him if he had been in contact with the Sayre family since Julia's body had been brought back.

"I saw Gillian once, a couple of weeks later," Mark said. "I had asked the owner of that shop she worked in to tip me off if she called to say she was coming in for her final paycheck. I wasn't the only one waiting—the guy must have called half the press in the area, hoping to get free publicity, I guess. She met all the reporters outside, said that she wished we'd look for Nick Parrish as hard as we had looked for her. And that was it."

Despite my pointing out my recent poor track record with vehicles, Ben loaned me his Jeep Cherokee, saying he would use David's pickup truck in the meantime. Jack did the driving. We nearly drove past the Sayres' large home—it used to be gray and white; it had been painted peach since the last time I had seen it.

I thought back; that had been just after Gillian had told me that Nick Parrish had lived on this street. I had spent a fruitless day interviewing neighbors—either they said he was pleasant but kept to himself, or they said they had always thought he was an odd duck. No one in this latter group could say why—leading me to believe that they had been influenced by what they had already read about him. No one in the neighborhood had any real insight into Nick Parrish, or could say where he had lived next, or what had become of his sister.

During the first year after Julia disappeared, the Sayres and I had seen one another fairly often. I had met Jason, and Giles's mother, a woman who was clearly not prepared to cope with a rebellious teenager like Gillian. I was shocked to realize that although I had spoken to Gillian in person on any number of occasions since then, and had seen her father a few times as well, I had never again talked to her brother or grandmother.

Months earlier, when Parrish had first made his offer to lead police to Julia Sayre's grave, I visited Giles at the company he owned. The moment I had arrived, he said, "He's told them where to find Julia, hasn't he?"

In the privacy of his office, I told him what I knew. He took it calmly, but asked, "Is there a chance he might be lying? A chance that it isn't her?"

Yes, of course there was, I said, having seen this sort of denial before. He asked me to keep him informed.

"Have you told Gillian?" he asked.

Dismayed, I said, "No, I thought I'd leave that to her father."

He fidgeted.

"She told me Parrish used to live on your street," I said.

"Did she?" he said absently. "I don't know. I never have kept track of the neighbors. The police did ask about it. I suppose that's how they were able to bring pressure on him."

"Did Parrish know Julia?"

"I don't think so," he said, frowning.

"She never complained to you about someone staring at her?"

"Perhaps she did," he said vaguely. "Listen, Gilly doesn't have much to do with us these days. I think she'd rather hear this news from you."

Reluctantly, I agreed to be the one to tell her.

But Gillian, in her usual manner, had revealed nothing of her feelings to me. She simply said, "Have you told my dad yet?"

I told her I had.

"He doesn't like to deal with anything unpleasant. Was he the one who asked you to tell me?"

"Yes."

She smiled, not at all cheerfully, but in the tight-lipped way a person smiles if she's right about something she doesn't want to be right about.

"You'll go with them, won't you?" she asked. "To find out if this woman in the grave is my mother?"

In one minute flat, she had broken down the resistance that neither the D.A. nor my bosses had been able to breach.

I rang the doorbell of the Sayres' house. To my surprise, it now played "Dixie." I heard someone scampering down the stairs, shouting, "I'll get it!"

Jason pulled the door open, seemed taken aback, then looked sullen. His hair was now cut fairly short and dyed a mix of black and blond. He was wearing a long, loose T-shirt and very baggy pants. "Oh, it's you," he said, his voice cracking.

"Jason, honey?" a voice called from upstairs. A voice too young to be his grandmother's.

Jason rolled his eyes. He was thirteen now, and much taller.

He seemed to make a sudden decision, quickly shut the door behind himself and said to me, "Let's go."

"Go where?" I asked, startled.

"Just go!" he insisted in his half-man, half-boy voice. He started moving off the front porch. "That your Jeep?"

"The one I'm using, but—"

He came to a halt when he saw Jack sitting in the driver's seat. "Who's that?"

"A friend of mine."

"Really?"

"Really."

"Looks kind of old, but cool," he said, starting to move toward the jeep again.

"It's all relative," I said. "The age part, I mean. Look, Jason—"

"Jason!" a voice screeched from an upstairs window.

"Oh, shit!" he said, glancing back at the house, then running toward the Jeep.

"Who is that?" I asked, running to keep up.

"Jason!" the voice screeched again.

He yanked the back passenger door open and jumped into the Jeep. "Dude!" he said to Jack. "Get me out of here!"

"Don't even turn the key, Jack," I said. "We are not going anywhere until he tells me who the banshee is."

"What's a banshee?" Jason asked.

"I'll explain that as soon as you tell me who this is that's coming out the front door of the house," I said, indicating a stylishly dressed, thin blond woman in her mid-fifties, whose noticeable efforts to turn back the hands of time hadn't even bent its pinky.

"That," Jason said grimly, "is Mrs. Sayre."

45

▲ ▼ ▲ ▼

THURSDAY AFTERNOON, SEPTEMBER 14

Las Piernas

"Jason, are you trying to kill your father?" the new Mrs. Sayre called out.

Jason's back went rigid.

Not noticing, she went on. "Do you know what he'd say if he knew you were getting into a Jeep with total strangers?" She stood back a little from us, eyeing Jack's scarred face, leather outfit, earring, and tattoos with disapproval.

"They aren't strangers," Jason protested. "This is Irene Kelly, from the newspaper."

"And what did he tell you about talking to reporters?" she asked. "Get out of that Jeep this instant! When your daddy gets home, you are going to get your smart little behind whipped!"

He reached toward his rear pocket, not to shield it, but to remove a slim black object. He flicked his wrist, and I saw that the object was a cell phone. A thirteen-year-old kid with a cell phone—in the Sayres' upscale neighborhood, I supposed every kid who was old enough to read a keypad had one.

"We'll see what my dad says," Jason said, and pushed a button.

"Yes, we will!" his stepmother said, sure of her ground.

"Hi, it's Jason," he said into the phone. "May I please speak to my dad?"

"More manners when you're talking to his secretary, I see," Mrs. Sayre complained.

"You should know," he sneered, causing her to turn red. In a more pleasant tone he said into the phone, "Hi, Dad, it's Jason. Ms. Kelly came over to talk to me and You-Know-Who is causing problems."

He looked toward me as he listened, his expression apprehensive, and then he smiled. He extended the phone toward his stepmother, who snatched it out of his hand.

"Giles, if you are going to undermine my authority with the boy every time I turn around—" She fell silent, and watched me. "And how on earth was I to know that? I see two strangers luring your son into a car, one of them looking like a Hell's Angel—"

She listened again, her expression darkening. She held the phone away from her ear while Giles was still talking, and pushed the off button. She snapped the phone shut, tossed it none too carefully to Jason, who made a fumbling catch.

"Mrs. Sayre—" I said, the name sounding strange to me, but she had already pivoted on her heel and marched back toward the porch.

At the door, she turned and called out, "If you do plan to kidnap him, please don't bother to send a ransom note." She slammed the door shut.

"Now can we go?" Jason said.

"Jack Fremont, meet my impatient friend, Jason Sayre."

"Hi—can we go?"

"Just where is it you're so anxious to get to?" Jack asked.

"Anywhere! Just get me away from her," he said.

Jack smiled at me and said, "Better get in, Irene. Buckle up, Jason."

Jason leaned back with a sigh when we finally pulled away from the curb.

"The park okay?" Jack asked.

"Sure," I said, then turned to Jason. "Is that all right with you?"

"Finally," he said dramatically, "someone asks me what I want!"

"Well?"

"Yeah, I like the park."

"When did your dad get married?" I asked.

"To Susan?"

"Is that your stepmother's name?"

He nodded. "She wants everybody to call her Dixie, but that's a crock—she isn't even from the South. She's lived with us since Gilly moved out. My dad was at her place before that."

"So she's not your father's wife?"

"She is now. They got married just after you found my mother."

"What?"

"Yeah," he said, looking away from me, down at his hands. "The day you came and told him about that killer, he called Susan up and told her it looked like they could finally get married."

Dumbstruck, I looked over at Jack. He kept glancing in the rearview mirror, not at traffic, but at Jason.

"As long as they couldn't find my mother, he had to wait seven years," Jason went on, kicking out his feet as if straightening his legs, but the look on his face said he wished his Timberlands were connecting with someone.

"Oh," I said, understanding dawning. "Because legally, your mother had not been declared dead?"

"Right. Susan thought my dad could have made the courts hurry it up, but Dad said it would be really bad for his business because people would be mad at him—because you had written all those stories and everything. So he had to wait to get his little hottie. Wait to get married to her, anyway. She wanted him to marry her the day after they said the body was my mom's. He made her wait a week."

"She used to be his secretary?" I asked, remembering the comment that had made her blush.

"Yeah."

We stopped at a corner market and bought some fresh fruit and a soda for Jason, bottled water for Jack and me. We drove to the large park that forms part of the eastern border of the city, found a shady spot, and began an impromptu picnic. Jason's cell phone rang; he spoke briefly to a friend and hung up.

"I guess it beats two tin cans and a wire," Jack said.

I laughed, but Jason asked what we were talking about, so we explained a little something about the olden days.

"And that really works?" he asked.

"We'll set up a demonstration a little later," Jack said.

He picked at the grass, then without looking up, said, "Did you find out something more about my mom?"

"Oh—no, I'm sorry. That's not why I stopped by to see you."

"It's not?"

"No. I just wanted to see how you were doing."

"Oh."

When he didn't say anything more, I added, "I also wanted to apologize for not coming by sooner."

He shrugged, frowned down at the piece of grass he was pulling on. "Why should you? You never even knew her."

"But I know your family."

He leveled a flat, cynical gaze at me. "Do you?"

I thought of today's revelations. "Not very well, perhaps—but enough to know that what happened to your mom has been hard on everyone in the family."

He laughed. "Hard on everyone? No way. I'm the only one who really loved her."

"I don't think that's true—"

"Who then? My dad? Oh, pul-eeeze. He was getting it on with old Suze. He probably thinks my mom's murder was the best thing that could have happened."

"Jason, I've seen—"

"His tears? He's a phony. And you know who's a bigger phony? Gilly. Learned it from him—only she's even better at it than he is. She even fooled you. She hated my mom. *Hated* her." He shook his head. "They hated each other."

"When she first met me, Gillian admitted that she had trouble with your mom, that there were arguments."

"*Trouble? Arguments?*" he said angrily. "You think it was all some teenage thing?"

It had seemed exactly that way to me, and to everyone I had talked to at the time Julia Sayre disappeared.

"So why did Gillian hate her?" Jack asked.

"How should I know?" he said, but with less hostility than he had shown me. "She's cold. She doesn't care about anybody or anything."

"For four years," I said, "Gillian has been the one to call me, to ask if there has been any news of your mother. In that time, other people have gone missing, but no one took the trouble your sister took to find the person she loved."

"Don't say 'loved,'" he snapped. "She didn't love my mother. She hated her. She was mean to me. She's mean to everyone. She's a user. She even used you, and now you're talking to me like that was something good. She just wanted attention. You gave it to her."

"When's the last time you talked to her?" I asked.

"Years ago. She moved out a long time ago."

"Do you miss her?"

"No."

"She hasn't been back to visit you since she moved out?"

"No. It doesn't matter. She's still weird. I see her every now and then—I mean, you know, see her when she's hanging out in different places. I saw her here once," he said, vaguely pointing toward another part of the park. "Didn't even say hello to me. Which is fine," he added quickly. "I don't want her to come anywhere near me."

"I'm sorry," I said, "I didn't realize . . . I didn't realize that you were so angry with her. Or with me."

And everyone else on the planet, I thought. But he said, "I'm not mad at you. Gilly fools people all the time. So does my dad." He sighed. "I wish I didn't live in Las Piernas."

"Why not?"

"Everybody knows what happened to my mom. Kids at school, it's like, the only thing they know about me. They either want to ask me about it—like, if it's true my mom's finger was cut off, shit like that—or they're all freaked out about it. I can't just be a normal person."

"They've acted like that for four years?" Jack asked.

"No," he acknowledged. "Just when it first happened. And now."

"So they might get over this?"

"Yeah, I guess so."

"Maybe they're just scared that the same thing might happen to their moms," Jack said.

"Maybe," he said. "But I still hate living here."

"Where would you like to live?" I asked.

"With Grandma," he said. "I miss her. I wish I could go live with her."

"Have you asked your dad if you could?" I asked.

"He says he would miss me too much. I think he's just worried about what people will think."

"Do you remember when Nick Parrish lived in the neighborhood?"

He shook his head. "I was little when he moved. Gilly remembers him. I think she used to go over there to see the lady or something."

"The lady? His sister?"

"Yeah." He hesitated, then said, "I knew it was Nick Parrish a long time ago. Before the cops knew."

"What do you mean?"

"I didn't know his name," Jason said, "but I had seen him."

"When?"

"Before my mom was killed. He was staring at our house one time when Gilly was baby-sitting. I was kind of little then, too—well, a third-grader, is all—but it scared me."

"Did you tell anyone?"

"I told Gilly. She went out and looked for him. But by then there wasn't anybody there."

"You didn't tell the police?"

"I didn't get too good a look at him," he admitted.

"What did you see?"

"I just saw this man in a car. But later, I figured it out—you know, when Gilly remembered he used to live on our street. It was too late," he said sadly. "Besides, who's going to believe a kid? It's like Gilly said, no one would take a kid seriously."

He reached into the bag of fruit and picked out an orange. He studied it in his hand, then hurled it hard against a tree trunk, where it landed with a pulpy thunk, then managed to cling to the tree for a few seconds before dropping to the ground. When I turned to look at Jason in surprise, he ducked his head, but not before I saw that his face was twisted up—in anger, but not anger alone.

"The other day, I threw something hard like that," I said. "I thought it would make me feel better, but it didn't, really."

"What did you throw?" he asked, talking to his ankles.

"A computer monitor."

He looked up, eyes damp but wide. "Get out!" he said admiringly. "A computer monitor?"

"Yes. Really stupid thing to do. Someone could have been seriously injured by what I did. I ended up feeling worse than I did before I threw it."

"So why did you throw it?"

"I was angry. Angry and blaming myself for things that had gone wrong, I suppose."

"Things that were your fault?"

"Some of them. Some were things that I really could have changed, could have done better. But a lot of it probably would have turned out the same way no matter what."

"What do you mean?"

"Well, for example, I thought I should have figured out what Nick Parrish had planned up in the mountains."

"How could you? Even the cops didn't know. A bunch of them died."

"Yes, and maybe that was my fault, because I suspected Nick Parrish of being up to no good. Sort of like you suspected the guy in the car of being up to no good."

"But maybe if I had told my dad instead of Gilly . . ."

"Was your dad home?"

"No."

"So maybe the man in the car would have been gone by the time your dad got home. Even if your dad had called the police that night, they would have said, 'Is the man in the car doing anything?' and if your dad said, 'No,' that would have been that. Maybe it wasn't even Parrish out there that night."

"Maybe," he said, without conviction.

"It troubles you anyway, doesn't it?"

"Yeah."

"I kept hoping that the thoughts that were troubling me would just go away. They didn't. So now I'm trying to talk about them a little more. It's hard."

"Really hard," he said, looking back at his shoes.

"Who do you talk to when you're upset?"

He didn't answer for a long time, but he finally said, "My grandmother, sometimes."

"Maybe you should call her a little more often. Maybe talk to your dad about visiting her for a while."

"Okay."

We picked up our trash—including the smashed orange—and left the park. Before taking him home, Jack stopped at a hardware store to buy a length of wire. Next he drove us to an Italian restaurant where he was apparently well known. Although the dining room was empty at this late afternoon hour, we were welcomed back into the kitchen, where Jack talked the busy cook into giving him the other essentials for a tin can telephone. The cook even washed out the cans, and added supervision to Jason's efforts to assemble the parts.

When it was finished, the cook urged Jason to take one end into the dining room while he held the other end in the kitchen. What they whispered back and forth, I'll never know, but it caused a great deal of amusement on both sides.

With some difficulty, and only with promises to return soon, were we able to leave without eating a meal. Jason was quiet on the way home, and when we pulled up in front of the house, he said, "Don't tell Gilly what I said about her, okay?"

"Okay," I said, relieved to see some sign of brotherly affection in him after all.

Jack told him that he'd ask Giles if Jason could go with him to the Italian restaurant some time.

"That would be fun," he said, but he seemed subdued, perhaps not believing Jack would follow through.

He thanked us and said good-bye, taking the tin can phone with him. As he walked into the house, I saw him speaking into one end, while holding the other to his ear, absorbed in some private conversation with himself.

46

▲ ▼ ▲ ▼

FRIDAY AFTERNOON, SEPTEMBER 15
Las Piernas

Nicholas Parrish surveyed his new workroom with pride. A vast improvement over the last one.

Again, he had to give his little Moth credit. His Moth had seen that he was hampered in his work, and had suggested this alternative. This was infinitely more suitable to his needs. The workbench was larger, there was a sink nearby, and even—to his delight—a freezer.

The dwelling itself was more comfortable than his last, but that was of little matter to him. He was not a soft man, after all. Like any other artist, he was most concerned with the space in which he would do his creative work. He had spent several days getting this place shaped up to his satisfaction—emptying the freezer of its previous contents and so on—and now—voilà! Perhaps it was not a studio worthy of his masterpieces— Alas, could there ever be such a place?—but he would be able to carry on very well here.

He could not help feeling a sense of pride in the way things were going lately. Irene was actually seeing a shrink! Obviously, he had her on the verge of a nervous breakdown. Delightful! What good were shrinks when one's terrors were real? She was terrified, all right! Just as he had promised.

Witness the woman's reaction to those bones! It made him wish he had stayed around to see what had happened when she got the roses.

He frowned, remembering Jack Fremont's arm around her. She was too free with her favors, to say the least. The woman was a real whore. Ben Sheridan, Jack Fremont, and God knows who else. Probably her own cousin.

He sat musing over what he might have to do in order to purify her of such defilement.

He stopped himself before the richness of those imaginings caused him to become overly excited. There was a great deal of work to do.

He studied his maps, mentally going over the routes he had already driven, considered once more all the possible hazards along the way.

He changed the plates on the Honda, and chose a blond wig for today's disguise. He had already called the newspaper, had already filled out the vacation hold form for the post office. The tools he would need for the first phase of his work were already in the trunk of the car.

He looked again at the small piece of paper the Moth had given him and felt a frisson. How had this information been obtained? The Moth was up to something. He did not believe the story the Moth had given him about this.

He disliked having to expend energy thinking about the Moth, especially at a time like this. He must stay focused.

He looked again at the markings on his map. Most were in blue. His eye was drawn to the single red mark.

He knew its exact address: 600 Broadway.

The Wrigley Building.

Home of the *Express*.

47

▲ ▼ ▲ ▼

SUNDAY MORNING, SEPTEMBER 17
Las Piernas

I hesitated outside the front door of the Wrigley Building. The arrangements Jo Robinson had made were not even close to what I had in mind when I had asked for a "return to work," and my pride was smarting. I knew Frank was watching from the Volvo, waiting to make sure I got safely inside. For a good ten minutes or so, I seriously contemplated going back to the car and asking him to drive me straight back home. Then I'd get Jo Robinson and Wrigley on a conference call, and tell them both to shove it.

Wrigley gave me twenty hours back at the paper, all right. He scheduled me to work a part-time graveyard shift, from ten at night until two in the morning on Tuesday, Thursday, and Friday—after deadline. To add a little additional punishment, I was also scheduled to work Saturday and Sunday from seven to eleven in the morning. That meant that on Friday nights, I had exactly five hours off before I'd have to report the next morning.

John gave me less than forty-eight hours of warning, saying my first shift was going to be the next Sunday morning. "I guess Wrigley assumes I have no plans?" I said. "That I'm just sitting here waiting for him to invite me to take complaint calls at the *Express*?"

"Do you have plans?" John asked.

"Yes, but not until later on Sunday," I admitted.

A phone call to Giles's office had finally resulted in getting Gillian's new number—his secretary had to find it for me—and Gillian had agreed to meet me on Sunday afternoon. Gillian was working as a waitress now, at a small café that served breakfast and lunch. "Just part-time," she had said. "I'm off after two o'clock."

"So you can come in?" John asked me.

"Yes, I'll be there. I guess he's determined to make me grovel."

"I don't like it, either, Kelly, but up until now, the fight has been to keep him from firing you. It's going to take some pressure from the board to get him to ease off on the hours. You know I'm doing whatever I can for you."

Knowing that John and others were making efforts on my behalf made me decide to go ahead and push the front door open that Sunday morning.

The building was all but empty, which, I decided, was not so bad. I didn't look forward to facing everyone who had seen me go haywire.

I could hear the phones ringing before I reached the top of the stairs. You work a Sunday morning, you listen to people bitch. They don't check to see which number is the one for circulation, which one for the city desk. So they dial whichever number they see first, and whoever sits in the newsroom takes complaint calls.

The calls were being picked up on the second or third ring though, and soon I heard voices. So I wouldn't be alone after all.

I stepped into the newsroom to see Mark Baker and Lydia Ames answering phones. I was puzzled. Neither of them should have been working that morning. Lydia waved me to a seat next to her.

Another line rang. I answered a call from a man who claimed that the guy who delivered his paper that morning had tossed it into a mud puddle. The man went on at length, never seeming to need to come up for air; the only thing making it bearable was watching Lydia and Mark comically gesturing and rolling their eyes as they each answered another call.

I finally managed to end the call with Mr. Mud Puddle just as Stuart Angert entered the room with a box of breakfast rolls and four cups of hot coffee.

"Welcome back!" he said.

"Thanks, but what are the three of you doing here at this ungodly hour on the Lord's day?" I asked.

"John told us what Wrigley was pulling," Mark said, "so we decided to change a few schedules of our own—with John's approval, of course."

"We didn't want to miss your first day back," Lydia said.

"You shouldn't be sticking your necks out for me like this," I said. "What if Wrigley decides to stop by?"

"He won't show up," Mark said. "He's scared to death of you."

Another round of calls came in. By nine o'clock they had slowed enough to allow us to talk to one another for more than two minutes at a time. I apologized to Stuart for wrecking his monitor.

"Feel free to use any of my other desk equipment the next time you want to launch a missile," he said. "I love the new computer monitor. Everybody's jealous of me."

"No, we're jealous of Irene. We'd all like to know how it feels to throw something at Wrigley," Lydia said.

"Not as wonderful as you'd think," I said.

This led to some all-too-serious "How are you really?" talk. I was evasive. They got the hint, and acting against journalistic instinct, let up.

At ten-thirty, I realized my shift was nearly over, and I hadn't even started sorting my mail. Lydia offered to help while Stuart and Mark covered the phones. I was able to give Lydia a few items that would need immediate dayshift follow-up. Some of it, I'd ask John to let me work on at home. Most of it could wait, or could be answered with a letter. I decided to save answering my e-mail for my first graveyard shift. One of the beautiful things about the Internet is that it's open 24/7.

Among the envelopes was a strange lumpy package with no

return address. Lydia eyed it doubtfully and said, "Now what are your strange fans sending you?"

I used a letter opener to slit it open and dumped the contents out with a flourish.

I watched a pair of panties fall onto the desk.

"My underwear," I said blankly.

For an awful moment, all I could see and hear was Nick Parrish in the mountains, taunting me, telling me he had my scent.

Then I heard Stuart laughing uproariously.

For a brief moment, I felt humiliated.

Then he said, "Jesus, Kelly, I've heard of having your laundry sent out, but this is ridiculous."

The humor of the situation struck me—Stuart was right, it was just a pair of underwear, after all. I started laughing, too.

Mark and Lydia seemed uncertain, but when Mark asked, "Shouldn't you call the police?" Stuart and I laughed so hard, they lost it, too.

When we had all calmed down a little, I said, "Hell, I guess I should call the police. But I think I'll call Frank first. I don't even like to think of what he's going to be hearing from the other folks at work."

Frank, as it turned out, didn't think there was anything funny about what had happened. Far from being worried about what kind of teasing he'd get at work, he insisted on being with me the rest of the day.

"But I'm going to see Gillian this afternoon."

"Fine," he said. "I'll be nearby."

I looked at the envelope while we waited for the police. Postmarked just before I took my leave of absence from the paper. "At least I made the little bastard wait," I said.

"I suppose I should cover this," Mark said, which started Stuart howling again.

Then I felt my temper kick in—not at Stuart, but at Parrish. "God damn it," I told Lydia, "Parrish sent that to me here hoping to humiliate me in an office full of coworkers. He thought I'd be terrified, while all of you would be wondering what my problem was. Well, I'm sick of it. Enough of playing defense. Time for the offense to take the field."

Stuart, overhearing this, said, "She's back, ladies and gentlemen!"

Lydia and Mark, on the other hand, cautioned me. "Don't do anything foolish," Mark said.

I turned to my computer and logged on. "I'll cover my own underwear, by God!"

"Put that slogan on the masthead!" Stuart said.

I started writing:

> What sort of loser thinks he can terrify a woman with a pair of her own underwear?
>
> Perhaps smarting from his previous failures, Nick Parrish has brought out his ultimate secret weapon. The man (I use the term loosely) has attempted to frighten me with an unlaundered pair of my own unmentionables.
>
> Nicky obviously has no idea what sort of horrors await the average woman on wash day.
>
> Here at the *Express*, picturing him hatching this grand scheme as he carried my dirty drawers around with him for three months has given rise to all sorts of hilarity.
>
> Nicky, who'd have thought you were a panty rustler?
>
> Yes, I know you'd prefer to go down in history as Mr. Evil Incarnate, and you've certainly done your best to make that moniker stick. But the world of the media is ever-changing, Nicky, and I'm afraid that here in the newsroom, that Evil Incarnate business has already been forgotten—you're doomed to be referred to as the Bloomer Bandit.

Lydia, reading it over my shoulder, shook her head and walked off.

But I was enjoying myself too much to care. It felt great to imagine what Parrish's face would look like when he read it. Here he was, trying to terrify me, and if things went my way, I'd make a laughingstock out of him.

I was on the verge of forwarding it to John, when for some odd reason, I suddenly I thought of Parzival. Parzival, whose good intentions did not prevent bad things from happening as a result of his actions.

Suppose Parrish decided to prove that he should be taken seriously? What if, instead of being utterly cast down and immobilized by my needle-sharp prose, the man grew so enraged he killed another dozen women to make us fear him again? Would I be able to live with myself then? Did I think for a moment that he would burst into tears and turn himself in, saying "I'll confess, just tell Irene Kelly to stop being mean to me?"

Then again, should I censor myself because in my heart of hearts I was afraid of Nick Parrish?

I printed out a copy of the story and gave it to Lydia, but told her I wasn't ready to file it yet, that I wanted a little time to think it over. I saved the story on a floppy disk, and then deleted it from the main system. If I changed my mind, I could hand over the floppy.

I called John at home to tell him what had happened with the package. "You're probably going to have some guys from the crime lab in here," I said.

"Oh, hell, Kelly, not even a full day back, and you've got the cops walking around in the newsroom."

As it turned out, the police weren't at the paper for long. Once they had taken the package and its contents, asked me a few questions ("When did you last have the garment in your possession?") and determined that the package had been mailed and not hand-delivered, they were on their way. They even mentioned that I'd probably be getting the van back soon.

I went to lunch with Frank, who seemed more quiet than usual.

"What's going on?" I asked.

"Lydia told me about the commentary you wrote."

I tried to read his expression, and couldn't. "I'm sorry she did. I was going to tell you, but I don't suppose you'll believe that now."

"I believe you."

"So what's the problem?"

"The problem is that you're infuriating a serial killer. Or in this 'everchanging media world,' had you truly forgotten that?"

"What do you suppose the answer to that question is?"

"Then what the hell were you thinking of?"

"I'm tired of playing it his way all the time, Frank."

"There are experts in forensic psychology who are working on these cases, Irene. People who study this type of guy for a living are on the task force. You ever think it might be a good idea to contact one of them before mouthing off to Parrish?"

"Listen, before we end up in a fight over this—"

"I don't blame you for getting angry. He's trying to control you and manipulate you, trying to make you feel afraid. He wants to be in charge. Do I think you should whimper in a corner? No. But standing up for yourself is one thing, and issuing an out-and-out challenge to the guy is another."

"I didn't file the story."

He sat back. "What?"

"Lydia gave you a copy of it, didn't she?"

He admitted it.

"Well, I didn't file the story. I have it on a floppy disk. I haven't made up my mind about it, but I guess I'm leaning toward not filing it." I held a hand up as he started to speak. "Don't—please don't say it's the smart thing to do, because probably it's also the cowardly thing to do."

Wisely, he didn't say more on the subject.

Gillian lived over a garage, in a small wooden one-bedroom apartment built during the housing shortage of the late 1940s. The garage was at the end of a long driveway and was detached from the large Craftsman house that occupied the front of the lot; the house had been converted into a duplex.

From the foot of the stairs we could hear her stereo; the Boomtown Rats singing "I Don't Like Mondays." An oldie. We climbed the stairs and knocked on the door. The stereo went off. Gillian greeted us wearing jeans and a bright yellow top; her hair was currently very short and black, her nails purple, but also much shorter than the last time I had seen her. Frank had briefly met Gillian once before, when she had inquired about a Jane Doe case he had been working on. She remembered him, though, and the specific case as well, although she must have asked about several dozen such cases over the past four years.

As they talked briefly about that investigation, I glanced around the interior of the apartment. It was oddly blank and austere for someone who dressed so colorfully; the walls were white and bare, the chairs and sofa were plain, and other than her stereo speakers and a potted palm, there were no other objects in the room. The stereo itself must have been in the bedroom. Nothing in this room to distract a guest from the host.

She politely asked us to have a seat, politely offered us something to drink, politely thanked me again for talking to her so soon after I had returned from the mountains. She said she was glad I hadn't been too scared by the bones in the van and asked if I was back at work yet.

Beneath these good manners was a not-so-concealed level of disinterest in us that made me wonder how she prevented herself from yawning in our faces.

I asked how she had been doing. She had been doing fine.

I expressed surprise at learning of her father's remarriage. She said she really didn't know Susan, but her father could do whatever he pleased with his life.

"Jason doesn't seem very happy."

"You talked to Jason?" she asked, showing the first sign of real attention to anything I had said.

"Yes," I said, "earlier in the week."

She spread her hands before her, palms out, and studied her nails. She looked up from them and said, "I don't have much to do with my dad or my brother now. I like it that way. They have their problems, I have mine."

I excused myself to use her bathroom, which was as plain and unadorned as the rest of the place. When I came back out, I was surprised to hear her laughing. I realized that it was the first time I had ever heard the sound of her laughter. It was an uninhibited, childish giggle. She was holding a folded piece of paper in her hand, extending it back to Frank with a smile.

Frank glanced back at me with a look that had guilt written all over it. He took the paper back from her and handed it to me.

"I hope you don't mind," he said. "I let her read your article about Parrish."

"Not at all," I said, but Gillian's smile had already faded.

We left not long after that. In the car, Frank said, "I'm sorry, I should have asked you first."

"Are you kidding? You're brilliant! I've never heard that kid laugh. I'm really glad you let her see what I wrote—maybe it helped relieve some of that burden she carries around—at least for a few minutes, anyway. She's usually so serious and remote."

"And here I thought the low-affect routine was just for me."

"It wasn't you," I said. "She's always like that around me, too. That's why hearing her laugh was so great—usually, nothing seems to get through to her. Jason says she's cold. I think it's her way of coping with everything that's happened. She just withdraws. And she's had plenty to deal with lately—after all this time, her mother has been found, but it's not exactly a happy ending."

"I don't underestimate what she's been through, but"—he gave a mock shiver—"I'm with Jason."

"I don't think you can go much by this act she puts on."

"I guess not. But you have to admit she's a little weird."

The whole family is strange, I thought. "You know, I've been thinking about Giles. I wonder if he was having an affair with his secretary before Julia was abducted. When Gillian first came to me, I focused all my attention on whether or not *Julia* was having an affair."

"Most likely, Bob Thompson took a look at him. A wife disappears, we usually look to see if the husband wanted her gone."

"Would it be hard to find out?"

"I think Reed Collins picked up the Sayre case—one they gave him after Bob died. He closed it out when the ID came in on her body. He probably has the file. They're using it for the task force on Parrish, and it still has to be prosecuted, of course. Reed will let me take a look at it."

"Giles seemed so upset when I first met him. Now, he's totally caught up in himself. The more I think about what his kids have said, the more I wonder if that initial grief was all an act."

"But connecting him to a guy like Parrish—"

"Parrish was his neighbor for a while."

"That doesn't mean he knew what Parrish was up to. Parrish isn't a hit man; he kills for his own pleasure."

"Maybe he's done both. I'm going to talk to Phil Newly," I

said. "Maybe he'll know if Parrish was in touch with anyone else, thought of anyone as a friend."

"Phil may have helped me to find you," he said, "but good luck getting him to take attorney-client privilege that lightly."

I called Phil Newly's number several times on Sunday afternoon and evening. No answer. I figured he might be away for the weekend.

That was one of my worries over the next few days—Phil Newly's phone ringing unanswered. I should have been more worried than I was.

48

▲ ▼ ▲ ▼

MONDAY MORNING, SEPTEMBER 18

Las Piernas

On Monday morning, while Jack was my sitter, we were able to pick up the van from the impound yard. I washed it more thoroughly than I have ever washed any vehicle. We took the Jeep back to Ben, who was able to use it in time to get to his first class. He seemed amazed that it came back to him in one piece.

I called Jo Robinson to complain about the hours she had arranged, and she told me that she had not expected that Wrigley would come up with this schedule. She was angry about it, but her calls to the *Express* apparently made no difference.

I kept calling Newly.

Travis called. He had been good about keeping in touch, although he was clearly having the time of his life with Stinger Dalton and as far as I could tell, was in no hurry to come back to Las Piernas. He had already soloed in small helicopters, and ecstatically related to me that Stinger was now teaching him to fly the big Sikorsky.

"So, are you still off work?" he asked me.

"No, in fact, I'm working tomorrow night." I told him about my unique working hours.

"That really sucks," he said, making me think he had spent a little too much time with Stinger.

"It's only temporary," I said.

"Maybe I'll come and visit you soon. I miss the dogs."

"Thanks." I laughed.

"That's not what I meant!"

"I know, I know. We all look forward to seeing you whenever you get a chance to come by."

I was approaching the first night shift with some trepidation. Normally, I wouldn't mind driving alone on deserted streets after midnight or working alone in an office on a graveyard shift, but nothing in my life was normal then. I had no doubt that Parrish would be stalking me on those streets, that Parrish would come to hunt me down in those empty hallways.

He'll hunt you wherever you are, I told myself. I couldn't hole up in the house forever. A life spent cowering was no life at all.

I was in that frame of mind when Frank told me he wanted to make sure that I was never unaccompanied at the newspaper on night shifts. I flatly refused to take a sitter into work with me. That argument livened things up for a few hours. He drove off, came back an hour later and handed me a cell phone.

"What's this?"

"My peace of mind."

"You expect me to carry this around with me—"

"And to have it on. Yes."

"Can we afford this?"

"It's cheaper than a funeral."

"Frank!"

"Okay, okay. Just carry it around for my peace of mind, please?"

I gave in.

I didn't do much of anything in connection with the Sayre case for the next week; I was too busy adjusting my sleep schedule and catching up with the paperwork that had piled up on my desk at the *Express*. Those first nights, the paper had already been put to bed by the time I arrived. I talked to the printers down in the basement, and to Jerry and Livy, the computer maintenance staff.

Frank tested me a few times, making sure I had the cell phone turned on, until I finally told him that if he didn't quit making me jump out of my skin by making the damned phone chirp, I was going to roll the thing between a couple of presses. That took care of that.

I tried calling Newly at eleven-thirty. No answer.

The newsroom was empty and quiet.

I was well on my way to being unnerved by that quiet when my cousin Travis called at 11:55 P.M.

"Go up onto the roof," he said.

"What?"

"We're coming to see you!" he said over loud noise in the background.

"Who is coming to see me?"

"Stinger and I."

"Great. When?"

"Right now."

"Now? Is this some practical joke, Travis?"

"Go up onto the roof of the *Express*. We'll be near there in about ten minutes."

"Are you nuts?"

"No, I told Stinger that you were going to have to work late at the paper and that you didn't sound too happy about being there by yourself at night. So we decided it would be fun to surprise you there. Stinger says there's a landing pad on top of your building."

"There is, but—"

"Who's going to know?" he asked, anticipating my objection.

"One of the computer maintenance guys goes up there for a smoke every now and then."

"Is he the type that would tell on you?"

"No," I admitted.

"Hurry, then! We're almost there!"

Wondering if Wrigley might call to check up on me, I set the phone on my desk to forward calls to the cell phone.

I took the stairs to the top of the building—a good workout—and opened the door marked ROOF ACCESS.

This actually opened on to another stairway. When I opened the final door, and stepped out onto the roof, I took a moment to enjoy my surroundings. It was good to be out in the open. The night air was cool but not chilly enough to make me long for a jacket. A slight sea breeze blew away the worst of the city smells. Sounds came to me—muffled traffic sounds, the hum of transformers and machinery housed on the roof, the sharp ching-ching-ching of the cables on the flagpoles, the soft flapping of the brightly lit flags (the Stars and Stripes and the California Bear). Within this mix I could also hear the steady pulse of an approaching, but still distant, helicopter.

Peering over the edge of the building, I could see some of the gargoyles and other ornamentation that in my childhood had put me in awe of this building, and had long since endeared it to me. I remembered the first time my father told me that this was the place where the newspaper was made, the *Las Piernas News Express* that landed so unfailingly on our driveway each morning, a grand publication that could have only come from so grand a place.

I reached over the waist-high guardrail and trailed my fingers across the sooty masonry, remembering my youthful veneration. "And look where that got me, old girl."

I looked up at the flat, featureless face of the skyscraper next door, a dark gray nothingness broken up only by an office light left on here and there. The Box, I sometimes called it. The Box had other names—so many, in fact, it kept signmakers busy changing the logo at the top every few years. For all its shiny newness, it had never filled all of its rooms. Some of the Wrigley's were empty now, too, but we had been around a lot longer. I stroked the stonework again.

I brushed off my fingertips and began walking. Although newer, taller buildings nearby have made it less spectacular than it once was, the view from the roof of the Wrigley Building is still breathtaking.

I wasn't at the highest point of the building; part of the roof held several structures—some of them fairly tall—that were clustered at the end of the roof nearest the stairway. A series of narrow alleyways ran between the housing for the huge air-conditioning unit, various utilities, the high mounting block of the satellite dishes and others. The flagpoles and a spindly lightning rod were on top of one of the tallest and longest of these, most of the space below used for storage.

Despite these obstructions, one could walk all around the perimeter of the roof and still see quite a distance. I didn't have time to take the grand tour that night—I could hear the helicopter coming closer.

I hurried to the other side of the building, and stood near an area with a special flat surface, painted with markings—the helicopter pad.

By now, I had seen the big Sikorsky. Its noise drowned out all other sound, a bright light shone down from beneath it, and a stinging cloud of dust and grime was raised in counterpoint to its slow descent to the landing pad.

I found myself grinning, pleased with Travis's skills, wondering what my mother's shy sister would have thought of her son's outlandish arrival. I waved and waited for them to shut down the engines, then to crawl out of the cockpit.

"Were you piloting just now?" I asked Travis, after we exchanged greetings, knowing full well that he had been.

"Yes," he said. "My first night landing on top of a city building!"

"Your first?" I echoed, then tried not to let him see how much that statement unnerved me. "You did great."

"Sorry about all that dust," Stinger said, shaking my hand. "Been a while since anybody landed here?"

"Yes. The *Express* used to have its own helicopter, but that was before budget cutbacks. Now the paper has a contract with a company at the airport. They'll come here and pick up reporters and photographers and take us to anything we need to get to," I said. "I think we were better off with our own, because we could respond more quickly, get to the scene we were covering without waiting for the contract pilots to pick us up. We're a little slower now. Of course, most of the time, Wrigley just wants us to drive to the scene."

"Hell," Stinger said, pointing back at the Sikorsky, "this will get you most places you need to go a damned sight faster than a car—especially on the L.A. freeways."

"Too bad you have to stay at work," Travis said. "I could take you for a ride."

"I'd like that," I said, "we'll definitely have to set that up for another time. How did you manage to call from the helicopter?"

"Pappy—Stinger's ground crew—stays in radio contact with us while we fly. He patches calls through from Fremont Enterprises to the helicopter, and vice versa. Most of the calls are Stinger's girlfriends—"

"Now, that's enough out of you, Short Stuff," Stinger said, although Travis was easily a head taller than he. "Time we were going. Irene's got to get back to work."

"But you just got here!" I protested.

"We might stay overnight in Las Piernas," Travis said. "Jack said he could put us up. We're just going to do a little more night flying and then go out to the airport after this."

"There's room at our place, too," I said. "Do you need the van back?"

"I might want to borrow it for a little while tomorrow. I'm thinking of making an offer on a place not far from your house."

Pleased by this news, I talked with him for a few more minutes about his plans. When I looked over at Stinger, his head was tilted to one side as he studied me. "When's your next night shift?" he asked.

"Thursday."

"Be back Thursday—same time, same station."

I laughed. "Giving Travis more practice?"

"Call it that," he said, nodding.

"Okay, why not?"

"Well, now that you mention it," he said, scratching his chin, "could be a reason why not. Here, let me borrow your cell phone for a minute."

I handed it to him, and he programmed a number into it. He handed the phone back, and showed me how to retrieve the number he had labeled "Stinger@FE."

"That's 'Stinger at Fremont Enterprises.' That will get you Pappy, and Pappy can patch you through to us. If your boss is hanging around or it's otherwise inconvenient to have a chopper landing here, give a call. Otherwise, we'll see you on Thursday."

They took off.

I walked back toward the stairway access in a much happier frame of mind. I strolled a little more slowly, and found myself thinking that staying at the paper was worth overcoming any obstacles one member of the current generation of Wrigleys might toss in my way. Otherwise, I thought, I might end up in a building that looked like the Box.

I had just reached that corner of the Wrigley Building rooftop where the Box came into full view. I stopped. Something was odd about one window, a window nearly at the same height as the level on which I stood. There was some light in that office, but not enough to work by. Stranger still—this light was moving.

Fluorescent ceiling panels don't move. A bright flashlight? Was I witnessing a robbery?

I had not rounded the corner that would place me in full view of the Box, and as the light bounced off the windowpane a few times, I stepped back into the shadows and took the cell phone out.

The light went out. I stayed where I was, kept watch on the window. Soon I saw a shadowy and indistinct figure standing close to the glass. I could barely make out the outline of this person. Nick Parrish?

Or was I only imagining him again?

I couldn't be sure. But I hadn't imagined that flashlight.

I crouched farther into the shadows and dialed the police.

49

▲ ▼ ▲ ▼

WEDNESDAY, SEPTEMBER 20, 12:15 A.M.

The Roof of the Wrigley Building

Next I called home.

"Irene? Are you all right?"

"I'm okay. Did I wake you?"

"No. I'm waiting up for you."

"You know how you said I should tell you if I thought I saw Parrish again?"

"Yes. Where is he?"

I told him that I had just reported a possible burglary in progress in the building next door, and quickly explained why I was on the roof. "But now I'm wondering if I should have mentioned Parrish after all," I admitted. "I don't want them to be unprepared if it is him."

"Get inside, and find Jerry or Livy or anyone else who's working there. Promise me you'll do that until a unit gets there. And alert the security guard in the lobby."

I agreed to do as he asked, and began my descent.

I had entered the second stairwell when I heard footsteps. I halted, listening.

I heard a door close below me. The metal rails were vibrating, as most of the building does when the presses are running. The rumble comes pulsing up from the basement, not loud at this height, but persistent. I felt my hand trembling in a different rhythm. I took the phone out again and tried to dial security, every little beep of the keypad seeming to blast out like a brass band. I waited for the call to go through, but nothing happened. I looked at the display—no signal. The stairwell wasn't a great place for reception.

I waited. I thought I heard another sound below me.

Jerry or Livy, I told myself. Moving from floor to floor to work on the computers. I waited.

When one of those three-minute years had gone by without my hearing any other sounds, I crept down to the next level and reached a doorway; I tried it—it was locked. I was frustrated, but not surprised. Even by elevator, these upper-level offices could only be accessed if you had a special key, and the doors to the stairway opened only from the other side.

I listened, and still not hearing any other noises, went for broke—completely unnerved now, I made a mad dash down the stairs. I swung around the last turn on the landing above the newsroom just as the door to the newsroom flew open. A man in dark clothing stepped out. He was pointing a gun at me.

I stopped, threw my hands up, and tried to say something. My mouth worked something like a guppy's, but no sound came out.

The security guard spoke first. "Jesus Christ, Kelly!" he said, lowering his gun to my kneecaps. "You just scared the shit out of me."

"Put the gun away, please," I said, wishing I could recall his name. "You're *still* scaring the shit out of me." Barely shaving, but he had a gun. Geoff, the day-shift guard, was nearing eighty (some swore it would be for the second time) and never wore a weapon. Guess who made me feel safer?

He holstered it, and hiked up his belt. "Your husband called. He said you had called him from the roof on your cell phone, but when he tried to call you back, there was no answer. He just got the phone's voice mail. So he tried to call your desk, but he got the cell phone again."

"This warrants an armed response?"

"Oh—well, as for that—just before I heard from him, I heard a call on the scanner—they think Parrish is in the building next door. I figured he might be after you, so I came prepared."

This was spoken with an easy confidence that did not indicate the slightest awareness that I might have been the recipient of a few rounds of whatever caliber he had in the clip. He was smiling now, and extended a hand, ready to assist me down the stairs. I let him guide me into the newsroom, where I all but collapsed into the nearest chair.

He picked up his radio and talked into it. "This is Unit One calling in."

When there was no reply, he frowned in consternation and tried again. "Unit One to Central. You there, Jerry?"

"Leonard?" came the reply. "You calling the front desk? What's with this 'Unit One to Central' horseshit?"

Leonard. How could I have forgotten that name?

"Do *not* use profanity on the security radio, Jerry! Totally against regulations. Totally!"

Leonard rolled his eyes and turned the radio off. "I better get down to the desk," he said to me. "Are you okay? You want me to get you a glass of water or anything?"

He hurried off to the water cooler before I could answer. A man of action, our Leonard. But I found myself starting to like him.

"I've got a bottle of spring water already started," I said, and he detoured with a smart about-face to fetch it from my desk.

"You should call your husband, let him know you're okay," he said sternly, handing the bottle to me.

"I will."

"He's with LPPD Homicide, right?"

"Yes."

"Hmm. Bring him by sometime. I'd like to meet him. By the way—that was cool about throwing the monitor and all, but don't break anything on my shift, okay?"

"I'll try not to."

A thorough search of the building next door did reveal that the office I had indicated had been broken into, although it did not appear that anything had been taken.

There was no sign of Parrish. It hadn't been easy to look for him in every nook and cranny of the Box, but no one on the Las Piernas Police force acted put out by the effort they had exerted. That doesn't mean they weren't irritated—but better trained than Leonard, they didn't threaten to shoot me.

When I came in to work the next shift on Thursday, there was a note stuck to the screen of my computer monitor:

> Kelly, please do try to work one shift without bringing the cops in here.
>
> *John*

I saved it to show to Frank the next time he asked me to let him hover over my desk.

Stinger was true to his word. On Thursday night, Jerry and Livy joined me to watch the landing, and were duly impressed. They then went downstairs to give Leonard a chance to take a look.

While we were waiting for the young man whom Stinger had (sight unseen) dubbed "Leonardo DaGung-ho," I asked them to show me what was done to sabotage the helicopters up in the mountains.

Stinger showed me the drain plug.

"Why do helicopters have something like this on them?" I asked.

"In the normal course of a day," he said, "moist air gets inside the fuel tank. The tank is made of metal, right? So as the metal in the tank cools, the water in the air condenses and drops into the fuel. Because water is heavier than the fuel, the water then goes to the bottom of the tank."

"If water is in your tank," Travis said, "and it gets mixed in with your fuel, it causes problems. When you start up and try to run, your engines might not run smoothly—they might misfire."

"So you open the valve and let the water drain out of the tank before you start up?" I asked.

"Right."

"So if it hadn't been raining, the Forest Service crew might have smelled all the fuel leaking out of the helicopters that night in the mountains?"

"Might have," Stinger agreed. "But what could they have done about it anyway? The person who sabotaged those helicopters walked off with the drain plugs."

"So the rangers couldn't have refilled the tanks without replacements."

"Right. The Forest Service and the cops have had metal detectors out, trying to find those plugs. I think whoever sabotaged them still has his souvenirs."

"They're small enough to carry in a pocket," I said.

"Yes, they are. You find those drain plugs, you've got Parrish's helper."

Leonard was bouncing with excitement when he met Stinger and Travis. "Wait here, man, wait here!" He hurried over to one of the rooftop buildings. A few minutes later, the helicopter pad was illuminated by a series of lights set into the roof itself.

He strutted back, hiking his pants again. "I'll show Irene where the switch is," he said. "You can land in style."

They thanked him, and stayed a few minutes more. Just before they took off, Leonard asked Travis, "How old are you?"

When Travis told him, his eyes widened, and he said, "Dude! Not much older than me."

He stood watching the helicopter long after they had taken off. "Thinking of giving up law enforcement?" I asked.

"No way. Air patrol!" He looked around the roof and said, "They said they're coming back tomorrow. I'm going to fix it so you can relax up here." He smiled. "Jerry's up here smoking all the time, so we'll make a nonsmoking section."

He showed me where the lights for the landing pad were, and then we walked back to the access door. I forced myself to look up at the Box. The window where I had seen the burglar was dark tonight.

"Too bad they didn't catch him," Leonard said, following my gaze.

"The burglar?"

"Parrish," he said.

"Maybe he wasn't there."

"He was there," he said authoritatively. "But don't you worry—I'm not going to let him come into the Wrigley Building—no way."

This from a guy who nearly shot me. But I thanked him, and then thanked him again a little later, when he sneaked us on to one of the executive-level floors and into the elevator.

Better yet, he let me on it again for the trip up to the roof on Friday. Nearly bursting with pride, he took me to "Café Kelly," as he referred to a cluster of four plastic chairs and a metal table borrowed from the cafeteria. "Don't worry, I got permission," he said. "These were in storage by the kitchen. They were glad to have the room." At his own expense, he had also purchased a cooler. He opened it to show me a six-pack of spring water.

"See? I even noticed your brand." He nodded. "I'm a trained observer."

"Leonard, this is very kind—but you didn't need to go to all this effort."

"Well, I like you. I like helping people. And maybe someday you might put in a good word about me, maybe have someone come by and meet me or something."

I smiled. "Oh, so it's a bribe to meet Frank."

He protested quickly and vehemently, until I told him that I was just teasing.

"Oh."

He still seemed offended. I made a big show of sitting in one of the chairs and opening a bottle of water and exclaiming over how great it was to have such a nice setup. He seemed pleased by all of this, and was soon back in his usual good humor. He heard the helicopter and turned on the landing pad lights, then stood entranced as the chopper blew dirt and dust all over Café Kelly. Afterward, he must have asked Travis a dozen times if the lights had helped him land "that baby."

His radio crackled, and he knocked his plastic chair over standing up to answer it. "This is Unit One."

"Unit One, this is Central," Jerry's voice said. "You ever going to give me a turn up there? I'm dying for a smoke."

"You should quit that filthy habit," he said, but excused himself and left.

I talked to Stinger and Travis for a while, learning that

Travis had decided to buy the house he had looked at. He told me that he was taking Stinger to meet my eighty-year-old great-aunt, Mary Kelly. "She wants us to stay there for a few days."

"I think you and Mary will get along fine," I said to Stinger.

Stinger grinned. "Travis tells me she's full of piss and vinegar."

"She is," I agreed. "She'll give you a run for your money, Mr. Dalton."

"She's already asked him about helicopters," Travis said.

"She wants a ride?"

"Yeah, but I mean, she wants to fly them, too."

"God help us."

Jerry came upstairs for his smoke, and Stinger and Travis soon left. They hovered, shining a bright light down on the roof, watching my progress to the access door the way someone might watch to make sure his date got safely inside the house. I waved to them and headed back down to the newsroom, reflecting on how much more tolerable this shift was because of their visits, outrageous as some might deem their method of arrival.

They helped me to get through this sentence Wrigley had passed on me, even allowed me to secretly thumb my nose at him. If Travis felt reassured that I was safe by checking up on me in this way, I could live with it.

The truth was, I did feel less vulnerable. Yes, I now parked close to the building and Jerry—on his own initiative—escorted me to and from the van. But these precautions were becoming routine. And each night as I passed the Box, I was becoming more and more certain that it had only been a burglar after all, and not Parrish.

The drive home at the end of these late shifts was always virtually free of traffic, but, like the newsroom, a little too shadowy and quiet. This night, fog had started to roll in, and as I drove down dark and empty, misty streets, I found myself thinking of science fiction shows where the protagonist somehow is the sole survivor of a neutron bomb attack or annihilation by aliens. He has the town to himself, but no one to share it with.

Well, I thought, I have someone to share it with—I should

call Frank. But I knew that just hearing the phone ring would be enough to make him feel a few moments of fear that I was in trouble, so I decided to wait. I was only ten minutes from home.

I kept hearing a soft, intermittent thumping sound from the rear of the van, and worried that the LPPD had damaged it somehow when they towed it to the impound yard. The exact location of the noise was elusive; I couldn't quite figure out what might be causing it.

I turned the radio on. A talk show was in progress. I listened to a so-called therapist berate a caller, who responded with masochistic groveling. It made me appreciate Jo Robinson. I switched to a jazz station.

I breathed a sigh of relief as I pulled into the driveway. I turned the radio off and was unplugging the cell phone from its dashboard charger when I noticed that its display showed that I had voice mail.

Shit! I should have checked it sooner—I pressed the button that retrieves messages, wondering if Wrigley had called to check up on me after all.

There were two messages. This did not bode well.

"First message," the automated voice of the phone service said. "Sent today at 12:11 A.M."

Not Wrigley, but John. Good news, actually. His message was that Wrigley had agreed to change my schedule to a solid week of late shifts, Monday through Friday. I would still only work part-time, but I didn't have to try to get myself out of bed on three hours' sleep to go in on Saturday morning. I would have the weekend off.

I listened to the overly pleasant recorded voice on the service saying, "To repeat this message, press one. To delete this message, press two. To save this message . . ."

I pressed two.

"Second message. Sent today at 12:16 A.M."

Expecting that the second one would be John trying again, I wasn't ready for what I heard.

Parrish's voice.

"It has been so long since we've talked, my dear. I really have missed you, but we've both been busy, haven't we? Tell me, is your phone cellular or digital? I did leave a *digital* message for you . . ." He gave a soft laugh.

"I wonder if you've taken a good look at yourself lately? You're looking a little tired. Not getting enough sleep? Careful, you'll wear yourself to the bone."

More laughter. I opened the door and got out of the van and stumbled toward the house.

"Now, even though you locked your doors like a good girl this time, I do need to let you know that locks won't stop me. I've left something a little perishable—or should I say, 'Parrishable'?—for you in the van."

I turned back toward the van and shouted for Frank.

"I think Ben Sheridan will enjoy it," Parrish went on. "Tell him I did. And tell him that I'm about to take you out of his reach."

There was a click. After a slight pause, the pleasant recorded voice on the voice mail service said, "To repeat this message, press one. To delete this message, press two. To save this message . . ."

But pleasant voices were beyond my hearing at that moment. I tossed the phone on the lawn as if I had suddenly found myself handling a snake; I hurried to open the sliding side door on the van.

Frank ran out of the house with Deke and Dunk. "Irene?" he asked frantically. "What's wrong?"

I pointed toward the phone as I crawled into the van and saw him go to pick it up.

"Irene, no!" he shouted, as I opened the refrigerator.

Too late.

A little light went on inside the tiny, aquamarine-colored space.

A human skull stared back at me.

50

▲▼▲▼

SATURDAY, SEPTEMBER 23, 2:45 A.M.

Las Piernas

I've tried, but even now I cannot remember most of what happened in the first few minutes immediately after I saw it. I vaguely recall that at some point Frank held me tightly by the shoulders and shouted at me, angry in his fear for my safety, his terror over imagining what trap I might have sprung by responding so unthinkingly to Parrish's taunting.

He was right, of course—I never should have touched it.

He tells me I responded to his ranting by calmly saying, "I thought he only cut off her fingers and toes. I didn't know she was decapitated."

"He didn't decapitate her! That's how we knew her hair and eye color!"

Suddenly unable to stand, I sat down on the porch steps.

He closed the van door, then sat next to me, keeping an arm around me as he called the police. Cody, my cat, came outside and sat on my lap. Deke and Dunk had our feet covered.

To some degree, the arrival of the detectives and the crime scene unit roused me from my cocoon of numbness, so that by the time they left I was feeling more myself. I had told them what I could—that Parrish had probably dialed my number at work, and the call had been forwarded; that the van had been locked; that yes, there were security cameras on the parking lot at the *Express*, but they were notoriously inadequate.

The officers called the paper, and learned that three weeks earlier, Leonard had dutifully reported that the camera that covers the parking lot had been vandalized. Wrigley's response had been to post a larger sign that said, PARK AT YOUR OWN RISK. OWNER OF LOT ASSUMES NO RESPONSIBILITY FOR LOSS OR DAMAGE TO VEHICLES OR THEIR CONTENTS. Nor for additions to their contents, evidently.

The next morning—technically, the same morning, but after we had been asleep—we found ourselves a little shy of each other; Frank for losing his temper, me for losing my mind. All the same we never moved far from each other, nor were we out of each other's sight for more than a few moments at a time. Gradually, feeling safer than I had at three in the morning, I began to relax, we began to talk, and by the end of the day, something like balance returned.

"I wish Rachel were in town," he said on Saturday night.

He wasn't longing for another woman—he wanted to hire a bodyguard. His partner's wife was a retired homicide detective and completely capable of kicking ass if need be. But Rachel's work as a private eye had taken her out of state that week.

Though there was a patrol car in front of our house, Frank wasn't just worried about my safety. "I don't want you to feel scared," he said. "You should have company."

I didn't object, which, as far as he was concerned, was probably the most worrisome thing that had happened that day.

On Sunday morning, I awoke to see him putting on his suit. "Sorry—I was trying to let you get a little more sleep. I have to go in. But Ben's going to come over with Bingle—okay?"

I told him that I'd enjoy seeing both Ben and his dog.

I thought I was telling him the truth, but while Bingle would have been welcomed to stay, by midday, I was ready to send Ben packing.

It was around one o'clock when I ventured to ask him if he was the one who was trying to make the identification on the skull.

"Yes, I am," he snapped at me, "and no, I don't know whose skull it is. I'd rather not guess. Especially not in front of a reporter."

"Go home," I said.

"What?"

"Go home. I am barely holding it together here, buster, and you keep making rude remarks. At least two dozen today, and I don't see any end to the supply you seem to have so handy. So get lost."

He frowned, and said, "If I've offended you, I'm sorry."

"Thank you very much. Very sincerely said. Good-bye."

"I'm not leaving."

"Yes, you are."

"No, I'm not. Stop being childish."

"Get the hell out of here!"

"If it were just for your sake, believe me, I'd go. But I promised Frank I would stay with you."

"If you don't get out of here, you won't have to worry about Parrish killing me. By the end of the day, I'll want to kill myself!"

"That's a horrible thing to say!"

"You're right, it is. And I accept that as the highest plaudit from the Master of Horrible Things to Say! Excuse me while I go to make a note of it in my special Horrible Ben Sheridan Diary! I keep it in our special Make Tribute to Ben Sheridan Shrine Room! Be right back—maybe!"

I stomped off into the bathroom and shut the door with a bang. I locked it and turned around.

Someday, when I am very wealthy, I am going to build a house with a bathroom that will allow a person to have a snit fit in it in true comfort. I wasn't wealthy that day.

In fact, everywhere I looked, there was some change we had made to accommodate Ben's disability when he stayed with us. My hands itched to pull it all apart.

I looked in the bathroom cabinet for something that I could break without feeling bad. Nothing. Not even a computer monitor. I sat down on the edge of the tub, head in hands.

I heard him walking quickly down the hall. His gait sounded

odd to me, as if he was favoring his right leg. I forgot about that when I heard him take hold of the doorknob and try to turn it.

"Don't you dare try to come into this room!" I shouted.

"Come out of there now!"

I took hold of a towel, stuffed it in my mouth, and screamed into it.

"Are you screaming into a towel?"

It almost struck me as funny. Almost.

"Open this door," he said.

I didn't answer.

"Are you all right?" he asked.

"Don't ask me if I'm all right, you insincere bastard," I said. "You don't really give a shit. I'm tired of taking crap from you. I'm tired of everything!"

I heard him walk off, then walk back. He was definitely limping.

Suddenly there was a loud bang, and the middle panel of the three-panel bathroom door splintered into pieces as Frank's long-handled flashlight came crashing through it. Outside, all three dogs were barking.

Ben's hand reached through the hole in the door and unlocked the doorknob.

I stared up at him in amazement as he opened the shattered door.

"Why in God's name did you do that?" I asked.

"I wanted to apologize."

It hit me first. I started laughing. He started laughing. I nearly lost my perch on the tub.

The doorbell rang. I went to answer it, wiping tears from my face. It was one of the patrolmen.

"Mrs. Harriman?" he asked, looking past my shoulder, then back at me. "We heard a loud noise—and the dogs. Are you all right?"

"Oh yes," I said, straining to keep my composure.

The officer looked at me warily.

"I made the sound," Ben said sheepishly. "I broke a door."

"I locked myself in the bathroom and couldn't get out," I said quickly. "Dr. Sheridan kindly rescued me."

"Oh," the officer said, and after a fleeting look back at Ben, left us.

We had cleaned up the wood splinters and tacked some brown parcel paper over the opening in the bathroom door when I saw him wincing and rubbing his thigh.

"Ben, rest for a while."

I half expected an argument, but he moved off to the couch. By the time I walked into the living room, all the color had drained from his face.

"I think I overdid it yesterday," he said. "Lately, I've noticed that's the only time the phantom pain really bothers me."

"You tried to keep up with Bingle's SAR group?" I asked.

He nodded. "I would have been fine, I think, but just when I got home they called to tell me about the skull, so I went into the lab, too. I stayed on my feet too long."

"So why are you keeping your rig on? Take it off."

"Some protection I'll be to you then."

"You're right—besides, it's better entertainment to watch you writhe in agony."

He smiled a little. "More entries for your Horrible Ben Diary."

"That bathroom door would probably still be in one piece if you had just admitted that pain was making you crabby. Give me your car keys and I'll get your chair out of the trunk."

"Do you still have that extra set of crutches here?"

"Yes."

"I'll just use those," he said, reaching down to push the release button on his prosthesis.

There were two basic sections to Ben's rig: the socket, worn over the end of his leg, and the Flex-Foot itself. A liner between his skin and the socket held the socket on by suction. A long metal pin extended from the bottom of the socket and fit into a clutch lock, which in turn was attached to his Flex-Foot. By pressing the button on the lock, he removed everything except the socket and liner. The socket and liner couldn't be pulled off, they had to be slowly rolled off. While he went to work on those, I got the crutches.

After bringing him an ice pack, I let the dogs in and fed them.

Frank came home, looking as if he was highly amused over something and greeted me by telling me that it was all over the department that his wife had alarmed the surveillance unit by getting stuck in the bathroom. Ben looked so mortified that I decided to hold off telling Frank the whole story until we were alone.

We invited Jack and Ben to have dinner with us. Afterward, we let Ben have the couch again, and he tried the ice pack once more.

We sat in companionable silence. Cody was on my lap, Deke and Dunk moved back and forth between Frank and Jack, and Bingle refused to let any of them near Ben. Ben had his eyes closed and was stroking Bingle's ears. "Tell me the rest of Parzival," he said.

"Jack could tell it better," I said.

"No, go ahead," Jack said. "You've read it more recently."

So I told of how Parzival went to Wild Mountain, and noticed that the Fisher King suffered some ailment, but having been warned by his mentor not to appear overly curious or to ask others too many questions, Parzival made no inquiries about the Fisher King's health.

I described the great feast in the hall of Wild Mountain, during which the Holy Grail itself was brought forth. Parzival noticed that all the people of the castle looked to him in anticipation, and he was filled with curiosity about all that he had seen—but remembering his mentor's admonitions, he asked no questions.

The next day, after a night of disturbing dreams, he awoke to find himself alone. Thinking it rude of his hosts to abandon him without so much as a servant to help him dress, he donned his clothing and went into the courtyard, where his horse was saddled, his sword and lance nearby. Angry now, he mounted and hurried to the drawbridge. But as he reached the end of it, someone gave the cable a yank, so Parzival nearly fell into the moat. He looked back to see a page, who cursed him and called him a fool. "Why didn't you ask the question?" the boy asked, shaking his fist at the knight.

"What question?" Parzival asked.

But the boy merely shut the iron portcullis and left Parzival with nowhere to go but away from the castle.

"What was the question?" Ben asked.

"Parzival has to go through a lot to find out what it was he should have asked," I said. "But basically, it was long ago foretold that only one person would be allowed to ever find the enchanted Wild Mountain, a knight who would end the suffering of the Fisher King by simply asking one question: 'What's wrong with you?' So Parzival blew his big chance."

"Does he get another one?" Frank asked.

"Yes, but it isn't easy. Parzival is so ashamed, he loses all faith in himself and in God. Eventually he regains it, and eventually, he meets the Fisher King again. He finally asks, 'What's wrong with you?' The king is healed, and everybody lives happily ever after."

"Thank God Travis isn't here," Jack said, almost angrily.

"Why?"

"I'd hate to have that be his impression of the story! You skipped the most important parts of it!" he grumbled.

Ben yawned. "Don't give her a hard time. I enjoyed it. And she's given me something to look forward to when I read it myself. Thanks, Irene."

Jack said good night, and Ben and Bingle went home. Frank and I stayed up a little longer, talking and not talking, more than satisfied with both, and with few thoughts of medieval poetry.

He fell asleep before I did, and I thought about the next day being Monday, and that he would be leaving again early the next morning. I decided I would try again to get in touch with Phil Newly and Jim Houghton.

Plans or no plans, it would still be a Monday. I started softly humming the song I had heard at Gillian's apartment—"I Don't Like Mondays."

That Monday would be one of my worst ever.

51

▲ ▼ ▲ ▼

MONDAY AFTERNOON, SEPTEMBER 25
Las Piernas

The Moth knew about the dog. Because of its work, the dog was trained to be friendly. And even if it had been asked to guard the house, the Moth had spent time getting to know it, and getting to know Ben Sheridan's schedule as well.

Sheridan had cut back on his work at the college. He was teaching the usual number of courses, but he allowed his graduate assistant, Ellen Raice, to handle more of the duties. Ms. Raice had been very forthcoming about Ben Sheridan's schedule.

Knowing when the professor would be on campus made it easy to figure out when to start coming by to talk to the dog. The dog was lonely when his owner was gone, and so he liked the visits, wagged his tail when the Moth approached.

It was really not too surprising, then, that the dog hadn't barked when the Moth once again broke into the garage. Dr. Sheridan had put a different lock on the back door, but not one that prevented breaking the door itself.

The Moth went into the house and carefully searched again.

And failed again.

Angry and frustrated, the Moth swept a gloved hand over a shelf full of videotapes, knocking them to the floor. This time, a little damage should be done. Swinging the crowbar, the Moth watched with glee as other things flew off the shelves—books, framed photographs. The most satisfying moment came when the iron bar hit the screen of the television set with a bang. At the sound of breaking glass, the dog started barking.

This had a slightly sobering effect. If the dog heard it, had the nosy old neighbor heard it? The old woman's attention to everything going on around here had already forced the Moth to park on another street, to climb fences to get here.

The dog kept barking.

Frightened, the Moth hid in the bathroom. After a while, the dog was quiet again. "What would Nicky say if you were caught?" the Moth asked aloud, but the thought was more irritating than frightening.

Nicky had been ignoring his Moth.

Angry again, but more under control now, the Moth opened the medicine chest, found Ben Sheridan's pain medication and stole it.

In the kitchen, the Moth did a search of the cabinets and quickly found the dog's food. The Moth opened a can of this, put a small amount of it into a bowl and began opening the capsules of pain medication over it. Mixing a dozen or so of them in well, the Moth put the cap back on the bottle and was about to take it—then paused. Wouldn't do to be caught carrying something with Sheridan's name on it, now would it? Spilling the pills out and pocketing them, the Moth left the container on the counter and went outside.

The dog did not perceive an enemy. This was a familiar person carrying a bowl of food. The dog was alert, and studied the Moth now. The dog was already interested in what the Moth had brought for him.

The Moth opened the gate to the run just slightly, then slid the bowl in.

"Good dog."

The dog looked up at the Moth, then cocked his head to one side. The dog stared at the food, licked his chops, but didn't touch it.

Was there some command it was waiting for?

The Moth opened the gate again, reached into the bowl and

took a handful of the food and held it under the dog's nose. The dog looked between the Moth and the food, then gently, almost reluctantly, ate the food out of the gloved hand.

This will take forever!

The Moth heard the neighbor's dog barking, then several other dogs barking as well. The big shepherd's ears pitched forward. Was someone approaching the house? The Moth hurried out of the enclosure. Scaling the high back fence, the Moth left through another backyard—a yard whose owners were without a dog, whose owners were never home during the day.

Reaching the car, the Moth closed and locked the door, then sighed, feeling safer now. Driving away, looking in the rearview mirror, satisfied that no one was watching or following, the Moth smiled and said, "*Adiós, Bingle.*"

52

▲ ▼ ▲ ▼

MONDAY AFTERNOON, SEPTEMBER 25

Las Piernas

Jack waited patiently in the van, using his cell phone to have a long talk with Stinger Dalton. This time, the police had left the van, but took my cell phone. They had promised to have it back to me later today, after they had made some recordings of Parrish's call.

I rang Phil Newly's doorbell a dozen times, and knocked until my knuckles were sore. Newly didn't come to the door. I told myself that I should simply accept that he was either not willing to see me or was out of town. I told myself that I should leave—but something kept me from going back to the van. At first, it just seemed to be one of those one-size-fits-all cases of the creeps. I tried to narrow it to something a little more specific.

The house wasn't just quiet, it seemed abandoned. There were a few handbills and a real estate broker's notepad on the front porch. And while the lawn and flower beds, which would be watered by automatic sprinklers, were green, the potted plants on the front porch looked dried out.

I walked over to the front window, but the miniblinds were closed. I thought back to my last visit here. No dogs. I opened the gate to the backyard. I called Phil's name. Nothing.

There were more windows along the back of the house. The blinds were down here, too, but one of them hadn't closed properly. I realized that it was the room where Phil spent most of his time. I moved closer to the window and peered in.

"What the hell are you doing?" a voice said behind me.

I jumped back, hand over heart. "Damn it, Jack, don't do that!"

"Don't sneak up on you when you're sneaking around?"

"Right." I looked back into the house, then at Jack. "Something's wrong here."

"What is it?" he asked.

"Look in there. What do you see?"

He looked, and said, "Nothing much. A couple of chairs, bookshelves, and a little table."

"A few days ago, there was a pile of books on that table, and he was looking at maps."

"When?"

I thought about it. "About two weeks ago, I guess."

"Irene . . ."

"He lives in this room. It's too neat. I can even see the marks the vacuum cleaner made on the carpet."

Jack shook his head. "You were in it once and you know for a fact that he never cleans this room? Don't you think it's possible that a cleaning lady or someone else with a vacuum cleaner has been through here in the last two weeks?"

"I don't know, Jack, you're probably right. But doesn't the house seem a little empty?"

"Maybe he went off to see his sister again."

"Maybe so," I said. "Maybe I'm overreacting."

But the more I thought about it, the more it made sense to me to worry about Newly's whereabouts while Parrish was on the loose. By the time we were back at home, I was convinced that someone should try to locate the lawyer.

"What is it you're imagining?" Jack asked. "That he's been killed? If so, where's his mail? Where's the pile of newspapers?"

"Newspapers!" I went to the phone and called circulation. They don't give out subscriber information as a rule, so I decided to do a little acting.

"Hi, this is Mrs. Phil Newly," I said, and gave his address. "I just wondered what's been happening to our newspaper."

The service rep asked for my phone number. After two seconds of mad panic while I fumbled to find it, I gave them Phil's. She looked up his records by using the phone number.

"Mrs. Newly, your husband canceled that subscription."

"He did!" I said in mock outrage. "When did he do that?"

She named the date—it was the day after I visited Phil Newly.

"Do you want to reinstate the subscription, Mrs. Newly?" the rep asked.

"I'd love to," I said, "but I'd better talk to Phil and see what he's up to first."

I called Frank. "Something fishy is going on with Phil Newly," I said, and told him what I had found out. "Did he give you the number at his sister's place?"

"I'm sure we have it here somewhere," he said. "You worried about him or suspicious of him?"

"Both. I suppose—it's a little difficult for the police to get a search warrant for a criminal defense attorney's house, right?"

"A little." He laughed. "I'll see what I can find out from his sister, though."

I received a surprise phone call at about three o'clock.

"Irene Kelly?" a male voice said. Familiar, but not someone I had heard recently. Then it struck me.

"Jim Houghton?"

"Listen, I'm a private citizen now, and I don't have to talk to any reporters. So stay the hell off my tail, would you? You and your PI friend."

"Rachel contacted you?"

"Yes. Now, she told me if I called you, you would probably leave me alone. So I've called you."

"Wait—I didn't call you because of the newspaper."

There was a long pause, then he said, "Oh no? Why then?"

"I just need to talk to other people who survived being up there."

"I didn't. You don't call it surviving when you aren't there for the action, okay? I wasn't anywhere near the place. I left with Newly, remember? So, I'm safe and sound, and you're safe and sound. So's Parrish. Good-bye, Ms. Kelly. And tell Harriman I said he ought to keep you at home if he wants you to live."

He hung up.

Jack saw me shaking my head. "What is it?"

"That call. I don't know what to make of it." I told him what had been said.

He called Frank, and told him that I had been threatened by a former LPPD cop. I grabbed the phone away.

"Not exactly, Frank." I thought a verbatim recitation of the call would calm him down, but Frank was as unhappy with Houghton as Jack was.

"I'm going to go over this guy's background with a microscope," he said. "And I want Rachel to tell me where she found him. I want him watched."

"But the department would have checked him out when he signed up, right?"

"Very thoroughly," he agreed. "But five years ago, when Houghton joined the LPPD, the name Nick Parrish didn't mean anything to us, so there could be a connection nobody saw back then."

Ben came by on his way home from work.

"Do you remember those videotapes of Bingle's training sessions with the search group?" he asked.

"Yes, the ones I brought to you in the hospital. You left them here after you stayed with us. Do you want me to get them for you?"

"Yes, please. I've watched the ones I have at home so often I could narrate them for the blind."

I got the box of tapes from the garage. "How is everything going?" I asked when I came back in.

"Fine—in fact, you should see the place now. I've made a few changes. Why don't you and Jack come over this afternoon?"

Jack was agreeable. We followed him over to the house. I was amused to note that rather than going in through the front door, the first place he headed was to the backyard, to see Bingle.

We followed him through the back gate, where he came to a sudden halt. I nearly plowed into him.

"Bingle?" he said.

The dog wobbled up on all fours, then lurched forward. He fell flat, but got up again, standing unsteadily, looking woozy. He whined softly.

"Hey," Jack said, "looks like somebody's busted into your garage again."

Ben ignored him. We ran to the dog run. Ben opened it and hurried inside.

"Oh God, Bingle!" Ben said, running his hands over the dog as Bingle collapsed in a heap. "Are you okay? Are you okay, Bingle? Shit! How do I say that in Spanish?"

By then, both Jack and I had crowded into the enclosure with him. I figured Bingle's understanding of Spanish was great for any number of dog commands but probably didn't extend to conversation. All the same, I understood Ben's panic, and told him, "*¿Estás bien, Bingle?*"

He asked it, and when the dog just lay there, Ben looked anxiously at me.

I glanced around and saw Bingle's dish, which had a little food in it—the food was still moist. I picked up the dish. "Don't you usually take this away after he's eaten?"

"Oh Jesus—I didn't put that in here! I haven't fed him yet this afternoon. I—I think someone has poisoned him."

"Let's get him to the vet," I said. "We should bring the food with us, too."

I drove as fast as I dared. Ben sat in the back with Bingle, talking to him, petting him. When we arrived, Bingle was hurried into an examination room.

Jack used his phone to call Frank and tell him what had happened, and mentioned the break-in. "No, we didn't even have time to look around inside the house." He looked over at me, then said, "That's probably a good idea."

When he hung up, he said, "Frank's going to try to get a unit over there right away, just to make sure no one else goes in or out, but they'll wait until Ben gets there. He's going to go home and make sure Deke and Dunk are okay—just in case . . ."

"Just in case this is Parrish's doing. Of course it is." I got up and paced. "Still, I think Parrish has a personal dislike of Bingle. He threatened to shoot Bingle when we were up in the mountains."

Ben was in with Bingle and the vet for a long time; Frank came by while we were waiting.

"Deke and Dunk are okay," he said. "I've put them inside with Cody and warned the surveillance team about what happened at Ben's place."

Ben came out, walking like a zombie. He sat down next to me, said hello to Frank, then told us that the vet had emptied Bingle's stomach. "They said that he didn't seem to have eaten much. But . . ." He lowered his head into his hands. "It all depends on what it was that they fed him."

"Is there any way to find out?" I asked.

"Probably not in time. He checked the food, it looked as if there was some sort of powder in it; mostly it was blended into the food, but sort of haphazardly. It wasn't anything caustic, but that's all we know right now. They want to keep him here—keep him under observation."

Frank said, "Mind if I talk to the vet?"

"Not at all. I need to get back to the house, to see if they left any sign of the poison . . ."

"A unit's there waiting for you," Frank said. "Just show them some ID."

"A unit?"

Jack's mention of the break-in had apparently never registered with him. We told him about the broken garage door.

"If you don't mind waiting for me," Frank said, "I'd like to be there when you walk through. I'll only be a minute."

He came out carrying a bag which held the dog food bowl.

There was a crime scene unit on hand—they greeted me by name—and much more investigative power than most citizens would get for a burglary call, but this break-in had merited special attention. Nick Parrish or his accomplice might have paid this visit. The police were giving the place a thorough inspection, looking for trace evidence, hoping to find something that might help them identify that accomplice or lead them to Parrish. Ben, who had numbly walked past the destruction in his living room, underwent a change when he discovered the empty plastic medicine container on the kitchen counter.

"Codeine!" he shouted, just barely restraining himself from touching it before Frank needed to warn him. "Codeine! I have to call the vet!" He started to reach for the phone, thought better of it, and momentarily looked lost.

Jack pulled out his cell phone, pushed a button to recall the most recently dialed numbers, found the one he wanted, and handed the phone to Ben.

Ben told the vet what he had learned, then looked at the bottle without touching it. He read off the dosage level, then said, "I just had it refilled over the weekend. It was for thirty capsules. I hadn't taken any of them yet. They're all gone." He looked over at the dog food can on the counter. "I think just about half of one can . . . almost thirteen ounces. Three hundred and sixty-one grams. It looks as if he didn't eat much of it. At that level . . . yes, I understand. Yes, a big dog, but not an adult's body weight." He listened for a while, then said, "Yes, I'd appreciate that." He wrote down a number.

He hung up and said, "All thirty at once is a heavy dosage—enough to kill him." His voice caught, but he went on. "They can't tell how much Bingle ingested, because it wasn't distributed evenly through the food. But he thinks that it probably wasn't so much, because Bingle seems to be doing better."

Later, Frank asked him, "What's on these videotapes—the two that really got smashed?"

"They're training tapes. When the Las Piernas Search and Rescue group gets together—including the cadaver dog team—we tape our sessions."

"So these are tapes of Bingle?"

"Bingle and the other dogs and their handlers. David is in most of these. I've been watching him and Bingle. I've only been to one session so far. The other handlers tell me that it's a two-way learning process, that Bingle is already trying to work with me, trying to read me as much as I'm trying to read him."

"These are the original tapes?"

"Yes, although David made copies for the other members of the group."

"Do you have a roster for this SAR group?"

"Yes."

"Good. I think we're going to want to see who was on these tapes."

"I can tell you that," he said. "I've watched them a lot."

Frank looked around at the mess. "Why don't you stay at our place tonight? Closer to the vet."

"I work tonight," I said, "but don't have to be anywhere tomorrow until the afternoon. I can help you clean up during the day."

"We'll get your back door boarded shut," Frank said, "and we'll be watching this place, too, from now on."

"Okay, okay." He laughed. "I'm sold. To be honest, I wasn't looking forward to staying here without Bingle tonight."

Ben gathered a change of clothes and put them in the back of his car. He was going to follow us back to the house. He started to get into his Jeep, then hurried over to the van. "Wait a minute," he said. "There are some tapes that didn't get smashed—the ones from your house—they should still be in the back of the van."

"Irene, I can see what we'll be doing before you go in tonight," Jack said, eyeing the twenty or so tapes in the box. "Want me to make popcorn?"

53

▲ ▼ ▲ ▼

MONDAY NIGHT, SEPTEMBER 25

Las Piernas

He was enraged. He didn't reveal it.

"Poor Moth," he said into the telephone, "you should have come to me in the first place, of course."

He was glad of the long cord on the telephone in the garage. It allowed him to pace as he listened to one lame excuse after another. Really, this was too much!

He halted in front of the freezer, ran his fingers over the lid. It calmed him.

"Yes, my dear Moth, but I already knew about that first visit to David Niles's home . . . you didn't doubt that did you?"

In truth, Nick had known nothing of the sort, but it wouldn't hurt the Moth to believe a little more strongly in his omniscience. He had been wounded and escaping to that rathole in Oregon when the break-in occurred. He should have wondered how the Moth had learned certain things about Sheridan.

"I have to hang up now," he said into the phone. "You and I must meet later. Left on your own, this would have been a hopeless mess. Luckily for you, I'm here to take care of you, my Moth. Wait for my call—and I mean that, little Moth. You must simply wait. You wouldn't want to displease me—would you?"

He listened with satisfaction to the Moth's pleading tone. "I thought not." He hung up.

He put the phone back in the cradle and returned to the freezer. He unlocked it and lifted the lid, enjoyed the rush of cold air that drifted up to his face.

He looked down at the frozen, nude corpse and said, "I know it's rather difficult to answer questions under the circumstances, my dear, but would you care to dance?"

He smiled.

"I *knew* I should have left your head on, just in case questions like these might arise. I have others, mostly about you-know-who. But you know, I think I have the answers to those questions anyway. You're something of a cold fish."

He slammed the lid closed and laughed uproariously.

It took him a few moments to regain his composure.

When he did, he put his gloves on and opened the freezer once more. He stared down at her a moment, then with one gloved finger, traced the outline of a birthmark on her inner thigh.

"You were his whore, of course, so he must have seen this. Did he love it, or did he hate it? Was it one of your imperfections or one of your charms?"

The plastic beneath the body crinkled as he lifted her. For a moment, he hugged her to himself, saying, "I'm so sorry we didn't have more time together, darling. But you can't blame a boy like me for trying to get a head!"

He admonished himself once his levity was back under control—if he didn't stop being so witty, the poor little darling would thaw before they found her.

He waltzed toward the car, clutching her to him.

His mind slipped a little then, and he thought of Irene Kelly, and his rage returned. "We'll show them, won't we, sweetheart?" he said to his dancing partner, and tenderly placed her in the trunk of the car.

54

▲ ▼ ▲ ▼

MONDAY NIGHT, SEPTEMBER 25

Las Piernas

We soon realized that watching tapes of Bingle and David was not such a great idea. After two minutes of the first tape, Ben turned it off and called the vet's office; Bingle was asleep, his heartbeat was normal.

Good news, but Ben looked miserable. He blamed himself, and wondered if he should have kept Bool, so that Bingle would not have been left alone. "Why won't Parrish just come after me?" he asked. "Leave the dog out of it."

Later, he said, "Bingle's not used to being caged at night. What if he wakes up and thinks I'm giving him away?"

Frank called to say that Houghton had been living near Dallas, in Irving, Texas. "Doesn't look like he's left the Dallas area in months, but we're still checking that out."

That night, Jack came with me to work, an arrangement John approved, sort of. "If it will keep me from having a uniformed cop inside the newsroom, fine," he said. "Just don't tell Wrigley. As it is, seeing all the police surveillance of the building, he's nervous as a turkey in late November. Called the chief of police this afternoon to complain about it."

"He'd rather have Nick Parrish in his newsroom?"

"I don't think he, uh, exactly believes the suggestion that Parrish is hanging out around here. Maybe he doesn't want to believe it."

I took Jack up to Café Kelly that night. When Stinger, Travis, and Leonard learned what had happened to Bingle, I thought Stinger just might go on a house-to-house hunt for Nick Parrish, with Leonard and Travis riding posse.

I asked him about Aunt Mary, and his mood changed immediately. "If I was twenty years younger, I'd ask her to marry me," he said with a grin.

When I got home, I discovered Cody had stretched himself out on Frank's chest, but the dogs were nowhere in sight. "They're in with Ben," Frank said sleepily.

I don't know if a dream awakened me, or if I heard Ben go outside. Either way, at about four in the morning, I knew I wasn't going to be able to get back to sleep. I dressed and went out to the patio, where Ben was sitting, already dressed and drinking coffee, petting Deke and Dunk.

"I called the vet," he said. "They say Bingle got up and he's barking. They think he's going to be fine."

"Great news," I said. "If he's barking, he must be getting better."

"Yes. I told them how to say 'be quiet' in Spanish. They said I could pick him up at eight."

"So here you are with a mere four hours to wait."

He smiled. "Right. At first I was too worried to sleep. Now, I'm too relieved. Ridiculous, isn't it?"

"No. You know I'm one of Bingle's biggest fans. And if anything happened to one of these guys, or Cody, I'd be a basket case. What's your schedule tomorrow? Can you catch up on sleep?"

"I'll be okay as far as sleep goes. I did sleep a little tonight—as much as I need. I'm supposed to be your . . ."

"Bodyguard?"

"How about—companion? What's your schedule?"

"I have an appointment with Jo Robinson in the afternoon.

Then I'm working from ten at night until two in the morning, but I think Frank is planning to relieve you from duty before then."

We sat in silence for a time. I thought about my assignments from Jo. I hadn't done too badly, but there was this Parzival business.

"Ben?"

"Hmm?"

"Before Parrish escaped—"

"Before the others were killed," he insisted, always annoyed at my attempt to avoid saying it.

"Before the others were killed," I conceded, "even before we found Julia Sayre, something was bothering you."

"What do you mean?"

"I mean, Ben—to quote good old Parzival—'What's wrong with you?' "

He looked away from me.

"I have a feeling it has something to do with reporters."

He didn't answer.

"Or was it an instant dislike of me, personally?"

"Of course not."

"Then what troubled you? What made you so angry? Why couldn't you sleep at night?"

"Many things," he answered softly.

I waited. He tried to fob me off with a list of the mass disaster cases he had worked recently.

"David told me about them," I said. "And while I'm not saying that I'd have the fortitude to work one of those cases, let alone as many as you have, David hinted there was something else going on with you."

"He did?" he said. "I'm surprised. David was usually better at keeping confidences."

"Don't try to make this about David. Unless you had some particularly awful experience with a reporter on one of those disaster cases, I don't think that's what made you snap at me from the moment I joined the team."

He hesitated, then said, "I'm tempted to make something up. It would be easier than telling you the truth." He sighed. "But after all you've done for me, the least I can do is be honest."

"You don't owe me anything. Tell me because we're friends, or don't tell me at all."

He looked out at the garden. In a low voice, he said, "It has a rather sordid beginning, I'm afraid. The end of a relationship. You remember Camille?"

"Yes—the blond bombshell who visited you at the hospital."

He nodded. "Camille is bright and funny, loves the outdoors, and yes, when we dated, I knew that every guy who saw her on my arm was green with envy."

"So what went wrong?"

"Me, I guess. She finally realized that I wasn't going to change in the ways she hoped I would."

"What was she hoping would change?"

"My work, mostly. She didn't mind dating an anthropologist, but she hated everything about the forensic work—the demands on my time, the thought of what I was doing, the smell of my clothes when I came home. She kept hoping that I'd weary of it, and take a position with a museum. I finally made it clear to her that I'd never leave forensic work, that it was important to me. She asked me if it was more important than she was, and I'm afraid I answered with my usual lack of tact."

"So you ended up moving out."

"Yes. I missed her a lot at first, but on the whole, I knew we were better off apart. I enjoyed living with David and Bingle and Bool. And I needed David's support not long after that."

He was silent for so long, I began to think he had changed his mind about talking to me. Eventually, though, he went on.

"A few weeks after I had moved out, Camille asked me to meet her for lunch. She said she had some things to give me, things I had left behind at the house—a few CDs and an old alarm clock. So we met and she gave them to me. She told me that she was seeing someone new. That hurt—my pride mostly, I suppose—but I lied and told her I was happy for her.

"Then she asked me what I was working on. I had no business telling her anything, but I was working on a case that had received a lot of attention. Five years ago, two young high school students had gone hiking in the desert and had disappeared. One partial set of remains was found, and it looked as if it might be one of the boys. I had been asked to work on it. I did, and I was close to making an identification.

"I was telling her what made the identification difficult—the passage of time, exposure to weather, animals damaging the bones, and so on. I said that I was going back to where the bones had been found and taking a team with me to see if we could recover more remains."

He shook his head. "Then she asked, 'Which boy do you think it is?' And—and I don't know why, but I guessed. I told her more than once that I wasn't at all sure. It doesn't matter. It was something that I never, ever should have done."

"She told someone."

"Oh, she told someone, all right. In all my self-involvement, I had failed to ask Camille who her new boyfriend was, what he did for a living. I believe the phrase he used in the first television newscast—which took place on the front lawn outside of the home of one of the families—was, 'Sources close to forensic anthropologists working on the case . . .' He was a damned sight closer to the source than I was at that point."

"Nasty thing for her to do to you—but 'hell hath no fury' and all of that. More than a little sloppy of him not to verify the information with someone other than your ex. But I can promise you, Ben, you are not the first man to leak something to the press by way of a girlfriend or spouse. Think of John Mitchell back in the Watergate days."

He looked at me and sighed. "If that was all there was to it, Irene, I'd be thanking God and counting it as a lesson learned."

"I don't understand."

"It was the wrong boy."

"You mean—"

"Yes, I mean a man and a woman and their two younger children, people who had waited for five years to learn what had happened to their son, their brother—those people had a reporter on their front lawn, asking them on camera if they had heard the news from the police yet, that their boy's remains had been found in the desert over a week ago, and that an announcement of positive identification was imminent."

"Oh, God."

"He also made statements about the condition of the remains that were almost word-for-word what I had told her."

"Making you feel worse."

"Not any worse than the family must have felt."

"How did you find out about it?"

"The coroner called and said they'd been asked to verify that an identification was about to be made. Carlos Hernandez, you know him?"

"Yes."

"He had seen it live on the five o'clock news, and told me to watch it at six." He shook his head. "Their faces as that reporter told them! Jesus! I'll never forget that as long as I live. By six o'clock, they had invited him into their living room and were showing him photos of the boy. Worst of all, I also knew that they would also feel a sense of relief and resolution after years of worry and wonder, and I'd have to tell them that it was all a mistake, that their son hadn't been found at all."

"And you figured you were the one who was torturing them, not that guy?"

"It was my responsibility! The coroner had trusted me with those remains. Trusted me to keep my mouth shut. Do you know where that trust comes from? From families like that boy's. They give it to Carlos, he extends it to me, and I betrayed it—and over what? A need to brag to a former girlfriend? Pathetic!"

"Human. And Carlos is fair-minded, Ben. He must have—"

"Oh, he was more than fair to me. I told him what had happened, fully expecting it was my last case for his office. He tried to help me—to help me! He gave me advice on how to handle the inevitable media frenzy that would follow. And it did. I must have said 'no comment' about a million times. The campus police had to keep reporters away from the lab where I do my work. There are no windows in the lab itself, but we had to have someone guard the door after one of the photographers tried to get a shot of the bones. Eventually, the media gave up."

"Ben, sometimes—"

"No, that isn't the last of it. The media gave up, but that didn't change anything for that family. They were naturally very angry. They asked to meet with Carlos and me. The press had told them their boy had been found, and we wouldn't comment one way or the other. They thought we were torturing them. But all we could say was that we were not prepared to make any identification at this time, and then promise them that they would be the first to know if we had any news."

"Which naturally made them think they were being given the brush-off."

"I felt terrible the whole time, but Carlos had made me promise that I wouldn't say more than that to them. They told Carlos that the reporter said I was the one that leaked the story. He told them, quite honestly, that neither of us had ever talked to that reporter, and no one that worked with either of us had ever mentioned the case to him. They weren't entirely satisfied, and spoke of getting an attorney, but fortunately things never reached that point. Carlos deserves the credit for that."

"What else did you do?"

"What?"

"I haven't known you all that long, Ben, but I know you well enough to realize that you wouldn't just say 'no comment' and wait for things to blow over."

"I would have, if it weren't for David. He got Ellen and some of the other graduate students together, hauled me out of bed in the middle of the night and said, 'Bool and Bingle want to go looking for bones in the desert.' We searched for six consecutive weekends. We found more of the first boy's remains. We were just about to give up when Bingle finally found the second boy's tibia—some distance from the first boy's. After that, we made a more intensive search and recovered more."

"Didn't that make you feel better about it?"

"Not really. It was better for the family, but I still felt miserable about what I had done. The outcome isn't the issue. Breaking that code of confidentiality was no more honorable on my part, just because we had found the second boy. It was just as likely that we could have searched and searched and never found him."

We sat in silence for a while before he said, "Although the blame is mine, really, for behaving unethically in that situation—"

"Ben, aren't you being a little hard on yourself?"

"Let me finish. I wanted to say—I do have a negative attitude toward the press. I was unfair to you. I apologize for that."

"Apology accepted. We aren't all as rotten as that idiot."

"I know, I know—but one guy like that one is enough to make you wary for life. There was a little justice, though—he isn't on the air anymore."

"I'm not surprised. And Camille got what she deserved with him, I'm sure."

"It didn't last, either. She told David that the guy broke up with her when I refused to let him 'cover' our searches. I felt sorry for her, really."

"Did you ever talk to her about it?"

"No. The only time I've seen her since then was when you were there, at the hospital. What would I say? 'You betrayed me'? To her, that would have been something like saying, 'Congratulations.' Besides, I betrayed myself."

"There's only one question left, then," I said. "When are you going to forgive yourself?"

He didn't answer.

55

▲▼▲▼

TUESDAY MORNING, SEPTEMBER 26

Las Piernas

I had gone back to bed and had about an hour's sleep when the phone rang. I looked at the clock. A little before six.

Frank answered the call. "Hi, Pete," he said to his partner, then listened for a while. He sat up and started taking notes. "Okay, I'll be there as soon as I can. Coroner's already been notified? Good . . . yes, I'll see you in a few."

He hung up, stretched, and started getting dressed.

"What's going on?" I asked.

He hesitated, then said, "The skull in the refrigerator? Looks as if he decided to let us have the rest of the body."

I shuddered. "Where?"

"Apparently, he's been keeping it on ice. A group of figure skaters got a rude surprise when they showed up at the local rink for practice this morning."

"He broke into the ice-skating rink?"

"Yep. First officer on the scene said it looks as if the body is frozen solid. No head." He paused in the act of putting on his holster. "Hope it's the one belonging to our skull. He'd probably think it was damned amusing to have more than one out there and mix and match them."

"You should tell Ben. He's been trying to do the identification on the skull. Maybe he'll be able to help out."

Frank didn't want to leave me alone, so he hesitated to ask Ben to go with him. So I promised not to write about events at the skating rink for the *Express*—whose editor-in-chief I was not much in charity with at the moment—and he decided I could come along and wait within the outer perimeter of the crime scene, where the heaviest level of police protection in Las Piernas would be available to keep his wife safe from Nick Parrish.

If the skating rink hadn't been fairly close to the vet's office, I'm not sure Ben would have followed Frank and me over there that morning. Sometimes, looking back on it, I've wished the two buildings had been farther apart.

There were several black-and-whites parked outside the rink; Frank went in first, while I talked to Ben in the parking lot. A few minutes later, Frank escorted me to what he had decided was a safe place to wait—safe for me, safe for the investigation.

This place turned out to be an overly warm glassed-in waiting area, complete with gas-log fireplace and a snack bar, a place where young skaters' parents and hockey widows might hang out. Personally, that day or any other, I would have preferred a cold, hard bleacher closer to the action. I couldn't see much from where I waited. The gargantuan officer Frank posted at the door didn't improve the view.

I could see that strips of flat carpet—usually used for awards ceremonies, so that nonskating dignitaries can walk out onto the ice—led out to a huddle of men that included Frank, Pete, Carlos Hernandez, and others. I couldn't see the body itself.

Ben was escorted in by a uniformed officer. When he saw where I was being kept, he gave me a little smile and waved.

He managed getting out to the huddle without any problems; the group parted a little, he went down on one knee to take a closer look at the body and suddenly started screaming.

He screamed words, but I'm not sure what they were, because the sound itself triggered a flood of memories, and made me think of him screaming in the mountains as he ran into the meadow—which made me try in vain to get past the behemoth in blue at the waiting area door.

The words didn't matter. I just wanted to get to Ben. Before long, I got my wish—Frank was bringing him into the waiting area. He had stopped screaming; his face was drained of color. Frank asked me for Jo Robinson's number as he set Ben down next to me.

Frank called and left a message with Jo's service. I held on to Ben, who seemed to be in a state of shock.

"What is it?" I asked him. "What's wrong?"

"Camille," he said numbly. "It's Camille. Out there on the ice."

"Who's Camille?" Pete asked, overhearing Ben as he walked into the room.

Ben didn't answer, so I told them that she was Ben's ex-girlfriend. "The woman he was living with until last January."

"Her skull," Ben said miserably, looking down at his hands as if they were foreign objects. "I've been handling her skull!"

Frank and Pete exchanged a look.

"How do you know it's Camille?" I asked.

I didn't think he'd answer; he looked as if he might faint. But he whispered, "Her birthmark. She has an unusual birthmark on her upper thigh."

I could see that Frank and Pete didn't entirely trust Ben's identification of the body, but they spoke consolingly, told him just to wait with me, and brought him a cup of coffee. I understood their doubts; Ben had experienced one loss after another, had spent a nearly sleepless night, and perhaps his reaction to the corpse had been a result of the strain he was under lately.

Frank flipped through his notebook, found Camille's address from his previous visit, and sent a unit to check on her home.

A little later, a uniformed officer leaned his head in the door and said, "They want you out there, Detective Harriman."

Frank glanced at Pete, then they left together.

Frank was back a few minutes later. He beckoned me away from Ben. In a low voice, he said, "Call John and tell him you aren't coming in."

"What?"

"Tell him you aren't coming into work."

"Why should I? Do you know how hard it was for me to get the few hours I do have?"

"Tell her," Pete said, walking up to us. "She's too damned stubborn for her own good."

Frank glanced over at Ben, then said, "Parrish left a note for you."

I felt my stomach clench, and my heart began to hammer against my ribs, as if it wanted somebody to let it out. But I looked at Pete's smug face, and suddenly my heart slowed. "Really?" I said. "What did it say?"

Frank's brows drew together. "Irene—"

"What did it say?"

He held out a plastic bag. There was another plastic bag within it; on this one, my name had been neatly written in black felt pen. Within it, a sheet of lined yellow paper from a legal pad contained a short message, written in very precisely printed letters:

No more presents, no more escapes.
You can't hide from me, Irene.
You can't go beyond my reach.
Next time, you're the one who gets iced,
much more slowly than dear Camille.
And Camilles are notorious for dying slowly—
ha! ha! ha!
Please tell Ben Sheridan that I enjoyed her immensely.

He had signed it with a flourish.

"Nothing anonymous about this one, is there?" I said, not as steadily as before.

"He left it under the body," Pete said. "Don't be an idiot, Irene. Stay home."

I glanced up at him.

Frank saw, a little too late, what was inspiring me.

"Irene—" he began.

"It doesn't change anything. I am going to work, Frank."

He started to argue, but I motioned toward Ben and said in a low voice, "For God's sake, we have until ten o'clock tonight to settle this. Let's not make it any worse for Ben by having a fight in here."

"Okay," he said, "okay. But we *will* talk about this!"

We were interrupted when Frank and Pete were called back out of the room. I could see Frank giving Pete hell as they went to meet the other detectives.

If Parrish's note left any doubts, before long, few people questioned the identity of the body. Signs of a forcible entry through a rear bedroom window were found at Camille's home; through that window, police saw overturned furniture and other indications of a struggle. Once inside, the officers also found a photo of Camille in a bathing suit; the photo showed the birthmark on her thigh.

While all of this was taking place, several of us tried to console Ben, but he barely acknowledged our presence. At a little after eight, the alarm on his watch went off. "Bingle," he said suddenly. "I can't leave him in that cage! I've got to go."

"Let me go with you," I said. "You're not in any shape to drive." Intentionally keeping any tone of challenge out of my voice, I turned to my husband and said, "Is that okay, Frank? I'll wait with him back at the house. If Jo Robinson calls, she can reach us there."

Frank frowned, but perhaps thinking he'd prove to me that he was going to be reasonable, too, gave in. "Okay, but I'm going to ask a unit to follow you—promise me you'll let them keep you in sight. Parrish is obviously focusing on the two of you right now, and I don't think it's wise for you to be alone anywhere."

No argument from me. There were certain givens, after all.

Bingle's exuberance over seeing Ben again went a long way toward breaking the awful spell his owner had been under. Ben thanked the vet, paid the bill, and we were on our way. Except for an occasional attempt on Bingle's part to ride in Ben's lap, the drive back home was uneventful.

Jo Robinson had left a message, and when Ben called her back, he spent a long time talking to her while I went outside with the dogs and Cody. Cody lounged on my lap while Deke and Dunk, apparently fascinated with whatever scents Bingle's coat had picked up from the vet's office, gave the big shepherd a thorough sniffing over.

By the time Frank came back that afternoon, Ben was able to answer his questions fairly calmly. Ben had a few of his own.

"Has anyone called her parents?" he asked.

"We've got someone working on that."

"Why hadn't she been reported missing?"

"She seems to have been at loose ends lately," Frank said, "and the truth is, there doesn't seem to be anyone who had regular contact with her."

"But she worked for an accounting firm—" Ben said.

"She left her job in June; apparently she's been looking for a new one, because on her desk she had mail from several places where she had applied for work. She had been filling in applications and had copies of her résumé on her desk."

"Since June?" he asked.

"Yes, we talked to her then."

Ben looked away, frowning. "I had forgotten—you had the ridiculous suspicion that she had tried to rob my house and office."

Frank didn't allow himself to be baited.

After a moment Ben said, "Sorry. Of course you had to question her. And maybe I didn't know her so well after all. I never thought she was thrilled with her work, but I'm surprised to hear she left the accounting firm."

I remembered her visit to the hospital, and Ben's final angry suggestion that she should be the one to think about finding another line of work. I wondered if that encounter had affected her more than any of us could have guessed. Having no desire to cause Ben further pain, I kept these thoughts to myself.

"People at her former office say she quit unexpectedly," Frank said, "but she may have been planning to leave for some time. She seemed prepared to be out of work for a while. She still had quite a bit of money in her savings account."

"She was good with money," Ben said. "Not just frugal, but also good at choosing investments."

"But her mail and newspapers—" I asked.

"The house has a mail slot," Ben said. "The mail would just pile up inside the house. We liked that feature when we used to go camping or traveling. No need to file a hold with the post office."

"Actually, we think Parrish did file one," Frank said. "He seems to have forged her name on it."

"But that still leaves the newspaper," I said. "Or didn't she subscribe?"

"Yes, she did," Frank said. "But she stopped the paper."

"Wait a minute—are you sure?" I asked.

"Yes, we checked with the *Express*. She canceled about a week ago."

"What I mean is, are you sure *she's* the one who stopped it?"

"What are you saying?" Ben asked.

"Do you know anyone who is looking for a job who stops taking the newspaper?" I asked. "They want to read the classifieds."

"She has a point," Ben said to Frank.

"Two possibilities," I said. "One is that she called to stop the paper at just about the time she was killed, which is the kind of unbelievable coincidence that makes you wonder if she was being forced to make the call."

"And the other?" Frank asked.

"Parrish called to stop the paper, to make sure no one started looking for her before he wanted her to be found."

"Yes, I suppose that's possible," he said. "But it doesn't get us any closer to catching Parrish."

"Maybe it does. I can think of another subscription that got canceled recently."

"Phil Newly's," Frank said.

"Yes. Nick Parrish is someone who has obviously made a study of police and forensic procedures. He knows what might trigger a missing persons investigation. A pile of newspapers on the driveway might be noticed by neighbors who don't even know the victim's name."

"I'll make another push to take a look at Newly's house. But as I've said, in general, judges don't like cops to take uninvited tours of defense lawyer's homes."

* * *

We went early to Jo Robinson's office. She had arranged to see Ben just before she saw me. "We should try to get a two-for-one rate out of her," I said, but needless to say, Ben wasn't in an especially humorous mood.

He ran over into my time, but I didn't mind. I thought that meant I might be able to cut it a little short, but no deal.

"How's he doing?" I asked, when she had closed the door to begin our session.

She smiled and said, "You don't expect me to answer that do you? This is your time. How are you?"

"I'm still working lousy hours," I said.

"They were supposed to be somewhat improved."

"They are," I admitted.

Now that my big gripe was out of the way, I sat studying my toes.

"Otherwise, how have things gone?" she prompted.

I told her about talking to the Sayres.

"Great. And have you thought more about Parzival?"

"A little." I mentioned that telling the story of Parzival's visit to Wild Mountain led to my talking to Ben that very morning. I related the gist of our conversation.

"Hmm."

"Hmm?" I repeated. It isn't easy to imbue a sound like that with sarcasm. I made it drip with the stuff.

She smiled again. "You know, I think your friend Jack was right. You forgot to tell the best part of the story."

"What do you mean?"

"What do I mean?" she repeated. She left out the sarcasm—all but a tinge, anyway.

"It's *not* the best part of the story—it's the saddest part. Parzival goes off in disgrace; he loses his faith. He tells others that he refuses to serve a God who has the power to always be merciful, but who instead is the . . . How does he put it? 'The godfather of all my troubles.' "

"Why would a good God let so many terrible things happen?" she asked.

"Right. Or let someone with good intentions cause so much harm?"

"In the story, how does Parzival feel as he goes riding off on his quest for the Grail?"

"Angry."

"Hmm."

I didn't bother echoing that one.

"Remind me," she said, "what must he do before he can find Wild Mountain again?"

"Regain his faith."

"Is that all?"

"No, there's more to it than that," I said, trying not to lose my patience. "It's a story about compassion, but not just toward others. That's what I was saying to you earlier—about talking to Ben this morning. Parzival has to be compassionate toward himself. He has to forgive himself."

"Oh," she said.

I was silent.

"Keep thinking about it, then. Now, despite the horrible hours, how did the return to work go?"

I told her about the support of my friends, the visits by Travis and Stinger, and about Leonard and Café Kelly.

"And since the problem with the van—"

"You mean the fingers and the toes and the skull?" I asked, showing no mercy.

"Any other contact? Any other times when you've seen him?"

I hesitated only briefly before recounting it all to her. "Oh, and I almost forgot the underwear business."

"Underwear business?"

So I told her what had happened on my first day back at work.

"You wrote the article, but you didn't file it?" she asked.

"Right."

"You were angry when Parrish sent this package?"

"Yes."

"But you fought an impulse to get back at him that must have been almost irresistible."

"When I considered the possible consequences, it didn't seem worth it."

"Do you remember what you said to me when you first came here, about feeling out of control?"

"Yes. I don't feel that way very often now," I admitted, then added, "does that mean I'm done?"

She laughed. "Keep thinking about Parzival, and we'll see what can be done about this urgent desire of yours never to see me again."

Frank ate dinner with us, and held off arguing with me about work. But in the middle of the meal, he got a call. He came back from the phone smiling at me, and saying someone had seen a car parked near the ice rink at about three that morning, and could describe it—it matched the description of a car that a neighbor had seen going in and out of Phil Newly's garage at odd hours.

"A dark green Honda Accord," he said, putting a hand on my shoulder, so that he must have felt my relief.

"Who saw it at the ice rink?" I asked.

"The driver of a delivery truck for the *Express*," he said. "Taking papers to a newsstand at a coffee shop near the rink."

"Did either the neighbor or the truck driver get a look at the person driving the car?" Ben asked.

"No, and neither of them got a plate number. But we're going to be asking around here and in your neighborhood to see if anyone has seen the car lately. Somewhere, somebody must have seen that driver. Best of all, Pete thinks we're well on our way to a warrant to search Newly's place."

A little later, Frank left to meet Pete—they had another lead on the car. Just before he left, he said, "I won't ask you to stay home. Maybe you'd be safer there than here. I don't know. Oh—and here—I brought this back." He handed the cell phone to me. "Battery is all charged up. Keep it on from the moment you pull out of the driveway, okay? A patrol car will follow you in, but Wrigley's been a little fussy about letting us on to the property—even so, don't work alone, okay? Tell Leonard I'll get him into the academy if he'll stay next to you all shift. I've called Travis and Stinger—they'll be stopping by. Spend the whole shift up on the roof with them if you have to. And don't leave the—"

"Frank, any more instructions and Pete's going to wonder what happened to you."

"I just don't want you to be there alone," he said.

"I'm going with her," Ben said.

"Ben—" we both protested.

"I can't sit around here all night. It would make me crazy."

I wasn't sure it was a great idea for him to be in the newsroom that night, especially since there might be a certain amount of activity there that centered on covering the story of Camille's death.

But he told me to remember that he was an expert when it came to dealing with the media—then smiled a little, letting me see that some part of his sense of humor was gradually returning.

Jack came over and offered to go in his stead, but by then Ben was entrenched in the idea of fulfilling his promise to Frank to keep an eye on me that day.

"You're both wearing on my nerves," I said, which didn't faze either of them.

"Okay, I'll stay here and keep an eye on Cody and the dogs," Jack said, much to Ben's relief. "If you change your mind about being at the paper, Ben, just call here and we can switch."

We hadn't gone very far from the house when the cell phone rang, making me jump. I fumbled a little, and ended up hanging up on the caller.

"Hell."

"Maybe it was Parrish," Ben said, in a flat tone of voice that made me worry about him.

The phone rang again. It was Jack.

"Why'd you hang up on me?" he asked.

"Inexperience."

He laughed. "Frank wanted me to let you know he got the warrant for Newly's house. Quite a surprise, huh?"

It was going to be a night full of surprises.

56

▲▼▲▼

TUESDAY NIGHT, SEPTEMBER 26

Las Piernas

Alas, my Moth, he thought sadly, watching yet another police cruiser make the turn toward his most recent lair, I will miss the peculiar comfort you gave me in better times.

The Moth had dutifully reported back that there were strange cars on the street, sedans that looked a great deal like unmarked police cars. Indeed, with his own eyes he had seen the Volvo of that cuckold detective, Frank Harriman—which of his wife's lovers had he so foolishly entrusted her to now?—make the same turn not long ago. Without the Moth's warning, he might have missed seeing that. Well, yes, he could admit that he might have been caught—even if they caught him, he would escape again. The police could be touchy though, when one had killed one of their own. Strange how they all banded together like that, how dear they were to one another. He grinned a little, letting himself imagine just what *that* might imply.

But soon he was thinking of the Moth again.

The Moth had been useful in many ways.

There were still one or two matters in which his Moth might be of help, but everything in this place was drawing to a close, and when he was finished here, the Moth must join the other devoted ones. It was only right. The least he could do.

Perhaps one day he would return to the coyote tree and hang a unique tribute there, in honor of the Moth. And a special one to the Ice Dancer, who was, he had to admit, one of his more spectacular accomplishments. Ben Sheridan's devastation was a thing of beauty. Oh yes, something special for the Ice Dancer, too.

Plans. There were always plans to be made. He loved plans. They kept his superhuman brain busy.

He had not expected the lair to be found at this point, but he was ready for anything—even the unexpected.

He had not expected, for example, that Irene Kelly could make him feel this combination of passion and anger from a distance. Usually, he needed to be much closer before his body reacted as it was reacting now. Her body was calling to his—calling, calling, relentlessly calling. He could feel it the way a deaf man can feel the beat of a bass drum, a pulsing, low, insistent vibration.

She would not leave him alone.

He could continue to outsmart the police as long as he chose to, of course, but he decided that it simply would not be healthy to wait, that she was obviously so longing to reach the sort of fulfillment that only he could provide, that he must be swift with his generosity. Tonight would be the night.

Deadline, he thought, and gave a daring little snort of laughter.

57

▲ ▼ ▲ ▼

TUESDAY NIGHT, SEPTEMBER 26

Las Piernas

I arrived a little early, wanting to take time to answer some of my mail and e-mail, but I wasn't given a chance to do more than find a place for Ben to sit. Shorthanded and bearing down on a drop-dead deadline—the final opportunity to make any major changes in the next morning's edition—the newsroom was a hive of activity when I arrived. John Walters was hoping to get a late chase in on a story Mark Baker was covering—the police investigation of Phil Newly's home. The building was already rumbling with the vibration of rolling presses. Page A-1 couldn't be held up much longer.

One of Phil Newly's neighbors had tipped the paper off, saying police were going door-to-door asking questions about whether anyone had seen the lawyer lately, or if they had noticed any cars other than Newly's parked near the house, or in his driveway or garage.

Other phone calls started coming in, including one from Mark. After taking Mark's call, John was pacing, barking out orders—most of the front page would have to be reset.

Inside Phil Newly's garage, the police made a number of gruesome discoveries, including a bloodstained workbench and circular saw, bone fragments, and other tissue. Inside a large freezer in the garage, they found a sheet of plastic covered with frozen blood.

There was no sign of the lawyer.

Frank's lieutenant was on the scene to handle contact with the press, and stated that Mr. Newly was sought for questioning. When asked if the lawyer was suspected of being an accomplice to Nick Parrish, the lieutenant said "not at this time." When asked if Mr. Newly might be one of the victims, he said, "Our investigation here is in its very early stages. We do not know who the victims are or how many victims there may be; we are not ruling out the possibility that Mr. Newly may be one of them." He gave a description of the lawyer and the lawyer's car—a silver BMW. The car was missing.

Mark's contacts within the department revealed other information. Two neighbors had seen a dark-colored Honda coming and going from the residence, although they had not been able to get a good look at the driver. The car had entered by using an automatic garage door opener.

Neither blood nor any signs of a struggle were found inside the house itself.

There were indications that Mr. Newly left the residence voluntarily—his toothbrush, razor, and other personal effects were missing. There were also signs that someone other than Newly—someone with blond hair, perhaps bleached—had been staying in one of the lower-floor guest rooms.

We got as many of these details into the paper as we could before the presses just couldn't be held up any longer. As will happen once a drop-dead deadline has been reached, the newsroom emptied out. John stayed just long enough to allow me to formally introduce him to Ben and to tell me he was still working on getting my hours changed.

"Oh, and, Kelly—this business with the helicopter that I'm hearing rumors of? Not on day shift, should you return. Wrigley's already scared enough of you, without thinking you're going to come in here like something out of *Apocalypse Now.*"

He headed out to try to catch a few hours of sleep.

The nature of the beast; no matter how well we had done this evening, the process of putting a newspaper together would start all over again in the morning.

Still, it was much more excitement than I had expected on my late shift.

Not long after the newsroom emptied, Ben went with me up the stairs to the top of the building. "I tried calling Leonard, to get us into the elevator," I said. "But he must be roaming around the building somewhere."

I explained about the elevator access key. "Needless to say, employees forced to seek psychological counseling for throwing heavy objects at the boss are not given this special key."

"I can manage the stairs," he said. "They're good practice for me." It was lots of practice, all right.

As we reached the final door, Ben said, "That wasn't so bad."

It was another pleasant night. I made myself look up at the Box. Nothing. No lights, no movement, not even the sensation of being watched.

"How can a helicopter land on top of all this mess?" Ben asked, looking at the rooftop structures.

"The landing pad is on the other side," I said. "Come on, I'll show you."

I took him along the perimeter to the helicopter pad.

While we waited for Travis and Stinger to arrive, I gave Ben the full tour. I pointed out several city landmarks that could be seen from the roof, and started to show him my favorite gargoyles. He didn't like leaning over the railing to see them, though, so after I had pointed out the wyvern, and the mermaid that was supposedly modeled after the present Wrigley's grandmother, I told him we could look at the others from the ground.

"That's the intended view, anyway," I said, as we settled in at Café Kelly. "Although I have to admit, I wouldn't have suspected you of having a fear of heights—not after seeing you walk steep trails in the mountains."

"I don't mind heights in the mountains," he said. "It's all the flat, sheer vertical surfaces in a city, I suppose. But you don't like being in the mountains, do you?"

I thought about this for a moment and said, "The mountains,

I love. It's the people I've encountered up there who've made me feel a little wary about going back."

"Parrish?"

"He's one of them."

"Tell me what happened that morning, before we were rescued."

"Want a bottle of water? You have your choice between that and water. A full selection in our fine establishment."

"Served with an open-faced plate of bullshit, I see. You're avoiding the question."

"For the moment," I agreed. "Listen, here comes the helicopter. Can you hear it?"

"Yes," he said with a sigh.

I got up to turn the landing lights on; Leonard no longer locked that door.

We had a pleasant visit with Travis and Stinger, who hadn't seen much of Ben recently. As usual, though, they didn't stay very long. With promises to get together soon, they took off again. "Travis is a fast learner," Ben said.

"Yes," I said, and started to move back toward the door to the roof.

"Hold on," Ben said, "I haven't forgotten that promise."

"I haven't either," I said. "I just want to be able to watch for Leonard, and for Jerry, the guy who comes up here to smoke. I don't want to spill my guts for everybody on staff. I need to be able to see the door."

I could see that he was irritated, but he went along with it. Before long, he was dogging my heels. I'll own up to sauntering. I was in no hurry to have this conversation.

"Christ, Irene," Ben said, passing me by. "I'm missing the last half of my left leg, and I'm going to reach that door first."

"Don't give me that," I said, "you've been working out. And I read that stuff you had about the Paralympics—someone wearing one of those Flex-Foot feet was within four seconds of beating one of Carl Lewis's records."

"My upper-body strength is much better than before the surgery," he admitted, "but I don't run every day like you do. Besides, much as you might want me to leap tall buildings at a single, artificial bound, we don't all get to be Super Amp, you know."

"Super Amp or not, you're nowhere near your full potential, and you know it," I said. "It hasn't been so long, you know."

"I know," he said, and stopped. He made a little gentlemanly bow when I caught up to him, and said, "After you. Delay all you like. It will not work."

I reached a corner and stopped. "Okay. I can see the door from here."

"Sure you don't want to go and open it?" Ben asked. "Maybe the smoker is on the other side with a parabolic mike."

"Look," I said, "you want to hear the unvarnished truth? I'm not anxious to relive that morning with Parrish. Sometimes I think if I ever see his face again . . ."

I didn't finish the sentence, because the door to the roof opened.

"Shit," Ben said. "I guess you were right about that nicotine fit."

But even with the blond hair, even from a distance, even in the darkness, I knew who had come out onto the roof.

It wasn't Jerry or Leonard.

I pulled Ben back around the corner, nearly throwing him off balance.

"What the—"

I put my hand over his mouth. "Parrish!" I whispered. "Run!"

He looked at me in panic and said, "Where?"

Good question.

58

▲▼▲▼

WEDNESDAY, SEPTEMBER 27, 1:35 A.M.

The Roof of the Wrigley Building

"Back this way!" I whispered, and we quickly ran into the dark and narrow maze of rooftop structures, turning another corner, and another, then hiding behind the air conditioner.

I hoped that Parrish would venture out to the more open end of the roof, so that we could get back to the door.

We heard noises, but it was hard to tell where they were coming from.

"We should split up," Ben said. "There's only one of him. He can't chase both of us."

"Unless he brought his helper." I saw a ladder on a nearby wall, one used for access to the flagpoles. "Wait here," I said. I scurried over to the ladder, climbed up as far as I dared and cautiously peered down into the little alley we had just traveled. Past our alley, but not far away from its entrance, I saw a strange sight, one that took me a moment to comprehend: a single light moving slowly, bobbing several feet above the ground. Then I realized what it was—Parrish had a camper's headlamp on, a flashlight that would allow him to keep his hands free for—for things I didn't want to think about.

I watched just long enough to determine one thing, then hurried back to Ben.

"He's alone, as far as I can tell. He's bound to come down this alley any minute. But I don't think we should split up until we have to."

"Okay," he whispered.

Then the cell phone rang, shrill and loud. It might as well have sent an electric shock through me.

I swore and fumbled to answer it. It rang a second time and Ben took off running again. I could understand his desire to distance himself from a woman who was wearing a homing device for Parrish.

"Whoever you are," I said into the phone as I ran in the opposite direction, "call the police!"

"Irene?" a man's voice said. Familiar, but who was it?

I turned a corner, heard footsteps. I ducked down another narrow alleyway and ran like hell. "Goddamn it, whoever you are, hang up and call the police. Tell them Nick Parrish is on the roof of the *Express*."

"This is Phil Newly, I'm—"

"Shit!" I said, and hung up.

Wonderful. Satan's minion now knew where to find his boss.

Parrish's headlamp appeared at the other end of the alley.

I turned another corner.

Dead end.

Okay, I thought, okay. Use the cell phone. Call 911, and even if you're dead, maybe they'll get here in time to save Ben.

I called, wondering which police department I'd reach. But the call was routed to the Las Piernas Police.

"Nick Parrish is on the rooftop of the Wrigley Building—"

"Hey, Nicky, you Mama's boy!" Ben called. "Come and get me!"

"Oh, Jesus," I said weakly. "On the rooftop of the *Express*. Send help!"

I hung up again. I moved forward, not sure what I'd find. No sign of Parrish. No sign of Ben.

I turned the phone on one more time, pressed the programmed button for "Stinger@FE."

I made the call as I continued my way back out of the dead-end alley. "Fremont Enterprises," a sleepy voice answered.

"Pappy?" I whispered.

"Have to speak up," he said.

"Tell Travis and Stinger to come back to the roof," I said and hung up, because I had just seen Ben run past the opening to the alley, and Parrish was not far behind.

I ran until I reached the opening, turned in the direction they had gone, and shouted at the top of my lungs, "Nick Parrish, you little weasel, I can't believe you fell for that dumb trick!"

I heard a small thud, and a light came from behind me. I whirled to see him standing not three feet away from me, grinning. He was standing next to another ladder. He wore a gun in a shoulder holster. That wasn't his weapon of choice, obviously—in his right hand, he was holding a knife with a long, thin blade.

"I didn't fall for any tricks," he said, moving the knife in a lazy figure eight. "You, on the other hand, were stupid enough to run right past me without looking up."

I backed up a few steps.

"You want to run?" he said, holding up the knife. "Of course you do. Especially now that I've killed your little crippled friend."

"You haven't killed him," I said, hoping I was right.

"How do you know?"

"No gunshot, no blood on you or your knife. As usual, you're full of shit."

"I don't think you're so certain he's alive. Call his name. See if he answers."

"You aren't going to get me to be the one to help you find him."

"I'll find him. He can't move as fast you can."

"Shows what you know. I don't think you can catch him."

"Oh, I can. Just as I caught his girlfriend, who completely lost her head over me. She was lovely. I'm so sorry I wasn't there to see his tears when he saw the Ice Dancer this morning."

"Wrong again, Nicky. He wasn't upset at all. She was his ex, don't forget. He really didn't give a rat's ass."

"Maybe that's because he's been boning you behind your husband's back."

Don't let him get to you, I told myself. Keep him distracted. Let Ben get away.

"Something out of your fantasies, Nicky? Or were you just trying to upset me? You'll have to do better. Of course, you don't know anything about friendships or genuine relationships, do you? You can't have sex with anyone unless you hold them at knifepoint, right? What woman in her right mind would want to get it on with you voluntarily?"

He laughed and lifted the knife. "If I wasn't going to enjoy your screams so much, I'd start by cutting out that tongue of yours. Maybe I'll start there, anyway."

He lunged and I leapt back, instinctively putting my hands out in front of me. I still held the cell phone.

"What?" He laughed. "You'll call the police? They'll never reach you in time. And you may rest assured that no one is coming up those stairs to the roof anytime soon. I've blocked the door to the stairwell, and even if they manage to push past that, I've secured the door to the roof from this side. A rather sturdy locking bar. Do you travel?"

The question was so unexpected, I didn't answer.

"Every airline magazine advertises these little gems," he said. "Something to supposedly keep you safe in your hotel room. This one is for industrial use. I've found it very handy on other occasions."

I tried to think of any other access to or from the roof. Only one side of the building adjoined any other buildings; a row of shops that were three stories tall.

"I have the only key," Parrish was saying. "You and Dr. Sheridan are my captives, you see. The locking bar won't hold forever, but it will give me all the time I need."

"You don't have as much time as you think you do," I said.

"Then let's make the most of it. Remember our little game in the mountains? Start running, Irene."

I took two steps, pivoted toward him, and hurled the cell phone with all my might. The phone didn't weigh much, but I hit the target, which was gleaming right at me and not more than ten feet away from me—his headlamp. He yelped and seemed stunned, which was fine by me. I took off running again without waiting to see if I had done any other damage.

I might not have done so well in the mountains, I told myself, but here it would be different. No altitude, exhaustion, or dehydration to slow me down. I was wearing running shoes, not hiking boots. The surface was flat and relatively free of obstacles. On the downside, I was running in a cage.

I thought of ducking into the room with the light panel for the landing pad, but I decided I'd be better off knowing where he was, and remaining free to move. One dark row of rooftop structures led to another, and every time I turned a corner, I was afraid I'd meet up with him.

Where was Ben?

I heard a helicopter approaching, then the sound of sirens wailing.

Suddenly it dawned on me that if Travis and Stinger landed again, they'd be in danger of being shot—or shot down by Parrish. Now I really needed to know where he was, and to warn them away. Where could I make sure they could see me, though, and not make a bull's-eye out of myself?

I headed for the flagpoles.

I climbed the ladder cautiously, but quickly, afraid I'd meet Parrish at the top or have him come at me from below.

To my relief, there was no one else up on this highest of the structures. I was about another twenty or thirty feet above the roof. I heard a sound below me, and saw that Ben was coming this way.

I took my eyes off Ben's progress when I saw the helicopter coming closer. Not knowing the official signals to get a helicopter to turn away, I made the universal shooing motion with my arms extended over my head, shook my head no and made a double thumbs-down motion. I even tried to pantomime a gun being shot at them. Some part of this bad mime show must have gotten through to them, though, because they pulled away, hovering higher, and to one side of the building. They didn't completely leave the area, though, and I was afraid Parrish still might shoot them.

I saw Ben's head at the top of the ladder and hurried over to him. "Get away!" he suddenly shouted, and seemed to lose his footing. He was grasping the top of the ladder, bent over the ledge at the waist, apparently straining to pull himself up.

I ignored his warning and ran closer. I peered over the edge and saw that Parrish, coming up the ladder behind him, had yanked Ben's right leg from the ladder and was trying to pull him off.

Parrish was not far from me, but now he had hold of both of Ben's legs with his right arm. His left hand grasped the ladder railing. He began trying to twist Ben off the ladder. I bent over the edge, holding the ladder rail and keeping most of my weight on the ledge. I grabbed Ben's belt, trying to counteract Parrish's twisting motion. The blood was rushing to my head, but with our combined resistance, Parrish wasn't making any progress.

Parrish moved up another rung, so that his face was inches away from mine.

"Now I have both of you. One hard tug, and over you go. Not bad for a panty rustler, eh?" He lurched up and licked my face.

I let go of Ben's belt and punched Nick Parrish hard in the nose. It started bleeding like crazy, and for a moment, he loosened his grip on Ben. Ben found a ladder rung with his right leg, while Parrish screamed at me in rage. I took advantage of what I hoped was a moment of near blindness for Parrish and reached for his gun in the shoulder holster. Now he did let go of Ben with his right hand, but not fast enough. I cleared the gun from the holster. He grasped my wrist hard, though, and I let the gun fall to the rooftop below.

He started to try to pull me over. Ben, who had stepped up a little higher, landed a mule kick in Parrish's groin area with his Flex-Foot; he apparently missed the nuts but not the squirrel, because Parrish grunted and let go of my wrist but didn't fall. Parrish quickly made a grab at Ben's legs again, but only managed to get a grasp on the prosthesis that had so recently wounded him. I grabbed the socket end of it, trying to pull Ben up, even as Ben held on to the top rung for dear life, kicking at Parrish's left arm.

There was a bright light above us, and noise and wind; the helicopter was overhead. I couldn't see them, but knew they could not get too close to us—there were too many poles and wires and other objects up on this part of the roof. The flags were snapping loudly, and the cables beat out a ringing alarm.

"To the left!" I shouted up at Ben, not knowing if he could hear—whether he did or not, he aimed his next kick better, coming down hard on Parrish's left arm.

Parrish lost his grip and nearly fell, but held on to the Flex-Foot as he tried to find his own footing. He managed to get his feet back on a rung midway up the ladder. Ben had moved his right leg up higher, out of reach, and was trying to pull himself up while Parrish kept all his weight on Ben's left leg. Still holding the Flex-Foot with his left hand, he grinned and suddenly let go of Ben with his right, swinging free. But instead of reaching for the ladder, he took hold of his knife.

"I'll make a double amputee out of him," Parrish said, his bloody nose making his speech sound odd. "But maybe I'll cut your fingers off first."

Involuntarily flexing my fingers, I felt a metal button beneath them. The locking pin release. I pressed it.

I heard a click and watched Parrish's bloodied face register a look of horror as the socket and Flex-Foot separated.

He made wild, futile stabs at the air as he fell backward onto the rooftop with a thumping crack.

He didn't move after that.

59

▲ ▼ ▲ ▼

WEDNESDAY, SEPTEMBER 27, 1:55 A.M.

Las Piernas

Ben pulled himself up onto the ledge. I sat up, dizzy after hanging upside down. We were both winded.

"Are you okay?" I asked.

He nodded. "You?"

"Yes. Sorry about your foot."

"It's probably okay. But after all that work to get up here, hell if I'm going back down there to find out if it's damaged."

"I think someone will bring it to you," I said, pointing to where the helicopter was landing.

At the same time, we heard a loud bang that made us jump—the SWAT team had made its way through the door to the roof. In no time at all, Parrish was surrounded. When he didn't move, they edged toward him.

"Irene!"

I turned from the scene directly below to that best-loved voice. Frank was stepping out of the helicopter, running toward us.

I waved and yelled, "We're okay!"

His face broke into a big smile and he ran faster.

Three members of the SWAT team made it up the ladder before Frank did.

"We're okay," Ben told them. "Is Parrish dead?"

"No," one said, "but damned close to it. Looks like he broke his neck. We're going to take him over to St. Anne's. It's just down the street."

Frank came up the ladder, carrying Ben's Flex-Foot.

"Thought you might need this," he said, handing it to him.

"Thanks," Ben said. "I was wondering how I was going to get down from here without it." He looked it over and decided that although it was a little scraped up, it wasn't badly damaged.

"I don't think my cell phone fared as well," I said. When I told him how I'd used it, Frank laughed and took me in his arms. "Parrish just didn't know what he was up against, did he?" But he was holding me tight, as if needing to reassure himself that I was okay. I held him, too. It felt good, the safest I had felt in a long time.

"Oh!" I said, coming out of that spell of comfort. "I just remembered something! Phil Newly called me, and it was forwarded from my desk to the cell phone. Can you find the number from the cell phone records?"

"No need to," Frank said. "Newly called us."

"The police?"

"Yes. That's how I found out you were here. Newly said he tried calling you, and you told him you were up here with Nick Parrish and were scared and asking for the police."

"Where has he been?"

"He said he's been hiding. He's been afraid of Parrish. He said after you got those bones and roses, he knew that Parrish was back in the area, and he took off. He rented a beach house down the coast, didn't even tell his sister how to get in touch with him. He heard the news reports tonight and decided to come home."

"So why call me?"

"He was expecting a hostile reaction from the police, and he thought you might help him meet with me before things got out of hand. I didn't tell him that you were the one that kept insisting we check him out. He's hired a defense attorney of his own, but agreed to meet with us tomorrow."

"Wait a minute," I said. "You found a bloody circular saw and more at his house, right?"

"Right."

"And those leg bones in the roses might have been cut with a saw, right, Ben?"

"Right."

"I met with Phil, and that same night the bones showed up on our doorstep. If he left *after* he heard about the bones, he left after they were worked on in his garage. If he's innocent, he must also be deaf—because he must not have noticed an awfully loud noise in his garage. Not to mention missing the peculiar sight of a bloody workbench while he was pulling his car out."

"Not necessarily," Ben said. "You're relying on news reports based on secondhand sources."

"Ben Sheridan—"

"No, I'm not trying to start a fight about the media. Frank, you were in Newly's garage and saw it with your own eyes. Was the workbench bloody?"

"Yes."

"If there was any blood, it probably came from Camille's body." He looked away for a moment, then said, "Or perhaps from the Jane Doe in the trash container. No matter what, that blood did not come from the Oregon woman's femurs."

"Wait a minute—" I protested.

"He's right," Frank said. "In general, dead bodies don't bleed, because the heart isn't pumping. You can drain blood from a body shortly after death, but the Oregon women were killed several weeks ago. Parrish removed the receptionist's legs where he left the bodies—a long way from Phil Newly's house."

"I examined those femurs," Ben said. "They weren't sawed when the bodies were fresh."

"So you think he's innocent?" I asked.

"I'm not saying he's guilty or innocent," Frank said. "So far, we haven't found any fragments at Newly's house that were an obvious match to the femurs. But we haven't even had a dozen hours to look around. Newly isn't in the clear. You don't find this kind of evidence without raising questions about the owner of the house. Newly still has lots of explaining to do."

When we got down from the ladder, I saw a familiar figure standing away from all the action, looking dejected. I walked over to him.

"Leonard? What's wrong?"

"I let you down," he said, glancing nervously at Frank, and then down at his shiny black shoes. "He pulled the oldest trick in the book on me, and I fell for it."

"What are you talking about?"

He sighed all the way from those shoes and said, "Parrish. Started a trash-can fire on the loading dock. When I went to investigate, he must have gone up the stairs."

"Any losses from the fire?"

He shook his head.

"Well, then, that's good, right?"

"I told you I wouldn't let him in here, and I did."

"He's been slipping past the whole department for months," Frank said, causing Leonard to look up at him. "No one would expect a lone officer to be able to stop him."

I formally introduced them then, and Frank went on to thank Leonard. "Knowing you were keeping an eye on things made me feel a lot better about her being here at night."

"It did?" Leonard asked, then quickly added, "I do my best, sir."

"All anyone asks," Frank said.

"Lone officer?" I said later, when Leonard had strutted his way out of earshot.

"I was afraid he was going to throw himself over that railing."

Once John Walters vented his anger over our wild chase on the rooftop occurring after deadline, he asked me to write a story for a special morning edition. I agreed to do it, over the protests of my entourage of protectors, because I wanted to prove to Wrigley that I wasn't going to be denied a place on A-1 just because he gave me post-deadline hours.

Frank, Ben, Travis, and Stinger refused to let me stay alone in the newsroom. Jack came over with a bottle of champagne and in spite of Leonard's warnings about explicit company rules forbidding alcohol on the premises ("I am not here, I am not seeing this," he said), we drank a toast to good friends, present and remembered. John joined us.

Parrish, we learned by taking a look at security tapes, had come into the building from the loading docks, wearing a baseball cap, carrying a toolbox, and moving purposefully past men who were caught up in the problem of delivering papers that were coming off the presses late. He started the fire near another camera, so that Leonard would be certain to see it.

I learned that he then spent some time making sure that it was going to be damned difficult for anyone to follow us up to the roof. He had barricaded the final interior doorway to the roof access stairs and put a heavy-duty locking bar on the door to the roof itself.

I called the hospital for an update. Nicholas Parrish was in critical condition with severe injuries, especially to his head and neck. If he died, I wondered if anyone other than his helper would mourn his passing.

"Ben," Travis asked, "with all of his weight on your prosthesis, why didn't the whole socket just pull off sooner?"

"It's held on by suction," he explained. "Unless I roll it off, it's not coming off. For obvious reasons, the socket is designed to stay on until I want to take it off. Which, to be honest, I'd love to do as soon as possible."

I filed the story and we left. Stinger stayed with Jack, Travis slept on the couch, Ben in the guest room with Bingle.

Frank and I didn't sleep much at first, but not because of nightmares. There was some drive in both of us that Dr. Robinson probably has some fancy name for, a syndrome or something, but we didn't need to name it. We had to be a little quieter than usual with such a houseful, but that was no big deal—we had already learned on a previous occasion that Bingle felt inclined to raise an alarm when he heard certain noises issuing from behind a bedroom door.

"I wonder if that's what first earned him the name *Bocazo*?" I asked Frank now.

"Who knows?" Frank said, concentrating on other matters.
We slept just fine after that.

But the next morning, I awakened with an unwelcome idea in my head, a suspicion I despised and yet no matter how I tried, I could not rid myself of it.

"Frank," I finally said, "I have a terrible favor to ask of you."

60

▲ ▼ ▲ ▼

WEDNESDAY, LATE AFTERNOON, SEPTEMBER 27

Las Piernas

The staff at St. Anne's had been wary of me at first. After all, I was the person who had put their patient here. But they had been reading about their patient for several months now, and knew who he was, so that when, after two hours, I had not tried to suffocate him, I began to overhear remarks about my amazing capacity for forgiveness.

A mistaken diagnosis if I've ever heard one.

I held a copy of Parzival, but I wasn't reading it. I was thinking about a search that was carried out that morning.

It hadn't taken me as long to convince Frank of my ideas as it had taken me to convince myself. While Frank made some calls, and Travis made breakfast, I scanned videotapes of Bingle and David working with their SAR group. I found what I was looking for, and showed it to Frank, which resulted in a few more calls. I made one of my own.

Ben woke up and joined us for breakfast; I asked him what time he had to teach his first class.

"I have a lab at two o'clock, but Ellen might be able to cover it if you need my help. What's up?"

"Frank received a report about a house where remains may be hidden. Can you bring Bingle?"

"Yes, of course. But we should have more than one dog to confirm it."

"Can you get Bool's new owner to join you?"

"I can try."

"If he can do it, here's the address where you'll meet."

"You aren't coming with us?"

"No, I have to be somewhere else this morning."

I could see that he wanted to ask more questions, but he seemed to sense my mood, and held off. He called Ellen Raice, and the bloodhound handler. This second call took a while, and when he hung up, he was smiling.

"What?" I asked.

"He said he's been meaning to call me. He thinks he may have been wrong before, and that Bool does miss 'that obstreperous shepherd' after all. He's having second thoughts about keeping him."

"Something tells me you've missed Bool, too."

"I have," he said. "In a lot of ways he's just a big silly dog, but he's very affectionate. A great tracker, too. David always said, 'If it's there to be found, then Bool will find it.' This handler said he'd teach me how to work with Bool if I wanted him back."

Frank called me at the hospital to say that the initial search with the dogs had been successful, and that they'd probably do a more thorough search that afternoon.

"One other thing," he said. "As soon as Ben gets the dogs settled in together, he's going to be coming by to see you there."

"He's upset?"

"Yes. I told him it was up to you to tell him what was going on."

"Thanks a bunch."

He laughed. "I'll come by as soon as I can."

* * *

"What are you doing here?" Ben half-shouted at me when he came into the ICU room where I sat next to Parrish.

"Lower your voice, Ben," I said. "They'll think you wish to harm poor little Nicky here."

"I do! I want to unplug the bastard!"

I sighed and closed the book. "You, Ben, are far more merciful than I am."

"Merciful?!"

"Think about it. He's trapped in the ultimate prison."

Ben's look of rage changed in an instant. He looked at Parrish and said, "He'll live?"

"Yes, it seems he will. He won't be able to move, or speak. They think he can hear and understand us, and he can open his eyes. He makes gurgling noises every once in a while. I like to think he's trying to say something."

"You like to . . ."

"Yes. Cruel of me, isn't it? I'm a little surprised at myself. Maybe someday I'll stop being angry at him for what he's done, and, like you, I'll wish him dead."

He took a seat, studied me. "You won't convince me that you're here to gloat."

"No," I said. "But as long as I have to be sitting next to him, I find I don't mind saying terribly mean things to him."

Parrish made a gurgling sound. Ben, hearing it, made a face.

"Awful," I agreed.

"Why are you here?" Ben asked again.

"I'm waiting for somebody."

"Who?"

"I'll tell you later."

"Irene—"

He was distracted by a slightly different sound from Parrish, a sort of a humming noise.

"What do you suppose he's trying to say?" Ben asked, looking at him warily.

I set the book down, stood up, and looked into Parrish's eyes. "What was it, Nicky?"

"Mmmaaah."

"Maybe he's calling for his mommy," I said, and sat down again.

Ben stared at me, then said, "Have you thought of calling Jo Robinson?"

I laughed. "I'll probably need a long session with her later. But don't worry, I'm not here to hurt Nicky or anyone else."

"Do you mind if I wait here with you?" he asked.

"No, at least—well, no, not at all. Mr. Nick's conversational abilities are rather limited."

Ben glanced at him, then said, "I wanted to have that conversation we keep putting off, but I don't want to talk about it in front of him."

"What's he going to do about it?" I said wearily. "Fantasize? Let him. He's finally in a condition where it's safe for him to do so."

"Irene—"

"Sorry, Ben," I said. "I'm feeling a little cynical today. Let me ask you about something else entirely—if you don't mind talking about this in front of Nick, here."

"What?"

"You said that David sometimes talked about—" I glanced at Parrish, and amended what I was going to say. "You said that he rarely talked about certain aspects of his childhood."

"That's right," he said, a little stiffly.

"Except to others who might have experienced the same thing."

"Right." He glanced toward Parrish.

"Did David ever tell you the names of people he talked to?"

"No. He would talk to me in general terms, or tell me about someone without mentioning a name. He felt that while . . . such a background should not be a source of shame, he worked hard to gain their trust, and so he would not betray their confidences. He had this ability to identify people who might have been through similar things, but David approached people gently, slowly. He didn't push them to tell him things. He earned their trust first."

He paused, then asked, "Why do you want to know about people he talked to?"

"I'm trying to understand someone I know," I said. "But maybe I won't ever be able to do that."

"You *are* in a cynical mood."

"Sorry, yes I am. Started when I woke up thinking of a song by the Boomtown Rats called, 'I Don't Like Mondays.' Do you know it?"

"Yes." He sang a little bit of the chorus.

"Exactly. It triggered a memory. The inspiration for that song was a shooting in San Carlos—that's in the San Diego area. A sixteen-year-old girl named Brenda Spencer decided to point a rifle at a schoolyard and embark on a sniping marathon. This was in 1979, when it wasn't so common for shots to be fired in elementary schoolyards."

"Definitely cynical. I do remember this story, though. She fired from inside her house toward the school for several hours, right?"

"Yes. And during that time, she killed two people and wounded nine others. When they asked her why, she said, 'I don't like Mondays.' "

"Jesus."

"She said, 'I don't like Mondays. This livens up the day.' "

"And this song reminded you of something else?"

"Yes," I said. "I like the song. Lots of people do. But it was written in the year of the shootings—a couple of decades ago, now. So until recently, it had been a long time since I had heard it."

He was about to say something when the officer outside the door stepped in and said, "Ms. Kelly? You ready?"

"As I'll ever be—thanks," I said. "Ben, I'm going to have to ask you to wait in the other room with Frank."

"Frank's here?" he asked, looking around.

"Yes. Don't worry. You'll be able to hear everything we say," I said, and reached behind my back.

"You're wearing a wire?" he asked in disbelief. "I'm not sure I—"

"Please, Ben," I said, "Frank can fill you in on everything."

He folded his arms.

The officer's radio crackled.

"Now or never, Mrs. Harriman," he said.

Ben didn't budge.

"Ben, if you trust me at all, get out of here now."

Reluctantly, he left with the officer.

I flipped a switch, gave my name, the date, time, location and said that Nick Parrish was present.

Parrish made his "Mmmaaah" sound.

I looked outside the glass wall toward the nurses' station. A person who was dressed exactly like a nurse but who wasn't taking care of any patients nodded to me. In another room, the reel-to-reel was turning. In my mind, wheels that had been whirling all day kept right on spinning.

The elevator door opened.

61

▲ ▼ ▲ ▼

WEDNESDAY, LATE AFTERNOON, SEPTEMBER 27

Las Piernas

I wiped my palms.

She approached cautiously, tentatively. She was dressed in a business-style woman's suit, the skirt at the most conservative length I had ever seen her wear. She carried a stylish leather handbag. I couldn't rid myself of the notion that she looked like a child playing at being a grown-up.

There was the slightest sign of surprise on her face when she saw me, but then she came into the room. "Hello, Irene."

"Hello, Gillian."

"I—I'm relieved to see you here, Irene. I'm a little afraid to be in here alone with him."

"Why come at all, then?"

"I had to." She looked back at me. "Did they search your purse when you came in here?"

"Yes," I said. "They've searched everyone."

"Why?"

"Someone might want to harm him. At this point, they're letting God get all the vengeance."

"Not just God—you, too. I heard about what you did."

I tried not to let that unnerve me.

"Maybe you'll think I'm some kind of freak for saying this," she went on, "but I had to see him. I had to see the man who did those things to my mother. Four years, I've waited."

"But you've seen him before," I said.

Her eyes widened a little.

"He was your neighbor, right?"

"Yes," she said, creeping closer to the bed. "But that was a long time ago." She leaned over, and looked into his eyes.

"Mmmaaah," Parrish said. She turned white and shrank back from the bed.

"Here," I said, putting an arm around her shoulders, "have a seat. He's not so scary once you get used to him—although I imagine he looks very different from the last time you saw him."

"Yes."

"About four years ago?" I ventured.

"No—yes. I mean, no, longer than that."

"Strange. Jason thought you saw him when he showed up to stalk your mom."

"What?"

"You know, the night you were baby-sitting, and Parrish's car was outside the house?"

"Jason said that? You can't believe anything that kid says." She shook her head. "It's sad."

I thought it was sad that I hadn't believed every word Jason told me about his sister, but I said, "Oh, wait, now I remember—he said there was a car, but you went outside and couldn't find it."

She shrugged. "Not that I remember."

"You know, I've been meaning to get in touch with you again, anyway," I said, moving between her and the door. "I thought you might help Ben Sheridan with his dog."

"The man who lost his leg, you mean?"

"Come on, now, Gillian, you know more about him than just that fact. You had contacted him about your mother's case."

"Did I? I contacted so many people. I don't remember. You said something about helping him with his dog?" she asked uneasily. "What dog?"

"Oh, you know this dog really well—Bingle. He used to be David Niles's dog."

She didn't say anything.

"I saw some interesting videotape this morning. You went out with the SAR group he worked with, right? I saw you on the tapes, talking to David, learning to work with Bingle."

"Yes," she said, "I thought maybe if I could learn to work with cadaver dogs, I could go out on searches for my mother."

"Your dedication to finding her was so inspiring," I said, and tried a small bluff. "Learning about forensic anthropology, and cadaver dogs, and even talking to Andy Stewart about how botanists can find unmarked graves."

"Like you said, I wanted to find her."

"Mmmaaah," Parrish said again.

"What do you think he's saying?" I asked.

She shook her head mutely, but those blue eyes were wide, frightened.

"They think he'll be able to talk again in a few days," I lied.

"They do?"

"Yes." Bigger bluff. "A neurologist was just in here, saying he's improving by the hour. That's why I'm waiting here. I'll have a question for him when he can talk."

"You will?" Gillian asked.

"Yes. About something he said to me not long before he fell. This has been on my mind all morning, and I can't wait for him to come around so that I can ask him about it."

"What?"

"You remember that article Frank showed you when we visited you at your apartment?"

"Yes."

"That's a great apartment, over a garage. On—what street is it?"

"Loma, near Eighth," she said, staring at Parrish again.

"I think Ben was over that way, earlier today—a search exercise with Bingle. Anyway, about that underwear story—"

"It was so funny," she said, giggling a little.

Parrish made a gurgling noise.

"You remember it that well?" I asked.

"Sure. It wasn't that long." She recited it almost word for word.

"Amazing. You know, it never ran in the *Express*."

"No?"

"No. That's why I was so surprised when Nick here quoted some of it to me last night. How could he have known what was in that column, if he never saw it?"

Gillian finally looked away from Parrish. "It must have been someone else—that lawyer they were looking for—"

I shook my head. "You, Gillian. You."

"That's ridiculous," she said quickly. "Why would I have anything to do with Nick Parrish?"

"I don't know the answer to that. But then again, maybe I do. Maybe I should have listened to what Jason said about that, too. That you're cold. That you genuinely hated your mother."

She folded her arms and leaned back in her chair. The look in her eyes was one of pure malice. "Nicholas Parrish said this, Jason said that. You say you never showed that article to anyone else, but I don't believe you."

"They've searched the garage beneath your apartment, Gillian. Frank got a warrant. The dogs were there while you were at work this morning. Even before they went inside, Bingle and Bool and a bloodhound named Beau were alerting to the presence of remains."

She went back to looking afraid.

"They were right, of course," I said. "There were remains there. Pieces that match up with the femurs of the woman from Oregon."

"Femurs?"

"Leg bones."

"You mean Nicholas Parrish had the nerve to use my own garage—"

"You won't be able to bluster your way out of this," I said. "They found your toolbox."

"What toolbox?"

"The one the dogs refused to bother with when commanded to search for Nicholas Parrish's scent. You were at the SAR training sessions, so you know how this works. Two bloodhounds were given one of Nicky's dirty socks, then asked to find him. They alerted all over your garage, even up in your apartment. But they weren't interested in the toolbox. The one that has the helicopter drain plugs in it—the plugs with your fingerprints all over them."

She started crying.

"If I thought those tears were for anyone other than yourself, I might be moved by them. Your own mother, Gillian!"

"You don't understand!" she said.

"God knows I want to!" I said. "You've got a reason? Just let me know it."

"You won't believe me."

"Try me."

"My own father never believed me, why should you?"

I let out a breath I didn't even know I was holding.

"Your father," I said, trying to choose my words carefully, "doesn't like unpleasantness, does he?"

"Unpleasantness?" she mocked. "No, he doesn't like to know about anything that's *unpleasant*. And my mother controlled him. She tried to control everyone. Jason, my dad—but not me—you understand? Not me! She tried—and tried—and tried—but I won! I did."

"How did she try?"

"How do you think?" she sneered.

I didn't answer.

"You think this is the first time I've been in this place?" she asked. "You should ask my dad about how 'accident prone' I was before Jason was born."

"But I thought hospitals—"

She gave me a pitying look. "Maybe it was all the time my mother spent chairing the Las Piernas General Hospital Auxiliary—you think? We didn't come to St. Anne's very often, but I knew what a nun was before I was five, and we sure as shit weren't Catholics."

"So you weren't always treated by the same doctor?"

Her lips curved into a cold smile. "You'd be surprised how far we had to drive sometimes to get to a hospital."

"Jason didn't know about it?"

"I'm not really close to my little brother, you know? I mean, we didn't have the same childhood—get it? He wasn't around for the scaldings, the fall down the stairs, things like that. I don't remember all of it. I was little. After Jason came along, she learned to work it so that I didn't have to see doctors—didn't leave marks. He just heard what she said—'Gillian's bad. Gillian disobeys. Gillian's out of control.' Out of her control, all right."

"If you were—"

"If. You see? Why believe me, right?"

"I was going to say, if you were a friend of David's—"

"I wasn't, all right? I just wanted to learn about the dogs. What has that got to do with anything?"

"Nothing, I'm sorry to say. So your father never saw her mistreat you?" I asked.

"Oh no. She was careful about that."

"And he wouldn't believe you?"

"No." She smiled again. "He said he didn't."

"Mmmmaah," came a sound from the bed.

"Nick Parrish believed you, didn't he?" I asked.

She nodded, looking over at him again. "Same thing happened in his house when he was a kid. Except his old lady went after him, left his little sister alone."

"So you went down to Mr. Parrish's house and told him what was happening?"

She shook her head.

"No?"

"No. I really didn't know him then. It wasn't until later, when I saw him watching the house. He remembered my mother, because she looked like his mom, but she was too young. He came back to see her when she was a little older."

"Mmmmaah!" he said.

"He was so good to me. And he had such . . . such power! He understood me. I knew it from the first time I saw him watching the house—before that night Jason told you about. I saw him. I was the only one who had ever been smart enough to see him before he knew he was being watched. No one had ever been able to sneak up on him. He was impressed."

"Mmmaaah," he said again.

"He was ready to make his move to fame. I helped him. It was exciting."

All day, in my thoughts of her, I had tried to see her as she was, not the way I wanted her to be. Not to see her as the victim she had been in my mind for so many years, but as the killer's helper. "How could she lend her aid to him?" I had asked myself again and again, thinking of Parrish's victims, their grieving families and friends—not just her own mother, but her younger brother among them. That she had been abused might explain her anger toward Julia and a great deal more, but with that one phrase, "it was exciting," she once again became alien to me. Whatever pity I felt for the child she had been, the young woman was someone I could not begin to truly understand.

I stepped back from her.

"How did you help him?" I asked.

"I told him where she was going that afternoon."

"And you were there when he killed her?"

She shook her head. "He wouldn't let me watch that one. But he showed me photos, later, after he saw that I was worthy."

"Worthy?" She didn't seem to hear or care about my revulsion.

"He's never had another disciple," she said proudly. "I'm the first. I told him I would make sure the world would know about him."

"With my unwitting help," I said bitterly.

"He made the plans, of course, but who would have known about him without me? I was the one who kept everyone afraid, who made them want to go to the mountains."

"So that we could see the trophies of his kills."

"You never would have known about him if we hadn't planned for you to write about my mother's death, would you?"

"Maybe not," I said, suddenly tired.

"That's why he buried her in her own place. I've seen it."

"What on earth would attract you to someone like him? Knowing what he was capable of doing—"

"Exactly! I knew what he was capable of. I could see his power. Even now—can't you see? He will get stronger. He'll be back. That's what he's trying to tell me. That I'm his moth, that the flame still burns."

"You're a moth? I guess you are. Moths are blinded by their fascinations, right? They fly too close to the flame, right? You're burning now and you can't even smell the smoke on your wings."

"You'll regret saying that someday," she said.

"He's not going to get better, Gillian. That was a lie. He's going to spend the rest of his life like this."

"No! You're lying now!"

"I think you know I'm not. Look at him. He's empty," I said. "Just like you are."

She stared at him in horror.

"You can't empathize with anyone, can you? Of all the things your mother destroyed in you—"

"Who cares?" she said. "I take care of myself."

"All that time, I thought you were being stoic—you aren't stoic, you're heartless."

"Whatever." She lowered her head on to her hands. "You're giving me a headache."

"You can't pity anyone, can you? Not even him."

She bent over, and I thought perhaps she really wasn't feeling well. But then she calmly reached beneath her skirt in a most unladylike fashion and removed a revolver. She stood as she pointed it straight at me. If she heard the commotion outside the room, where one gun after another was suddenly being trained on her, she gave no sign of it.

"Am I the one who misled you?" I asked. "Or did the all-powerful Nicky?"

"Mmmaah!"

She spun toward Parrish. I tackled her from behind. We went sprawling onto the floor, crashing into chairs. The gun went off, a deafening sound that kept me from hearing anything for a moment.

We were in a dog pile within seconds—and someone in a uniform had wrestled the gun away from her.

The air was full of the smell of gunpowder, and I felt a strong pair of hands helping me to my feet.

"Are you all right?" Frank asked.

"Yes."

I heard someone reading her rights to her. I turned to look.

As they marched her off to the elevator, she looked back at me. She gave me that same pleading stare that had haunted me for four years.

The one that had fooled me for four years.

"Don't do that to yourself," Ben said, walking up to us.

"What?" I asked.

"Don't blame yourself."

I didn't answer—a woman officer came into the room just then to take the wire off me. She started telling me what a great job I had done; Frank, watching my face, told her—in his polite way—to hurry up and take the equipment and leave me alone.

"Are you sure you're all right?" he asked when she left.

I nodded.

"How about you, Ben?" he asked.

"Not so great at the moment," he said.

"One of us is lying," I said. "I think it's me."

Parrish gurgled.

I walked over and looked down into his face. His eyes were bright with something like laughter.

"Don't take too much joy in that, Nicky. I'll get over whatever is bothering me."

His face twitched.

"Ten years from now, when you're still staring at the ceiling, wishing you were dead—or maybe just wishing someone would come in and scratch your nose for you—I want you to remember what I did on behalf of your victims. I saved your life."

"Mmmaah! Mmmaaaahh!"

"So long, Nicky. I hope you live to be a hundred."

62

▲ ▼ ▲ ▼

WEDNESDAY, OCTOBER 18, MIDNIGHT

The Roof of the Wrigley Building

Three weeks later, I was up on the roof of the *Express* at midnight, looking out at the city. I was still working part-time, odd hours. I had canceled several of my appointments with Jo Robinson and told John not to hassle Wrigley about changing my hours.

I liked the slow shifts, I told him. They weren't really slow; I had a lot to catch up on.

That was true—but I never seemed to get around to catching up.

There was a restlessness in me. I found myself looking at the travel section instead of reading my mail. I started looking at real estate ads, too. I wondered if I could talk Frank into moving somewhere else, doing something else for a living.

Frank would listen to my suggestions, say, "That's a possibility, but maybe this isn't a good time to make that kind of decision."

I don't like to think of what might have happened to me in those weeks if I hadn't been married to Frank Harriman. He didn't push or nag; he spoiled me rotten. I guess I needed a little spoiling. With him, I felt as if there were no secrets that couldn't be told, no fears that couldn't be voiced. There were evenings of confiding in him, they kept me from losing whatever balance I had.

The days consisted of routines of avoidance. I knew I couldn't continue treading on the surface of life, knew that I needed to dive back in. Easy to say.

Up on the roof that night, the autumn breezes were warm. "Mild Santa Ana conditions," the weather forecasters called it. That meant that the smog was blown away by desert winds, the days were a little too hot, but most people wouldn't feel as crazy as a true red wind would make them. It meant the view was better than usual. I could see Catalina, the distant lights of Avalon.

I should go back down to my desk and work, I thought, taking another long pull from my water bottle. But that would mean being indoors. Didn't want to be indoors, not just yet.

I heard the access door open and tensed. Probably just Jerry or Livy, maybe Leonard. Jerry and Leonard always greeted me with the same joke—each would say that he was just making sure I hadn't jumped. Livy never said that, but I think she was more certain that I wouldn't end up on the pavement in front of the building. Not my style. I refuse to do anything that will force anyone else to use a hose to clean up my departure.

Tonight's visitor to my aerie rounded the corner—I was surprised to see Ben Sheridan.

"Up late, Professor?" I said when he came nearer.

"Up high. Mind if we move a little farther away from the edge?"

"Not at all. Come have a seat at Café Kelly. We no longer feature helicopter floor shows, but the water is fine."

"Sounds good to me."

We sat down and propped our feet up, both original and replacement models.

"You owe me something," he said, taking a drink of water.

"I haven't forgotten. If you really want to hear it, I'll tell it."

"Yes, I do," he said.

So I told him what had happened in the mountains that morning, when Parrish had threatened Bingle and shoved my face into the mud, and chased me through the woods.

"My God," he said when I had finished. "Jesus, I wish I

could have helped you. I feel terrible about it. If you hadn't been worrying about keeping him away from me, you wouldn't have even been near him. And I know you were worn out because of—"

"Stop it! If you want the truth, *that's* the reason I never told you about what Parrish did that morning. I knew you'd feel this ridiculous sense of guilt, as if you could have done anything about it, as if it were your fault that it happened, instead of Parrish's."

"Oh?" he said. "You mean, I'd feel the way you do about my having to undergo an amputation?"

I was dumbfounded. "I don't feel that way," I said at last.

"Bullshit. You hide it better than you did at first, but you still blame yourself."

I started to deny it, then changed my mind and rushed headlong into the fray. "As a matter of fact, I do! Talk about shielding! You know it's my fault."

"What? I know no such thing. I know Parrish shot me. I painted that bull's-eye on myself, as I recall—in fact, I distinctly remember that you called out to me, tried to prevent me from running into that meadow."

"Yes, yes," I said impatiently. "But who took forever to find you out there? Who didn't know how to properly care for the wound? Who didn't give you enough Keflex?"

He stared at me incredulously and said, "Keflex?"

"Don't try to lie to me! At the hospital, they said that was the drug they were giving you to try to stop the infection. Only it was too late. And the whole time, I had Earl's pills, and if I had given you more—"

"Wait! Do you mean—do you think—don't tell me that you've spent all these months believing that!"

"It's true," I said.

"Irene, the bullet damaged the artery. That's why they amputated. Not because of infection."

"But they gave you—"

"Yes, they gave me something to fight the infection, but do me a favor and ask Dr. Riley to tell you what sort of intravenous megadose of that drug they were talking about. That infection was beyond anything that could be stopped by tablet form doses. Earl's *entire* prescription couldn't have stopped it."

"Then why did you bother taking any of it?"

He looked pointedly at his left leg and said, "You do what you can with what you have."

I couldn't speak.

"As for getting to me in time, we both know you did the safe, smart thing and waited until Parrish was gone."

"But maybe I could have—"

"Irene! You damned idiot! Listen to yourself."

I shut up.

"Tell you what," he said. "If you reveal to me now that you have a medical degree, that you had surgical tools in your back-pack, and that we were actually very close to a sterile operating room up there in the mountains, I will start heaping blame upon you for not saving my leg. Otherwise, stop feeling bad about your role in all of this. You're the person who allowed me to keep my life, not the person who caused me to lose part of my leg."

I felt tears rolling down my face. "God damn," I said, wip-ing them away. "I never used to do this. I really hate it."

"Are you saying that so I'll know you're more macho than I am?"

"What?"

"You've seen me cry."

"You went through a lot."

He laughed. "Just me, and all by myself, right?"

"No, but—"

He made a T of his hands—the "time out" sign.

"Yes?"

"We, the jury, find the defendant, Irene Kelly, not guilty. Not guilty for trusting that Gillian Sayre was telling her the truth. Not guilty in the matter of the deaths of her friends and com-panions. Not guilty in the loss of Ben Sheridan's leg. Not guilty for any other thing that went wrong because she was human, or didn't know everything that could possibly be known about the universe and its inhabitants."

I blew my nose.

"Thank you, your honor," he said. "Court is adjourned. You are now free to forgive yourself."

I went back to Jo Robinson, and I told her that I knew what was wrong with me. I stopped fighting the process of taking a look at my way of thinking about things, and before long, I was back at work and not seeing her anymore. Just as I was starting to enjoy it.

Gillian Sayre is still awaiting trial. Phil Newly, cleared of all suspicion, once toyed with the idea of defending her, but decided to stick with his retirement plan. Lately he has sent e-mail to me about once a week, telling me about his new life. He says he might do a little pro bono work now and then, but is enjoying the slower pace.

Jason Sayre sends e-mail, too. He's living with his grandmother. He likes to write to me, he says, because Jack and I are the only ones who will talk to him about what happened. Jack, who has all but asked if he can adopt him, visits him fairly often; they still talk on the tin telephone.

Giles Sayre sold his business and moved with his new wife to a town not far from the one where Jason lives, but seldom visits his son.

Jim Houghton came back to Las Piernas. He had been spending time with a retired airplane mechanic who had taught Nicholas Parrish how to fly and repair small planes. Using information the older man gave him about Nick Parrish's favorite places to fly, Houghton discovered where Nicholas Parrish had buried his sister. It was not far from a desert airstrip. The body was not alone. The recovery and identification of the other remains is slowed by concerns for worker safety. There has been a renewed interest in missing persons cases in towns where Parrish once lived.

After giving police information on the location of the graves, Houghton came by to apologize to me. I told him that it wasn't necessary, that I had stood trial in the same courtroom he had himself in, and that all charges had been dropped against both of us. We talked for a long time, and I gave him Jo Robinson's card. I don't know if he ever called her.

* * *

Nicholas Parrish remains at St. Anne's, although the district attorney, who looked over the original deal and decided a guilty plea and life imprisonment might be fine after all, is looking into the possibility of having a judge rule on the matter, and moving Parrish to a state prison hospital. If not, and if there is a trial, I know some people who will testify against the defendant.

Frank and I bought Ben's Jeep when he decided David's pickup was better suited to his needs. The Jeep is big enough to hold the two of us and the dogs and camping gear.

Sometimes we go camping alone; sometimes with Pete and Rachel, or Tom Cassidy and other old friends. Quite often J.C., Andy, Jack, Stinger, and Travis join us up in the mountains. Ben comes along, too, with Anna, his new girlfriend, a woman he met on the SAR team. We all liked her from the start; she doesn't have any difficulty fitting into our chaotic camping style. She has two dogs of her own. Camping with Stinger Dalton and six big, rowdy dogs is always chaotic.

Bingle still leads the pack.

He still barks.

I still insist on sleeping with the tent flap open.

But we all sleep through the night.

Notes and Acknowledgments

▲ ▼ ▲ ▼

While the southern Sierra Nevada mountains include many meadows, ridges, and other features that may resemble those in this book, the landscape in *Bones* is fictional, as are the ranger station and other settings.

Readers who are interested in the tale of Parzival will find it beautifully retold in Katherine Paterson's *Parzival: The Quest of the Grail Knight*, or may prefer to read Professor A. T. Hatto's scholarly introduction and translation of the full work by Wolfram von Eschenbach, *Parzival*.

Several forensic anthropologists took time from their hectic schedules to answer my questions and to comment on the manuscript. I'm especially grateful to Paul Sledzik, Curator of the Anatomical Collections of the National Museum of Health and Medicine, Armed Forces Institute of Pathology; Marilyn London, Department of Anthropology, National Museum of Natural History, Smithsonian Institution, and Forensic Anthropology Consultant to the Rhode Island Office of Medical Examiners; Diane France, Director, Human Identification Laboratory, Colorado State University; and William Haglund, former Chief Medical Investigator, King County Medical Examiner's Office, Seattle, Washington, Senior Forensic Consultant for the United Nations Criminal Tribunals, and Director of the Forensic Program for Physicians for Human Rights.

Bingle and Boolean were inspired by several real cadaver dogs, whose trainers and handlers were extremely generous with their time and help. Many thanks to Dr. Ed David, Deputy Chief Medical Examiner for the State of Maine and the trainer and handler of Wraith and Shadow, Maine's two cadaver/crime scene dogs; Beth Barkley, SAR/cadaver dog trainer and handler of Sirius, Czar, and Jadzia; the handlers and dogs of Search Services America—Mike and Kelly, Eileen and Reilly, Ross and Maverick, George and Smoky, Blair and Thor; Deputy Al Nelson, bloodhound handler and trainer, Jefferson County (Colorado) Sheriff's Department and member of NecroSearch. Additional dog information came from Linda McDermott, Chair of the K-9 Unit of the Angeles chapter of the Sierra Club, and Orbin Pratt, DVM.

My thanks to Vaughn Askue, who has more than thirty years of experience as a pilot and Technical Support Manager for Sikorsky Helicopters; Deputy David Kitchings, Pilot, Los Angeles County Sheriff's Department Aero Bureau; Dave Nalle, Assistant Captain, Kernville Helitack; Ranger Judy Schutza, Kernville Station, U.S. Forest Service; Nick Agosta, TNG Helicopter Company; and Noelani Mars, Professional Helicopter Pilots Association. I'm grateful to Hal Higdon, senior writer, *Runner's World* and Benji Durden, Olympic marathoner, for their helpful suggestions regarding the effects of altitude, terrain, and other factors during Irene's run through the mountains. Thanks also to Dr. Ed Dohring and Dr. Michael Strauss, orthopedic surgeons; Dr. Marvin Zamost; Joan Dilley; Wayne Reynardson, list owner of AMP-L, and the members of that list; Todd Cignetti; Flex-Foot, Inc., especially Jeff Gerber; David Barnhart, C.P.O.; Michael Pavelski, C.P.O; Mary Kay Razo, school psychologist; Dale Carter, Latin Blood Books, Professor Emeritus of Spanish at California State University, Los Angeles; Steve Burr; Debbie Arrington; Sharon Weissman; Tonya Pearsley; Sandra Cvar; and Dr. Christine Padesky and Dr. Kathleen Mooney of the Padesky Center for Cognitive Therapy—

friends who responded quickly and enthusiastically when I told them Irene needed therapy.

My family and friends have been supportive as always, and I again thank my agent and my publisher's hardworking sales reps.

I am deeply indebted to my editors, Laurie Bernstein and Marysue Rucci, for their perceptive comments and many hours of work on the manuscript.

Carolyn Reidy, thank you for your kind words of encouragement.

As for my husband, Tim Burke—I'm having holy cards printed.

Part One: Ten Years Ago

I

Sunday, June 3, 11:35 P.M.
Las Piernas Marina South

Blissfully unaware that the moment everything would change was near, they were bickering.

"You should have to do the kitchen, Seth," Mandy said, drying a tumbler. "I shouldn't have to do it just because I'm a female."

"Female," Seth scoffed, securing the latch on a compartment beneath a berth. "Not like anyone could tell you are. You're still an 'it.' "

"An *it*!" Mandy snapped the towel at the seat of his pants. She hit her mark, then squealed in dismay as he turned and easily grabbed her weapon away from her.

He grinned as he saw the belated realization dawn on her face—it had been a mistake to attack him within the confines of the yacht. She cowered, waiting for his retribution. He laughed and tossed the towel in her face. "Half the other girls in ninth grade have bigger boobs than you do, Pancake."

She shoved at him, and as he fell back in mock surrender, he knocked over a set of cookware she had not yet put away. In the silence after the crash and clatter, they each covered their mouths and repressed laughter.

"Quit the horseplay down there!" their father's voice called.

Seth glanced at the companionway, but his dad was too busy with his own work above to continue scolding. Seth looked at his watch. They probably wouldn't be at his dad's house until almost one o'clock in the morning—they had a lot to do before they could even take their dad's new boat back to number 414, its own slip.

Seth knew that some boat owners would have taken their yachts into the slip at any hour and cleaned up there, but his father never showed such disregard for others. Whenever he got into the marina after nine or ten o'clock at night, Trent Randolph, in consideration of the live-aboards whose boats occupied the slips nearest his own, always docked here first, near a bait shop at an isolated point on the far end of the marina. "You wouldn't turn on bright lights and wash and vacuum a car at midnight on your driveway at home," he would tell friends who asked about this habit. "People live even closer together here."

They hadn't taken friends with them this time. This weekend's sailing trip to Catalina Island had been fun—especially, Seth thought, because it had just been the three of them. Trent Randolph had finally dumped Tessa, his low-life girlfriend, not long ago. Seth hated her. She was the one who had split his folks up two years earlier, but that wasn't the only reason he didn't like her. She bitched about Seth and Amanda constantly, and Seth was almost positive she was playing his dad. He had no proof, but once or twice when his dad wasn't around, Seth had overheard her talking on her cell phone in kind of a lovey-dovey voice, all sexy and everything. And he knew she hadn't been talking to his dad. So maybe his dad had caught her at it, too—or just finally wised up.

He knew his dad wouldn't get back together with his mom. He knew they weren't happy together. And he wished he could stop wishing they would get back together anyway.

Better to think of good times. Like this weekend. Seth, Mandy, and their dad had even spent a night camping on the island, something they had not done since the divorce. "It was like he could be a dad again," Mandy confided to Seth when they left Avalon. He had rolled his eyes, not willing to openly agree with her. One reason he liked the new boat was that he figured his dad had used it to get rid of Tessa—Seth recalled that she had been just about as pissed as his sister had been pleased with the yacht's name—*Amanda.*

"I still say you should help with the kitchen," Mandy whispered now as they picked up the fallen pots and pans.

"It's a *galley*, not a kitchen," Seth corrected. "You always say it wrong."

"Whatever. You should have to do it."

"Quit whining or I'll make you clean the head."

"The bathroom?"

He nodded.

"Why call it 'the head' and not, you know, something like, 'the ass?' "

"Don't be a trash mouth, Mandy," he said, turning away so she wouldn't see him laugh.

"It's not trashy. Even donkeys are called asses."

He wouldn't take the bait, and so they worked quietly for a few minutes. They heard their father's footsteps as he moved overhead, heard the thumps and thuds and other sounds of gear and life vests being stowed, rigging secured, decks hosed and scrubbed. Seth carried the two duffel bags filled with camping gear toward the hatch, setting them near the companionway to be carried up later.

He was athletic; broad shouldered and tall for sixteen. Dark haired and green eyed, and a little shy. Mandy could make him blush furiously by using one of her nicknames for him: Mr. Babe Magnet. "Every girl who becomes my friend develops a major crush on you," she once complained to him, "unless she already had one on you and became my friend just so she could get next to you."

"No, they like you for yourself."

She shook her head and said, "Right. Try to catch the next flight back to planet earth."

He still thought she was wrong. At fourteen, she was slender but gawky, more bookish than he. The only reason he had started lifting weights was because he worried that, without his father in the house, the duty of fighting off her unworthy would-be boyfriends would fall to him. He expected them to arrive by the busload once his redheaded little sister filled out a little. The only after-school fight he had ever been in—the one their mother chalked up to "Seth adjusting to the divorce"—had actually started when the other kid made a "see what develops" crack about Mandy. Seth had pummeled him.

"Where does this go?" Mandy asked, startling him out of his reverie. She was biting on her lower lip as she held up an oven mitt. Fretting over exactly where everything belonged. He didn't blame her. No use shoving things any-old-where they would fit. Their dad was a neatness freak. Seth showed her the compartment where such things were stored, then went back to work on cleaning the head.

"Mom's probably called Dad's house," she said as Seth started polishing the mirror. When he didn't respond, she added, "She's going to be mad."

"Mom's always mad," he said, not pausing in his work. "He'll take us to school on time tomorrow. Don't worry. She doesn't need to know we're up this late on a school night—right?"

"Right," Mandy agreed. "But if she calls—"

"Even if she finds out, she'll still have to let Dad take us every other weekend."

Mandy gave a little sigh of relief, a sound not lost on her brother.

A noisy fishing boat pulled up nearby. They could hear the loud thrumming of its engines. A little later, above them, mixed in with the engine noise, they heard voices. Male voices. Their father, and another man.

"Who could that be?" Mandy asked, moving toward the companionway.

Seth shrugged. "The guy from the fishing boat probably."

The voices grew louder. They heard snatches of conversation, their father's voice as he strode angrily past the hatch: ". . . trouble . . . get up . . . not what police should . . . you think I'm going to . . . then . . ."

"I'm going to see who it is!" Mandy whispered.

"Some politico," Seth said, using a term they applied to most of their father's newest associates. "Can't you tell? Dad's making a speech to him."

"At midnight?"

"They bug him at all hours. Stay put."

They both listened, but the men seemed to have stopped talking.

"I'm going to go see," she said. She was up the companionway before he could stop her. The men were still quiet, so he thought Mandy was probably too late anyway—the other man had probably left. He squirted some toilet bowl cleaner into the bowl and began to scrub—let Mandy get in trouble for not working.

He heard a loud thud and wondered if his dumb sister had tripped. He listened and could hear quick footsteps—too heavy to be Amanda's. His dad running? He thought he heard her yelp. He stepped out of the head, listened. Hell, maybe she did fall.

He started toward the companionway just as she came stumbling down the ladder. Her face was white, and she was clutching her throat. A bright red wash of blood covered her hands, her arms, the entire front of her body.

"Mandy!"

Her eyes were wide and terrified, pleading with him. Her mouth formed some unspoken word just before she collapsed in a heap at the foot of the ladder. As she fell, her hand came away from her throat, and he was sprayed with her warm blood.

"Mandy!" he screamed.

There was a cut on her neck—blood continued to spray in smaller and smaller spurts from it.

"Dad!" he yelled. "Dad! Help!"

He heard hurried steps and looked up, expecting to see his father. A pirate stood at the top of the ladder.

The man who looked down at him was wearing a black eye patch over his left eye and carried a glinting piece of steel—though it was a small knife, not a cutlass—and the man's dark clothes were modern.

Seth turned and ran in blind panic toward the bow. But there was no escape except through the hatch, and no shelter—except the small head. He dodged into it, turning to close the door on his attacker just as the knife came slashing. He raised his hands in defense, and the knife cut across his fingers. Screaming in pain, he whirled and threw his back against the door, catching the attacker's arm. The attacker shoved hard, moving one step in. Seth ground his heel into the man's foot. The man gave a grunt of pain and pulled the foot back even as he slashed with the knife, cutting across the front of Seth's neck. Only as he reached up with bloodied hands to cover the wound did Seth catch his own reflection in the mirror. Realizing that this was how the man had aimed the blow, Seth jammed his shoulder against the man's arm, pinning it against the wall. Then he hit the light switch. He felt dizzy, but forced himself to stay on his feet. With a fumbling grasp, he used his less injured left hand to pick up the open plastic bottle of toilet bowl cleaner on the sink counter. He put it up to where the man's good eye was peering in—and squeezed the plastic bottle between the wall and his palm.

He didn't think any of the chemical had hit the man, who must have seen it coming, because he jerked back, cutting Seth's shoulder as he pulled the knife arm from beneath him. Free of this obstruction, the door slammed shut and Seth's weight held it closed. He dropped the cleaner even as he fumbled with the lock, his fingers slippery and barely functioning. He managed to grab a towel, to hold it against his neck, but soon he could not stand. The pain was intense, and he felt himself weakening, his own blood warm and sticky and dampening his shirt. He wedged himself between the hull and the door, even as the attacker began slamming against it.

The door shook beneath the blows. It would give, Seth thought. He tried to yell, but found he couldn't make a sound.

Suddenly, the pounding stopped. The small room swam before him. Seth bent forward, trying to fight the feeling of faintness. No sooner had he moved than the wood where he had rested his head splintered inward with a bang—split by a small ax. The attacker must have taken it from their camping gear. The man yanked the ax from the wood. Seth tried to drag himself away from the door before the second blow came, but found he could not. He brought his hands back to the towel at his throat, wondering if the ax's third blow would slice into his back.

Suddenly, he heard music—not music, really, but a short series of tones, a repetitive, insistent, three-note call—the sound of a pager or of an alarm on an electronic watch.

Do-re-mi-do-re-mi-do-re—

Seth heard the sound cut off. He waited, every muscle tense, for the ax to strike again—but the third blow never came.

Over the next few minutes, Seth drifted in and out of awareness, but a low rumbling made him open his eyes. The fishing boat was leaving.

He began to feel cold and sleepy. He must get up and help Mandy, he thought, but in his pain and light-headed confusion, he could not locate the door latch. Still holding the towel against his neck, he groped along the wall with one hand and managed to turn on the light. He found the latch just as he lost consciousness.

II

Monday, June 4, 1:56 A.M.
Las Piernas

Wearing rubber gloves, the Looking Glass Man checked all the blinds. On a less eventful evening, this last night of using this apartment would have filled him with a sense of regret. It was so perfectly suited to his needs—at the back of the building, over the carport, where no one would notice his footsteps across the floor late in the evening. The tenant in the only adjoining apartment worked the graveyard shift. Still, he moved quietly.

The old television set was off; he had never watched it. The stove was clean but cold; he had never cooked on it. The meager, outdated furnishings in the apartment bore the marks of previous owners and tenants. The next tenant would not see any sign of his use of it. There was nothing he was so careful of as where he left signs of his presence.

He evenly sprayed the disinfectant over the surface of the gray Formica tabletop, then wiped it with a white paper towel, moving his gloved hand in controlled, overlapping circles. He placed the towel in a white plastic bag.

When he was certain the surface of the table was dry, he took out a notebook with a stiff, cardboard cover. It was the sort of notebook one could find in any college bookstore, a black-and-white marbled cover binding graph paper, used by science students to record experiments.

Inside the cover, on the first page, he had written a quotation:

God is in the details

The quotation was from a famous architect—Ludwig Mies van der Rohe, who had designed the Seagram's Building in New York. The Looking Glass Man considered himself to be a kind of architect, too. When he had started the first of these notebooks, at the age of sixteen, the entries had been so benign—nothing more than recorded observations of little social experiments, his attempts to monitor the reactions of others to certain stimuli. But even then, perhaps intuitively, he had placed the quotation on the first page of the notebook. He now had many of these notebooks and had written this same quotation at the front of all of them. His faith in the importance of details was unshakable.

He turned to a blank page and, using a mechanical pencil, began to record data in block letters. Each letter took up one square of the graph paper's grid, the tip of the pencil lead never crossing a blue line. He wrote a heading, "ANTI-INTERFERENCE," then noted the date and time for a series of events, from the time he boarded the fishing vessel *Cygnet* until the time he left it. It was difficult not to rush ahead to the most exciting minutes, those few spent on the yacht, the *Amanda*. He forced himself to work in a precise manner, recounting every one of the God-laden details in chronological order.

He left a row of empty squares beneath the last of these, then wrote:

TIME ELAPSED IN CRITICAL MODE: 18 M 51 S
FATALITIES: 3
RATING: 4

AREAS OF IMPROVEMENT: TOO SLOW W/ THIRD VIC; NEARLY SUSTAINED INJURY FROM CORROSIVE WHICH WOULD HAVE REQUIRED MEDICAL TREATMENT. SUCH TREATMENT MIGHT HAVE BEEN REMARKED BY PHYSICIANS AND LATER CONNECTED TO CRIME SCENE. TOO EMOTIONAL. SLOPPY!

He paused and lifted the pencil, turning it upside down so that he could see the tip, and gently turned the pencil barrel so that the lead was at the proper length. He then continued to write.

COMMENTS: DID NOT LIKE WORKING WITH CHILDREN. NEVER WILL FORGIVE RANDOLPH FOR FORCING THIS SOLUTION.

HOWEVER, MUST NOT THINK OF THIS. MUST CONSIDER THE NUMBER OF CHILDREN SAVED BY THE DEATHS OF THESE TWO ADOLESCENTS. SHOULD BE ABLE TO CONTINUE NOW. SMALL SACRIFICE, ALL CONSIDERED.

He reread what he had written, checking for errors. He found none. Accurate records were so important. If one were to truly evaluate the effectiveness of his activities, one could not rely on memory. He knew the discovery of any of the more recent notebooks by others would greatly increase his chances of being prosecuted for certain of the activities recounted in them. It was a risk he had to take, though, in order to proceed in an orderly manner.

His hands began to perspire beneath the gloves. He disliked the sensation it caused.

He retracted the pencil lead, closed the notebook, and put it and the pencil into a briefcase. He went into the bathroom, fought off a sudden nausea, then quickly went back to work. He emptied the remaining disinfectant into the toilet and flushed it twice. He put the empty bottle into the white plastic bag.

He caught his own reflection in the mirror over the sink and paused for a moment, studying himself. He stared hard into his own eyes, looking for observable changes. It was a habit of his, staring at himself in the mirror. His sister used to chide him, calling him the Looking Glass Man. But while he admitted a fascination with faces, especially his own, it was with detached interest and not any real admiration that he studied his reflection.

Who was that looking back at him from that silver surface?

The Looking Glass Man.

He switched off the bathroom light.

He gathered the bag and the briefcase, stepped out onto the landing, and locked the apartment door. Over the next few days, the apartment would be painted, the carpets cleaned. The new tenants would move in by the tenth.

He should not allow such trifles to disturb him, he decided. He had greater problems to consider. Crime and punishment. He thought of the photograph in his wallet, but he did not take it out. Thinking of the photograph always made him think of the judge—Judge Lewis Kerr. Kerr must be watched.

He allowed himself a small, soft sigh, then walked downstairs to the large metal trash bin. At last able to remove the annoying gloves, he added them and the roll of paper towels to the white bag, and placed it in the bin. The bin was quite full.

Trash day, he thought. Just another trash day.

Monday, June 4, 2:15 A.M.
The Las Piernas Marina

"Maybe your snitch was wrong," Elena Rosario said.

Philip Lefebvre did not reply. He continued to watch a yacht moored to a dock near a bait shop.

"Lefebvre?"

He turned, then followed her gaze toward her partner, Bob Hitchcock, who was walking toward them. The narcotics detective's hands were in his pockets as he approached them, his head down. Hitch was a big man beginning to go soft around the belly and beneath his chin—and Lefebvre thought he was going soft on the job as well, coasting whenever he could. Any extra effort would have put Hitch in a shitty mood, and the fact that this surveillance call hadn't panned out had ticked him off.

Rosario was easier to work with, but harder to read, more reserved. And unlike Hitch, she wasn't a burnout case. When Hitch had argued against coming down here, she had said, "You want to tell the captain why we didn't follow up on a lead concerning Whitey Dane?"

Hitch had caved—they all knew this was exactly why he was being forced to work with Lefebvre in the first place. As much as Hitch resented having someone from homicide assigned to the task force on Dane, there was nothing he could to about it.

Whitey Dane, long suspected of being behind a number of local criminal activities, including drug dealing, had proven slippery—although the police department had occasionally crippled his operations in the city, their efforts to bring charges against him were futile.

Every attempt to make progress in investigating his activities had met with a reversal. Informants were murdered or disappeared, undercover officers were unable to get anywhere near Dane himself. Rosario had told Lefebvre that most of her two years as a narcotics detective had been spent on a team that had tried to gather enough evidence against Dane to put him out of business. Instead, over that time, he had branched out from drug dealing and vice into other types of crime—and increased his influence on local politics and businesses.

Following a recent outbreak of violence in an area controlled by Dane, the task force was expanded—Lefebvre, a veteran homicide detective, had been assigned to work with it.

"So they've given us the golden boy," Hitch had said. "You sure you can stop giving interviews long enough to work with us?"

"He's already more aware of Dane's little oddball habits than you are," Rosario had said. "And you're just jealous because you think he's getting into that reporter's pants."

"Irene Kelly is a good-looking broad. So tell me, Lefebvre, what's she like in bed?"

Lefebvre had regarded him coldly, but said nothing, and after a moment of uncomfortable silence, Rosario had said, "You were asking who makes the silk vests Dane likes to wear . . ." and went on to discuss Dane's affected way of dressing.

As she watched Hitch coming toward them now, she sighed. "Tonight seemed so promising."

Lefebvre thought of the call that had brought them here. Just before midnight, he had received a tip from an informant, a mechanically disguised voice saying that Whitey Dane would be paying for the hit tonight, aboard his fishing boat, the *Cygnet.* Whitey and the shooter were due back to the marina at any moment. The informant seemed to know what he was talking about—he knew Whitey's slip number—305.

Lefebvre had paged Rosario and Hitch, who already knew exactly where Whitey kept his boat, and the three of them hurried to that section of the marina. Sure enough, the slip was empty. And so, for the past two hours, they had awaited the *Cygnet*'s return.

The slip stayed empty.

"We're at the wrong marina," Hitch said now, addressing Rosario and avoiding eye contact with Lefebvre. "The whole time, the damned boat's been in the other marina."

"The Downtown Marina?" Lefebvre asked.

"Yep."

"But this is where he usually keeps the boat?"

"Yes. We've been watching this guy for three years, and I've never seen him do so much as gas the thing up in the Downtown Marina."

"Was Dane—?"

"Didn't see him at all. And Mr. Eye Patch isn't exactly difficult to spot in a crowd."

"Anyone still watching the boat?"

"Yes, but until we get a warrant . . ." Hitchcock shrugged.

"You know we'd be turned down again," Lefebvre said. "Not enough to go on yet."

"You sure your snitch said here?"

"Yes." Lefebvre looked back toward the yacht, as if this conversation no longer interested him.

Hitch bristled over this dismissal. "Call came in anonymously?" he asked.

"He already told us it did," Rosario said, impatient with Hitch's mood. Hitch gave her a dark look, but she ignored it.

Lefebvre's attention remained with the yacht. "Is that yacht moored legally?"

"What, you want to leave Homicide and join the Harbor Patrol?" Hitch asked.

Lefebvre turned to Rosario. "Is that yacht—"

"How the hell should we know?" Hitch interrupted.

"No," Rosario said. She turned to Hitch. "I like to sail," she said, "but in case you're wondering, no, I don't want to join the Harbor Patrol either."

Lefebvre quickly hid a smile, but Hitch noticed his amusement.

"You might end up working there anyway," he snapped at his partner.

Lefebvre started walking down the dock, toward the yacht. Leaving Hitch behind, Rosario hurried to catch up with him. "Why are you so interested in it?" she asked.

"Rats with wings," Lefebvre said.

"What?"

"Seagulls," he said, walking a little faster. "They usually stay put for the evening, right?"

She then saw what he saw: birds were gathering around the yacht. "Maybe the bait shop—"

"That's what I noticed. The birds are ignoring the bait shop and going for something on the boat deck. And whoever's belowdecks hasn't come out to see what they're interested in."

"*Amanda*," she said, reading the neat lettering on the stern. "Somebody has bucks. She's a beauty."

She said that before they came close enough to see what was aboard.

First Lefebvre saw the blood, and then the man lying not far from the hatch. "Call for backup," he said. "Wait here on the dock." He stepped aboard amid noisy birds and flies, shooing them off as he moved cautiously toward the body.

Hitch had the only radio. He was still sauntering along.

Rosario shouted to him to make the call.

Lefebvre quickly checked the victim—the body was cold. As he headed for the companionway, he saw Rosario stepping aboard. He sighed with exasperation. "Put your hands in your pockets and don't step on any of the obvious pathways—or in the blood."

"I know enough not to mess up a crime scene," she said testily, but obediently put her hands in the pockets of her slacks. She stared at the dark, open gash on the victim's throat and turned pale.

Lefebvre watched her, then said, "If you're going to be sick—"

"I won't be."

He said nothing else to her; he had already turned to look down the companionway. He swore when he saw the girl's body, then drew his gun and moved awkwardly down the steps, doing his best not to disturb the bloodstain patterns. Rosario took her own weapon out and came closer.

"Oh, no," he heard her say. "Oh, no. Oh, no."

More faintly, from the docks, Hitch's voice: "Christ Almighty!"

Rosario shouted, "Get on that radio, you fucking asshole! We've got at least two dead—one's a kid."

Lefebvre kept moving toward the battered door to the head. He pushed on it—it only opened a few inches, something heavy was on the other side. Through a narrow, splintered slit that had been hacked into the door, he saw more blood—and then the boy. Lefebvre quickly holstered his weapon, got down near the floor, then reached inside. He pushed in a little farther, and touched skin—cool, but not the cold of the bodies behind him.

For one brief instant, the memory of the cooling skin of another young man flickered across his thoughts, but he closed his mind to it.

Not this time, he swore to himself. *Not this time!*

And in that moment, he felt a faint pulse.

He turned to Rosario and shouted, "Still alive! Get an ambulance here!"

Even as she began relaying this to Hitch, Lefebvre saw the ax. He grabbed it and heedless of Rosario's shout about prints, swung it hard but with precision, striking the wood near the upper hinges. With the fourth swing, the door began to give—he dropped the ax and turned, catching its weight, slowing its outward fall. He gently lowered it and, with it, the boy.

Lefebvre gathered the unconscious young man in his arms, keeping pressure on the bloodstained towel at the boy's throat, holding him close to warm him, speaking to him in a low voice, a desperate litany of "Stay with me, keep fighting, come on!"

Rosario found a sleeping bag among some camping gear near the companionway and brought it over. She covered the boy with it, helping Lefebvre bundle him within it, but when she touched the boy's skin, Lefebvre heard her sharp intake of breath.

"Lefebvre," she said gently, placing a hand on his shoulder.

He shrugged it off. "Stay with me!" he repeated to the boy, bending closer to him, as if shielding him from her lack of faith.

"Lefebvre," she tried again, but when he would not relent, she moved closer, holding on to a boy he knew she believed to be dead, silently adding her own warmth to his.